Departure

William Chapman

ISBN: 978-0-9837178-0-5

For Tom and Teri, brother and sister

1

Boots make your feet soft. Soft, white, sun-baked sand seared Michael Lander's feet, having lost all their years of barefoot-youth callous. Still, walking across Ocean Beach, surfboard under arm, was the easiest thing he ever had to do. Trying to look all-ways cool, in spite of screaming feet, was a much easier absorption of pain than washing away the perpetual acid besieging his heart and soul, while drowning his conscience. One main ingredient of that acid was Army boots. Give them the proper cadence and direction and they would march off to war. His were aimed for Viet Nam, forty-eight hours to D-Day. Just get to the shorebreak, take one stroke and there would be no connection, in any dimension, to anything on land. Surfing is perpetual fun, an interminable lullaby, even throwing in occasional lumps, cuts or thrashings. Near drownings aren't fun but, with honed luck, he's only had a half dozen since his first memory in life, playing in waves. Ever since, he's felt that water is his protectress, the more dramatic and powerful the better, when seeking harbor from emotions.

This wasn't the twenty-first year he'd ever envisioned, a designated golden age for an American kid. You could vote, yes, but, more immediately gratifying, you could also walk into a bar and order a drink, legally. Time for the lobos of each generation to attempt to publicly rewrite the rulebook of gonzo behavior. Though the anthropology of zanies is far from complete, the overall record book had survived most generations intact, with but a few anecdotal addenda to the American social fabric. These mid to late 1960s, the rulebook was being severely rewritten, from all sides. Revolution riddled the air. Perhaps, more accurately, it was societal civil war. A cold, mean civil war driven by a hot outbreak in a hot jungle of the enduring Cold War between communism and democracy. Perhaps there was no rulebook to be rewritten. Disaster doesn't always arrive with rules or reason. War-starters, mystics and demons charge in, from where wise men and angels flee in dread. And survivors dream their way out, when all else fails.

One early symptom of the cultural revolution was chemical warfare. A drug attack. When Landers went away to the University of California at Los Angeles, in nineteen sixty-three, drug use amongst his friends had been limited to popping a few "whites, a.k.a bennies", Benzedrine – to cram for exams or to extend an all-night Tijuana drinkathon – or "reds", barbiturates, for extra-stupefication. Neither appealed enough to even try them. Rumors had it that a few of the wild kids smoked marijuana, a very few had even tried heroin, neither new territory in Americana, but not openly popular either. That first summer back from college, Landers cautiously guarded his reputation that he had smoked pot, up there, where its taboos were picked apart pseudo-intellectually, with new proclamations of it being mind expanding as well as a safer hedonism than alcohol. Some of his back-home friends guarded their clean reputations, too. Until they all showed up at the same party where a twelve-armed hookah held the altar surrounded with bean chairs and cushions, with wah-wah guitars and strobe lights gyring the mind. The previous decade's casual style standard, plain cotton T-shirts – white or blue and J.C.Penney's only – were growing curvy collars and fluorescent paisley patterns. LSD, peyote and magic mushrooms, all legal on the streets then, had overrun fields of euphoria once ruled by Bacchus. Purists, in the early days, even abstained from alcohol like it was a banished, evil tyrant of the soul.

For introduction to the new dementia and some pocket cash, Landers had joined a few of his friends from a fraternity in an experiment on mind-altering drugs at the Wadsworth Veterans Hospital, across a military cemetary and a freeway from the UCLA campus, an adjunct to the Medical Center. Often it used students and vets as lab rats, voluntary and non-voluntary, by candy, default or deceit. This recipe: three psychedelics and two placebos, once a week for five weeks. This would be the first time Landers ever walked into the front door of a military establishment (he'd snuck around back hundreds of times to go surfing). They gave him a sugar cube soaked in perfect LSD, then told him to play in the guarded garden and a scientific toy and music room. No problem there, except on the placebo days. Psychologists observed and down-briefed, then handed him a twenty-dollar bill on the way out. All concocted and paid for by the Central Intelligence Agency.

Second cannon of the revolution was a new drug too; the birth control pill. Finally, armed against heredity, legions of women were making up for all those lost centuries. No worries, one shot of penicillin cured all. Guys might have been surprised, but girls weren't, that what they'd been guarding all those years weren't so much their repute as their tendency to get pregnant. Abortions were illegal and there were horror stories by the score of women being scarred, left unfertile or dead in backrooms and back-alley Tijuana clinics.

The third shot of the civil revolution was fear...or was that always really the first wave of the set. This far-off war in Viet Nam was escalating, exponentially. Nobody seemed to quite understand but they all debated it, often and vigorously, pre-armed with ironclad opinions. Overwhelmingly, previous American lore was if the armed forces were getting shot at, everyone lined up behind the flag and marched. Any opposing voices had to be traitors to the other side. That's what the first doubters of this war were called, loud and often: traitors, degenerate cowards, godless communists. The nation being rebelled against was "The Establishment". It included almost anyone in the government or corporate bureaucracies, and absolutely anyone in a uniform. "Don't trust anyone over thirty," was the battle cry. But *mantra primera* was "drugs, sex and rock-and-roll." Parents, unanimously, were appalled.

Above all, for Landers, he wanted out of the Army. Desperately, he wanted out. He didn't care much for the military. He hated the war. He didn't want to run, though, he just wanted to disappear. The surf was only place he knew to do that, if only for a few hours. Crossing the beach, the only distractions from the surf were girls sunning all about, chatting, reading or just being beautiful. Adding thrust to his libido, this was the year the string bikinis started arriving on lithe bodies which, last summer, were barely showing navels. Guys hadn't responded in kind. Showing up in skimpy trunks was reserved for the military or guys of questionable gender, and would get a local banned, forever, from the social scene. This was based on fashion and vanity, not on modesty. Surfers are notoriously sloppy in displaying untanned flesh just by being oblivious to how low their baggy trunks ride or while often changing clothes in the wide open with the towel-around-the-waist technique. Surf trunks are to a surfer what a saddle is to a cowboy. Style evolved from function. Tie strings adjust them exactly, so that they hang loosely on the hipbones for mobility, but multiple stitching in the waistband keeps them from stretching even a fraction more, so waves can't yank them off. The turbulence in the impact zone of even small surf and the abundant reefs quickly shred all but the toughest fabrics. Sail canvas and nylons were all that seemed to work. Add a pocket for wax and maybe a few bills and enough length to protect thighs from chafing. Lots of surfers only owned one pair of trunks and wore them everywhere, many even slept in them. In winters, Landers and friends always had a pair hanging from the back pocket of their jeans. The canvas ones Landers currently wore were faded and frayed, green with black trim, which he'd received as a Christmas present by his main girlfriend, several years earlier. Two subsequent girlfriends had protested this byway to the past, but weren't going to win the point without producing a better pair of trunks. Hailed by a group who included half his high-school cheerleading team, lushly unadorned in square-inches of cloth, Landers paused to chat. He would have basked awhile in this garden of fresh skin, all golden tanned with soft blond fuzz, except the hint of arousal caused him to break off contact. Lingering dreams still might have betrayed him except a large set of waves powering through the pier flacked those fantasies.

The main difference between Landers walking across Ocean Beach, as he had thousands of times before, is this time he had the odd haircut; he was military. Even a three-week, non-regulation mustache grown during his current leave of absence would fool nobody. Next day, he was scheduled to report to the Oakland Departure Center for troops flying to Viet Nam. Waiting for a friend to catch up, he burrowed his feet deeper, down to cooler sands. The pain recalled a time in junior high, when the surfers took to cutting out the bottoms of their tennis shoes, and one scorching day standing in gym class roll call on fresh asphalt had delivered an equally painful message, even through late-summer callous. It started a run of memories of pain and happiness, and made him wonder

4

which were universal and which unique to this water-oriented community.

Watching a fight brewing over near a jetty recalled rights of passage for teenage boys, to prove their combative nature against sailors or, for even more points, Marines. Since a fresh crop poured weekly out of the Navy and Marine boot camps, just over the hill, romping to test drive their newly toned physiques, targets weren't in short supply. Many of the recruits were in shape for the first time in their lives. They were taught battlefield tactics, not the dance-up moves to a street-fight, so many didn't fare so well against the known toughs who picked most of the fights. To add to the normal distribution of combative athletes and thugs in any neighborhood, the hardcore surfers and fishermen around here had been in superb condition since grade school, and many fought for the sport of it. Every generation, the Ocean Beach and Tunaville toughs, from over the hill, would take it out on each other, but usually end up friends. Some military pugilists more than held their own and older Marines, particularly those of World War II or Korean War vintage, were given wide berth.

These were all matters of lore for bragging and non-constructive amusement. By the mid-sixties, a drastically more urgent piece had been placed on the military game board; the Viet Nam war was escalating fast, with all its uncertainties. The constant obsession of most young men, and the women who loved them, was how to cope with the draft board. What exactly were the real duties, when the enemy was no threat whatsoever to American soil; to serve and possibly die or to dodge and at least survive? Civilians, then, thought the military was of unanimous resolve to win. They would have been wrong. The military majority was splitting too

Walking and watching the long set of waves, only an occasional radio sound breezed by his consciousness. Tunes of the day wafted by unnoticed but not the half-hourly count of the daily dead in Viet Nam. His stomach boiled up. A familiar whistle from behind was a welcome distraction. Caves, one of Landers's best friends, was catching up to him, also with board. Caves is actually a diminutive of Caveboy, from his youthful propensity to exploring sea caves, above or below water. Landers hadn't ever much cared for any dark, claustrophobic spaces, nor for the crabs, eels or spiders that might be there. Even though he regularly had to swim in caves to chase a board or get out of the water, and almost always surfed over shallow reefs, he felt he could ignore what was down their easier the less he looked into all those crevices. If it came to filling dead time, between surfing, he was much more prone to climb the cliffs and dive off the tops of caves. Caves, with no more greeting, matched Landers's pace. Unlike Landers's quiet observation of everything around him, Caves reacted to almost everything. He flirted with every girl he could, with considerable success, and stared down any potential fraternity or military types. Landers almost wanted to apologize to one group of Marines, having learned enough to break down any growing-up prejudices about the military, at least on an individual level. Mannerism and posture told a lot, as did the subtleties of sidewall haircuts, even with those horrendous Marine jarhead jobs that must have been a bad joke that nobody would admit to; they certainly didn't make anyone look fiercer…though fervor is probably the real message. That he even thought about this stirred him to wish for his status six months prior. Biggest worry would have been scraping together the rent and pass a test or two. Then all he'd have on his mind on a day like this would be surf until the sun set splendidly, then turn back and watch the full moon rise over the rose-lit shore.

At the water, Landers and Caves met two surfers coming in. Always standing out, was a massive Hawaiian named Smoke with islander tattoos around his calves and upper arms, his hair in a ponytail, first one ever seen around there on a guy. They other guy, Dubay, wore a week's grizzly beard, hair to the shoulder all splintered and frizzed by perpetual sun and salt, first in junior high to refuse to cut it, back when only surfers tried that approach. There were only a handful of local surfers back then, mostly survival-by-scratch, with lived-in bodies and souls. Official proclamation was if they'd ever squandered enough time to get good at riding waves they were lined off as beachbums for life. So-called proper society, and police, deemed them contagious, better off removed than they should corrupt the children. These four had all had random interviews with the cops since grade school, deserved or not, fights on the side, items in status of questionable abandonment were gone missing around them. Out of the water, parties and girls were the primary target. On the other side of the hill, Landers was quieter, much less aggressive, and mostly stayed out of trouble. He always did well in school and crossed politely across the full social spectrum. A prodigious reader, he'd been chided plenty, but with some wonder that he could sit or lay on the beach or cliffs for hours, projected away into words; storyland if it was on his time. To date, he had been in abject love once – two years, with heartbreak tacked on for a third – had had a few designated girlfriends, several passionate seasonals, an inveterate flirt through it all, and lost in the grasp of lust every gap in between. Yet also through it all, his soul was locked in trust to his best friend and deepest unprofessed love, Katrina, right then up at the University of California at Berkeley.

With his hand, Smoke smacked Lander's board in greeting, "Hey, Michael, long time no check you out. What's slidin', Caves?"

Caves replied, "Takin' him for his last surf for awhile."

"Caves, come on, can it..."

"Ain't no secret spot," Dubay said. "So you got orders for the Nam. Bag it. Should've pre-bagged it. Like me an' Smoke. We just enlisted for the Marines, one flat day. Showed up for induction in trunks, period, stoned beyond dimension. Man, they were purrr-plexed."

"Yeah, Dubay chooses to choose off every jarhead in sight. Declared we were there to main and defame without blame or shame, so let's flame up the game. Four of them jumped him, with full malice."

"Smoke peeled them off, rag-dolled 'em, two-at-a-time and chucked them over a counter. They declared us irrevocably undesirable in six fun-filled hours. All quite ideal."

"Three back-to-back TJ all-nighters, a dozen cups of coffee to wash down a dozen bennies was all it took for me. Popped their blood-pressure gauge," Caves added his escape story. "They could see my pulse in my thighs. Shoved me out the back door, afraid I'd die dead on the spot."

Landers mused, "Maybe I should've tried something. Way back when."

"When's now," Smoke said, meaning it. "Paddle on over to Kauai. You already know the main mob. Army come nosing around, family kick their ass off the rock, right now, brah, I say so. And I am hooiey to all there, brah."

"Yeah, these flabby flatlanders and their bombin' bullshit. All they do is take our tax money and hand us back grief," Dubay said. "Southern Bible-whiners think we're all perverts. Back-Easters think we're all dumb. Rest of 'em think we're shallow as pancakes and hate us for breakfast. But stick a cigar in their mouth 'til their voice rasps

7

and let 'em grow a gut until they can balance beer on the top of it and they're badder than bad. 'Til it's their turn. Man, millions of 'em claim they know a war story, but there's only twenty guys in the world will paddle out in thirty-foot surf."

"Whatever it is that that says," Landers interjects.

"It says they're all just jealous 'cause they can't surf. So leave 'em be. Why can't we just annex Baja and redraw the border east of the Sierras. Except grab a six-pack of islands and maybe Vegas for the flat days."

Caves picked, "Oahu, Maui, Kauai and Hawaii."

"Who invited you over?" Smoke said. "Alright, but only since you got all the starlets."

"They can go ahead and ship us more girls. 'Course the girls will just come on their own," Caves said. "And what are our other two islands?"

"Tahiti. Or maybe the rest of Polynesia, group package. Plenty of da-kine virgin reefs out there," Smoke said.

Dubay added, "Maybe Australia later, plenty of waves there, too."

"Yeah, and armies of agro surfers," Caves said. "We'll visit them. Their girls even like Americans. Actually think we have manners. Shows you something."

"I'll take Manhattan," Landers said.

"Huh?" the others proclaim, in trio.

"Line from a song. Actually, it'll give us an Atlantic trading post."

"Let 'em keep Atlantica. It's too skinny. What do they bring, besides uptight attitudes? Give me Pacifica. We already have way more people. Maybe that's why we're mellower. Nothing to prove."

"Hm," Landers thinks, torn between being analytical and simply playing along. He throws in, "And as for war, the only good war is a cold war."

"I'll ride that wave," Smoke says. "Should be a UN department of cold wars. You get a bitch on, go formally declare it; propagandate away until you can't remember why you started. Then say aloha to no more-a-war-a."

"Presto," Landers said. "Though having brought it up, this Cold War's a little expensive. At the cost of making a thousand or so nukes a year."

"Hey, buzz head, we're dreaming here," Caves said. "No wonder you say you never dream about surfing. Probably afraid you'll get stuck inside and never get back out. Why can't you ride daydreams without analyzing or trying to scare everybody? Or apply the conscience crap?"

"So Michael, that Manhattan project; nothing against tubes but I don't want to share mine with a subway. Does the Atlantic even have surf?"

"Yeah, on the Ireland and France side. Those hurricanes gotta be good for somethin," Caves said, "Can you get one to go right at New York City?"

"Maybe, the hundred years storm. I'll be there," Landers said. "Meantime, let's go out, before the tide kills it."

Caves mused, "Wish to God it'd just get big beyond belief, spook all the war creeps back to the fatlands, for ever."

To this proposal they all, "Amen." Landers and Caves head to the water.

"So what are you gonna do?"

"I don't know. I wake up every day like there's ten pissed-off lobsters in my stomach. It all seems wrong."

"Massive understatement. Does anyone really expect to see any Viet Cong paddling sixty thousand rafts across the whole wide Pacific to surf O.B.? They do I'll snake every wave. Bet your board that the tide won't show, before that one comes down."

"I got to forget about all this," Landers said, walking over and jumping into the riptide to paddle out. The emotional tides pulling on his psyche had no timing or sense. These were the three toughest and loyal guys in all his close acquaintance. Sure there were guys much bigger than Caves and Dubay, but not in heart; and the ocean only cares about endurance and strength per mass. He couldn't imagine a human stronger than Smoke; to weigh 300 pounds and surf like a Bolshoi star alone is astounding. For the other three to even be discussing politics would be unique and, despite the banter about their evasion of the war, they all knew there were serious consequences yet to be paid, nor were their consciences close to absolved. Even the heavyweight boxing champion of the world, Muhammad Ali, wouldn't fight in this war.

The pro-war contingent had already claimed the flag all for themselves and irrevocably enlisted, "God on our side. Fight for your country or you're a coward and a traitor." Not easy words to hear, when they're aimed at you. When does a reasonable reaction to fear become intelligent survival and when is it cowardice? Fear is relative and surfers have the purest media to all know all each other's limits. There are waves nobody on earth will paddle out in, even if they appear to be rideable. Some highly skilled surfers won't go near overhead waves, while modest-skilled pitbulls will charge 30 footers and pull it off by just committing and not getting bounced off. Commitment is everything in big waves; because you want to at least make it to the bottom of the face and penetrate the surface or you're just one more bubble in the explosion. Guys who commit to the heavy drops have their own mutual respect, which doesn't contra-positive to disrespect for someone else who knows their limits; as long as they don't put down people with smaller limits, or lie too much. Pushing the shock edges of fear and willingness to accept the frequent poundings forces familiarity with mortality, which usually causes respect of all life. Managing extreme fear opens your heart chakra whether you want it to or not. Landers hadn't yet run into waves that anyone else would paddle out in and he wouldn't. He almost preferred stormy, messy conditions over clean days, for the constant variety and not having to wait out the lulls. He hadn't seen huge Hawaiian surf, though every couple years San Diego and Northern Baja push the max size and conditions anyone will ride. Central California and farther north do it regularly. He always wondered what too big would be for him and was willing to go looking. After high school, many of his friends moved to Hawaii, for good. Needing to work, for college, had kept him from following, so far.

Ignoring someone who had no apparent courage shouting coward at you was the hardest part. Shrill as they could be, many pro-war folk were sincere, maybe even right. Harder to take were those thinking they or kin were endowed with some status too lofty to risk their own blood. Often, way too often, they were the most strident. Doubters kept asking whether it made any sense if settling someone else's civil war was worth tearing apart America. What if the country was wrong? What then? Without any doubt the country was weaker; not just for losing bodies but for having its heart split in two.

Ocean Beach is on the sea side of Point Loma, a geo-eccentric corner of America, and the most mellow attitude neighborhoods of one of America's least stressed cities. Technically, one could claim if they traveled several miles east and south, to Imperial Beach, where just across a slough and the perpetually polluted Tijuana River was the border of Mexico, they'd be a few miles further south in America; though not further southwest. Better to climb high up to the old Point Loma lighthouse where one was reassured that the United States ended dramatically. Tall, golden cliffs drop off in three directions. Look down at the top of your relaxed left hand, the Point would be your thumb, some nine miles long, aimed due south, with the open Pacific to the west and south. Look back east, slightly to the left, on the index finger would be the lights of downtown San Diego dancing across five miles of harbor. Looking slightly right, across ten miles of the Coronado Bay, the lights of Tijuana twinkle in the hills. Both were spreading outward towards the mountains, with hundreds of new lights a day.

Having gone to live ten miles inland, to college, and much further inland in the Army, hadn't made Landers grasp how different he was than dry-landers, as it was happening; until he came back. Inland, he lost his sense of direction and, worse, weakened his sense of being. San Diego had always been a water-oriented town, the Point much more so. Given its long dry seasons, native tribes would have to have stuck close to the river, but found endless bounty in the bays, marshes and shallow reefs. Since the ocean is almost always between fifty-five and seventy degrees, any air temperature below fifty or over eighty is extreme and rare. That first ten thousand years must have been lovely. Jóan Cabrilho of Portugal landed on Point Loma, fifty years after Columbus had sailed into the Caribbean. That he had dismantled his boats at Panama, walked over to the Pacific and rebuilt them was much more impressive than that he had simply gotten here first. The peninsula was an island then, cut off from the mainland as the San Diego River split through marshes into the port harbor to the east and False Harbor to the north.

The Point still thinks like an island community. The riverbed, the Navy and Marine boot camps and the airport blocked civilization to the east. Behind them were the vast Convair airplane factories, where the Liberator bombers of WWII were built. Most of the rest of San Diego is over on the other side of the Pacific Coast Highway. All up and down the West Coast, chauvinist humor asked why would anyone want to cross over PCH anyway, ever. Plenty of beach towns up the coast were considered worthy destinations, but Los Angeles and San Francisco were like sisters who left home for culture and city lights. For all that San Francisco might want to claim in fine dining and intellectual punch with an East Coast flavor, and that L.A.

recreates the world with glitz and workaholic zeal, San Diego takes its status in physical energy; mellow mood but once you start moving, go at it. Social groups are much more prone to form around how people play, not by how they work, nor influenced as much by money. Surfers with surfers, fisherman with fisherman, team jocks with team jocks, boaters with boaters; though sailboats and powerboats apart. Crossover was not only tolerated but encouraged. Landers, competitive by nature and driven to work-hard, play-hard, had charged them all. He moved comfortably across the entire spectrum, from the old-money San Diego Yacht Club to the Dog Beach surf locals in the poorest corner of Ocean Beach.

Having gone to a Catholic elementary school in a neighborhood dubbed "Tunaville", where almost all the kids' parents were fishermen, mostly Portuguese with a smattering of Sicilians, he was quite at home on the fishing docks and boats. It did have its rough niches and tough people, but was a vital, self-sufficient community. Commercial fishing was dying, however, mostly because of foreign competition. Yachts and sportfishing companies were grabbing all the docks. Many thousands of wayfarers from all over the world, for four centuries, had docked or anchored here and lived on boats. Farther out along the bay is upscale La Playa, called the most stable Zip Code in California by the Post Office. Along the upper rib are the Wooded Area and Loma Portal neighborhoods, where almost every house has a postcard view of the harbor. Over on the ocean side, the homes of the Sunset Cliffs look out over those six miles of picturesque cliffs onto dozens of quality surfing reefs.

Sunset Cliffs melds north into Ocean Beach − O.B. as it is nearly always called − where Landers and friends wiled away their summer days. While most of the rest of Southern California's colorful and scruffy beach towns were yielding to money and gentrification, O.B. survived unaffected through a posture of feinted indifference to materialism. It is as much a state of mind as a place, time barely changes. You can drive as slow as you want and blocking traffic a minute to chat with friends is totally acceptable, unless the surf is really good, and then going surfing is the most noble thing to do. Being able to hold onto a full-time job − or even having the desire − are not required for respectability. Point Loma being the southern end of the Southern California Bight − the north end being Point Conception, several hundred miles north − dragged into the perpetual southward outer currents, so was colder offshore and could hold onto the coastal overcast longer than anywhere in Southern California. Bohemian from birth, artists, writers and musicians abound. Beatniks had taken to it in the fifties. Hippies were flocking there in the sixties. Bikers and other outlaw types had found, long ago, that their machines, tattoos, leathers, rivets and spikes turned heads only if their artwork merited a second glance. Drinking was legal on the beach, but squatters with attitude who abused the privilege were driven off, not as quickly by the police as by the locals. Back then, fighting on the sand was frequent and seemed more or less legal, as long as no weapons were visible and the contestants quit before the lifeguards got there; never in a hurry.

Newport Avenue runs inland, away from a long concrete pier. The first block is lined with bars, surfboard shops, several head-shops flanking a police sub-station, and casual cafes. Breakfast being the busiest meal of the day. Walk up that first block with a chip on your shoulder and you could expect to have it swacked off every ten steps. Walk with a casual smile, day or night, and you'd get by safely, every time, with smile and wallet intact. As long as they weren't jerks and flaunted it, marijuana smokers were overlooked, even by the police who at least acknowledged they were much less likely to stir it up than the drunks. In the midst of it all, average families raised healthy kids and let them run freely through the whole scenario, unattended, even when very young. That some strayed was a given statistic. Drugs and crime did thrive, mainly in the "War Zone" between Newport and the "big jetty", a several miles long rock pile, which creates a boat channel for Mission Bay and doubles as a levee to keep the San Diego River from flooding. Interstate 8 dumps out here, all the way over from Georgia, a western escape route for so many looking for a whole new dance. Symbolically, that jetty is a taboo sign, warning back staid control freaks, with "US OUT OF OB"ever a bumper-sticker favorite. If the Post Office thought La Playa was staid and stable, the street proclamation was if O.B. got any weirder they wouldn't deliver mail there at all.

Fifteen minutes south of downtown San Diego is Tijuana. It isn't so much a foreign country, it's the poor side of town, though with several oases of culture and wealth. Intimacy breeds a lot of griping, both ways, but criticism from outsiders is treated like an insult to the family. The work force of fifty thousand that crosses the world's busiest border crossing, every day, will work long hard hours, with seldom a complaint. The false myth that Mexicans are lazy says a lot more about the old-world bosses or new-world tyrants than the workers. Respect and fairness beget wonders. To Americans in need of eternal revelry, especially minors, TJ was a place to drink and dance all night only, back then, kids under eighteen had to sneak in, to get by the American check-point. Walking along the beach, waving to the Mexicans headed north was almost always successful, but a sure thing being to paddle a surfboard over from the Sloughs. It was then still the TJ of legend. All seven ingredients for sin were available on every block. Danger lurked in every crack of the sidewalk, the most dangerous of all being the corner dealer's brother with a badge. After a right-of-passage tour or two of the raunchy strip joints, usually in their early teens, for the most part the locals left these to the sailors and college kids driving down from L.A. Surfers, along with most regulars, gravitated towards the Long Bar, narrow but a full block long, in *Norteño* motif, where pitchers poured freely and *mariachis* played non-stop. Bands of angels must patrol Revolution Boulevard, that any kids ever get home safe. Beyond Tijuana is Baja California, a thousand miles on both sides of spectacular cliffs and deserted beaches, where surfing, fishing and kicking-back are as good as anywhere on earth. Just saying, "Baja", brought a smile to local faces.

Military is omnipresent around Point Loma. The last four miles of the Point is off limits to civilians except for a single road out to the ten-acre National Monument surrounding the old lighthouse, at the tip. Along the sides of that road is a cemetery, with a hundred thousand identical military gravestones in neat rows. San Diego Harbor having been considered the probable next target after Pearl Harbor – detailed battle plans had actually been drawn, with a date set and then cancelled – massive battery emplacements, dozens of old bunkers and rows of trenches still etch the landscape. Landers and friends had played in most of them in their pre-teens; war games. He claimed hiding and capturing prisoners as his forte. The Pacific Fleet headquarters is also out there. The whole area has labyrinths of underground command and storage centers. Local myth has them stuffed with nuclear and all other degrees of ready weapons. Darker local myth has it that after the Pentagon, Point Loma catches the next flurry of missiles.

Familiarity does not always build reverance. During World War II, the British sentiment for the American soldiers was expressed as, "Overfed, overpaid and over here." Though there is a broader respect for the military's reason for being – with patriotism not always made as part of the argument – kids growing up around the bases were trained by the kids before them, from first consciousness, to want them gone. The parents of this baby boom were war weary, and much more mature and world-informed than any American generation had ever been. Yet they were also very tired of thinking about it, so not a lot of war wisdom was passed on to the kids. Nobody ever took a poll; much of the resentment was pure prejudice. Few people really made much of a fuss about any of it; that's just the way it was.

In return, the short-term rotating military personnel had no particular connection to the place, though they proclaimed they did as a propaganda protocol. It appeared to the local populace that the military felt no obligation, moral or practical, to tell the truth to any civilian. Every low-altitude sonic boom, oil spill or act of disorderly conduct was denied, at every level, with no board of review. All along, plenty of locals actually went away into the military, even a few for life. All along, there were civic and commercial parties who lauded the fact that San Diego was a Navy town. Others argued that the cost way outweighed the benefits; that all that prime waterfront would be much better put to civilian use.

"How did you ever get drafted?" Landers had been asked hundreds of times. "You were in college. You had a deferment, as long as you wanted. You were smart, weren't you? What the hell happened?" What had happened was he had been surviving financially up at UCLA on a physics scholarship, along with part time jobs. Only he had started taking mostly literature courses. Not that he had lost a love of science, he just realized that to excel would mean sitting in labs twelve hours a day, for life. The day that realization hit him, he instantly understood why his friends who were otherwise extremely bright didn't do well in math. If you weren't going to excel, why waste the concentration effort. First day of his senior year, when he walked into the scholarship office to pick up his check, Landers was told it was being held back a semester, until he reapplied in a new major. A clerk told him he had been intentionally "duplicitous and ungrateful". He hadn't meant to be duplicitous; he had simply lagged on changing his major. At UCLA, general advice was never deal with the administration at all, unless prepared to wait a half-day in lines. This was bad advice, in his case. A timely meeting or two with a counselor might have kept the scholarship and warded off the draft board. He couldn't afford school otherwise. His family couldn't help, though they would have for every dime if they could. His father had recently died of cancer. He'd left only medical debts. Blindsided, fifteen years of school progress cut off, in a few short words. Landers drove up along the coast, hanging out with various friends a few days at a time, until he wondered if his heavy mood – even though he tried hard to hide it – was wearing on his welcome. Arrived home in San Diego, three weeks later, he opened a letter from the Selective Service Office, which ordered him to appear for induction into the Army, the next day.

Most guys got at least a six months countdown. Three months notice warning to take a physical exam, three months to process the results. Only Landers had already passed his physical two years before, because of a paperwork mix-up; his own fault, assuming the glitch would fix itself. Since the military didn't even realize then that they were in for a real fight yet, and could be somewhat picky, it would have been easy to fail the physical back then. So many did. Wet your bed, have any drug in your system, be or pretend to be homosexual, claim to walk in your sleep, take pills and drive up your blood pressure, simply act like a lunatic. But by 1966 a potential soldier could walk in the Los Angeles physical exam center with purple eyes, a needle in every vein and a police blotter a foot thick. They'd seen it all, "Come on in, son, we've got just the place for you." There were still plenty of scams to get out, legal or not. Money and/or political clout could get a favored son into a reserve unit with no chance of ever being activated. Get a lawyer to find you a town whose draft board could be compromised, or could get you registered in a small town where their draft quota was always filled because a local son had no choice but to go in, if they ever wanted to live with their family again. Running to Canada was always an option; they valued freedom of conscience over this war. Mexico, though close and inexpensive, wouldn't work. They'd ship you back on the first realization of why you were there. Landers didn't want to run anyway. He was naive, or vain or stupid enough to think he could actually show up for induction and convince the Army that the war wouldn't work well, for him. He even debated the officers at the initial military oath swear-in that he wanted a codicil added that he was also swearing to uphold international law, specifically those mandated by the Geneva Conventions. Perhaps he caught them by surprise – they yelled at him in protracted chorus – but either he wore them down or they were getting bored, so they even told him he could orally amend the oath, and he was ingenuous enough to think this mattered or would ever make his file. Mostly, he was stalling, waiting for a miracle.

Getting selected for the infantry, right off, was the reverse of a miracle. By intransigent behavior or perpetual incompetence, a clerk, driver or mechanic could get shipped back home from the military labeled "undesirable", which would fade from the record, in a few years; not as dire as "dishonorable discharge", which would last for life. By 1966, the trend was to transfer undesirables to the infantry for a second reading; over where enemy bullets were the inducement to comply. Infantry could overlook anything short of certain social felonies, and still might proffer a few more chances. Plenty of judges offered prison or the infantry. An assault conviction, for one, might not be such a bad quality. Almost everybody in the infantry wanted out, no questions asked. In 1966, there were few ways out, short of self-affliction, beating the VC to the punch. A few wars back, refusing to go to the front lines would get you up against a firing squad wall, on the spot. That Viet Nam wasn't a declared war negated this fate, but refusing to go to the field still would only get you time in the brig, only to be sent out there again anyway, upon release. Plus, the bad time would not count against the tour.

Paddling out through the surf washes all this away. Landers raced over to try to catch the last wave of a set, but a kid beat him to be a bit deeper to earn position, so Landers slipped over the top, only to spot the set of the day outside. Most of the sets were a foot or two overhead, this looks almost double overhead. Caves popped over the wave too. They made eye contact, each knowing no one else in the water could have seen it. They casually paddled a few yards further out, but as soon as they're over the next wave and out of sight from the crowd, they paddled hard as they can to get a ten yard jump on the pack. It's almost not enough. They barely ducked through the first four waves. This puts them into that surfing breathing gamble of paddling hard as possible, to not get caught inside, but leaving just enough breath that if they do get caught they can still hold their breath for a potential beating; which could be many waves, if the set goes on and on. Landers would barely make it through one, while Caves, off to the side, was in position so spun and caught it. Faced with the last wave, Landers paddled to right under the shadow of the pier. The wave hitting the bottom of the pier exploded over him, burying him in whitewater. Taking a few blind strokes and standing before clearing his eyes, his board shot forward in perhaps the most mystical moving sensation a human can have. Free-falling over the white water he made a long bottom turn to catch back up with the smooth green face of the wave and carve his wake in it, half way down the beach, maximizing every opportunity for more speed. He pulled out smiling, then laughed to see Caves clobbered trying to catch the tail end of the next wave. These few weeks of leave, with daily-double surfing sessions, had gotten him back in the physical shape he was used to, before going into the Army. During basic training and jungle infantry school at "Tigerland", Ft. Polk, Louisiana, he did extra push-ups and other exercises in the dark, or just plain ran harder when he didn't need to, to stay in almost as good of condition. Now he felt smooth, like he could go on forever, racing back out, again and again, for four hours. Just don't think about any of it.

2

On the other side of Earth, by calendar under the same Moon cycle but culturally somewhere between the Bronze and Iron Ages, the boy Te awoke. He stirred on his woven sleeping mat. Again he had had it, his living dream. More a conscious feeling than a dream. Some kind, old figure seemed to be just watching him in his sleep. Nothing ever happened and nothing was ever said, simply he never felt so protected and content. Never had he told anyone about it, as it wasn't his wont to tell of his dreams anyway. Yet, he'd heard that everyone had a spirit protector and figured that maybe this was his spirit protector. He wouldn't want to tell anyone about that either. Whatever or whoever it was, it never moved or spoke during this dream; it didn't seem necessary. This dream seemed to understand him.

Beside him, the vine, wood, and bamboo floor stretched and creaked. Already awake, his little cousin Mya pushed herself to her feet. "Why is she always up earlier than all of them?" thought Te. "She has nothing to do until the older girls and young woman are finished pounding the rice husks." Mya, at four, was already better at getting her own way than any of Aunt Rama's other children. That she did it through wanting so much to be involved, never through pouting, made her almost impossible to resist.

Sometimes Aunt Rama seemed to be awake earlier than Mya. But Te wondered, did she ever totally sleep? Nothing ever seemed to happen that she wasn't aware of it. This morning Aunt Rama had already been up, already brushed back the ashes over the ceramic fire pit, already picked out a live cinder that had settled into the sand base. She laid in the twigs and branches, in the order they were set out the night before and blessed them in a prayer to Yang-Long, the middle-plane deity of the trees, to let their smoke be blown up in the winds as a gift to the Nyang, the gods of the upper plane.

Blowing on the cinder until it glowed, she held one twig against it. When it kindled, she thanked all the spirits of all the planes for fire, once again. She thanked La Pom, the Goddess, for her family, praying for the soul of each one, as she picked out their nine sleeping forms in the near total darkness. One by one, she isolated the sound of their breathing; knowing who would wake up sick, who scared, or who happy. She moved over beside the children. With a sigh of pride and a new type of fear, she touched Te's crown, so softly.

"You've come to us to be picked, Te. I heard the rumors in the darkness. The spirit winds were here last night. They've found you. They've never felt like this before. In all history," she said as if talking through her dreamtime into Te's dreams. "Why, when you're only ten…doesn't matter, does it…history doesn't care about ages." Yet Te heard the spirit winds, and her in his awake time, though not knowing at all what she was talking about. She lay back down and sorted out the day's labyrinth of tasks, in her mind.

Mya was moving now. Te groped for her blanket with his skinny feet, but his cousin Zi already had it twisted around his own good foot; his other being a gnarled fist of flesh, from polio when he was three. Sometimes Te envied Zi that lame foot, "He never has to carry water." Envisioning an unheard of, wondrous village, where water ran in bamboo pipes, down through every house, he felt pulled into that water and into a dream of floating above a raging mountain stream. As it split into three paths across a slippery, flat sluice, he was dunked into it. Sliding and spinning, he was laughing, then trying to grab on to anything to stop himself as it poured into a green-black granite hole, sucking him under, down with the surge. Yet it was warm and comforting, as if he tumbled like a willing feather through a warm, bubbling phantasmagoria of light and colors; as if falling back into an all-loving womb, before there were any choices in his life.

Sounds of rhythmic pounding soon woke him again. One by one, throughout the village, the women and girls started pounding the rice in ground-out indents gouged into heavy ironwood logs.

Though they all kept to the same rhythm, Te knew every one by her own distinct thump. His older cousin Lieu, at twelve just a few years older than him, had the nearest and most distinct, a ringing tone, which reverberated through their entire hooch. With his eyes still closed, he could imagine her holding her pole high, in prayer to Yang-Sori, the god of the rice fields. Her slender body would arch back, stretching as far as she could, then strike down with the pole, which was as tall as her, crushing the rice with its rounded knob-head. That pole, given to her at birth and blessed by old Amba, would be the only pole she would use for all her life.

Amba was so old, and so much wiser than anyone could imagine. Ever since Mya was born, Amba had had Mya's pole set aside, in her hooch, carving over time all the sacred symbols Mya could come to encounter in her life, particularly those symbols of her protective spirits. She had even cut Mya's pole herself, when Mya was born. Some said that Amba already knew Mya would be the next shaman of the village, but others said this was not so, there were no other specific signs. She loved Mya, who was already the prettiest, everyone agreed; pretty because of those clear, piercing eyes, ever grasping at everything in a sense of wonder; eyes like Te had never seen, but only because he'd never seen the reflection of his own eyes.

It was time to be awake. Focusing slowly, in the dim light, his eyes followed a complete circle around the intricate, woven bamboo walls. He knew all the square and diamond patterns and every variation. Adjusting his loin cloth tighter, and straightening out the flap-over pieces of black fabric, he sat up, then rose slowly, stretching high to the ceiling and offering himself to the day.

Cocks started crowing. "Useless birds," Te thought, "They never lay eggs and who needs to be told the sun is coming up?" But Old Amba forbade anyone to ever kill them for eating; only for sacrifices. One time he had questioned this out loud and great-aunt Meyra heard him. She said don't ever contradict Amba, because she was their *njau*, their shaman to the spirit world, and losing protection from the spirits might allow a *molai*, an evil spirit of the forest, to slip into his mind while he was dreaming and devour his soul. He'd told that to the other boys and they laughed, though they'd been warned of *molais* too, and asked Te how was it, living with a witch. Te wasn't sure exactly what made one a witch but didn't think Meyra was one, though she was usually of a sour disposition, except when cooking a feast. She loved a feast, didn't matter to which deity or spirit.

Te moved to the door and watched Mya squat there on the elevated porch, tossing handfuls of kernels into the rounded indents for her sister, then scooping out the pounded remains into a large flat basket from which she sifted the husks from the kernels. Continually, Lieu pounded the rice, never missed a beat. Pounded with her feet apart, knees pushing outward, tightening her virgin hips, pumping in a smooth, rubbery dance. Her skirt of black ramie with red pinstripes shimmied, barely hanging from her hipbones, looking ready to fall at the slightest catch or tug but it never did. Flexing muscles in just-bulging breasts pulled tight the skin, baring her ribs as she raised her already powerful shoulders. "Strange things," Te thought of breasts. "End up shriveled sacks of skin, folded down over wrinkled bellies. Are women born dim? If they weren't dim why would they choose the life they did; always laboring with the pounding, or working the fields, or tending with children, or just squatting in groups, talking incessantly. How could there be that much to talk about? They had to do heavy labor too, carrying loads on their heads, which they seemed to be able to do longer than men. At least men got to go off into the forest to hunt for herbs, vegetables, nuts and fruits as well as small animals, snakes, lizards and large insects." Some women did this too, when they weren't satisfied with what the men brought back.

Everyone was stirring now. Te looked back in at the old people, Mehra and his uncle's parents. His own grandparents were dead, his grandmother having been taken by black-water malaria many years ago and his grandfather having died in some mysterious way he was never told. This was when he was two, around the time when his father was killed and his older sister and mother had disappeared though he knew nothing of that, either. He was never sure of anything about what happened, because the *Kra Polie*, the council of elders, forbade anyone to ever speak of his those times or of anything else beyond this village; not even of his mother. She'd never committed a dishonor, he was sure, and even felt she was alive, sometimes. Te had a great power of instinct that he assumed was normal. However, it was just because of this instinct that Amba and even the *Kra Polie* seemed unnerved about him, though he never knew of this concern.

Aunt Rama stood and took it all in, with the slightest smile to Lieu's and Mya's enterprise, took the notched pole that was their only way of climbing up to the raised hooch and slid it off the corner of the lanai. Without using her hands, she stepped slowly down the deep notches carved as steps into the steep pole. Every night it would be pulled back up. The hooch was atop tree-trunk poles high enough that a man could walk under it. They stored firewood under theirs. It's walls and floors were of woven bamboo, in the particularly intricate style of their clan, with a variation only their family used. In that tribe's style, the reeds of the steeply slanted roof were thatched. Slowly, nodding to the matriarch of the family next door, she walked out to the edge of the village, to where the women's dung holes were.

Though he hated his first chore of going for water, Te wanted to get on his way, this morning. Shouldering a pole with twenty gourds netted to each end, he hurried down the pole, jumping most of the way. He trotted towards the perimeter of the twenty-five hooches that made up his village. His family's hooch was the largest of the six hooches of their clan, the Jolong. The Jolong took most pride in always having been the best artisans, musicians and storytellers. The largest structure of all was the spirit house, with Amba's modest hooch right beside it. In front of the spirit house was the open village center. Around this center was a square of the ten homes of the Nie Drong clan, the ruling and by far the richest of the clans. One extended family of Nie Drong lived in a long-house, with forty people. Out around the perimeter, with no particular order, were the significantly smaller hooches of the Biu clan, who did most of the difficult and unpleasant labor. Some of the Biu were slaves to the Nie Drong, for not having been able to pay back debts. Under their homes were kept the pigs and chickens, which mostly belonged to the Nie Drong. Varying in size and intricacy of detail work, all the living hooches were basic rectangles with a-frame roofs. Only a few had ells for different branches of an extended family. Their possessions, mostly woven cloth for various ceremonies and ancient bottles, which served sometimes as money, were stored in baskets and woven trunks, along the walls. Tools, a couple spears and a crossbow were leaned on a rack by the door. Living activity centered around the hearth, where various ceramic crocks were stacked on a shelf and mats were arranged for eating and doing indoor work by a few short tables. In the south corner, where light came from the doorway and a window with a woven cover, were several spindles and looms. Next to it was an area for various crafts, including making jewelry and woodcarvings. Out on the lanai was another work area for working heavier woods and making pottery.

Much more elaborate was the spirit house, three times as tall, with intertwined weavings of the various clans' styles, including clans which weren't part of the village anymore. Its elaborately woven walls were taller and the high roof bowed up on both ends. Even the roof had a decorative crosshatch design made by binding and selecting different color reeds and vines in the thick, layered thatching. All the poles supporting the floor bore carvings, with the lower designs being taboos against unacceptable humans, as well as warning off any possessed animals or forest spirits. Even while giving polite praise, the next rings prayed to the maleficent deities to not bring anger or any unhealthy conditions to this place. On the upper rings were larger, deeper designs welcoming all the deities of the higher plane. Its broad lanai was partially shadowed by the overhanging eaves. Amba's lanai didn't actually touch this lanai, but she could step across the slight gap; only she was allowed to enter the spirit house this way. All others had to climb the elaborate pole ladder, which only was lowered for holy events.

In the village center, in front of the spirit house, was the spirit pole, the true focus of the village's collective *ae*, or soul force. On it were carved symbols of all the known planets, stars and constellations, as well as the symbol names for each day of the lunar month. They had no alphabet. All the various deities and spirits had their symbols engraved. Higher plane gods, the Nyang, were up top and went all the way around the pole. Lower plane Nyang had their symbol on one side or the other. Nyang-Long (Lord of the Trees), was drawn twice; once to ask permission and bid forgiveness for cutting this actual tree, once to give thanks and ask that it be blessed, as well as thanking him for all the trees of the forest. Below all the signs of the deities, each clan and family notched in their important identifying designs.

As Te ran past the last hooches of the village, he could hear Aunt Rama call him, "Te, Te, it's too early." But he pretended not to hear and kept running. Aunt Rama had scolded him for going down to the water place before the others, but this time he was anxious to get there, for no reason that he understood. "It's still dark down there," she'd chide. "The dark spirits might still be around. Or even Mr. Tiger."

Through the rows of bean hedges and vegetable gardens, Te ran. Running up the tilt pole and hopping over the last water buffalo fence, he start descending down the bamboo steps into the glen. For a second he paused, looking to either side of the path into the dark jungle wall, looking for any detail that might move. He shuddered, thought of Rama's words. But the last feelings of his waking dream were of him being so safe and comfortable in a water world, he felt compelled to get down into the water, to regain the feeling. It was dark down there but he continued anyway, down the slick red clay trail, grooved smooth by years of wear from the broad bare feet of his tribe. No other humans had ever walked here.

At a corner of the woods the trail dropped steeply over a bank. Teak-block steps led down and around a short scarp to a graceful bamboo bridge, hung across a rivulet like a spider's web. On the other side, a system of large bamboo pipes funneled water down into a system where shorter, bamboo pipes protruded from twenty different places, one for each family; though the Biu families often shared pipes. Below each bamboo pole was a teak floor, caged in by bamboo poles. Water poured pure, splaying on the floors or going straight through holes, to run down into the stream. Fresh and cool, the water came from the springs. Springs that were gifts of the Ra spirits. When this village was formed, even before they chose where their hooches would be, each family had picked where they would draw water, asking guidance and a blessing from the family's guiding spirit. The Nie Drong clan had the highest pipes, mostly along a separate branch of the glen. Te's Jolong clan picked next and his family had actually picked the very lowest place, not usually favorable but only because it was in a deep, private grotto. He filled half the gourds. Then he reached above him with a stick and turned a bamboo sieve to be under the waterspout, which spread the flow from the pipe into a soft, wide, endless shower.

Still wet, he continued down off the trail into the streambed. In ankle deep water he made his way under bared roots, knowing every footstone across a deep, rushing eddy. Nobody else ever went this way, there was no need to because it was thought it never went anywhere. Plus the spiders back in there were particularly ambitious. But last month, while chasing an enormous violet butterfly that seemed to tease and lead him on, Te followed it as it seemed to have a special chart through the spider webs. It perched up on a ledge rock and he pulled himself up on a lower branch to look at it closely.

He had no desire to catch it, just wanted to see it up close. Seeming to enjoy his attention, it rested only a foot from his face, as if slowly fanning him with its wings. When it flew off, he leaned his head over and could see a grotto and a still pool around the bend. Wanting to be the first explorer, he told nobody else, but just waited until he could be here alone. So here he was, dodging and weaving through the spider webs, which he was very afraid of, but curiosity led him on. By bracing his legs across a narrow divide he sidled around the last turn. Leaping from boulder to boulder over a slow, gurgling run he made it to where the stream merged with a larger stream. The powerful combined flow charged down the "rapids to the end of the world", which could be seen from above, and even heard from the village, during the monsoon.

To the left of the split was the pool he'd glimpsed, much grander than he'd even imagined, crystal clear and seemingly bottomless. By far the stillest water he had ever seen, almost a perfect mirror. Almost no sky was visible overhead, because of overhanging giant ferns and thick shrubs. Up hundreds of feet higher, it was all overshadowed by a tremendous ficus tree, which shaded the entire watering area. Though the light was dim, it seemed so peaceful, with all the roots and banks covered by a thick, spongy layer of moss and tiny-leaf ferns, woven into a deep, green carpet.

Te leaped to the far bank. He squatted and waited. When the first morning breeze wafted by, he felt a chill as if spirits were passing. Mystery shivered up and down his spine but he felt no fear so was sure it he was a good spirit out for a place to play or just be at peace. He wasn't sure if he really wanted to meet a spirit but there was so much told of them his curiosity was always peaked.

From the corner of his eye a movement flashed. A small flat rock skipped a half dozen times across the mirror pool, until it stopped briefly on the surface, just spinning in place a few turns until it sank. Then the only movement was all the circles growing and crossing each other. Where the rock came from was only a giant *kuba* spider web in the farthest, dark corner. This terrified Te. Had the spider thrown the rock? It pulsed there, in the middle of its web; so large it could place a leg on either of his shoulders and clear the top of his head with its belly. Sometimes he had nightmares of a spider doing this. He had never seen one so large, nor nearly as furry. But he was always told the *kuba* spiders were great friends to men. They ate insects, many, many mosquitoes and sometimes birds.

Then the giant web shimmied, even though the spider was motionless. Te started, ready to run away. But some movement in the darkness behind the web made him stay, in curiosity. Slowly, as the increasing light reflected off the pool it lit the back of the cave. As he stared, he made out the unmistakable figure of a man, standing there. Though instinct would be to run from any stranger, because he'd never seen anyone in his life who wasn't from his village, the web seemed to act as a barrier, keeping this figure from coming after him. Something actually drew him closer. When he was but five paces away, he could make out the face of an old man, older than anyone in his village, even older than Amba. Yet there was something reassuringly familiar about this figure, particularly as the light from above cleared the ridges and the man's eyes glistened in an unmistakable smile of recognition and understanding. With both hands, the man pinched the two main supporting strands of the spider web and moved them, reattaching them to a thin root. Now there was nothing between them.

Te bowed, as did the old man, not just as a normal greeting, but somewhat longer, denoting more trust and honor than any elder had ever shown to Te before. He said, in a deep, clear tone, "Finally, Te. Finally we meet."

Te asked, "Who are you?"

"Xem. You've never heard of me, have you?"

"I've never heard there was anyone else, at all, who didn't live in our village. All other beings are either animals or spirits. Are you a spirit?"

Xem chuckled, his straggly whiskers amusing Te by the way they danced. "Oh, no more than any other person is a spirit. No more than you."

At this Te smiled, for this was great adventure. Everything about this encounter was extraordinary, but mostly that this oldest of men seemed to recognize, respect and laugh with him.

"Come on in," Xem said, walking to the back of the cave, so that Te would not feel trapped. Te hesitated slightly, but his curiosity was stirred by this deep cave, which nobody in his village knew existed. Unlike most caves he'd peered into this hadn't dirt for walls, nor roots hanging down. All the walls were of glistening granite. Distinct lines of many colors crisscrossed the sides and ceiling, with tiny crystals and mica shimmering all around. On a slightly raised stoop, Xem squatted, indicating with his hand for Te do the same.

Te squatted, just a few steps in from the web. For a moment they both just looked at each other. Everything was familiar about this face, to Te. Familiar not in detail but in feeling, an emanation of comfort from a good dream. Almost perfectly round was Xem's face, even the lines and wrinkles were part of this roundness. His broad, flat nose offset eyes that danced from sparkling clearness then deepened into a meditative glaze.

Uncomfortable at this long silence, Te asked, "How did you make the rock stop and float like that? Was it magic?"

Xem laughed at the fearlessness with which Te formed questions. "It's good you ask the first thing to come to mind. Questions scare rigid people. No that wasn't magic, it was the way of things," he told Te.

"But rocks don't float. Or is that wrong?"

"No, that's not wrong. But don't be afraid of being wrong. By acknowledging that what you had thought, just before, was wrong, is a way of learning."

"Then if that was a rock, and rocks don't float, why wasn't it magic?"

"You have the natural Jolong way with logic. The Jolong were always the smartest clan."

"What clan are you?"

"We'll get to that later. Let's get back to your previous question. That rocked skipping was simply a technique of throwing it flat, at the right speed, with just the right spin. My action was simply a type of play, to get your attention." Te smiled that an older person would even consider playing with him. Xem became more serious, "Though water seems soft, it actually has a silk-like skin. Take a narrow piece of bamboo and fill it to the top. Notice how the top of the water will arch slightly. This isn't magic either, it's also simply the way of things."

"Can you do magic though? Is there really magic? I want to be able to do magic."

"Are you quite sure of that? Whether magic exists or not, there's never really proof because the ways of things are never reversible, nor exactly repeatable. There are even those who say there really is no magic, only original fate, by design. Be aware that if you ever have the ability to create magic, never play with it or take it lightly, in any way. No matter what your intention, any time you borrow magic from the universe you owe it back to one spirit or another. Don't be sure that the spirits won't trade your debt. Maybe a gentle tea herb you borrow magic from for a stomach ache might trade your debt to a tree spirit, who might trade it to a tiger spirit, or worse."

"Even to a *molai*?"

"I don't think about *molai* and neither should you. No spirit can enter or eat your soul if you don't in some way invite it in. Even saying the word gives them more presence in your life than they had just before. When any thought of an evil demon, or of a mean lower spirit or even of an untrustworthy divinity comes into mind and starts going around and around in a memory loop, I try to think of an instant waterfall falling on me. Let it all wash the image instantly from my mind. If it won't go away, I repeat the dowsing over and over, until I can form a new thought. If it an emotion persists, I visualize peaceful falling water, while turning my eyes from side to side, under closed lids, as long as needed. Only exception is when I owe an apology and have not been able to make it. I'll maintain that thought but hold it aside until I can complete the apology. Try to make amends as soon as they will be gracefully accepted. Apologies, if they are sincere, make you stronger and protect you, from spirits as well as people."

"I want to apologize to aunt Rama for running from her voice this morning. Do you owe any apologies?"

Looking long into the distance, Xem finally answered, "Yes. So many that I will never be able to give. There is the one greatest apology owed of my life, which might still be possible. Perhaps you can help me, some day. But not today and we haven't forever. There are things I want to teach you. First off, since I can tell that the silence ban of the *Kra Polie* is still in effect, you have been taught that this is the only village on earth. That is far, far from true. Just be aware of that for now, but never speak of it, to anyone. I'll tell you about the outside world, later. For now, be thankful you are safe within your current world. Most important and most immediate, from this minute on, never, ever speak of me to anyone in the village or it might be very dangerous for you."

Te understood this already. He knew there were people who were very suspicious, very mean, and very deceitful. This he knew not just from the myths but from his own observations. Still, he asked, "And dangerous for you, too?"

Old Xem barely smiled, as if inwardly and said, "I would not be in any more danger than I am now, from the decrees of the *Kra Polie* of your village and a few others as well. But threats from humans are the least of my worries. Let's spend another day talking about history and politics. Do you know what I mean by politics?"

"It's something to do with who gets to make up the biggest chores and hand out the greatest punishments for disobeying. And who gets to receive presents, for reasons I don't understand," Te said.

Xem laughed slightly at this, but not mockingly. "That is the general idea, yes. Right now, though, let's not learn about ideas; let's learn real skills. How well can you swim?"

"Not so well, but I can stay afloat as long as anyone, by filling up my stomach with air."

"Good, this is the direction I want to go. Let me teach you to breathe so that you can stay underwater much longer. Get into the pool."

Te did this without hesitation, though only in the chest deep water that was inside the cave. He was surprised how warm it was. Xem said, "Now, take a deep breath and show me how long you can stay under."

Wanting to impress Xem, Te took several deep breaths, slipped under the water and tried not to come up until he absolutely could not manage any longer. He shot up quickly, with a gasp."

"That was actually very good, considering you're doing it all wrong. Try this. Take slower breaths, and pay more attention to exhaling all the tired air. Even push in your stomach and diaphragm with your hands. Not too fast, which would help if you were only going to do it once, but I want you to learn to do it over and over. After you've been down only ten counts let out a few bubbles. This seems wrong, I know. Your body will think so too, and for a second it will tense up, as if panicking that all your air will be gone. But it won't be gone. After a second or two, that panic will be gone and you'll feel quite comfortable for another ten counts. Before the lack of air starts to feel very uncomfortable, let out another small breath. Same first panic, same comfort after that. Keep doing this over and over. Try it a few times."

Te did try this a few times, as he was always quick to grasp new instructions. First time he had his timing off, but did manage to let out four or five mouthfuls of bubbles, before he became too uncomfortable and shot up quickly.

"That was better than the first time, but not longer. Did you have the feeling, after the first few bubbles went out, that you were quite peaceful?"

"Yes, the second and third time too."

"Good, now believe that will be true, every time."

So Te tried the whole process again, three or four times. Each time he became more excited, because he was staying under much longer than he'd ever done. It was almost like dreams he'd have of being able to fly under water. On the fifth time, he became so relaxed, that Xem became concerned, and came over, reaching under to tap Te to make sure he was still conscious. Te was still conscious, waving softly with his hands. For another thirty seconds he stayed under, coming up without a gasp, and with a big smile, "Wow. I can't wait to show..."

"Yes, you can wait. Don't show that to anyone. You might practice it if nobody is looking, but don't show anyone."

"Why?"

"Because I know the Nie Drong clan. Don't let them know any secrets you might have, ever. One day or another, they'll use them against you."

"You don't like the Nie Drong either, do you?"

"Let's just say I don't trust them. It's not a good thing to speak of groups of people as if they all had the traits of some individual in that group."

"And there are other villages beside ours? How many?"

"That was a jump. Too many to consider. And vastly different than your village. With people who look and behave much different, though they're all human. But leave this for another day. Do you know how to tell the new moon?"

"I think so."

"Well make a point that you do, exactly, and come back here on the next new moon, earlier even than this time, if possible. And we will talk of many more things. I hear the other boys, coming. You must get back, before they see you returning."

"Is there nothing I can share or take with me, from today?"

"There is nothing you can share. Maybe someday, but not yet. Not nearly yet. There are three people you and I will be meeting, though. From a land far across the Earth. Two I've met; they've been near here, before, only a few years ago. The third is yet to be revealed. Most likely will be in Dreamtime, when the Nyang will it."

"Have you ever been to Dreamtime?"

"So have you," Xem said, and looked more deeply into Te's eyes than he could have ever imagined an adult doing. And looked profoundly into him like an equal, if even that – subject to not knowing that Te could be higher, in an eternal hierarchy. On the current matter, he added, "No, you can't tell anything, but there is something you should take. On your way back, dive down to the bottom of the pool and find the rock you saw me throw. You'll recognize it because it has a red drawing on it. Hide it in your loincloth and never let anyone else see it. And add this simple idea to your prayers, if you haven't already been taught it. No matter how evil or vulgar some person or event may seem, always remember that, in our universe, where everything is sacred, there is no such thing as profane. But go, don't try to digest that now. Go, Te, go with the gods, that they lead us to peace." He bowed slightly, as did Te, who turned to go, quickly. Behind him, Xem reattached the spider web and slipped back into the shadows.

Diving into the pool outside the cave, he didn't think he could ever reach the bottom. But he tried his new breath-holding technique, even though it didn't work so well when he was swimming. The rock was easily found on the sand. He stuffed it in his loincloth and arose.

As fast as he could, he scrambled back through the ravine. Just before the other boys could see him, he scurried out but he hadn't time to wash the mud off his knees and hands before he was spotted. A slightly older but much bigger boy called down from the bridge. This was Pim, the village chief's son and a leader of the Nie Drong boys, who all acted superior. "Hey, Te, what are you doing, down in the mud? You must think you're a leech." Quickly he and a few other boys came down the trail, to just above Te.

"I dropped one of my gourds and it drifted down the stream. I tried to catch it."

"What was down there?"

"Nothing. Nothing but a bunch of giant spiders. Want to see?"

"Sure, show me," Pim said in his normal bully tone.

Te was surprised his bluff didn't work, and was even more anxious when Pim pushed by him and seemed like he was going to try to get through the narrow ravine. With Te and a few other boys right behind him, he soon reached a tangle of spider webs that Te knew hadn't been there just minutes before, even though he had said they were. In the first, largest web was the giant *kuba* spider, or one just like him, pulsing menacingly. It even hissed. They all turned and ran back, continuing up the bank. Calmly, Te stopped at his family's water place and continued filling his gourds.

From way up higher, some of the other Nie Drong boys who had been watching all of this started harassing Te, which was not unusual. One called, "You better watch out, for coming down here alone. Mr. Tiger's will have you for a snack. Or a *molai*."

At which several of the boys started chanting, "Molai, molai, eat your soul. Bury it in a *poo-poo* hole." After a few verses they laughed at their own fun and turned their attention to themselves.

This didn't bother Te much. Being one of only a few boys of his age in his clan, he was used to being teased. Yet it did start him thinking about if *poo poo* was a profane word. Older people told them not to say it, not like this anyway. Or would having a soul buried under excrement be a profane concept? It seemed like it might be. How could it not be? If the gods gave people everything, why couldn't they give them profanity? Nothing was clear about any of this. Yet he felt a great warmth, for this grand secret. Without knowing how or why, he knew his life would never be the same.

3

Right at sunset, Caves, who had finished his own session hours ago, paddled back out, came up alongside Landers and sat up on his board. High, eastern tropical thunderheads mushroomed over the mountains, sucking up off the great Sonora desert from a Sea of Cortez hurricane, glowing corals and pinks through the rainbows in the spindrift skimmed off the breaking waves by the offshore winds. Shore lights shimmered in between. Refracted to way-overscale, a gold-blood moon came easing over the top of the Point just as the sun spread out in a wide scarlet ribbon, then melted through the horizon, echoed by the green flash. There's so much dramatic beauty out in the surf-line, it rarely needs to be discussed.

"Let's go, the girls are at my house, prepared to go loony. Everyone who thinks they're anyone is there."

"Last thing in the world I want is a hundred good-byes."

"Don't matter, you're coming. Six chicks, personally, told me they are going to write you in their 'had him' diaries, tonight. And I'm gonna scoop up the ones you can't get to."

Landers laughed, "How likely is this lie."

"Ain't like I'm above lying, but this one is the naked truth, no pun to be had. I never claimed to have any idea what the hell girls could ever be thinking, but tonight they're *toda loca*. Not my job to tame them. Only thing I really don't understand is why they'd try for your skinny ass before they'd grab a big ol' hunk of me."

Landers laughed. He paddled with Caves along the cliffs for a quarter mile. One last look around reassured him why they'd named the place Sunset Cliffs. Separately, they rode bouncy waves into a tiny cove, quickly scampered up the cliff before the next wave came, using worn handholds they'd carved years before. Caves hung over the edge, grabbing a rope hidden up under a cave. He pulled up a trap with half a dozen lobsters, half of them of questionable size. He took them all. Being off-season it was poaching regardless. Several other surfers were surf-casting and had landed a two-foot white seabass, several corvina and a twenty-pound halibut. "No way you just pulled those in right there," Caves challenged them.

"Yeah, right, asshole, we brought 'em live, in a tank, from over from Tunaville, and put 'em in that tidepool just for your viewing pleasure," was his sarcastic reply.

"I'm impressed," Landers said, and he was.

Right at the top of the bluff, Caves' house was partially hanging over the edge, likely to be one of the next to tumble over the ever-crumbling cliffs. A barbecue improvised from a dismantled shopping cart was piled high in fresh albacore, yellowtail, yellowfin and bluefin, caught that day, twenty miles out on skiffs. Dozens of partiers were on the lawn, which ran up to the cliff's edge, drinking beers and margueritas. Most wore swimwear, with t-shirts or bikini tops optional. Age range from five to fifty. In the scene that assembles around surfing, ages don't matter, only a common spirit. Drugs were cutting into this age blend, however. The older surfers were indifferent to marijuana but had no idea what to think of the powerful psychedelics. They didn't understand how perfectly healthy kids could go from wanting to do nothing surf all day long, to blotto forever, in only weeks. Used to be it took years of drinking to achieve that effect. Landers went around the side and rinsed off in the outdoor shower, a hose hooked up in a tree. A younger girl he recognized but couldn't exactly place walked right into the shower with him, pulled off her top and gave him a death-grip hug. "Michael, I gotta talk to you." He held her back a bit, "Oh, hi, aren't you," he said, looking around to stall and embarrassed that several people were watching, including whom he recognized to be her older brother, "Aren't you Roderigo's much-younger sister? Like, fourteen. I wouldn't mind going to jail right now, but not for that. Plus, I don't think your bro appreciates it much." She looked at her brother, did a brief pout, picked up her top and swang it at him. Walking away, she flipped them both off, saying, "Fifteen, and old enough to be old enough." Landers opened his palms out, to say it wasn't his doing. Roderigo just shrugged, laughed and raised his beer.

Landers poured a beer from the keg. He tossed a tortilla on the barbecue and heaped it with samplings of fish, then piled on onions, lettuce, tomato, avocado, *ceviche*, and *jalapeño* laced salsa. Even while eating, he just kept moving, nodding and smiling to friends but weaving around individuals who might start a conversation. Inside, the party was getting looser. Lit by multi-color lightwheels and lava lamps, decoration was cheap Persian rugs on the floors and beat-up, roomy chairs and couches, draped with wool blankets. All other wallspace was plastered in surfing photos, with a few psychedelic concert posters and hyper-figurative Tijuana paintings on black velvet that glowed gaudy in the black lights. Couples were making out in every possible locale. A makeshift band was playing, on no particular tune but with a driving, inescapable rhythm. A girl he'd dated a few times in high school pulled Landers into a slow dance, even though it was a fast song, and seemed to be starting up what Caves had been advertising. When her boyfriend came around looking for her, she backed off quickly with a wink and a smile. Upstairs was a large room with windows on all sides, lit by candles, lots of them. Caves, Roderigo, two other surfers and a dozen girls were propped up on the floor cushions and bean-bag chairs, around a multi-armed hookah, kept constantly packed from a large bowl of rough but potent Mexican marijuana.

"High time you showed up for high time, "Caves said, with a mind-fading smile and his eyelids drooping nearly shut. "First, though, you gotta kiss all the girls, just to see who might kiss back." He kissed a couple around him, for demonstration purposes.

Somewhat reserved but not unaccommodating, Landers made his way around the circle. They all kissed back, with intention. These were all girls Landers had known since junior high. A couple he'd dated a few times, most of the others he'd tried to put moves on at one party or another. Two girls, Colleen and Francina, his favorites and two best girl friends, not counting Katrina, pulled him to sit between them. They held on tight, but their kisses were more as warm greetings than tongue-filled journeys the other girls in the room had tendered. Always having been sweet-looking but wild-at-heart surf chicks they were taking on exotic, gypsyesque looks, with beads, turquoise jewelry and loose, hippie dresses, sans underwear. They stuck one of the hookah tubes in his mouth. Landers took a deep draw, held it, exhaled, then took another. He closed his eyes and let it swirl his brain a bit. At least it seemed to erase some of his feeling of being totally apart from the whole scene. He smiled, without forcing it.

Colleen pressed, "What are you doing to us, Michael? First you go away to college for three years, now the war. What next, Wall Street? Ever consider reapplying yourself to common surfer anarchy?"

Francina added with a squishy hug, "Don't go gettin' killed now. You know Billy Roderigo, don't you, from over at Windansea? He just got back." Roderigo was on her other shoulder.

Given the shower scene, Landers just smiled and nodded. Roderigo was a top surfer from La Jolla. They'd sat outside the surfline and chatted between waves, dozens of times, but they'd never actually met on land.

"Yeah, so how's Michael get out? Get too crazy?" Caves asked.

"Too late for that," Roderigo said. "No such thing as too crazy, once you've got orders for a line company. The Constitution and Bill of Rights, all that free choice, pursuit of happiness stuff, it don't apply no more. Shit, everybody in the infantry wants out. Ain't no out. Myself, I had a good time in Nam, but I was a truck driver down near Saigon. You do get some pretty hairy convoys, but otherwise it's a party and a dry bed, almost every night. Having done it, though, my life's gravy now. Having the government off your back is a monster relief. Get paid three years of college. Only drag is keeping my hair short for four years, for Reserve meetings. One thing about infantry, you won't have to go to reserve meetings. They let you out clean; they probably don't want you. Which isn't a good sign. If I was you, I wouldn't risk it. Not for this one. Shit, who got me started on this? You're gonna hate when you get back, when they get you rapping. Hook me up to the pipe. Shut me up."

"What are you gonna do?" Colleen asked.

"I have no idea. But I have a day and a half to decide. So how 'bout there's gotta be something else to talk about. Anything."

From downstairs, they hear an all-to-familiar commotion. Growling, Caves jumps up. Landers would have waited for a report, but Caves nods for him to come with him. Landers follows, as do the others, except Roderigo and a few of the girls.

With blood on their shirts and fresh scrapes and bruises, Dubay and Smoke were parading around the living room.

"Heah, what the bejesus is goin' on?" Caves asked, but knew the answer upon instant surveyance. "Primo, who'd you draw this time? Not the Marines again. We're trying to maintain a party mode, here, if you hadn't noticed."

Shadow-dancing for effect, Dubay reported, "It was b'itchin', man. We were cruising by the biker bar, not the Hells Angels hang, the black leather, muscle freaks one, when some tweaker started pimpin' Smoke's ponytail. Some redneck swabbies, just passing by, thought it this was good sport too. Smoke picked up one of the swabbies and tossed him through the doors. Then knocked two more over a couple of bikes.

"Just as the rivet rabbits were organizing, inside, Dubay jumped on one of their bikes and drove it right in the door, taking out three of them, right now. I had to follow."

"Only the others piled on me, until Smoke started yanking them off and mauling them by the score."

"He took down a half dozen," Smoke added though as if it was no big deal.

Ever animated, Dubay said, "A whole caravan of fun, man. When we walked away, the bike boys and swabbies were organizing a posse. Anybody feel like going and deorganizing them?" About a dozen guys seemed ready to join in, complete with a swatch of epithets, but a skinny surf kid came in the door, reporting, "Forget it, the cops are already down there and the owner had you guys followed. I say we got about two minutes 'til the raid."

Caves was disgusted, "And the party was just starting to kick in. Alright, everybody, grab everything you brought and run. I gotta be gone too, so nobody stays. Everybody, now, go."

His announcement was unneeded, this drill was well rehearsed. Scooping up bags and six packs, people scrambled out every door and window. As they went out the back door, Colleen and Francina grabbed Landers and Caves, but Caves resisted, "No, I gotta get my wagon out of here or they'll confiscate it." Colleen and Francina would have joined him in his wagon, only Roderigo's little sister and her girlfriends piled in. Not liking this casting, the girls held onto Landers and headed across the alley and through an apartment courtyard to Colleen's car, left over on the next street as a normal getaway precaution.

By the time Caves got to the corner, the police had already blocked off the party street. Party guys and girls were scattering in all directions, with the bar patrons and swabbies pointing them out for the police. Having sized up the various groups, the cops, for the first time in local memory, actually seemed to be on the surfers' side, ignoring the bar owner and his pals screaming for vengeance. Caves tried to drive by a cop, but he casually waved them over, to park across the street. Realizing his was in big trouble, with his car loaded with beer and young girls, all likely to be stuffing pot down between the seats. Caves slowly sauntered around to the police so they watched him and not the car. As Caves had instructed them, the kids all took off running, carrying all the evidence. They would have made it away clean, too, except a bag of a dozen bottles crashed and beer foam ran all over the place. The police instructed Caves to sit on the sidewalk and went across to investigate.

Already beyond the police barricades, with power to the pedal, Colleen inspected the contents of the paper bag she'd grabbed. "Alright, a six-pack and a bottle of wine.

"Excellent grab. I got the pipe and a bag of grass," Francina added to the inventory. "How'd you do?"

"You guys are lot faster than I am," Landers complimented them, although it would not actually have been his nature to pick up a bag that wasn't his.

"The Army dulled your senses, you're just out of practice," Colleen said. "It would be nice to find Caves, it is his grass. First place he'll go is out to the cliffs to dump off all those gremmie chicks." Right then they saw Caves, in detention. "Oh-oh, this calls for a rescue mission."

"I don't think, maybe...oh well," Landers started to say but Colleen slammed on the brakes. Francina pulled off her blouse – she did have a bathing suit top underneath – jumped out and hung it over the back license plate. Slowly, she cruised towards the cops, advising Landers, "Lay down in the back, we got this covered. Cops are easy." Even though Caves saw them and nodded for the girls to get out of there, Colleen stopped. Francina called to the officers, "Hey, guys, we heard there was a big party down here. You know where it is?"

Eyeing the girls, a welcome eyeful at that, the cops approached, trying to be flirty. "Sorry, girls, you're too late, it's broken up. Better move on. We have to hang around and check out some complaints."

"Yeah, well check this out," Francina proclaimed, whereat she dropped her shorts and shined her pretty white moon out the window, about three feet from the cops' faces, yelling "Any complaints now?" Not having a page in their manuals for this one, the cops were momentarily lodged in perplexity.

Colleen floored the accelerator, yelled, "Hey, pigs, get back in the bag!"

For effect, Francina added the popular epithets, "Eat shit and mold. Make love not war."

Jumping in their car, the cops spun it around, to take chase. They shouted at Caves and another surfer detained on the sidewalk near him, "You guys stay right there, we'll be right back."

As the cops sped off Caves smiled. "Yeah, we'll be right here, loungin' away. Meantime, let's participate," he said to the other guy. They grabbed a couple loose beer cans and launched them at the cop car, the cans exploding foam all over the windshield. This redirected the cops' attention. They tried to make another U-turn, but the street was so narrow they had to make several maneuvers to get free. By then, Caves' and Colleen's cars were long out of sight.

A few minutes later, Colleen and Francina led Landers by the hand down a dark path to Francina's tiny bungalow, buried in blooming wisteria. It was tucked way back in the trees behind a La Playa mini-mansion, owned but not inhabited by Colleen's parents, who'd had to rent it out to make ends meet. She said, "I'd love to see their police report. 'Blinded in beer foam, by the light of the moon.'" They laughed. Inside, the girls didn't bother with the lights, but went straight to lighting a dozen candles. Colleen rifled the record collection, placing a one-inch stack of soft rhythm discs on the stereo changer. Francina tossed several pieces of clothes off the bed onto the only piece of furniture, a padded chair, and she arranged the pillows to sit everyone close together. She nudged him onto the bed and both girls corralled him in the corner. Colleen opened beers while Francina rolled a joint.

Bemused and amazed by all this progress, but not wanting to highlight any of its implications, Landers commented, "You guys deserve the surfer medal of honor."

"After all the times you guys rescued us, it's the least we could do," Francina said.

"Yeah, remember those Marines in TJ? Or all those drunk surf rats up in Huntington? They were some gnarly beasts, too. Especially their chicks. Classify that one as a pure kamikaze mission. Speaking of which, ever had a kamikaze hit?"

"I don't know, but it better not hurt."

"You tell me how much it hurts," said Colleen, mischievously smiling as she sat over him, facing him. She lit a joint, took a deep hit, said, "Exhale," then, after he did, put her mouth over his and blew the smoke into him, following it up by her tongue with no doubt of its very immediate intentions. By the time they came up for air, Landers was panting, inside his head was a spinning swirl of lights.

Before the phantasmagoria faded, Francina playfully shoved Colleen off the bed and took her place. In the middle of her kiss she rolled aside and pulled him with her, straddling and squeezing his thigh between her legs.

"Y'know, you girls really do know how to get a guy high."

"We've only just begun," they sang in chorus. Francina began unbuttoning his shirt, slowly kissing each revealed inch. As Colleen got back on the bed, she artfully undid her blouse, then playfully, tried to push down the self-reviving tent of his surf trunks. As if to find out what was causing them to keep popping back, she stuck her hand under the loose bottom. Once she captured the perpetrator, she pretended she was going to choke it with both hands.

Inching up towards ecstasy, Landers just fell back. "This is a fresh take. Ever since junior high school, I've made a number of honorable efforts to get even a decent kiss from either of you."

"Indecent, you meant," Francina corrected. "Which, coincidentally, does happen to be just my kind."

"Yeah, Michael, say, if you'd taken the time to dial a phone and have actually asked either of us out, and actually came up and rang the doorbell, did the parents thing, as on a real date, you might've...well let's put it this way; you were the only guy in tenth grade who I would have considered to repair my virginity problem."

"But baby, take a look at her now."

41

"Put that mirror up to your own little late-night deposit box. Anyways, Michael, honorable, my ass. I don't think the Eagle Scouts offer an honor badge for performing the coarse grind on the dance floor, late into the party, after several beers and expecting automatic closure. That was your normal proposal. For face, you know we gotta present some sort of challenge, at least for the guys we know," Francina said. Not letting words interfere with her intentions, she took his hand and put it on her thigh, just above the knee, then didn't let go until it started wandering in the right direction. She moved on to kissing him, fervently.

While she moved on to his neck, he said, "Back it up. Weren't both of you kind of my steady girlfriends, in ninth grade? I was pretty much falling in love; and I said it, too. As I recall, didn't you both kinda dump me, back to back?"

"At least we had the courtesy to dump you. We weren't exactly in to singularity, those days. Would you rather we cheat on them on or cheat on you? Plus, it was for older guys. With cars and stuff." Francina said.

"Oh right. I see. I knew there was a nobler position here, somewhere."

"Crybaby. Do you want to win this argument, or do you want us? I know just how to shut up a crying baby," Colleen said, proving the point by pushing her breast into his mouth, though she teased him with it a few times. He was content, in warm wet silence, but the girls weren't.

"The real point is, and you totally missed it as usual, was that Katrina wanted you. What's more, she deserved you. You're too much a brain snob for us anyway. And what's even more, she waited for you, while we were spreading the news to every cute guy in town. God, I miss her. She's worse than you. Since she went up to Berkeley, I've seen her all of twice, in three years."

"Would you come back to her parents?" Colleen asked.

"Her Mom's okay. A bit bland, but okay," he said, "I'm confused. Katrina, what? What are you telling me?"

Francina started to answer but stopped a second to watch Colleen, who was back to pretending to be amazed that the tent in his trunks won't stay down when she keeps pushing it. As if she was mad at it, she slapped it, lightly, a few times, then undid the ties. In a display of delight she mimed finishing off the perpetrator forever by biting off its head. Francina, slightly pouting like she wanted to be first, eventually completed her thought, "We're telling you, you two have sniffed around each other for six years, like lost puppy dogs; and never, ever looked to see how close you were following each other."

Colleen disengaged her mouth a second, to add, "Our overall analysis was that you were both too goddamn shy," then returned to matters in hand. Not to be outdone, Francina led his free hand to pull down her pants and ever onward, defining his progress in escalating moans.

"I'm not all that shy. I've approached a girl or two. What about Janine? First day she showed up, I walked across a whole empty dance floor alone to introduce myself? Out of the blue. Didn't we go steady for a year?"

Tiring of these distractions, Colleen looked into his eyes, from very close, her pupils wide from other than intellectual excitement but she was still engaged enough say, "There's a difference between properly shy and being raging in heat. Admitted, when you are horny, which is very often, you do act. Rather stupidly, for the most part. As for Janine – and not even commenting how stupid you are to even bring her up – maybe you think you made the moves, but from our point of view she chomped on you like a seal on a seabass. And if she ever tries it on anyone else I like, I'm...aw, never mind. I hate Janine. Fuck her. No, I mean, fuck me. I love you."

Twisting off on his own take, he said, "I still don't think I'm all that shy. With Katrina, yes, maybe, but only because I respect..."

"God, you are the worst I ever knew for getting stuck on a mindset. As for Katrina, next time you see her, try starting with your desires and saving the respect for a slow day," Francina said pelvically zooming in, since Colleen seemed of likewise intentions. "And watch that fuzzy little thing, Colleen. You snaked me on the appetizer so I got first dibs on the main course. And, Michael, don't read too much into this. We just...just decided you deserve a present for doing this war thing...and we might not ever see...well...you know."

This was the one subject he particularly didn't want to get on. "I'm still not sure I'm going to go." The girls both backed off a bit. "So, that is the only reason."

"I just can't see you getting in trouble. You go to Canada or jail, where's your life going to go from there? You got too much going for you to start off on the ultimate black list."

Francina added, "Yeah, all these other guys just went in crazy and got thrown out, but most of them are half crazy."

"Caves isn't. Dubay, neither; well, a fun kind of crazy. Smoke's the most aloha guy I ever knew. He just likes to fight, sometimes."

"Synchronize aloha and fighting for me, please. In ten words or less."

"He never hurts anybody, bad. Just likes to see the moment of realization on their face as they go skyrocketing through the air that a round Polynesian shouldn't be mistaken for puff. It is an interesting spectacle, sometimes."

"Michael, you are generally civilized but the truth is you do have a cloudy background of taking more than a hands-off interest in mayhem."

"Only as long as nobody really gets hurt. Or when a bully needs their bluff called."

"Shut up, Michael" Colleen said. "We'll miss you, that's all. I'm only glad that if someone's gotta fight, it's you."

"Huh, is that a compliment or a wish? Plus, I'm hardly the baddest dude around."

"Pound for pound, you're right up there," Francina said. "Mainly, it's 'cause you fight smart."

"Yeah, you know how to get out of it when you don't have a prayer. Although you have stood up to a couple of big lumps a few times, when I thought you should've been praying...or running."

"I haven't been in a fight since I left here. Maybe I had an overdose of teenage invincibility once, but I'm feeling very vincible now. Plus, fighting stopped being fun when I realized I was getting strong enough to really hurt someone. I don't need that on my conscience either."

"Heh, don't play conscience games. Want us to?" Francina said. "This isn't our usual, you know. It's my one and only time for this. Sharing ain't my style, nor are nude girls anywhere near me. In fact, Colleen, where do you think that hand is going? Fine, and keep it off there. I'm not waiting any longer." She pulled him down on top of her, wanting her entrée now. Colleen took to scratching and licking his back. This wasn't his usual either. After a minute of luxe way beyond his experience, he came in Francina. They worked the night over, until all lay still, in bliss and exhaustion. Going away presents.

44

4

Just before dawn, Landers awoke. After a brief wondering if he'd really untangled himself from dreams, he gently untangled himself from Colleen and Francina. He wanted to shower but didn't want to wake them, so sprayed himself down with the yard hose, wearing his trunks. Without drying, he put his T-shirt on and walked down to the bay. He just wanted to feel safe, if even for a few moments, and nowhere else did he ever feel so safe as here, especially in the pre-dawn quiet, the still water backed up by the deep, soft green foliage of this plush bayside neighborhood. Watching the last lights of downtown reflecting as lines on the mirror-smooth water, he walked along the narrow, unimproved path between the sand strip and the the bayside homes. Announcing the sun, the whole sky illuminated to violet, the cloud images reflected almost perfectly in the bay. Through this burst of color a flat-gray Navy cruiser slid out of the harbor like a wall of silent death, with no apparent urgency but likely was off to war. When he'd viewed this scene from his paper route – getting up at 4:30 A.M., 365 days a year for four years – he didn't need to read the headlines to know there was some Cold War crisis going on. The air would hum loudly as all the active Navy ships would churn out the harbor and drop anchor off Coronado, so as not to be all taken out by one Communist missile. Though motionless, the current would point the hundreds of bows all in the same direction and they'd look like a snapshot of a high-speed armada.

It must have been a minor holiday, he wasn't sure which, and a few homeowners had put American flags out in front of their homes. One woman announced to him, as if challenging him to refute her intentions, "I'm putting up the flag for all you servicemen. This is what I'd like to do to all those draft dodgers and peace creeps. Four generations of my family have fought in wars." Whereat she made an exaggerated motion of plunging the pole deep into the sand. Again, his mustache and slightly filled-in hair certainly hadn't hidden his present state of being in the military. Not feeling any need to take a position for or against her, he could still feel the anger as if the pole had stuck in his heart, exactly not the distraction he needed. He turned to the water for diversion, swimming halfway out into the bay. Slowly, he breast-stroked back, watching the whole five mile emerald green wall of Point Loma light up as the sun's first rays moved from top to bottom, making the white houses glisten and their bay windows echo the sunrise in small squares. This was all so beautiful. Was he defending it or losing it forever? He lay floating on his back, to go into a state of total immersion from his senses. Soon, he became cold and swam in, accelerating to an angry full sprint the last hundred yards.

He walked home, taking his time so that his mother and sister would have left for work before he got there. On a quiet street of modest homes but lush foliage, he walked slower and slower. Seeing this house dropped him to new lows of sadness. It seemed so unfamiliar, like his family's stuff shouldn't even be in there. He had little attachment to it. His mom and two sisters had moved in there while he was away. After his father had died the year before, they hadn't been able to afford the nicer house up on the hill in which he'd grown up. On his brief visits back to town, he stayed with friends, and dropped by only to visit his mother and sister, rather than wanting to sleep in that house. There hadn't been any truly peaceful good memories in there. More loneliness, as if he didn't have a connection to anywhere, was all it gave him. He felt no self-pity, knowing that having lonely positions about where the world was really going was a sign of the times. Yet the number of people he felt close connections to was becoming smaller and smaller. After taking a quick shower and shaving, he put on some loose corduroys and a T-shirt and started packing away the last of his personal items into boxes. He felt someone watching him. Spinning around, he saw his sister Marny, a few years older, leaning against the doorjamb, watching him, on the verge of tears, but doing everything she could to fight them back. She said, "I figured you'd try to sneak in and out, while we were at work, so I doubled back...I had to say goodbye."

"I'd have come by your work. I just couldn't take another scene with Mom. We'd argue. Then she'd cry...then...she wouldn't want to go through it either."

"I don't know. You know, she's really not totally convinced about this war."

"Never know it by her arguments."

"Older people remember all those wars that counted. They don't believe that after all America's gone through, that we can possibly be wrong. She tries. Just...things die hard."

"I know. Do I act like I know any answers here?"

"She won't admit it to you, but she really doesn't want you to go."

"I'd like to think no mother would."

"Nor would any mother want any stigma that'll stick with you for life. But if you took off for Canada, she'd go for it."

"I'm not running; to Canada or anywhere else."

"Why not, Michael? So many guys find so many ways out. Why should you go? You're so bright, so talented."

"You know, those guys I went through training with, few of them are all that bright, few are particularly talented. They're mostly caught being poor. It's a crazy irony how the poor end up being more patriotic than the rich, though saying so seems to be inversely proportional to being it. Being too special to go isn't an excuse I'm considering; not that I'm even trying to develop a case for being in any way special."

"I know...It's just, God, I'm a regular church-going, conservative Republican Christian and...and," she couldn't say any more and broke down in tears. "Oh, Michael, what is going on? Who is America right now?"

"I don't know. Only thing I do know is everything I always took for granted is just mocking me. I gotta go."

"Leave your stuff there, I'll put it away," she said, then went off to answer the ringing phone. She came right back, with the phone in her hand, her hand covering the mouthpiece. "It's Katrina's dad." He shook his head that he didn't want to talk. "Sorry, too late, I wasn't thinking. I told him you're here."

Reluctantly, he took the receiver, "Hi...Actually I'm just leaving for...Yeah, I'll try to stop by and see her, at Berkeley. Alright, be right there."

He hangs up. "Dammit, I really need this. I just want out of here. Not 'cause of you. Just, with Dad dead and Mom working that shitty job, and Suzie off at Aunt Kate's..."

"We'll get it all back together. Soon. Surviving is in the family blood line." She lost the battle with the tears. They started pouring, instantly and profusely.

"I know. Just...I don't know how to leave this. I never do. Every time I went back up to school, I was depressed...but this time, shit...." Tears caught him too.

"I know, I know. It sounds so trite, but there's just so much evil in the world right now, and it seems to be winning. Just go."

In a way, walking the few houses up the street to visit Katrina's parents helped with his sadness, because anger took over his emotional phase. Even though he'd never outwardly fought the tide of the kids around there in despising the Navy as the popular course, he had met a number of sailors over the years who he'd liked and even enjoyed. Katrina's father wasn't one of them. A cold, gray military machine was the only side Landers had ever seen of him. He could never stand the way he ordered Katrina and her mom around. He knocked on the screen door. Arthur's voice, in the familiar commanding tone, said, "Come in. I'll be right out." Landers entered, walked into the living room, pausing only to look at the pictures of Katrina on the wall and piano. He started, that Katrina's mom was sitting silently in her chair all this time. Arthur entered, with a smile and two beers. He handed one to Landers, giving him a hearty handshake."

Bemused, Landers only said what he thought, "A beer. In the morning, no less. That's a switch."

"If you can fight overseas you can drink beer in my house. You know, Michael, of all that beach crowd Katrina and you run with, you're the only one we could ever stand."

"You don't know them all. Some...well, they are who the are." He had no desire to make or win any point.

Arthur wouldn't have been listening anyway if it didn't match his long-ago locked opinions. "Well, all I gotta tell you, Michael, is of the thirty years I put in the Navy, the time I cussed the most but remember the fondest, was the time overseas."

"Yeah, wished I was Navy. At least they put their bases on oceans."

"They aren't all that fabulous, believe me. Plus, months out at sea, on any ship, gets to be a bitch."

"No disrespect meant, I just wasn't born to be military."

"I respect that. Because it's honest. I didn't think I was either. But by the time the war was over, there was baby Katrina on the way, and I had no other job. Five more years, then Korea, by then I had half a pension earned and was reasonably secure, then...well, that's how a life goes. I don't regret it."

"I just want out, then back to mine."

"Whelp, keep your head and your butt down, the rest of you'll follow suit. That's about all the advice a sailor can pass on to an infantryman. It's a weird war. They all are in there own way, but there must be a reason. That's why America's still here, there always turns out to be a reason."

Landers' mind drifted on this one. Getting ever more fidgety, he said, pushing for a way out, "Well, I really have to get moving. I gotta catch a plane. You wanted me to take something to Katrina?"

"Just some books. You know how she loves to read. These are a few on what valor really means. Michael, you're as close to a brother as she's ever had. She'll listen to you long before us. That Berkeley scene...we never wanted her there, with all those rabble rousers and cowards an all. They're downright commies, some of 'em. I'm afraid they'll influence her."

"Katrina? God knows, she takes in everything. Always has. But when it comes to making a decision, you can bet the bank it's going to be her own."

"I know, but...well, just try, for us."

"She'll get the books, I promise." He took them and shook Arthur's hand again. He walked over and shook his wife's hand, too. Still not saying a word, she alternately shook her head slightly up and down, then right to left, then up and down again. In her husband's presence, Landers never expected her to be anywhere but left hanging between what she wanted to say and what she thought she should say.

When Landers walked back to his house, Caves was sitting on the hood of his beat-up old, station wagon. "I figured I'd catch you here some time or other. Trying to sneak out of town again, huh."

"I'm about O.D.'d on good-byes.

"You don't have to be in Oakland till tomorrow afternoon. Let's go surfing."

"Naw, I want to see Katrina, before I go."

"Yeah, I know. How were you planning on getting to the airport?"

"Hitchhiking. That's the one thing looking military's good for. If you can ignore getting yelled at and dodge the people trying to rip you off." Without discussion, he threw his bag in the missing tailgate window.

At the airport, Caves pulled over in the shadows, lit a joint, took a long hit, passed it, exhaled and said, "You know I'm not much for wading into the sentimental swamps. But if this was a real war, I wouldn't let you go off without me. If you do go, and get captured, you know we'll come get you, one way or another."

Landers blew out his hit in laughing, "You guys are nuts enough you'd probably pull it off too."

"I know screwing up, on purpose or otherwise, isn't your style, but just this once...get out of it. Whatever it takes. Bring us back the wildest story you can. It's in you. Do it."

"It'll work out okay...somehow...some way..." Landers drifted off. He took another hit, held it, blew it out slowly, grabbed his bag, made the Hawaiian hand signal for "all's cool" (thumb and little finger up, the rest down) and headed off for the plane.

At the ticket counter, he asked the clerk, "Can I change my reservation to military standby?"

She gave him a wry smile, "You're pushing it. I don't usually fall for that trick, especially when the plane's booked. But considering where you're going, yeah. Here, sixteen dollars."

"Thanks, that doubles my lifetime bankroll."

"It won't have to go too far in Oakland. I hear they don't let you go roaming."

"You must book a lot of these."

"There are happier departures. Good luck." Having said that, her expression went blank, wanting out of the thought. Landers walked on, wondering if there was any way out of every encounter coming down to torn emotions.

On the plane he actually looked for a potentially numb seatmate, but there was only one seat free, next to an elderly man. His whole life, he'd easily gotten along with people of all ages, even seeming to gravitate towards older people, but battle lines of this whole un-civil war were most pronounced between age groups. He didn't feel like being preached down to on his misguided generation. "This taken?" he asked the man.

"Sit. You're getting away with murder on the haircut. Can't be Marines. But I'm thinking infantry, so it can't be Navy or Airforce. Which leaves, Army."

"Darn, is it really that obvious. Although, you're the first to pin it down to infantry."

"Takes one to know one. It starts with the first thing you're looking for is a place to hide or escape. Can I buy you a beer?"

"Yeah, sure, thanks," Michael nodded. Somehow, this was the first person he'd felt relaxed and uncompromised around, in his entire three weeks of leave. They drank one beer and the stewardess served them a second one, without asking. They chatted about the inconsequential but drifted quickly into the inevitable. After prodding Landers for his feelings, his steady gaze stating he wanted only the truth, the man started off on his own feelings, "Once people are afraid of thinking, or afraid of the truth, or both, they either assume they've already got everything in order or assign that ultimate order to someone one else, or to some set of laws before them, or to God, then they lock down rigid. On spiritual existence they can just say, 'Well, the prophets got it direct from God, so that's that. God hasn't had anything more to say to humans for two thousand years. It's all in the Bible.' But people proofread that Bible, not God. What if he would want to add a few dropped points or delete a few incorrect ones? Some people say the founding fathers of America had everything there is to know about government fixed solid, two hundred years ago. They were brilliant, but that didn't mean brilliant people after them couldn't fine tune. Hence all the Amendments. It's natural to be afraid of what horror might be right over the next ridge. But it might be also be a wonder, and being afraid to look is based in fear, ignorance and laziness. The farther along your are on the downcount of life, protecting what you've got keeps making more sense. You figure you've earned some peace of mind. That doesn't mean you have to squelch all those behind you. Call me reckless...they sure did when I was young...but I'd be bored to death with any new generation that doesn't want to taste everything there is and rewrite the whole menu. The wilder the better, as long as they leave out the violence and self-destruction. But then, after you've watched a few variations, you come to realize most are yelling about the same old shallow stuff. First, it's breaking loose from authority, parents, whatall. The weakest kids just say nothing matters, anyway, so why should we respect anything; let the anarchy bell ring. The stronger ones form some idealism or other, to attack the hypocrisy of those who lord over them. The next generation of ideals and truths mostly come from that group; from the ones who stick with it. But in too many cases, their new vision is self-serving if not just plain trivial. Come a few years of working, financial setbacks and maybe a wife or kids on the way, most of them totally flip-flop. Blinders intact, they pick the safe, obvious road. That includes protecting self, family and nation, whichever order. Strong stuff, keep it, it's right; assuming the nation is a good one. And good and perfect aren't exact synonyms. Is this war really about survival of nation? So far, it's more about breaking families than saving them and I don't see that trend reversing. As for self, well, for the foot soldier you're issued two selfs. There are no more trivial choices. For your generation, unlike for mine, the popular course isn't inevitable – not to say that the course is ever simple. But for your generation feeling that something is extremely wrong isn't shallow. And you might be right."

"You have know idea how good it is to talk to someone older who doesn't think I'm a traitor for even considering not going. Especially someone who's been there."

"People want to believe their country is right. That's not complicated. Though the guys who've really been out there getting shot at are rarely the ones hiding behind flags and looking down on the hesitant, with inequivocable righteousness. With nothing left to prove in the loyalty and valor arenas, you want to visualize a world where all the soldiers, on all sides, turn to the leaders and say, hell no, we won't go. Mr. Hitler, if you're so right and you got a beef against Mr. Stalin, you go over there and punch him right in the nose, yourself. Keep us common folk out of it, this time. Three years on the front lines, in my case, makes being right into a fragile proposition. And it's hard to get over the feeling that they signed you off as expendable."

"Especially in this war."

"War's war. Except it at least ought to be for defending your own. The Vietnamese attack us? Not likely. Plus, you just don't go dumping our army on the continent of Asia, period. Eisenhower couldn't say that enough. Gotta know it's some politician dreamed this one up. That hothead Kennedy kid, maybe. Ah, that may turn out unfair. This time it's more likely the arms manufacturers. Maybe it always is. At least their goals are clear, as much as they try to disguise their tactics."

"The important tactic is how to get out. Not just for me, for the whole country."

"Sorry I brought up the word, but since we're on it, tactics here stink. First place, let the other side wear themselves down more. World Wars I and II, shit, some of our best allies were near stomped out of existence, before we got in. And here, here we're beginning a war with a country most people don't even know where it is."

"Finally, I meet someone who seems to care about all this as much as me. From the same perspective, anyway."

"Don't always rate how much people care by what they do. Avoidance and denial are perfectly valid survival skills, in their proper time and place. In your case, rule number one for an infantryman is you are the keeper of your own emotions. Whether you're attacking or retreating, lead with your own heart, but keep it protected, from inside and outside. Regardless of what you are eventually going to do, right now you go in there and let them know how pissed off your are. Tell 'em now, 'cause if you do it after you come back and they don't like what you've got to say, they'll just label you as a crazy vet; just go away. So right now is the time, don't go easy. How do you kids say it, blow their minds. Get mad at hate. Get mad at evil. This is that ultimate decision. This is a shear line in the rest of your life. You're a surfer, you said, so a wave has caught you. You're going right on the wave, or left, but either way, there's no way back to the takeoff peak. It doesn't exist anymore. You're overwhelmed, I can tell. I sure as hell would be. We don't know how history will judge the draft evaders but we know how they'll judge the dead. Give them a medal, if you want, but they're still dead. And pity those who end up maimed and outcasts, like lepers in limbo.

"If you do ultimately decide to go, here's a couple secret weapons I can give you. I don't know your religious or spiritual persuasion and don't want to even get into it. But believe in your connection to a higher existence, regardless what you want to call it. Believe that they're paying attention to you and they believe in your worth. Don't wear out your welcome with perpetual prayers and incantations though. Save your prayers for when you're truly in danger, and believe in them. Prayers without emotion in every breath are nothing. Believe like you're on a magic adventure with a purpose, even if you don't know what that purpose is. Otherwise, one time or another, probably a lot of them, war will beat you down so far you'll wonder why there is any purpose for humans to exist at all.

"And in your dealings with the Army, right now, before you actually go, feel safe knowing that anything you're going to say or do, and any other dark marks in your military past, will be forgiven in total, once you get to the front line. Out there, you have a different brand of bravery to prove. Anyone here calls you a coward, keep reminding yourself, 'It takes a coward, or a fool, to judge someone else on how they act or don't act, before they've got their mind made up.' So say your piece now. Whatever you decide, don't go easy. They messed with your mind, you mess with theirs, awhile. And if they ask why, you tell them Platoon Sergeant W.B. Meadows ordered you to do it. And I know what a coward means. It means giving up only because you don't have the will to go on."

Feeling his pulse rising and his heart racing, he stopped, surprised at catching himself blurting so many thoughts and feelings, in one burst. Regaining his calm, his eyes had a guru-esque twinkle. The plane had landed and stopped. They held a long firm handshake, gazing deep in each others eyes...a lot of anger, a lot of fear, a lot of love for life. As if he still felt doubts coming from Landers, the man reiterated, "Don't let it fester your whole life, wishing you'd said your mind. Let 'em know you're angry. Let 'em know good soldiers are rare and not to be wasted. Don't...go...easy."

Landers thanked him offering to buy a round. The old man, more riled than he ever expected or wanted to be, simply shut down his availability.

.

5

Te's meeting the stranger, Xem, in the cave, was pure adventure and mystery. Everything about his life was now so different, but he did his best to show no changes in his nature. Everything he'd ever been taught or had assumed was up for questioning. He wondered who amongst the adults, or even other children, could know anything about Xem or all those other people he said existed. He wondered about how things were built or made and whether they had been invented by the people of his tribe or by others. Tools and jewelry, where had they come from, were they gifts of the Nyang, to be copied and enhanced by people, or from somewhere else altogether. Particularly, bottles took on such an air of mystery. His family had almost fifty, in large baskets, no two of which were alike. Yet nobody in his village knew how to make even the simplest ones. Were they not direct gifts of the Nyang to the ancients, as he'd been taught, or were they from other peoples? Looking at them he wondered who those people could be. After a few days, Te showed new interest in the moon, and asked great-aunt Mehra to teach him the names of all the nights of the month cycle. Mehra was considered to have the greatest knowledge in his clan, though seldom did anyone ever approach her, as she was usually in a surly mood, except when cooking, so Te did know enough to approach her when she was preparing an offering to some spirit. She was surprised and flattered. She told him how everyone knows when the full moon, *truq*, is coming and they expect all nature to be astir. But it's the no moon, *nhil nha*, which causes more confusion because nobody pays it any attention. Yet the universe is actually more disturbed then, and people seem confused and unable to communicate. Few learn to expect it, even though it is the time when the soul energy, *ae*, starts to increase again, so they should learn to be aware of this and use it to their advantage. She taught him exactly how to know when the no moon would come, and offered to wake him that morning, because the sliver of new moon can first be seen in the west, right at dawn, just before it sets. Since Xem called it the new moon and not the no moon, as Te had always been taught, he thought of it with Xem's name, but made careful to call it the no moon, to Mehra. Though he was glad she put so much emphasis on the no moon, the last thing he wanted was for her to be awake that morning. As it turned out, her memory was leaky and she'd forgotten, it having been almost two weeks since she'd taught him and quizzed him on the 30 moon names.

That night of next new moon, Te was afraid to go to sleep, that he wouldn't wake up in time. Eventually, he did go to sleep, and he had that dream of the figure who seemed to watch him, like a guarding spirit again, only this time he was almost sure he recognized the spirit as Xem. Directly, he woke from this dream, and even though it was absolutely dark he knew to get up. As quietly as he could, he arose and soft-stepped from the hut, hoping Aunt Rama would think, if she heard anything, that it was one of the old people getting up to pee. He didn't put down the pole, but merely jumped down. The water gourds, which he'd meticulously prepared the afternoon before so they wouldn't rattle, rattled anyway. He thought he did hear Rama say his name, but he ran quickly.

At the path down into the water area he stopped. It was absolutely black, down there. Though as scared as he could be, still, he started feeling his way down the steps, touching ahead with his bare feet. This wasn't difficult as he knew the trail so well, but it took awhile. By the time he reached the bottom, daylight was having some effect and he was glad because he wasn't sure how he was going to get through the spider webs in the ravine, without being able to see at all. But the spider webs were spread apart, so that he could walk right through. His thought was that Xem must have been through here and cleared the way.

When Te reached the cave, Xem was right there, and again moved the *kuba* spider's web, for Te to enter. They bowed, both not able to resist smiling. First thing Xem said was that the elders didn't allow the children enough play time. They were entirely too controlling. He inferred that this was probably the doing of the Nie Drong clan, who always seemed determined to control everything. As Xem taught Te to skip stones, Te picked up that this was perhaps the first time an older person had taught him to play. Under Xem's guidance of which stones to pick, then the throwing technique, soon Te had reasonably mastery of both a forehand and backhand spin. Te asked if could show the other boys and Xem said he could, but he said it would be better if the first time he tried it would be with others watching, and him pretending that it happened only by accident. He assured Te they would be greatly impressed by how fast he figured out what happened and became the best skipper the quickest, but not to be vain for this.

Then Xem made Te show him how long he could hold his breath underwater. Even though he'd only had a few chances to practice, when the other boys weren't around, Te had the system down to only letting out tiny bubbles, every fifteen seconds or so, so that he could stay down several minutes, with ease. Xem told him he was quite impressed, as he was honestly in marvel that a boy could use this technique, so well. Assuming the cross-legged, traditional meditation pose, he showed Te another breathing technique of totally relaxing and taking only the slightest possible breaths, with his upper lungs. He described to Te how to move his consciousness up through the main power centers, the chakras, of his body. Then he taught him the sensation of taking a few deep breaths as if he was glowing right through his skin and becoming a bodyless cloud, with a shape slightly large than his body but no distinct boundaries.

Even though he knew he was a great teacher he had never known anybody to learn each step of this technique faster than Te. Not only was Te gifted and bright in the first place, but he had few preconceptions about anything. After Te spent some time in this boundary-less state of well being, Xem asked him to open his eyes, but try to retain the feeling. He asked Te to show him the original skipping stone, the one Te had fetched from the bottom of the pond. Te retrieved it from his loincloth. Having looked at it many times, in secret, he mentioned that he had never seen a sign like that and asked what it meant. Xem said, "We'll get to that, just hold it tight in your hand and put it over your heart, so you will be protected by the same spirit as me, as we go to this next stage." Xem removed a small ivory box from his travel pack. Saying a prayer Te didn't understand, he opened the box. From it he took a petrified spiral cochlea and attached bones, from an ancient human's ear. He said, "Now, stare at this spiral. Stare without blinking, without thinking. You will go into a heavy trance, but don't be afraid, because while under this trance I will teach you many things." Even as he said this, Te was already becoming hypnotized. "Even though you will be in a different level of clarity, you will retain all that I tell you. Even though you don't need to go through this process to learn, it will protect you. Because if you ever mistakenly reveal anything I teach you, and it would be almost impossible that this doesn't happen, some day, you can always say you saw it in a dream. Because this will feel more like a dream than being totally awake. This spiral is an ear-bone of a powerful ancient shaman. It was turned to stone by a far away god, not of our people, eons and eons ago. I received it as a gift from a powerful shaman from a tribe across the great water. That is a story for another day." With that, Xem made a circle with the bone and punctuated his ritual with a slight tap on Te's third-eye place.

Even though Te was fully mentally aware, while being hypnotized, he had nothing in his experience to explain it. His tribe did not know about externally enhanced hypnosis, even though Amba and a few others could reach profound states of meditational departure. He asked, "What happened, did I go to the spirit plane?"

"There is no possible way to leave the spirit plane, as souls are eternal. This wasn't even an expansion, in the way that you will be learning to increase your *ae* by different types of meditation. What just happened was a focusing of the concentration part of your mind, while at the same time disconnecting your consciousness from your feeling senses. I learned it from a holy man from a place called France. Another topic for another time. The part of your education, which has been frightfully neglected, maybe even dangerously so, is your lack of knowledge of how your tribe came to be so isolated from all the other people's on Earth. The Kra Polie in your village are doing your generation a great disservice in claiming you are the only humans in existence. I'm sure they claim to other adults, who are forbidden to pass on this knowledge, that it is to save you children from dangerous encounters with other people, but it is just another Nie Drong trick to control everybody. No, your tribe is not even nearly the only tribe of Myong. Myong happens to be the common word used to differentiate our tribal type from all humans; *mol* or *man* or human, it means the same thing. In the great order of all peoples, we Myong – though possibly the oldest peoples – are one of the smaller and most remote groups. By design, your village is one of the most isolated of all.

"The beginning of how this came to be was because of a strange twist of love, often the most treacherous of human emotions. Amongst the Myong there are 33 major tribes. Two of the great tribes, each having many villages, are the Bahnar to the north and the Jarai to the south. Five generations ago, a prince of the Jarai tribe had fallen for a girl from the Bahnar, at a trading fair up in the north mountains. Their seeing each other was absolutely forbidden, by the elders of both their villages, as they weren't even from the same caste.

"As have an ever-expanding list of lovers before and after them, they gave up all but themselves, and eloped to the high mountains. That both were favorites of La Pom, the Goddess, she led them to chance upon a wonderful hidden valley. They asked her in prayers for permission to be wed. Nine months later, they had a child. When they came back with the child to the fair the next year, they hoped they could use this child to bring the tribes together. Instead, there was a great argument, which led to a fight, in which one of the Jarai of a noble family was killed. A great shaman stopped it from being an overall battle, right there, but only by proposing that both the boy and girl and their child would be banished, forever, as well as the man who had killed the Jarai noble. This man was sent off immediately and it was suspected that he lost any connection to his head as soon as he walked into the woods. It was reportedly shown back in the Bahnar lands, in secret ceremonies. If this was so, the Jarai never sought retribution, as in some degree this was seen as justice. The man was a troublemaker anyway.

"As for the lovers, neither of their families could bear never seeing their child again. So they asked for and were given permission to form a new tribe. They were allowed to take everything they could carry on their own backs, with each family getting a water buffalo to drag some heavy things, and with a second female calf thrown in to make a better chance for breeding. This was not an easy beginning, because the Bahnar and Jarai don't even speak the same language. Even naming their tribe wasn't easy and it just remained being called, the New Tribe, as at least those words were similar in both languages. In their year together, the two lovers had concocted their own combined language, as well as having become extremely adept at living in the woods. In affect, they came to lead the tribe, which numbered twenty people. This whole escapade didn't start well, as they couldn't find their way back to their own home. They had had the presence to mark the way back, but the monsoon had so swollen one stream that, in trying to find a way around it, they went up the wrong ridge into a different range of mountains altogether. After days of wandering, they came across an almost equally inaccessible valley. They decided they had to settle somewhere for the rest of the monsoon and began building shelter. After the monsoon, they tried to find their way back to their original home, but for whatever reason of the Nyang, La Pom did not aid them again. After several unsuccessful attempts they gave up, because by then the new village was well established. Their old home became known as the Lost River Valley and in lore it grew to be described as a lost paradise and the most wonderful place on earth."

Te spoke up, "I've heard of the Lost River Valley. Although I know the Kra Polie say we're not supposed to talk of it. It's supposed to be on another plane, next to heaven."

"That would be a personal opinion. My opinion is that it exists, and not so far off. For whatever design of fate, my life has been one of many wanderings, and even now I am on a long mission, which seems like it could go on for the rest of my life. Maybe it's getting closer to being fulfilled, but there's so many strange forces involved. I suspect you've never heard of a person called 'The Wanderer', have you."

"No. Well, actually one of the Biu boys used that name once, but we weren't sure if he was just talking about some evil *molai* spirit. He was scolded so severely by the chief's wife, S'Yu, that nobody ever said it again. Jom, the chief, would never cross his wife in any way, as she so much more domineering.

"I assure you I'm not a *molai* nor has my soul been consumed by one. Thought it might be troubled, at times, my soul is quite intact."

"Then you are The Wanderer. And, what, you're from our village?"

"That's another story. Let's stay with the New Tribe's story, for now. For years they lived without contact with anyone, and nobody looked for them, as all the other Bahnar and Jarai tribes were forbidden to make contact with them. Theirs was a peaceful tribe with clever craftsman, excellent musicians and, more important, highly-educated tellers of the great Hamon legends. Otherwise they might have drifted from having any cultural heritage at all. Yet, they became so isolated only the elders even remembered anything about where the other tribes were, and how they were different. Inevitably, as the tribe grew and started wandering farther and farther, the great grand-children of the original combining couple, came in contact with people of the Ha Lang tribe. This was a surprise to everyone. When told about these 'other people', the New Tribe elders forbade the young people to go down there again. This was not heeded, and the young people made it the fashion to sneak off to observe these 'other people'. They even began trading with them, in secret. When they started showing up with new knives, the elders were jealous and angry. But they let this new tradition of trading go on because in the New Tribe, although they had extraordinary jewelry makers, nobody knew how to make proper tool metals. In fact most of their old knives were almost worn away and they were having to reinvent stone tools. Soon they established a trading fair every year, but down in the Ha Lang territory. They would make a great effort to sneak back to their own village without leaving tracks.

"Eventually, word of this newly relocated tribe got back to both the Bahnar and Jarai tribal councils, at a time when they were virtually at war with each other. They were different in so many ways. The Bahnar speak in the language which came from the Mon Khmer gods, by the great river to the west of the mountains. The Jarai received their language from the water Nyang. In fact many of the earliest tribes of their peoples carved great canoes and sailed off to become the peoples of the thousands of islands in the great ocean, called the Pacific. Some went east and became known as what the great council of all peoples call Polynesians. Some went south and mixed with other peoples in another place of a thousand islands, called Indonesia."

"Wait, what is an ocean. What is the Pacific?"

"Oh, Te, where do I start. Imagine a lake so vast the fastest bird couldn't fly across it in a month. You can't even drink it, as it's so salty. There are monstrous fish in it."

"Fish as big as people?"

"Oh yes, hundreds of times as big. Fish that could and would eat people."

"Oh," Te said in sad bewilderment. "I knew there was more world than just here, and Amba even says it's round like the moon, but we were taught only spirits could go there. It must be very dangerous."

"Yes, it can be dangerous. Everywhere can be dangerous so always give thanks to the spirits that protect you. Now, show me the rock I gave you." Te opened his hand. Xem took off a heavy lace around his neck and took a rock similar to Te's, from a bead-woven cover. He held them side by side, to show that the symbols are exactly the same. "The symbol is the divine inscription of the Yank-Dak, the water Nyang. It was burned into these rocks at the temple of the Dragon, who is the Nyang-superior of all the individual water Nyang."

"Who lives above the celestial mountains with Bok-Hoi-Doi, the Creator, and the other Nyang of the higher plane."

"It's good they are at least teaching of the Nyang. These stones have great power to protect from evil, be that in your earth plane or in on the dream plane. Now repeat this prayer three times." And he taught Te a prayer of syllables he'd never heard. Xem continued, "It is a prayer to the Dragon, who will be able to find you in your dreams, when it is time, if you have the stone on your person. Never show the stone to anyone. Not that anyone in the village who would even know what it meant, except possibly Amba." On saying this, Xem seem profoundly moved and was silent for several moments.

Having time to think, Te asked him why, if there had only been the two families in the original village, why there was now three clans.

Xem told, "As nature would have it, before long, love was mixing things up again. In mixing with the Ha Lang tribe, which had much more visible wealth that the New Tribe, soon some of the girls were seduced by the Ha Lang men. There were marriages and a few babies came to the tribe. Almost all of them were from the same clan, which was not an accident. There was a clan in the Ha Lang, whose name was changed in the New Tribe's language to be the Nie Drong clan. Their elders had purposely told their most clever young men to seduce the New Tribe girls, so that they could gain power within this New Tribe. That is the way of the Nie Drong.

"Even all the Nie Drong from that Ha Lang tribe weren't all originally from the same clan. After a dozen had married in, there was none of the great clans of the highlands who weren't related to someone there. A few of those clan names would be, oh, let's see, the S'Iu, Kiom, Hlai, Hing, He, Jom Piu, Yup, Y Jut...ah, I'm lost and rambling, there are so many. Maybe someday we'll go over them but much later. For cultural reasons that would bear study, but you don't need to know them now. And of course the clans cross over between the other great tribes of the mountains, the Renga O, Katu, Jeh, Sedang, and there's more of them, too.

"In the village of the New Tribe the original two clans were of course the Jolong and Biu, who had great respect for each. Since the newcomers from the Ha Lang were all Nie Drong, they had many more possessions. They had another name, in the other villages, which I won't even say, that you might learn to prejudge them as acting like your village's Nie Drong. There are many who resist the dark side of their clan's manipulations and become great and honorable people. Their majority almost always behave the same, however, and all across the mountains they have been notorious in trying to control everything. They're very wealthy, not by their own work or creativity but by banding together and figuring out ways to divide all the other clans. Politics and deceit are their primary skill. They form secret societies that spy on and sabotage any opposition. They make up or change all the rules they can, to exclude any others from any chance to make decisions. They pool their wealth and are aggressive to make what seem like generous loans, but then make it impossible for the borrowers to pay them back."

"I saw the Nie Drong do that," Te said. "One of the Biu men was loaned an extra buffalo by the chief's family. And he used the buffalo to work the chief's cousin's field. Only the chief's cousin never paid the Biu man, so he couldn't pay the chief. Except the chief didn't make his cousin pay. He took that Biu family's buffalo and now they have to work for the chief, forever. Plus he gave the buffalo he took to his cousin."

"Exactly. Unjust as even that may sound, their worst trick of all is in trying to make all the shamans be of their clan. Fortunately, the Nyang have something to say in that matter. But the Nyang don't always seem to respond, or else their responses aren't interpreted correctly. There's no doubt many shamans were picked by the secret societies, not by the Nyang. There are cases where shamans not loyal to the Nie Drong leaders were removed, or poisoned directly."

"They'd have to be crazy. Wouldn't the Nyang punish them for eternity?"

"I don't answer about eternity nor predict for the Nyang, but I do know there are people out there who are so crazed for power they will try to cheat the Nyang, in this life. It can't wear well in their other lives. Other shamans they couldn't control were accused of being possessed by *molai*, demons who have eaten their soul, or of being *rolung*, who are sorcerers or witches who make pacts with *molai*s or some middle-plane spirits, to possess souls of humans. They'd put them through trials by ordeal, which were often rigged that if the accused person survived that in itself was taken as proof they were guilty, so they were punished anyway. When the Nie Drong have a shaman under their control, they're quick to call themselves holier than everyone else. If they break the moral rules they overlook it, but are always accusing everyone else of moral depravity. Hypocrisy, is the word for this. Questioning their moral authority often leads to the accuser being buried alive or having their head chopped off."

This was all very upsetting to Te, so much so that Xem paused a moment just to watch him. Te blurted out, "Why did you ever have to come here? Why would I want to know about all these types of evil? I don't want to know about evil."

"I didn't come here to bring you evil. Things are about to change in your village. It's getting to be time to pick the next shaman."

"Why should that concern me?"

"How could it not concern you? It can be the greatest of times in the village but also a most dangerous time. It may be the only time in your life it happens. And it could be you who is picked, which can make it doubly dangerous."

"I don't want to be picked."

"It's is not for you to choose."

"But Amba is a Nie Drong. Why wouldn't she choose a Nie Drong?"

"It's not for Amba to choose, either. Amba will listen to the Nyang, before any humans. She is very fair and very brave."

"How do you know that?"

"I just know. And whoever is picked, she will protect. So will all the Biu and Jolong, because when they work together they are much stronger than the Nie Drong. The Biu are the strongest, because they do most of the hardest work. But they do tend to enjoy their rice wine, and are often arguing amongst themselves."

"I've noticed. And they're the best fighters, though the Nie Drong sometimes win because they don't fight fair," Te said. "But all my best friends are Biu. They're the only boys who are nice to me."

"The Biu are good-hearted, that is their way. Your Jolong clan have always been the artisans, the musicians and the story tellers. They're also the smartest. But just that they always try to think individually and to make their arts new and better has them often working in their own directions. All the while, the Nie Drong are always plotting and mocking."

"Always plotting and mocking," Te confirmed, looking down with a frown. "Here's what I don't understand. There are all these kids in our village, and more babies are born than people die. So why isn't our village bigger and why isn't there anybody between the ages of thirteen and twenty-five?"

This was not a question Xem wanted to think about, right then, but he knew it had to be told. "It will take a while to explain, better leave it until next time. You should go. The boys will be along soon and you cut it too close last time. Thankfully, the spiders were working together that morning."

Te had time to fill all the gourds and be almost to the top of the ridge, before the other boys arrived. Indeed there was some mention, by other boys and aunt Rama, of why he went down there alone, but he gave no answer at all. That Te could be extremely stubborn was well known. Trying to get him to change his mind was so difficult, few wanted to try, at least not very often. His perception of everyone was so changed; he didn't feel close to anyone any longer. He even started looking at everyone more intensely, to figure out who was more Bahnar and who was more Jarai. His life had become so complex and confusing. Some days he found himself wishing he could be as old as Xem, because all this new information made him seem to understand less about everything.

6

Having stashed his duffel bag in a locker at the Oakland bus station, Landers caught a bus up to Berkeley, the flagship campus of the University of California. He'd been there half dozen times before, for visits. It felt and looked like the great university that it is, with imposing buildings, century old landscaping, Spartan quads but designed to make every entrance look important. Passers-by – from horn-rimmed professors, to sliderule-packing nerds, to full-bore hippies, to Greek classics, to janitors and gardeners – all had mastered the pensive look. All frozen in timeless academia. Frozen there except for the one thing Landers wanted to avoid. Remembrance of war. The omni-present peace symbol (a drawing of a pie with two large pieces on the top and two small ones on the bottom) and other anti-war slogans were plastered everywhere. Knowing Katrina was in class, he found a dry lawn in the shade and closed his eyes, trying to get lost in pure momentary sensation, an all-aural universe: the wind in the trees, the shuffle of feet, the occasional snippets of conversation with ideas attached. All his young years he'd dreamed of being away at college and he wanted back into that feeling only, for this particular moment, without the ideas.

But his thoughts clicked on, betrayed again. He remembered how he'd almost gone to Berkeley, as the obvious next choice once he decided his earlier goal of Cal Tech was defunct, but not because it wasn't the Mecca of all science. At a high-school math team contest there, he looked around and made his own mathematical evaluation that the ratio was about a hundred guys for every coed. He sought a more complete education. Earlier on, he'd thought college should be one of those Ivy League sanctuaries but, even if he could have gotten a full scholarship, the cost of even getting back there scared him. It's a long hitchhike, though that alone wouldn't have stopped him; he didn't even know how he'd pay for a winter wardrobe. NYU seemed ever so cool but same problem. He knew he was a city-boy at heart and if not N.Y., then L.A. Ultimately, why he changed, in the last minute, was that he was already suspected his long-term ambitions were diverting. It was was a single line in a New York Times article that said UCLA had one of the best creative writing departments, at that time. Part was a very unscientific poll in Playboy that rated it as having some of the prettiest coeds in the country. Sold.

Science and math had always come easier to him. Particularly physics, because it didn't require memory work to get A's. Nothing wrong with his memory, but memorizing did usually require sitting still, never his forte unless he was rapt in a book with information incoming faster than he could think about it. His love of science and analytical thought came from his father, who had been a top aerospace engineer. At home he and his compatriots talked science and drank, heavily, to the wee hours, nightly. Landers jumped in to both the conversation and perpetual chess tournament. Born just as WWII was ending, the fathers of most of his class were engineers and scientists, conscripted to design planes rather than fly them; or fight below them.

From his mother he'd been as avidly led to music and the arts, so that he envisioned becoming a scientist daytimes and an arts aficionado at night. Even that he was also physically driven, be it surfing or all other sports, he didn't mind sacrificing surfing for awhile, but if that was also available, so be it. If he'd actually spent time at Berkeley first, it might have won. Its purist intellectual air was that alluring. It wanted to look like a serious school, to itself and to the rest of academia. UCLA didn't much care what anyone else thought; gaudy lipstick was not considered a mind eraser. It looked out to the rest of the city like L.A. looked out at the rest of the world, as its empire-to-be, and if the world wouldn't see that ambition through the face of frills, all the easier. Both schools had complete departments in all majors but UCLA favored the fine arts and medical-related sciences, while Berkeley focused more on the physical and social sciences. It and the city of Berkeley, a definitive college town but on a huge scale, meld into each other as if being one continuous entity. Dress – at least until the current social reinvention – was classic Ivy or deliberately down-mode proletariat, camouflage for the adjoining Telegraph Avenue scene. Though there were pretenders, UCLA didn't buy the way Back-East collegial snobbery that style and substance were mutually exclusive; it was fine to be Venice boardwalk funky in the AM, San Marino staid in plaid by sunset, and Sunset Strip cross-chic by neon.

Spread out linearly, like much of Los Angeles, UCLA is a commuter island at the base of the Santa Monica Mountains, below Bel Air, amid the lush gardens of the finest homes in L.A., where few students or professors could afford to live. Its enormous medical center borders the Westwood quarter, more a barrier than a connector. Westwood was fast becoming such a hip and popular shopping and theater destination that a tourist might not even know a huge university was right up the street. On campus, related departments are in tight groups along the overall line. Sciences, engineering and math on the south, mid and east campus are the law school, business school and humanities. Northwest end of campus is its own carnival, where social life spun around the Gypsy Wagon, an outdoor eating quad under flowering jacaranda trees, between the art, music, theater, English and film departments. Landers hung out here, in spare time. The Gypsy Wagon was showtime, echoing L.A.'s droll *raison d'etre*; wake up every day and go do something nobody ever dreamed of before. Normally dreams were more Landers's style, not counting the current nightmare.

Just forming this thought caused him to open his eyes. Right then, walking down the path towards him was the one person he would always want to see. Long dark curls, tall, with a relaxed but refined posture, thin in the right ways; his model of classic beauty. Her Celtic eyes were green with thin golden cat streaks and blue-black outer rings around the iris. They would pin him stiff and critique him more profoundly and honestly than he had ever allowed anyone else. Then she could be so quick to retire into an internal castle; the signal being she'd put on those oft-worn, clear lens, clunky glasses, that she thought helped ward off the frequent tide of guys trying to monopolize her attention. She wore a sensible sweater, jeans and sandals, slightly on the irreverent side but still serious enough to show up at the part-time jobs she needed to support herself. Scholarships paid her tuition and some expenses but her father had cut her off from family financial support, when she chose Berkeley as her college. The only part the two kept distant from each other were their hearts. Having watched each other go through all the vain, silly, rainy and rainbow stages of teen amour was their main protection from falling mindlessly in love with each other. Neither would ever want to go through a breakup. Their souls had been interlocked all along, though they wouldn't have used that wording. She almost walked right by him, until he called her name, softly.

She froze. All she could do at first is stare and bite her lip. Every other time she'd heard that greeting she lilted happy, now it was all angst and sadness. They fell into a deep embrace. "Oh, God, Michael, oh God." Tears in her eyes, she finally cranked up her best smile. "It is always good to see you." They kiss, a bit too contracted for just best friends.

"I was getting into a hiding mood but it turns out you're the only one I really want to see. If we could disappear together, for a long time, I wouldn't need anything else. Excluding that possibility, here's the next best thing, presents from home."

He handed her the books and she laughed at the irony of the shoddy substitute. Barely glancing at them, she stuffed them in her backpack, which was not a fashionable way to carry books at the time. One quality she did glean unabashedly from her military upbringing was practicality. Then she took one book back out and outright tossed it in a trashcan. "That one I know. It's on beyond petty, but could still be dangerous anti-knowledge in the wrong hands. I hereby expunge if from its earthly existence. I'll breeze the others. Sometimes Arthur doesn't understand his own propaganda and lands an interesting fish tale. Mostly though, they're horror tales from the right wing, which wouldn't alone be non-entertaining, if he didn't have such dreary taste in writers. Even creeps stumble on unique ideas within their wee isolated hours of focused obsessions."

"One obsession we're observing is once your hands touch a printed page your subconscious offers you no rest until all those words have been absorbed."

"One obsession my hands are not letting go of is you. They can't take you if I won't let go." She did continue holding his hands with both of hers, but bored soon of this fantasy. "Damn them, and damn my father for making me so aware of their totality."

"Yeah, ol' Arthur, he had me over for a beer."

"Huh! Now there's a switch."

"My words exactly. I'm learning people go through a whole lot of switches when they don't expect to ever see you again."

"Michael, morbidity does not wear well on you."

"I'm not weighting the matter, I'm just noting people's attitudes." He laughed to himself. "Sometimes I actually like some of it."

"Would that 'some of it' include Colleen and Francina?"

"Man, details do travel fast in femal-ia, don't they."

"Oh, are there details to fill in? You skipped a beat. I haven't talked to them. I do happen to know they are on a bit of a bacchanalia and not likely to let a longtime, missing trophy slip away. Never mind, I was just surmising. I'd rather not know, preferring to remain resting-reassured it's forever impossible to stay one twist ahead of whatever goes on in your so-called mind...So, is this D-day?"

"Tomorrow."

"Well, then let's dig up Sarelle and some other people you know and do something like a party."

"I'd rather just hang out with you."

"I would too, but I'm kind of involved with Jeffrey again and we have a study date for later. He's not all that understanding in the first place but this Army thing is way outside his scope of comprehension. If Sarelle and I both guilt him into a mandatory party mode he'll knuckle under."

Their shared expression is all the communication they needed to relay that this would be far from an ideal scene, short or long term. She let one hand go, but kept a tight grip on his hand with the other as they walked. At the edge of campus they walked a few blocks down Telegraph Avenue, Berkeley's main street. Though charming architecturally, all lined with bookstores, coffee houses and urbane but affordable restaurants, it always had a dense air. Intellectuals prevailed, yes, but had to be guarded against a deluge of street people who were showing up from all over the country. Some were anti-war stalwarts, others but hippies looking for their own types. What were all those lost souls looking for? Drugs were *de rigueur*. Trippers were everywhere, with flowers in their hair and bliss-fogged eyes; until the bliss faded to blasé. Dealers and freeloaders were frequent players of the circus. In Berkeley tradition, however, to be socially mobile one still had to be able to proffer some articulation, at least clever if not truly intelligent. Nobody knew what the drug revolution would bring, but it didn't take a social scientist to sense this droll dreamland would warp into a community headache. A few blocks off campus they turned up a tree-lined residential street and stopped a few doors from Sarelle's sorority house.

Landers stalled, "Why don't we just keep trying to phone her."

"Sixty girls on three phone lines! Next time it won't be busy is four A.M."

"Suits me. Oh, alright, but I always feel like I'm in a glass inspection case, in these houses."

"Because you are. You're plenty cute, boy, just imagine what they're really visualizing. Stop, delete that; all your libido needs is more food for fantasy. Be strong now, eyes dead ahead. Ignore the natives in the bushes. That jungle warfare training had to be good for something."

That she was a Navy brat made it easier for them to joke about military matters. Back with the other soldiers it had been easy too, but that brand of dark humor rarely carried well with most civilians. "Yeah, watch me low crawl, right in to door," he said. He walked, feinting his best slink step for a few yards, but then went nondescript when he reached the over-manicured yard.

The instant he rang, the door opened with three hair-helmet coifed girls guarding the threshold, all head to toe, outer and under, wearing exactly the same clothing labels, item by item; only the tints were varied. Accustomed to looking through uniforms, he could notice they were well-structured lasses; DNA did matter in the process here. The tallest asked, "Yes, are you here to see someone?"

"Why not? Sarelle. Is she in?"

"Was she expecting you?"

"No, the phone was always busy. Tell her it's Michael Landers. We're old friends since junior high."

"Oh, I didn't know that," the short girl asked, as if they all spoke from one consciousness. "What fraternity shall I tell her you're from?"

"Yeah, ah, make that Upsilon Sigma Alpha."

They exchanged confused glances on this one. The middle girl spoke for them, "Well, he said he wasn't from here." They spun and walked off in unison. Landers wandered the foyer, browsing photos from various parties, all with the letters of some fraternity gold-embossed on them. Separately, two girls poked from around a corner and lingered long enough for Landers to smile first. Reserved but much looser than the others, they smiled back, with no cut-off point. They do move off, upon siting the triumvirate returning, but both glance back. The tall one spoke for the trio, "We figured it out, U.S. Army. That's funny. But this whole Viet Nam thing isn't funny. It's insane. What about all those poor, country do-nothings and Mexicans and black gang kids who all just love to fight. Even they could finish off all those commies, once and for all."

"I want to send all the peace demonstrators and hippies first. And hope they don't ever come back. It's horrible, they'd send a clean-cut college guy like you."

"The Army clean cut me," Landers said.

"It's just not right. Why won't they quit? Don't they know who we are? Maybe if we bombed China...oh, I can't think that way. I just don't know what to say," the small girl said.

"You've said enough," Landers finished for her, because they were making him very angry, not so much for their political takes or social insensitivity but that they were disparaging a lot of his Army friends.

Luckily for all, Sarelle, came down the stairs, wearing jeans and loafers and hastily pulling on a stylish sweater. A petite blonde, very cute in a teenage way, which she recognized, and pushed herself to prepare her brain for when a ski-jump nose and bubbly cheeks wouldn't mature fashionably. That she picked her boyfriends from the science brain-pool rather than the frat pulchritude patch didn't endear her with her sorority sisters, particularly this vanity pack at the door. On seeing him, she paused for a heavy beat, but continued down, gracefully, to give him a hug and a kiss.

The middle girl said, "If you're from the same school, I don't suppose you're going to be seeing a certain someone we sisters aren't supposed to associate with, are we?"

"Don't worry, we sisters are very discerning," Landers said.

"Well alright, I suppose. Do remember though, the new codes still don't allow jeans on campus," the small girl said, as the three pinned Sarelle.

"Yes, I know. But I also thought the new codes did away with these butler-ette squads guarding the front door."

Outside, he commented, "Nothing personal, but that place is lagging a bit behind the times."

"Yeah, by definition. Which isn't bad, of itself. Don't grade the whole batch on the three ugly stepsisters at the door. They're just desperate for attention. Or control. Which are inextricable by nature. Lot of the other girls are actually quite cool. The war thing has split the place right down the middle. The whole Greek system was never so tenuous. They've never heard of bodies dropping out, not like they are now. Scary result is those left inside are way too pure. Nature abhors an inbred."

They reached where Katrina was waiting in the shadows. Landers said, "Mission accomplished. None too soon. I actually almost expressed myself."

"The safety zone is getting to be rather compromising," Sarelle sighed.

"So quit. Counter-rejection of those who select by rejection is fair game."

"Not when you're in the grip of economic blackmail. My parents say, they pay where I live they say where I live. I'd do it your way, but with all your jobs I have no idea how you even pass, let alone get all A's. Of course, when you can read at the speed of light...Ah, a bed's a bed, when all you do is get up, clean up and walk out the door. That said, it's party on 'til dawn."

"Small, private party, to be more specific," Landers refined. "Us only."

"Well, we have to see if we can disclude Jeff first. Correctly," Katrina said. "I do owe him that."

They found Jeffrey at a local sidewalk cafe, with half a dozen other students. Very deliberate about his whole existence, Jeff covered the social middle-ground. Slightly long hair but a neat moustache, slightly-frayed jeans but a traditional suede jacket, ivy-league shirt but tailored from blue twill work-shirt cloth, desert boots from Brooks Brothers. Both Landers and Jeff were compromised, on sight. They'd met before and actually got along well, but Katrina's bond to Landers always made Jeff ill at ease. Landers had always contained himself from making any comments about whom Katrina dated, unless he knew pertinent shady background stories. Jeff was fine, but he didn't want to share her right then, nor even with Sarelle. Yet, in the first few comments of the introductions, the group decision was that since midterms were just over they had apt cause to drink a lot of beer. This train wreck was unavoidable without wholesale rudeness.

For various reasons, not the least of which was several of the attendees were her adjoining neighbors, Katrina's place was voted as the site. Her apartment was considered a rental marvel, partly because it had character galore and partly because of an accidental discovery by Landers, two years before. It was in the garrets of an old Victorian mansion converted into a half dozen apartments. Hers had been the smallest, although most charming. In his curiosity, of which he had ample, particularly in the category of wondering what held things together, Landers had noticed that one wallboard was attached by little more than the splitting paint in its corners. He peeked behind it and found two more raw spaces identical to hers, only that one had to duck through low places to get to them. Although only the bathroom was an airspace separated by a door, because of this configuration she now had an extra bedroom and an office. Thrown in were two cozy, isolated window alcoves for private reading spaces. Altogether, quite spacious, by student standards. Ever industrious and an inspired makeshift decorator, when Katrina worked it over it suggested comfortable elegance. Furniture was seasonal students and professors castoffs, reupholstered by her. Kitchen items were the only thing she'd gotten from her parents. Her father had allowed Katrina and her mother a budget to buy "sturdy" ware at the Navy and Marine post exchanges in San Diego. They put together a coordinated set in a near-Bauhaus style. Her mother actually had a cultured upbringing, but only offered it up to Katrina outside the realm of her husband. Style scared Arthur in the usual way that ignorance breeds fear.

On the first time they'd met, in seventh grade, Landers had nicknamed her the "Reading Machine". One summer day at Ocean Beach, she had approached this skinny but toned and tan kid, with peeling nose even under layers of white zinc oxide, hair longer than she was used to, all weathered and streaked by long over-exposure. Though not timid, she was normally unimposing and shy, from never having lived anywhere more than two years straight in her life, and knowing well the stigma local kids often put on military brats. Yet, get her on the subject of books and she was avid and fearless. She wasn't impressed so much by his easy presence that might have attracted a girl wanting instant social stature, but that while all his friends watched the surf and chatted with the girls, he had been lying among them, finishing up reading "Portrait of an Artist as a Young Man". This magnetized Katrina to have to know him. Doing something she'd never done before, she walked right into the group, sat beside him, and asked him if he really understood it. He said he liked it, especially for all the amazing words and usage he'd never seen before, but didn't know where it was all going. It had come from a reading list his Dad had compiled. Though amazed that this angel from afar was right there beside him, after awhile he went surfing and left it with her. By the time he came in, maybe three hours later, she had read it all and then explained it to him. This stirred his own contrarian side and he took exception to some precepts, launching the first of hundreds of debates on literature and all else, with his friends amazed how animated he became; moreso how he became oblivious to them and even the surf. He was captured by those piercing eyes that seemed to have so much more world knowledge and experience than him. Had he not had a girlfriend, at the time, they would probably have started off as in-love as two thirteen year olds could be. Oddly, not only was Landers's girlfriend not jealous of Katrina, she made it her mission to establish Katrina as centerpiece of the whole social scene. Only years later did Landers and Katrina figure out that that girlfriend was more in love and lust with Katrina than him. He'd wondered why she never cared much for "making out", which all the other kids were exploring with fervor, yet she was so affectionate in Katrina's presence, letting her fingers wander to places they never did at any other time, sometimes "accidentally" brushing Katrina and sometimes almost pushing them to kiss and touch.

One thing Katrina was rich in was books. By her third year at Berkeley, the word on her book collection was legend. Even jaded senior professors found their way to her apartment to admire not only the quality of the editions, but her taste in literature, often quite obscure. From her mother's parents, Katrina had inherited twenty boxes of leather-bound or otherwise in prime-condition, first-edition classics, including a set of the best printing of the Harvard Classics, which she'd read by her senior year of high school. Her grandfather had showed her which first editions to look for, never to bend back the binding or pages, to use plain butcher paper to replace the dustcovers and to keep them in drawers until she was finished reading, then put them back on to preserve them in mint condition. From age five until fifteen, when he died, he would show up in his old Plymouth, in whatever corner of the country her father was stationed in, and they'd drive all day long hunting through used bookstores and rummage sales, though surreptitiously, because Arthur resented his father-in-law's "over-educated" airs. Sometimes, they'd live together on the road for weeks, between her father's permanent stations or while her Mom was in tight temporary quarters. College towns were always their favorites and they had explored hundreds of campuses and libraries. He'd missed college because of war, early marriage and the Depression, but she saw him as the smartest and best-read person she ever met. Even in her four years in Europe, in two installments, she was foraging through dark, dusty university basements and bookstores. Katrina did indeed love her father, because she knew he provided for them from a genuine position of devotion, even if it was in his super-militarized fashion. Yet, she always anticipated her father's returns with trepidation, not for any physical danger but for his life mission to control everything, especially her imagination. Grandfather was a diamond mine of the imagination. His legacy was in every nook of her apartment. It was not uncommon that half a dozen serious readers lounged silently around her place, some of whom she hardly knew. Often they shared favorite books or left them there, where they'd have "good friends". The result was her library grew of itself, quite selectively, by a dozen or so books a week. Her collector side loved this but her reader side felt a slight but comforting angst, as her long list of must-reads grew ever longer. Time became more and more precious.

Setback in a deep niche was an electric radiator which she'd fashioned into a *trompe l'oiel* fireplace, using crinkled tinfoil and votive candles in rose-tint holders to lights cut-out cellophane fire tongues dangling from mono-filament,. Her art collection was mostly cutouts from magazines, with frames implied by layered cardboard. Her main room's "parlor art", as she described it with a fun inflection, was Fauve through deco-moderne, the guest wing Impressionist back through Renaissance, the halls and alcoves eclectic miniatures, the office contemporary. The *chef d'oeuvre* was her own, only oil painting from a summer-school art class, of a slightly figurative abstract style somewhere between Kandinsky and Friesz. Nobody else was more amazed than she about how finished it was, being her first try at a serious painting. Her favorite piece, and only other original, was a pencil sketch of her by Landers, not particularly accurate or skilled but it indubitably portrayed her in her best, looking-over-her-reading-glasses with a "yeah, so I'm smart but I can kiss" expression. She knew exactly what he'd wanted to capture. All of her.

Even though she had a warm smile for anyone who deserved one, Katrina was not an avid schmoozer. While others klatsched in coffeehouses and beer bars, she might be in the room but would be aside, reading. Although she might make an appearance at parties, if she couldn't tag into conversation that wasn't trivial, she'd soon duck out. She did enjoy entertaining at home, for small groups. Without being material or vain, she was very proud of her home. As a kid she never had anyone over to the house, except a couple closest girlfriends. Dad was too imposing, Mom was too quiet to be inviting, and the place felt more like a family barracks than a warm home. Her hideout was the garage, where she kept all her books up in a loft, built by her and Landers. Although the walls and ceiling were bare frames with tarpaper, she covered them with wallpaper and fabric; this was her palace. Her favorite place to read was in her dad's old Model T Ford, which he promised to restore to factory condition, after he retired.

As the ten partiers worked their way over to Katrina's, individuals popped into stores and came back out with bags. Half of them were under twenty-one so they pooled their money for beer, with Landers and Jeff to be the buyers. Assessing their insufficient contributions, Landers spent the last of his cash. Near Katrina's, he handed the bags over and disappeared up an alley. When he caught back up with them, going up her staircase, he had a large bouquet of whatever-me-nots and greenery he'd found on his foray. Katrina accepted them with a smile and extra notch of sadness in her heart. Landers garnered genuine smiles of esteem from the other four girls. He appreciated the attention but never was able to flirt with abandon, within Katrina's eyesight.

Plenty of crackers, cheese, dip, raw veggies and even a large pizza, all displayed like a Tuscany feast by Katrina, dressed up with greens and some of Landers' flowers. This crowd came ready to drink so when Jeffrey pulled out a joint, both Sarelle and Katrina moved in to stop him. Sarelle said, "Do we really know all these people, well? Let's wait a bit." They weren't particularly worried about being busted for breaking a law that wasn't enforced anyway, but an irony in the schism of the times was that drinkers and dopers didn't necessarily mix well.

Thankfully, for Landers, he wasn't featured as focus for this soiree, so his plight didn't become any particular halo of attention. Politics was always fair game, but this crowd considered itself too educated to not add an academic, historical thesis rather than to simply blast the day's headlines or scoundrel of the moment. Still, the war topic kept bouncing back like a perpetual yo-yo. Landers found himself drifting. By midnight the last of them were out the door, except Landers, Jeffrey and Sarelle. But then two other men walked in, without seeming to feel they needed an invitation. Reading the expressions on the girls' faces, Landers knew they weren't strangers, but weren't welcome, not right then.

"So this is where everybody is. Wasn't a very inclusive invitation list, I take it," the shorter man said. His accent, mop-down-the-forehead haircut, and dress announced him as from New York, intellectually proud and probably Jewish. Though brusque, his tone was more a call to debate than antagonistic, so Landers had no immediate feelings of like or dislike, but wished he wasn't there.

On every level, the other guy's entire presence gouged at intuitions and sensibilities. Though his features were unremarkable, his wind was sour, by body and vocal language. His clothes said maybe he tried to look to-mode, but with no fashion sense at all. What stood out to Landers was the shirt, like the only style and fabric one could buy in an Army PX. Without a greeting for anyone, the newcomer helped himself to a beer.

Sarelle said, "Hi, guys. This wasn't a party, just a spontaneous sociological combustion only quenchable by beer. Ah, let's see, Jeffrey you know all the concerned parties. Landers, this is Arnold and Werner."

"Glad to meet you," Arnold, the shorter man said, offering a sincere handshake and looking Landers in the eye, with no preconclusions, "It's Arnold Glifkin, to be technical, attorney at large and anti-draft specialist."

"Glad to meet you," Landers said. "Maybe I should've met you six months ago."

Werner said, "And I'm an Establishment hater at large; anti-Viet Nam specialist. We heard there was a soldier in trouble. Which must be you. You ready to throw a wrench in the gears of the war machine?" This all came out in empty staccato, almost rehearsed and hit Landers like a dare. Considering a dare as almost always a cover for cowardice, he tried not to show any posture of disdain but did put his hand out. Without conviction or eye contact, Werner barely shook it, with affected distaste, as if even a basic handshake was an Establishment trapping.

Finally responding to Werner's challenge, Landers said, "I don't much feel like being guillotine filler, right now. I just want to disappear."

Arnold said, "It's not hard to put you on the subway to Canada."

"AWOL does me no good. Eventually it just goes back on my time. And getting my time back is the goal at hand."

"We could actually get some mileage out of this angle," Werner said. "We could play up a guy already in the military, trying to bust the system."

Katrina cut this line off, "Michael's the one who needs help, not you."

"No individual is above history," Werner said. "Speaking of changing history, are you two still thinking about working for that newspaper and reaming the war mongers?"

Landers clicked on this beat, "What's he talking about?"

"Oh, it came up, about Jeffrey and I doing some writing for a paper. In San Diego, no less. The Berkeley connection supposedly adds some credibility."

"And leave school?" Landers detracted. "You're nuts."

"It's a sacrifice but if you want to kill the demon, you have to go for the heart. San Diego is the heart, from both the military and the war manufacturing base. And the public there actually promote it."

"Have you ever been there? It's not quite that simplistic. Nowhere is. For starters, the average local has a long head start in grudges against the military."

"Who cares? What matters is now. I do assume nobody here is too conformist to call themselves a revolutionary."

"You seem the one most tracked on a one-party line. Conforming doesn't motivate me much; it's not like I haven't been known to paddle out, when everyone else is paddling in."

Werner scoffed, "Is surfing the depth of existential values we're talking here?"

"For the record, surfing is experiential, not existential."

"As if anybody else knows or cares what the hell you're talking about. I'm talking about saving the people."

"I'm all over an honest cry for help. And I'm not shy to point out the Emperor needs more than a new diet. But I'm not so keen on whining just to ennoble personal suffering. Mine or anybody elses."

Werner, stocky and considerably taller than Landers, took up a physically assertive stance, like a bully about one second from striking out. Any bully posture would turn on Landers's most ornery side, but that this guy had pushed his way into Katrina's house and was acting like such a brute was turning him livid. By old habit, he started shifting weight from foot to foot. Katrina knew well what this shuffle might lead to and pinned Landers with her eyes, to not even think of throwing a punch. Even though he was thinking more of blocking a punch, he did realize he might appear thuggish, a street side of himself he'd tried to espunge from his image, ever since he'd started college.

It was Jeffrey who jumped in to alter the mood, brandishing his way over scale joint with a smile of great accomplishment. "This right here, folks, is the indisputable, totally revolutionary, unadulterated, leave no prisoners unstoned, one toke over the line, wacky wonder weed. Any takers?...Is it all right, Katrina?"

"Go ahead, just let me open the windows," Katrina said, "I'm not counting tonight as normal." She handed Arnold a fresh beer and the mood softened. Sarelle even turned down the lights a bit.

Jeffrey lit up, with an air of the connoisseur. Inhaling, slowly, to light it evenly all the way around, he exhaled this first puff, to clear the fumes from the lighter, then took a full hit and passed it to Katrina, with a nod.

"Thanks, but no thanks. It tends to turn me overly sentimental and I'm about as drenched in sentiment as I want to be, right now." She passed it to Landers.

"Well if you're not, I guess..." he stalled, her phrasing hitting home.

"Some party pack this is," Arnold said. "I'll take it, and I will gladly fill in the dots, with an extra hit for each of you." He only took one big hit, however. Katrina took it back from him and held it out to Landers.

"Go ahead, don't be so noble, my behalf doesn't need it. It does at least put a smile on your face."

Landers did take a hit and, while still holding it, made a facial expression to Arnold of, "Thanks, quite tasty."

Sarelle helped herself to two mild hits and passed it to Werner. Nobody else was paying much attention but Landers noticed that Werner made an exaggerated sucking, yet the ash on the joint didn't glow, at all. There was no purposeful detective thinking going on, writing if off as the not uncommon person who felt smoking grass made them look "in" but who really didn't care for it. It did increase his suspicions about that this guy was phony, but for what cause?

"So where do you stand?" Werner started up again, since everyone else in the room seemed disinclined to flex degrees of outrage with him. "Either you're going over there to kill children or you're helping us tear down the U.S. war-crimes factory."

"I've still got twelve hours to decide the rest of my life. I'm waiting for a sign. 'Til then, I'm trying to enjoy the moment." Landers said. "Suffering has no particular, appeal. If you've got the time, go ahead. Somewhere else would be ideal. Out of curiosity, though, I'm wondering exactly what it is that you're tearing down?"

"We're going to annihilate all the institutions of suppression, page by page, brick by brick. Anarchy is the only rule. It's time for total revolution."

"Being a rebel has a peal to it. Isn't it supposed to be an American instinct, to replace something that isn't working with something better. I can nit-pick away, on a bad day, but I don't have a wholesale plan in mind to rewrite the entire system. For sure, I'm not an anarchist or a nihilist. Nihilism is for losers, period. If they drown in their own cesspool I'm not inclined to want to watch. And anarchy sounds like bliss but could only work if every individual had total respect for all other individuals and their property. Since the group you're trying to govern happens to be humans that evolution doesn't seem complete, yet, does it. For instance, do you have any respect for anybody else?"

"We're here specifically to help you, and all you do is dump trash on us," Werner said. "The only answer, now, is attack the system, with everything we've got."

Arnold was enough of a lawyer to realize that Werner was losing the jury's sympathy, if he ever had any. "C'mon, Werner, he's got talking points. Full frontal attack is for mass rallies. His seems to be a specific case, at a distinct turning point. Let's define that position before we dis-incorporate it."

As if a stuck phonograph, Werner rattled "We're saving America from corporate hell. I don't need my ass kissed for gratitude but I don't see how some people can't care enough to cooperate. Now is not the time to let down the guard. If we show up at a rally, with a soldier in uniform denouncing all this genocide, the press would report every word of our message. We could get it on live TV, nationwide even."

Not at all shy about locking swords intellectually, Katrina was reticent to jump into ionized, cyclical debates, when mindsets were pre-fixed. Still, she was the most angry person in the room, partly protective for Landers and partly for having a party she didn't invent nor want turn into a battleground. Although having far more long-term reasons to be against the military system than any of them, from that exposure she had also picked up an aversion to losing self-control. As calm as she could, she said, "Say we try to waltz this number, not stomp it. He is not putting out a general SOS, particularly not for pity. His position is he's supposed to report tomorrow, to be shipped out. Plus he's in the infantry. Arnold, if you, right now, can think of a precedent for legally stalling that action, perfect. Let's hear it, concise, without elaboration. Otherwise, I'd rather say goodbye to my friend, peacefully. The party is over. Sorry you weren't invited, but this was not planned."

Arnold, indeed an ardent lover of emotional debate but not an admirer of personal grudge matches, backed off, "Understood. Sorry, we did walk in here rather presumptive. Truth is, too, Michael, you're way beyond our distant-early-warning system. I'll take it up with some other legal eyes, but military law is a well-insulated, nether-world unto itself. If we can dredge up any stalling tactics, I'll call Katrina. Ah, Sarelle, can we talk a minute, though?"

"Yeah, sure. I'll walk you out," Sarelle said. "Mind going a bit ahead of us, Werner?"

"No. Because I got more important places to be, with people with a passion for the right cause."

Without good-byes or a thank you, Werner left. The mutual, nearly silent sigh of relief was evident. Sarelle took Arnold by the arm and walked him out.

Landers commented, "Well, at least he's memorized all the right jargon. His main cause does seem to be himself, though."

Katrina apologized, "Sorry, Michael. That wasn't my idea for a party favor. Social graces are bit loose around here, these days."

"Leave it to Katrina to euphemize a total asshole into simply a social mis-grace," Jeffrey said.

"A skill I'm trying to learn, myself. Confronted by a total junker pretending to be a Deuzy, I have often a bad habit of kicking tires.

For which I apologize, Katrina; you hardly need to. Thanks for defusing them so succinctly. Actually, Arnold seemed okay."

"Yeah, he is," Katrina said. "Except that he doesn't have an off button. He's trying to date Sarelle and she's trying to decide if she can take the constant heat. Law school is in her future and he is one of the new stars at Boalt. He starts teaching precedent law at Stanford next semester. It's not altogether heartening that he didn't bite all over your case; he loves fresh bait. Sorry, didn't mean to bring that one back."

"It's not like it doesn't crawl out of my own conscience every few minutes. And the intervals are decreasing in proportion to time left. I've about run out of tactics. Guess I just show up and continue to try to talk them out of the whole war. So far, they're overwhelmingly unimpressed."

"You can never beat the military by boring them to death," Katrina said. "In that category they're already dead."

"I'd be glad to revive them, but there's not many tricks they haven't seen, or at least imagined."

"Don't give them that much credit for creativity. For instance, I'm pretty sure they don't have LSD totally categorized. Just float right on in the front door dancing the Nutcracker Suite and watch them scatter. Better yet, go wandering around a supermarket parking lot mumbling like you're trying to find Ho Chi Minh's house. I'll call the MPs, myself, and have you picked up. Then you're not really AWOL, or even seriously disorderly."

"From the one who is always ever-so-careful, you do manage to pull some whacky rabbits out of your hat," Jeffrey said.

"Undetected diversion against the military does happen to be one of my specialties," she said. "Sincere confusion from within will always spin them out. They expect you to be afraid of war and constantly try to make you afraid of them, but they don't know what to think when you're not scared of anything, especially including yourself."

"I'm impressed by the concept, but I'm filing it for now; it's about tomorrow," Landers said.

"True. So, subject deleted. In fact, delete the last twenty minutes, boys, anyone for a fresh beer? And re-light that joint, I'll have some. A drastic alteration of dimension seems appropriate."

Hearing only this last line, Sarelle returned, with head and hands bobbing in the international body language of indecision. "Dementia

83

is more like it. Wouldn't it be a joy to have your head, heart and body in the same dimension, for just one instant." She made eye contact with Katrina, who nodded for Sarelle to follow her.

Once they're out of earshot, Jeffrey said, "Don't worry, they'll have our entire gender recategorized, in no time. They're quite a duo. And you too. You guys just don't fit in any social box I know. Not that you look at all square, you are hardly standout counter culture. And you for sure don't think nearly as straight as you look."

"Yeah, well we've all kind of played the social game on the crossover inclusion plan. Stick to a look too tightly, any look, it may work fine in one group but keeps you out of others. Plus we've all had jobs, for years. As for 'square', I took significant aversion to that concept, way back when they tried to get us to swear an oath in Cub Scouts, something about 'be square and obey the laws of the pack.' I hadn't fully formed the thought yet, but I knew a control situation when I saw it. If being square meant being under uniform control, unh-uh, they got the wrong kid."

"Is that where the word square came from?"

"I don't know, really, it's just my first encounter with it, as a character depiction."

"Hm. Having always lived the Bay Area – in the 'in' neighborhoods at that – where the popular dogma is that anything south of Palo Alto is considered Neanderthal-landia, you three have given me a new perspective. I do love San Francisco, but it's easy to get stuck in one box. You wander too far into any other box, you might not get back in. I'm being drawn to New York. Or even L.A., which you don't ever mention around here."

"San Diegans put down L.A. as much as Frisco does, if that's possible. But you gotta admit, while S.F. might appreciate the arts, it's L.A. that creates them, at least with an eye to the outer world. Dago doesn't even appreciate them, much. Looking north, you can feel like San Diego is the older brother who stayed home, while L.A. and Frisco are two sisters trying to outdo each other. Despite the chorus from the purposely uninitiated, L.A. has ample soul and breadth – but you gotta look for it and smile a bit, like you found it or at least have a sense of humor for excesses – and not be distracted by all the flash and splash. Frisco has clear substance, but you have to sneak by all those "The City" snobs, self-put to put all else down. My patience gets leery at that altitude. That whole border circus on Dago's doorstep casts a stark perspective. You appreciate what you have. Lifestyle-wise, San Diego is freer and, at times, surprisingly more libertine. Especially in O.B.. Best you leave your preaching robes at home. Caste lines aren't as extreme and they aren't as impassable. And they don't mind a party, even if it gets a bit loud; or even lewd, in that most the locals did the TJ sleaze crawl somewhere along the line and have at least witnessed a much broader sample of when is the sex game titillating and when is it depravity. Bottom line, I'll take any of the three over anywhere else. Though the New York magnet always has its pull. Every time I see those streets in the movies I want to be there."

The girls returned. Katrina is mum, but Sarelle had a bemused glint in her eye. She poured herself a wine, turned the lights down even lower, put on a slow, sexy dance record and lit the stub of the joint. "Come on, Michael, let's dance." She pulled him up, put both his hands behind her waist and gets right to work with her own fingers, behind his neck. Picking all the red beats of the rhythm she practiced a full-body contact, rub-a-dub. Somewhat shy in others' presence, particularly Katrina's, he backed off a bit, but Sarelle recognized a weakness when she felt one and does have the wherewithal to persist. Katrina maneuvered Jeffrey so they're not looking towards the other two. Landers's resistance began to go awandering.

He did ask Sarelle, close to her ear, "Let's see, this is the same party, right? What'd you girls just talk about?"

"Oh, girl things."

"Girl things like whom?"

"Oh, girl things like you. You and I are supposed to start making out, real good, right now. Like this." She's not kidding. Beginning with a rich kiss, she backed him into the corner and straddled his thigh, definitely matching all points with firm counterpoints."

When she paused to catch her breath, he asks, "Just pretend I'm curious. Are you on a mission?"

"What, you don't want me?" she teased, with body and soul.

"You know that as well as I do. I could name several previous examples, with no success...Why do keep running into myself saying that, lately...I do have this vague recollection of you slapping me off my feet, on the dance floor, at the junior prom. Nothing like public humiliation to spice up a memory. And you were the one who initiated that particular movement, as I recall."

"It wasn't the movement which, I confess, was mine all mine, but you just happened to be the first boy whose hard-on pressed up against my tender loins. Since then, I've weathered the shock. For example, your thrust is not exactly shocking me, right now. In fact, my mission plan is fading, no, fading, yes, fading, umm, fading, fading. No! Lock gyroscope on original objective. Here's the flight plan, full course. I'm supposed to fizz you up, a bit. Because Katrina figures Jeffrey won't leave with you here, unless I've staked out all claims on your collateral. So figure, right now, she's telling him that she's too self-conscious to sleep with him, with us here, no matter what we're doing. The endgame being that she wants to sleep with you. But, and this would be a major 'but', so that you don't get any visionary ideas, she said to give you a full-frontal de-libido-otomy that this does not include sex."

"Yeah. I love girls when they get so scientific. Let's see now; as object B of plan A, you get to get me throbbin' and bobbin' so she can ice me down. Am I a man or am I a sponge?"

"Michael!" she said with the tone alone stating that the one thing he should never doubt was Katrina's sincerity, nor how much she loved him, be it romantic or not, nor how far she would go to protect him.

"I know. I know. For the record, I believe your intentions were purely scholarly, all along. And you do your job so well."

"And I'll keep right on doing it, until he walks out the door. I gotta be thorough and I gotta be noble, you know." She got so noble she soon came on his leg and he was fighting to not be far behind.

Neither of them even heard the door close, but they did hear Katrina's, "Ahem," right behind them. "Let's not over-emote here, friends."

"Too late, I done emoted," Sarelle said. "Take him, he's all yours. Should I go?"

"Maybe you should stay. To thwart prying eyes. Being in step with the paranoia of the times. Plus, your presence will enhance my self control."

"Alright, I'm on the den couch. If I get restless I might wander off in an hour or so. I do have to be in a lab at six-thirty; that's A.M. So, goodnight. And so Michael, I guess this is...God dammit. Just...just...I don't know. This whole fucking war is getting way too personal. It's not fair. I read all the romances. I dreamed all the right dreams. Isn't this where I'm supposed to get to wave a little handkerchief and cry myself into a puddle. No. Instead, I'm just pissed off. Pissed off if you go. Pissed off if you don't. One of these days I'm really going to blow up in somebody's face." She was crying and shaking. Catching herself, she gave Landers a very brief kiss on the cheek and ducked out of the front door. Katrina and Landers knew they had exactly the same feelings about this, so don't mention it.

"Well, ah. I guess we ought to...What did she tell you?"

"That we're sleeping together, and that's it."

"Is that okay?"

"Yeah, that's okay. There's absolutely nowhere else I'd rather be."

Shyly, she led him into her bedroom. "Turn around, while I change." She quickly changed into a full-length flannel gown and sat on the bed. "Okay." He turned back around. That he glanced at the clothes she hastily piled on the chair, with bra and panties showing, which made her blush that she hadn't been more careful.

"What am I sleeping in? Do you have any pajamas?"

"Ah, no. Your pants, I guess."

"Fine by me, but I've kind of been living in them for the last three days. They're not exactly filthy but..."

"Oh, hell, just lose them. The outer ones. There's an extra-baggy T-shirt in that hamper." She got in bed and turned away while he changed and turned off the light. He got under the covers and moved close enough to put his hand on her waist.

"Michael, I am so, so exhausted. My heart is way too drained to talk about anything. Can we just have a kiss goodnight, and go to sleep?"

She rolled towards him, laid back and looked up at him, fighting back the glistening tears in her eyes. He stared down at her, so close in the dim moonlight through the window, struck that this is more beauty than has ever filled his vision. Slowly, ever so slowly, they approached, to kiss. When they did, it started out as lips barely touching, but she puts her fingers through his hair and, trembling, pulled him towards her. Their tongues mate so instantly and eternally that the sparkle knocked him away. "Katrina. Katrina. This is way too many years of wondering, all exploding way too fast. I can't start this, and then stop. And I don't want to feel like I'm part of your romantic duty, even though I know you're not ruled by duty.

I'm just way too confused to make it as magic as it would have to be. So are you going to be insulted if we just stop."

For a long time, she stared into his eyes, reading, much clearer than he, all the conceivable parameters of their moment. "I'd give you anything, right now, Michael but, yes, I would rather wait until it's about something besides us not being able to stop ourselves. Some better day, there might be our place. But if it's everything tonight, and nothing tomorrow, I'd find myself analyzing it into mush. At least one imaginary outcome is that it would put such a Gordian knot in either or both of our hearts that we couldn't just be friends. Even the hint of that, I couldn't bear. I am so distracted and so, so scared, and I know I'm not a millionth as scared as you are. What scares me more is knowing that you attack when you're scared. Just for me, would you learn to hide. That is not the same as being a coward. Don't turn and run. Just hide, even if that's just going blank, until it's your time to come out. And right now, let me hide you. Just hold me. Hold me all night." She gave a quick goodnight kiss and turned away from him, but pulled his arm around her and locked it tight between her breasts. On the instinct of stopping a scream, she bit on his hand, enough to taste blood. His silently screaming with her pain exactly completes the communication.

He curled up tight behind her. Nothing had ever felt more like pure love than Katrina in his arms, all wrapped up warm in flannel. She wiggled a bit to be totally cocooned, which placed the natural reaction very close to home.

"Michael, watch it," she said.

"It's not like I'm in control here."

"Alright. Just don't move. Goodnight. I love you."

"I love you. Goodnight."

And they went to sleep, though it took awhile.

When Landers awoke at daybreak, neither had moved. Before opening his eyes, and even knowing where he was, he had the most powerful instance of peace and well-being he had ever known. Opening his eyes, though, it all hit like a battering ram in the gut. His flinching woke her, sleepy-eyed with a soft smile. "Oh, yeah. Shit. God, you know I just had the most beautiful dream. We were flying together, anywhere we wanted. Then we'd land, until if it didn't seem right, we'd take off and fly again. I could ride on your back like I used to do when we went bodysurfing. That was so young, huh."

"We had the same dream. So much more real than any dream I'd ever had."

"Don't get out of bed yet. Lie on me. Clothes on. But don't move. Just lie on me. I want to feel your heart beating and your breathing." She rolled back and he did lie on her. She just barely moved her legs apart and let him lie between them. Instantly, he was hard, and everything was felt. "Don't move," she said again, starting to cry, softly. For fifteen moments they lay still, until the alarm went off. She said, "I've got an hour before I go tutor this girl in French. I can't miss it, there's nowhere to call her. Want to fake denial and talk about nothing that matters?"

"That's exactly what I want to talk about," he agreed. They walked to a nearby coffee shop and had a quick breakfast. Purposely, she waited until the last second to say, "I gotta go. Have you decided yet?"

"Nope, short of some amazing sign, I just go report. Then, feel it out."

They stood, hugged and kissed briefly. Neither wanted to make any more of it. Walking backward, she shook her head, starting to cry again. "Let me know," is all she said, turned and walked away quickly.

Having three hours until reporting time, Landers just started walking. He walked indiscriminately through residential and business neighborhoods, walked until he wondered where he was and what time it was. On a business street, he flagged down a taxi and said, "Oakland Bus Station, so I can pick up my duffel bag, than Oakland Army Base."

"Yeah. Viet Nam bound?"

Landers didn't respond, his mind was reeling.

The driver drove a bit and started back up, "So, what's your specialty, eh, buddy?"

"Army. Ah, I mean, infantry."

"Shit, shoulda said so. Infantry rides free, in this hack." He flips off the meter. "S'over in Korea, myself. Not infantry, but I'd o' done that shit if they'd o' asked me. Not like these kids today. All hippies, faggots, draft dodgers an' protestors. Popping all kinds of drugs. An' their girlfriends singing about all these flowers and beads and free-love. Bunch of goddamn sluts and whores, if you ask me. How the hell'd they think they got to be free in the first place?" He spat out the window for effect. Landers' face showed a twitch of anger. The driver continued his rant, "Yeah, shit, you guys outta kill all those slant-eyed commies, then come back and kick the snot out of all these peace creeps. Pinko pansies, every one of them. Infantry. The real fighters. Yeah, you should'a told me. I'd o' kicked the meter sooner."

"Know what, take me back up to Berkeley."

"Berkeley, for what? What the hell you wanta do up there with them fuckin-think-they're-all-geniuses commies? Say, you aren't pullin' nothing weird, are you?"

"It's not me, it's fate. When I was looking for a sign I was looking for some bright light or stark angel. I didn't expect it to be a parrot spewing blind hate. I'm starting to feel a little mad at hate. And a lot mad at evil. And I'm not feeling like going easy. I don't know who's who yet, but it's seems like the right time to blow a few minds."

At first, the driver started to pull over but glancing back at Landers didn't tell him anything he really thought would justify this, nor did he have any understanding of what he'd just said. He conspicuously flicked the meter back on, speeded back up and spat out the window.

Back outside Katrina's house, Landers found her gone, though he suspected that. He paced around for a few minutes, until he saw Jeffrey walking up the block. As matter-of-factly as he could, he asked if Jeffrey could find some LSD. Jeffrey went off to try. Landers was still pacing when Katrina returned.

Her emotions were nothing but twisted, "Hi...Didn't you have an appointment somewhere?"

"Yeah, but I ran into a representative of the one side I for sure don't want to come out ahead. So, I'm trying your plan X."

"Me and my big mouth. This damn sure isn't a responsibility I want anywhere on my resume. Come on up." She walked ahead, not acting like she wanted to make any conversation.

Jeffrey returned, just as they were entering Katrina's door. He said, "Voila, man, this is the purple monster shit. Made personally by a chemistry prof. He pipetted it onto this sugar cube ten minutes ago, and said you better eat it within fifteen minutes."

"This isn't your textbook, dreamy trip setup," Katrina said. "You're sure?"

"I'm not close to sure of anything. But if I think about it..." he stops mid-sentence and swallows the sugar cube. "Well, goodbye to life as I've come to know it. And I can't lay any more of this on you. So I'm straight off to the supermarket parking lot, before this kicks in and I lose all track. If you still want to make that call..."

"Yeah, go on. If for no other reason, now, than I'd rather you be safely locked up by the MPs. Just promise me that you will not take a swing at anybody, no matter what."

"I promise. Goodbye."

Profoundly disconsolate, she let out a deep sigh of discomposure and simply walked off, leaving the two guys awkwardly misplaced.

Jeffrey, already walking off, said, "Ah...yeah, good luck, man." He started after Katrina but she waved him off, backhanded, without even having looked to see who might be following.

7

As Landers starts off towards the supermarket, he was consumed by the Russian roulette of how fast would the drug come on, and how powerful would it be. That it supposedly did come from a top-rung biochemist helped him believe that he didn't have some true poisons scorching his system. Besides his initial trip at the West L.A. V.A., Landers had tried it three other times. Once with a girlfriend, they'd massaged each other and made love and all night. That was as magic as it was supposed to be, their vibe clouds totally entrained. Once with close student friends in a cabin up in Beverly Glen, a tight neighborly enclave nestled in a long Santa Monica Mountains canyon, just up above UCLA, with a significant bohemian and intellectual concentration. They'd laid around listening to music and took short jaunts into the lush, semi-tropical fingers of the canyon. He took the time to feel the advertised spiritual bursts of connection to all things, and was unashamed that the popular love mantras kept rolling off his own tongue. What were heralded as LSD's mind-expanding natures became clear to him. It removed the automatic functions of the central nervous system, making you see that nothing is solid, just like they'd claimed in physics class. You could see and touch pure energy clouds, all kept in a vibrating order by a myriad of standing waves. Living things pulsated with swirls and paisleys and veins of blood-like bubbles, just like it seemed life energy should look. No pure hallucinations, as such, no figures appearing that weren't there at all, more that everything was transformed. But as the drug wore off, even if the so-brilliant mind loops didn't seem so brilliant, anymore, there would never be a way of going back to the concept of normal perception being just a self-tuning TV screen. There were now other dials to be dealt with: tint, audio, scent, tactile. But there are no hold knobs, be it vertical, horizontal or, especially, time. The last acid trip had been at a Monday, midday, raunchy and rowdy surfer party, in a family neighborhood off Sunset Cliffs. All with music blasting, girls running around in bikini bottoms and often not much else, every design, device and degree of psychedelic enhancement. Then there was that one guy who kept driving his station wagon around the yard with people hanging all over it, radio blasting. Mostly triggered by the fear that the police would raid the party, that time he'd become truly paranoid, that he was losing control of his emotions and his whole nervous system was being pulled apart. Paranoia of ever feeling that paranoia again, and the fact that he didn't care much for the post-trip, profound exhaustion, had led him to decide that his LSD days were over.

Until now. Now everything is present tense. Perception and reaction rule over protracted thought. Walking towards the market he can already feel his jaw tightening and the cylinders of electricity rolling around between his thumbs, fingers and palms. Feeling dizzy and very warm, even though the day is chilly, he takes his sweater off from over a T-shirt. Because the rush comes on so quickly, it makes him scared if he'll be able to keep control, at all. By the time he reaches the supermarket, energy bubbles are running through veins of trees, all patterns want to be fluttering paisleys, and the cars all cat along like living cartoon figures. He's sure a headlight winks at him. Another car laughs. This is a whole new dimension he's never been to before. To not stand out, he tries nonchalantly sitting on a wall, planning to wait until he sees the MPs, to start carrying on, a bit. With his time sense totally distorted, even the first few minutes of waiting seem like days. Every few seconds, he keeps calling himself back to attention, by trying to count to twenty. Being so distracted from outside and inside, he never gets close.

Cruising up the avenue is the expected military police wagon. In it are Mayborough and Clives. Both like to be thought of as city hip to the marrow. Mayborough is black, from the Bedford-Stuyvesant area of Brooklyn and Clives is white, from a rough Irish neighborhood of South Chicago. It was similarly misspent teenage years which had landed them in

93

the military. After recidivist runs of minor scrapes, judges had offered them some time in jail or a clean slate, if they enlisted. After their battery of aptitude tests, both were picked for the infantry, with the option of being in the MPs if they added another year to their tour. Thinking they would go to Germany, they took the MP options. Both went straight to Oakland where Mayborough, after two years, had risen to the ranks of Specialist 5, equivalent to the lowest degree of sergeant. Clives lacked the discipline to ever get beyond PFC. Not liking to feel like cops, at all, still they feel lucky that as long as they're marking time, driving around with each other is the best they could hope for. Deemed too freewheeling to do duty where image and decorum matter, their seniors recognized, very reluctantly, that they were the best field partners in the whole Bay Area. Having grown up on the other side of the authority game, both are adept at sorting out true criminals from simply drunk and disorderly soldiers. Having empathy with the customers allows them to have few problem prisoners. To relieve the boredom, they function as an ongoing, droll, self-entertaining duo. Music from a hot-wired tape deck blasts Motown, with fidelity.

Clives, who couldn't care less if what comes out of his mouth makes any sense at all, has picked up a palette of somewhat blackish mannerisms and a vaguely New Orleans patois, for no other philosophy than it felt right, says, "Where is this ass-jivin' mudda-fuqua. It's too *belle du jour* to be shakin' down any of this marshmallow shit. I say we find he took off running into the Berkeley, and we're in hot pursuit, way out of radio reach. I need a fresh *paté* of coeds to let my *bon temps roulez*. I further suggest we do it in civvies, so we can properly infiltrate the perfidilles."

"No, shit, Clives, that's a definite plan B. As for Plan A, I hope this turkey ain't rabid. Can't be entertaining no lip-foamers today, no bedamned way. What I'd really like to do is to score us up some smoke. I bet there's sixteen tons of prime-time, right on this block."

"Chances are. 'Cept, lest I say again, ignoring the feat of repetition, that your average student pusher-man ain't likely to procure unto us; not flyin' these threads. Oh-oh, there's the scene of the crime. Dum-dee-dum-dum. Drive by fast, in case there's snipers."

They cruise by, honestly scanning the area, barely getting a second's glimpse to see Landers' back, where he is still sitting and trying to be low key. Since he'd been described as having a mustache and dressed in a sweater he doesn't register. Landers hasn't seen them. Mayborough says, "Don't see him. Don't want to see him."

Clives adds, "An' I don't even see nobody staring at nobody else. The fool in question is either been way over-sold or is way gone from the goings on."

"I think you're on to something. Let's loop the coop, a time or two."

"Yeah, then let's be gone, anon, to Plan B and beyond."

Landers spots them. He knows he can't flag their attention, but does stand up. Too late, they're gone. More upset and confused than ever, he starts walking. First instinct is to try to retrace his way back to Katrina's. Now the drug is raging. The whole sidewalk is snaking and people walking by look fiendish, as if their hair whips around like snakes and their skin is peeling back. Almost by accident, he finds Katrina's building. He knocks, but gets no answer. A girl who had been at the party coming down the hall recognizes him. Sensing distress, she nods, but turns away. His reading of her slightly protective stance is that she's freaked at what must appear to her as a wild-eyed demon. Quickly he leaves and walks, with the vision that he still has to get back to the supermarket. This is easier than finding the apartment. He's getting used to the power of the drug, accepted that it's probably peaked, and convinces himself nobody's paying any attention to him, at least as long as he keeps moving.

Seeing a phonebooth, he decides to try to call in a report to the MPs, himself. With the numbers skittering all over the page, he takes five minutes to find the number in the phone book. He has to hold his thumb on it to keep it from wandering off. That's the easy part. He keeps losing track of what he's dialed. Afraid he'll lose his only dime, and truly not wanting to enter a store to ask for change, he stops after a few numbers, hangs up and tries again. Over and over. Frustrated, he does have enough presence of mind to write the numbers, in large figures, in the margins of the phone book and cross each one off as he dials it. It seems to ring so long, he's shocked when a voice actually answers. All he can iterate is, "Supermarket.

Crazy GI. Berkeley." Feeling drastically estranged from his own voice, he hangs up.

Relieved a bit and feeling safer in the booth, he holds the phone to his ear as if having a conversation. Finally, he takes a deep breath and the time to ride with the drug, to just relax and not worry that the whole universe is vibrating, pulsing and flowing. "Flow with it", is the hip term for the process, and just thinking it smoothes out his whole disposition. A warmth of well-being flushes up through his body as if he can feel his heart pulsing in every cell. For a moment, he even feels that he is doing exactly the right thing, that everything will turn out fine. But a city police car cruising by kicks him back into a paranoid state. After the patrol car is gone, he goes back over to his corner of the parking lot and pretends to read a found newspaper, but constantly scans the traffic.

Doing larger and larger loops around the neighborhood, Mayborough and Clives get a call on their radio. Mayborough listens on the handset and responds, "Roger, we've been looking for an hour...We haven't seen anyone acting crazy. Not fitting a GI profile, anyway. Over...Roger, we'll go back. Over." He hangs up the handset and turns to Clives, "Man, you believe this shit. Someone else just called."

"There's something serious weirdly about this one."

Back at the supermarket, they drive the aisles. They spot Landers, ever fidgeting away. Clives says, "Now this li'l dumpling here, *voila*, he'd look sublime in a straightjacket of any color."

Mayborough takes up the patter, "Sublime, you say, but dress him in gray? No way. Damn, this guy is kiting higher than Supercat. Don't skit him. Go slow-mo. I am not of the proper disposition for a marathon."

"Smile. You're on Cand-acid Camera," Clives says, easing out with a calm, vague smile on his face. Mayborough exits the other side. That Clives is so looming, round, pinkish and pale, and Mayborough so thin and dark with a slight lifetime embedded uptown avenue strut, strikes Landers as humorous. They haven't turned off the music, and are approaching him in step with the rhythm, so the drug's power morphs them into dancing 'toons. Landers cracks up laughing and can't stop. They look at each other, serious now. Landers slightly composes himself, to say, "Oh, g-g-great, there you are. I thought I was at the wrong bus stop. Next stop Ho Chi Minh Trail, right. Left. Right, left and halt."

The MPs look at each other and roll their eyes. Mayborough says, "Look, man, are you in the Army?"

"Yes, sir. The US American Army. Taken prisoner, articles of war, just name, rank, serial number...Landers, Landers, private first class, serial number seven, ah..."

"That's alright, we'll look it up ourselves," Clives says.

Mayborough takes command, "Alright, soldier, let's go for a tour."

Clives asides, "What we got, right here, is the, pre-genuine fruit-of-the-mudda-fadda-loom."

They move in, cautiously. Landers mains himself as relaxed as he can, holds his arms out, a bit. Clives is about to go for his cuffs, but Mayborough taps his arm, to forget them, sensing no confrontation. They each take Landers firmly by the elbows and put him in the back of the wagon. As Landers steps inside, they pull out his wallet, check his military ID and remove the piece of paper with his orders. Clives checks the ID and returns it and the wallet, while Mayborough scans the orders, "Hell, no wonder he's gone airborne, from the ground up," Mayborough remarks, after glimpsing at the orders. He's Eleven-Bravo, Central Highlands. I'd be there with him. Can't be a total screw-up; he's already made PFC, right out of AIT. Hell, I say we give him a parade." They get in and drive off.

Inside the wagon, the walls are quilted, stainless-steel, refracting every light change of every bump and turning the space into a 3-D kaleidoscope. The crosshatch patterns projecting through the security grill digitalizes this effect. The MPs aren't worried about propriety on this one, so they crank their music up again. All this comes across to Landers as a personal psychedelic extravaganza. With a hint of a goofy smile on his face, he applies boogie to the beat.

The MPs alternatively watch him, entertained though ever leery. Clives suggests, "This guy don't know a minute from a monument. I say we don't call in we found him. Let's see, my guess, is he'd be lookin' to take one last peek at a couple long-legged ones. I suggest that's where we search first."

Mayborough nods agreement, then continues the nod into a bob to the beat. They cruise around the Berkeley campus, checking out girls, but are always leery of being picked out as a target for the anti-war folk. Clives looks at the orders again and starts, "Ah, man, look'at we did. The dude's AWOL as of thirty minutes ago. He'd 'ave been in on time if we'd 'ave taken him straight there."

This registers to Landers and he reacts scared to the acronym, AWOL. Absent Without Official Leave. Though he had no clear plan, he knew this as one level of offense the Army can use to trigger a wide range of punishments. Anticipating this anxiety, Mayborough says, "It's okay, we'll fix you up for it." They head for the Oakland Viet Nam Departure Depot.

Fifteen minutes later, they pull up to a large warehouse, with rows of concrete brick barracks beside it. As they let him out, they put Landers in handcuffs. "Sorry, man, I hate these things," Mayborough said, "but it makes the situation more under our control. Which, all things considered, is where you want to be. And if there's anything pretending to be an intelligent thought there in your brain, suppress it. Right now, dumber is better." Inside the large human warehouse are some five hundred very bored and broody soldiers, mostly fidgeting, bitching or sleeping. At twenty different tables, lines wait to have their files processed. All turn to watch Landers be led in by the MPs.

Having more than an anonymous interest in this parade are three privates, sitting against the side wall. They are Smith and Johnson, black teenagers from up North, and Jones a white kid from Oregon. They had been with Landers at Ft. Polk, Louisiana, in a jungle warfare training unit dubbed "Tigerland", where everyone was next-stop Viet Nam. All were on the same schedule over, only to different infantry units. Unlike in previous wars, the Army did its best to separate troops who knew each other, except for the early units that were shipped over in mass. The three privately exchange concerned words.

The MPs lead Landers to the central processing table, where sits a grizzled staff sergeant, and standing behind him is Captain Pearson, the unit CO. Seemingly for his own entertainment, the sergeant bellows, "What in the good name of shit do we have us here?"

Mayborough hands over Landers' orders, says, "PFC Landers, reporting for RVN departure."

Overplaying his disgust, the sergeant reads, then says, "Yeah, look out VC, we're sending you a damn flower child. But meantime, Landers, it looks like you're a bit AWOL."

Mayborough says, "Actually that's because of us. We picked him up at a bus stop and he'd have made it in time. But he didn't have his wallet so we drove him around for an hour trying to find it. Which was an adventure unto itself."

"Spare the details. So, Landers, what the hell do you call that uniform?"

Clives answers, "Sergeant, he is either one dumb private soldier or he's tripped out on drugs."

"Looks like both, to me," the sergeant determines. "Alright, so he's not AWOL. We'll process him through, then you boys get him, for awhile. We don't want to look at him. Men check in here, not fucking fruits and cabbages."

The sergeant hands Landers' papers to a clerk, who goes off to find his file. The MPs have Landers sit on a bench, over near the door to the restroom, which happens to be close to Smith, Johnson and Jones. The MPs wander away a bit, to smoke. In looking around, Landers does make eye contact with his friends, which clicks on a familiarity of thought processes and behavior control. He flicks his eyes towards the MPs, indicating he'd best not communicate with them, at least not then.

A clerk comes to lead Landers over to where they are giving immunization shots. At the sight of the needle, Landers destabilizes and starts to walk away. The MPs close in.

Having been closely watching the situation, Captain Pearson steps in and says, "It's alright, we can give him his shots another time. Sit him back over against the wall and, you, walk his papers straight through." The clerk goes off and the MPs lead Landers to the bench, right where Smith and Jones are sitting. They slide apart, letting Landers sit between them. When the MPs go back to relight, Smith and Jones try to start up an out-of-the-corner-of-the-mouth dialogue. Smith says, "Landers, what you got coming down on you, here?"

Landers is silent, wanting to talk but not sure of how to express himself. Jones asks, "Hey, man, they fuck you up or what?"

"No," is all Landers gets out.

"You're in some world of deep shit, ain't you?" Smith asks.

"You could say that. Very pretty shit though," Landers says, starting to giggle. He can barely control it.

"Man, what the dude is, is chasin' the moon," Jones diagnoses.

"That would be the symptom, wouldn't it? Eh, man, got any more?"

This starts Landers into muffled, laughing convolutions, but clearly he's trying to stop. Noticing the commotion, the MPs walk over.

Mayborough says, "Hey, what's goin' on? What're you guys doin'?"

"Nothin' but nothin'. Just what we supposed be doin'," Jones says. "Your man here is flip floppin' out."

"Nah, he just wants to go to the head," Smith concocts. "Can't you see his bladder's bouncing round inside him."

"Clowns. Landers, you gotta go to the head?" Mayborough asked.

Landers nods, yes. Watching this, from a few benches away, Johnson stands and walks toward the restroom.

Mayborough tells Landers, "So go, man. This outta make the sharpshooters hall of fame."

Landers stands and starts to walk off. Clives questions, "Huh? You're letting him go alone?"

"Hell, he can't sneak out of there. If he can't piss on his own, I'm sure not holding his goddamn cock for him."

"Suppose he tries to commit suicide?" Clives asks.

Mayborough eyes Johnson, just about to go into the restroom, "Hey, private, this guy tries to kill himself, give a holler, hear?"

"Yeah, long as he keeps it to himself," Johnson says. "He gets amorous, I'm kicking his ass." He goes in and Landers, on bouncy legs, follows. The MPs, Jones and Smith just shake their heads.

Inside the head, Johnson waves Landers over to sit in the stall next to him. These stalls are only chest high. Johnson asks, "Man, what in all hell are you up to?"

Landers wants to try but only says, "It's ah, kind of hard to explain."

"So let us help you. You want us to bust you out of this shit?"

"No...isn't like that. Better you guys just stay out of it."

"You want to get out of Nam, don't you?"

"I want the whole U.S. to get out of Nam."

"Right on, brother. You know, I wouldn't have said that when we were down in Tigerland. But three weeks of leave let me see we had our asses brainwashed. This is Class A bullshit; a lot of fat-cats get rich on this scam-ass war and they don't care nothin' if us poor folk die in it."

Mayborough enters the head, looking angry, "What the hell's going on in here? Landers, finish up and get back out there."

Landers stands up, zips himself, which takes a few tries, and goes to wash his hands, but starts tripping in the mirror. Johnson tries to leave, directly.

"Go on, Landers, quit tripping in the mirror. Just go back out there. And you, soldier, stay right here."

"Me?"

"Who you think I'm talking to, dickhead?" Mayborough says but softens his tone considerably, when Landers has left. "Alright, bro, you gotta tell me something about this dude."

"I don't usually go to the john to make friends."

"You know him. I saw you three guys maneuvering to get close. You guys go through basic together? AIT?"

Defensive, Johnson tries to clear his way out, "I didn't do nothin', man. I'm goin' to Nam, ain't that enough to clear me of getting my ass harassed, least for the moment."

"I'm not harassing you. Look, forget this MP suit, go straight up with me."

"I don't know the dude."

"All's I gotta do is ask for your orders and match 'em up. Is he a full goof or should I do him right?"

"Why should I trust you?"

"I don't know. But, man, I'm straight from the streets of Bed-Sty. Just marking my time, 'til I'm back. Being a cop, military or any other way, ain't my natural mode. I might be able to help your man, if you want to help."

Johnson considers, a bit, "Okay. He's one of our main running partners. Totally upright dude."

"I thought he might be okay. He's up to something, besides being stone beyond belief. Is he cool?"

"In what way?"

"You know, man, can he be trusted?"

"He's far from a square, if that's what you mean," Johnson says, but then catches Mayborough's drift and laughs. "Wait, bro, I know what you're after. You're after his mo-fu'in' stash. T's what it is."

Mayborough also laughs, slightly, "Hey, I'm not going to rip him off. I don't meet nobody to buy nothing. Just want a little of the weed. I damn sure don't trust these other MPs, except for my man,

Clives, out there. Street dealers won't sell nothing but manure to anyone they think is military."

"Alright. Get him to sit by me and I'll tell him to work with you. But if you find something, you gotta make a reasonable effort to get some of it back to us. We're goin', goin', gone berserk, locked up this zoo. But don't be ripping him off, I'm serious. We will find your ass. We don't step lightly on loyalty."

"No sweat, bro, I be clean."

Johnson adds, "Most important, you gotta see what you can do to get him out of the whole Army. Without nothing too crazy on his record."

"That's not easy, these days. Specially with infantry. There is only one place that can change his status, without criminal proceedings. The S-2 psychiatric observation ward over at the Presidio. Which is not easy to get in. We'll see."

"Whatever you can do. Because he is down-to-the-soul...Bed-Sty, huh? Just up the river. Brownsville, myself."

They exchange the mode expression of acknowledgment of the times, slapping each other's hands, twice, which the blacks started but whites of hip persuasion have commandeered it at will. There was no consensus name: dap-splap, slap-off, touch or simply slap were all used along with unique jargon from every neighborhood in the country.

Outside, Landers is sitting against the wall again. Captain Pearson nods for Mayborough to confer with him. They've had numerous occasions to discuss odd transfer conditions, considering the thousands of men going through this depot every week. It's clear they respect each other. Captain Pearson asks, "What do you think about this one?"

Turning on his succinct diction voice, Mayborough says, "I don't know Captain. He is different. Those are his buddies from Tigerland, over there. They think he's basically an okay guy. Totally clean record, up to now. Whatever he's stoned on is way beyond my personal experience. I'm guessing some mega-dose LSD, but who knows anymore. And that's my main concern. What if the drug has barely even kicked in. I hear there's stuff out there that lasts three days, with a drastic depression likely to follow. I don't feel altogether right throwing him in with the normal drunks, up at my place. I'm not reading him as right out crazy, but I think S-2 should have a look at him, for at least their minimum week. Can't hurt and the war sure's hell isn't gonna end in that time."

"Alright, I'm with you. I don't understand anything any more. It's supposed to take a doctor to sign him over, but our only doctor is gone. I'll fix the transfer. But I don't want to hear any crap about him getting knocked around."

"Sir, you may hear that about some other MPs, but that is not now, never was, and never will be our style."

"I wasn't implying it was. Sorry," Captain Pearson says. "Carry on."

Johnson, Smith and Jones have settled in around Landers. Nobody else is paying any attention anymore.

Johnson says, "This MP says he's gonna get you transferred over to some place called S-2. Apparently they can reevaluate you there. That suit you, for now?"

Landers' mind is scanning scenarios faster than his logic can react. He starts to say something, a couple times, but doesn't fully form a sentence.

"You aren't grasping this, are you?" Johnson said. "Which tells me how stoned you really are, because you grasp the core fast as anyone. But hear this straight. The E-5 MP and I kind of talked about a deal. You don't like it, just keep playing dumb and don't bother. He does seem like just your average brother on the block. And he's dyin' for some pot. He mentioned maybe you could score some. And he says he'll try to sneak some back to us. You down on that?"

"Huh," Landers responds, "Sell to the man? I don't sell to anybody." This registered enough to comment on but not to deeply consider the concept.

"The goon on the moon could tell how decommissioned you are," Johnson says, "Which is logical; but these aren't logical times. Feel it out. It might improve how much effort they put into getting you into the right place, with the right twist. It's not goin' down clean, bail. Nobody'll be down on you either way."

"I'll see. It's so backward it might be right," Landers says, as if lack of reason is the only thing that seems to make sense.

Several clerks convene on Captain Pearson. He signs some papers and carries the file over to the MPs.

Jones says, "Man, looks like they already got you processed in. That right there is worth it. We've got three more days. Of all the depressing places the Army gots, this is the bonafide worst. Hope those MPs get us some weed."

"I'll see what I can do," Landers says, feeling compassion for his friends, and wanting to help them any way he can. "Now I'm feeling torn up that I'm not going with you. I still might end up there."

"It don't matter. Nothin' matters for nothin', no more. We're all split up soon as we get to the Nam anyway," Johnson says. "Just take care of your own self. That's all any of us can do, now. Just manage to stay alive. Just one year."

With Landers' files in hand, the MPs come over to get him.

Without even bringing up the subject of the pot, they put Landers in the van and cruise over towards Berkeley.

Mayborough finally brings up the subject, vaguely. "Your friends talk to you, back there?"

"Yeah. I'm thinking about it."

"No problem, I don't know if I'd do it," Mayborough says.

They do drive slowly through the Berkeley neighborhoods. Observing the scene out there, juxtaposed against what he'd just witnessed, makes Landers angry enough to not care what the results will be if it will maybe ease his friends moment. "Alright, I'll do it. But it's not like I can have you walk in with me."

This is agreed, so they cruise to an obscure place, down the alley from Katrina's house.

Clives seems the most dubious. "I gotta say, May-bro, you do play a few loony tunes, but this is the do-re-mi of inanity."

"I wouldn't let us walk into my friend's house either. He'll come back. Won't you man?"

"All I got left in the world is my word. Why would I give that up?"

They let him out, very cautious that noone is watching and start circling the neighborhood. Disoriented again, that he's on his own, Landers almost walks straight to Katrina's. His instincts tell him he better at least be evasive, and zig-zags through some buildings. He runs into Katrina, picking up her mail in the foyer. All she can feel is strain. "God, Michael, you are turning into a human boomerang. These good-byes are draining me."

"I don't know how if I can explain this too well. Some MPs are trying to help me."

"Please, I hope they're not outside."

"No, they're down the block. Can you get twenty dollars in weed together? Reasonably good stuff."

"I hardly know good from junk and you know I don't ever have any of my own. Is this LSD talking or is it plain, normal crazy?"

"Yes, but what isn't? Is Jeffrey around, or maybe your neighbors. It doesn't have to happen, but it seems like it's a fair trade."

"For what?"

"For them not being required to be nice guys. And maybe help my other friends. If you don't want to, I can easily understand."

"Glad you can. Because I can't believe you're asking. Okay, but just wait in the foyer. I'll see if any neighbors are home."

She takes his twenty dollars and disappears. In just a few minutes, she returns and hands him a bag. "So, now I'm a dope dealer. A moral a day, dies away." With her having said that, even though she holds out the bag, he doesn't know if to take it nor not. She stuffs it in his pocket, saying, "Just my little way of contributing to the insanity at hand. You should probably, go, huh. Mainly, because I can't stand any of this."

"Thanks," Landers says. "If it makes you feel better, a few lost souls may get a few minutes of relief." There's no more to be said than the sadness in their eyes already relates.

Landers walks to a safe pickup spot, just around an alley corner. After they drive safely away, Landers hands the bag through the grate. The MPs are impressed. Mayborough says, "Check it out, big-A buds and all. For only twenty bucks."

"I'm moving out here, for sure, when I get discharged. I couldn't buy this for five hundred back home. Here's your twenty."

"Hang onto it," Landers says. "On the technicality that I'm not selling to you."

"Makes sense. Thanks," Mayborough says. So let the good times roll one up."

"Right here?" Clives asks.

"Why anywhere? We are the Man, man."

With loose papers that were in the bag, Clives rolls up a sloppy but singular joint. They smoke it. Effectively wasted, they bop along, with the music blasting.

Their command radio crackles, "Four-Alpha, this is Hotel Quebec, over."

Clives reacts, "Ah, shit, man, you deal with it. I can't talk on the radio, stoned."

"No sweat, Maybro's the name, announcin's my game," he picks up the handset. "Hotel Quebec, this is Four-Alpha, over."

"Four-Alpha, where are you? Over?"

"On our way over to the Presidio. We're taking the prisoner to Sierra Two. Over."

"Sierra Two? Why? If he's just drugged up, bring him here. We'll lock him up, fine. Over."

"Wasn't our call. The Charlie Oscar in Oakland said we had to take him to S-2. Over."

"Which doctor signed it? Over."

"Wasn't one. But I'm not overriding the CO. This guy we got here's a mumbling tumbleweed. Over."

"Roger. Take him over. And don't take all day getting back. Out."

Setting down the handset, Mayborough is ever more pleased. "Yes, sir-ree, sir, be right on back. Only I envision nothing but traffic jams, way up ahead. Let's find a long one. We're in for some significant fun."

Clives rolls another joint and they smoke it, ever bopping along, with the van wide open to air out the smoke. At a traffic light, as a city police car pulls along side they roll up windows as quickly and inconspicuously as possibly. Mayborough gives them a casual but professional courtesy salute. The two policemen nod back. One cop starts sniffing. Mayborough picks this up, reacting instantly, he over-exaggerates sniffing, himself. He looks all around. There are two hippies across the street, on a bus bench. Mayborough nods toward them, knowingly. He says, "You civilians just don't even try anymore, do you? Let these hippies smoke pot right out on bus stop."

Not particularly affected, the passenger cop says, "Don't worry, we get to stuff our share. Watch." The driver pulls a dramatic U-turn, stops right by the hippies and both cops jump out.

Inside the MP van all three men laugh themselves into stitches, but Mayborough takes care to make a few quick evasive moves in case the police figure it out and get ambitious. Soon they cross the Bay Bridge, all three duly impressed by the beauty of the whole scene, as storm clouds move across Mount Tamalpais, highlighting the sunlit Golden Gate against their dark ominous surge.

For awhile, they drive around the north end of San Francisco. Around the corner from a convenience store, Mayborough pulls over and stops. Clives goes in and returns with three beers. They go up and sit at a hidden picnic table, in Golden Gate Park. The storm clouds move in quickly, so they get back in. Mayborough says, "Well, it was a fine picnic. On to the next stage. Man, I be so, so glad, to be so done with all this shit. Two more months. Hope, you find a way out, Landers. It's just not a good time to be a young American male, is it."

They drive into the Presidio Army Base, a picturesque fort of formal barracks and administrative buildings, tucked in among tall pine and cypress groves, adjoining the parkland beside the Golden Gate Bridge. Much of it was built long before the turn of the century. Clives comments, "This is the one place in the whole Army world that I'd come even if I wasn't in the Army."

Landers would reaffirm this but having smoked the pot, he's back again as stoned as ever, with his tongue feeling like it fills his entire mouth. This causes a brief panic but somehow the trust he has in these two strangers, with no innate grudges against society and content to merely pass their time amused, calms him back down.

They pull up to the main building of the Presidio's Letterman Hospital, a long, impressive structure in a Craftsman style, with manicured grounds. It could pass as a fine hotel. The condition of many of the soldiers in the vicinity might have distressed Landers further, had he been able to take in much more than his immediate situation. There are lots of amputees, guys in wheel chairs and on gurneys with all variations of bandages, and plenty of guys with no obvious problems other than general soporific diffidence. These come in all ages.

"Well, that's it, man, we gotta turn you over. It's not a done deal, getting you in. Let us do the talking."

Through a series of halls they march Landers. They give his files to an administrative nurse, who's more impressed by her small stage of power than in any other factor of her job. She skims the files and seems to want to stop them cold.

To preempt her, Mayborough says, "Just look at him. This guy don't belong in the Fruit Bowl, nobody does."

Disparagingly, she casts her best scowl, "We don't use that term in front of the patients. But then, protocol doesn't seem to be your strong suit."

A young doctor picks up on the tension and approaches, "What's happening here, nurse?"

"They say a CO over in Oakland sent this man over. I'm trying to tell them only a doctor can specifically send him to S-2."

The doctor looks over Landers, checking his eyes. "What's he on?"

To downplay his own awareness, Mayborough affects a more "undereducated" accent and mannerisms, "Well, I'm no type of expert on drugs, sir. They're inventing 'em faster than the manual writes 'em up. He's so stoned he can barely remember his name. I s'pose it's somethin' real, real strong, maybe even that LSD stuff. Or beyond."

Long since exasperated from the deluge of all types of characters in all types of traumatic circumstances, the doctor signs the papers, adding, "Alright, put him in S-2. Don't want to take chances. Who knows anything, anymore. Gentlemen, would you mind escorting him?"

Going back outside, they escort Landers towards a different complex of buildings, with a well-defined tighter security. The sobering air of the entire institution has Landers thinking more and wondering what is he actually getting into. He asks, "What is this S-2 place, anyway?"

"A psyche farm. The spec you out," Mayborough says, normal voice. "These days, they're overwhelmed, but they really do have a rep for trying to do the right thing. If you're genuinely wild and wacky, they can shrink-wrap you. I doubt that's your case, at least by our eyes. We do have an instinct for these things. Plus, your file and your buddies back there say a lot more than the last few hours. They could discharge you on the spot, as incompatible to all things military. Your problem is your record. It's too good. One thing, though, if they let you out without changing your status, play every trick you can to get sent back to Oakland. Or if over here, into a holding company called the Suicide Squad. Do not break any serious rules and get yourself thrown into the Presidio Stockade or even the MP holding station here. The one guy you absolutely do not want to meet is an MP named Macree."

"One dangerous, serious asshole, by the standards of every MP in the region. And a few others of them represent the congress of assholes all too well themselves."

"Don't lash out at anybody. Generally, just play dumb. It seems like you already know that."

"Yeah, man, the smartest fruit in the bowl is the potato. Nothing affects it. And it's all root, so you can't kill it."

"What 'ave you been smokin, Clives," Mayborough says, which starts them all laughing. But they quickly take stock to stop, in case anybody is watching.

Landers says, "I don't know why I deserved this help, but thanks."

"No thanks needed," Mayborough said. "Extreme times; you got to go to extreme measures. Society just stuffs you where you don't belong, sometimes. I know...only too well."

At the gate to the psychiatric wing of the hospital, the MPs perfunctorily hand Landers over to a stern, cautious hospital staff. They take him into a high-security area, with double-up gates. Scared, drained and suddenly the loneliest he's ever felt, Landers acts listless and mute. They lead him down a long hall, with locked doors along either side. They cross a yard where both the staff and inmates have a distinct cautiousness about their manner. Upstairs, they pass by a seemingly normal barracks though there are heavy grates outside the windows. A dozen or so men sit or lie on their bunks, with a few reading or playing cards.

In a shower area, they order Landers to strip down, take all his clothes and tell him to take a shower. He's given an outfit that looks like work pajamas. An intern appears with a tray on which are two paper cups with capsules in them. Landers won't take the cup of water nor touch either of the pills. They shrug and move on to the next degree, which is the two larger interns hold him, while the other prepares a needle. Landers almost panics but quickly surmises the capsules is still a viable alternative and takes them. They escort him into an administrative wing, where the doors also have heavy locks and reinforced windows. Ever since the MPs handed him over, Landers hasn't said one word. They let him into the last room and close the door. One waits outside.

Inside, the room could be a family doctor's office, a bit Spartan but not at all imposing. Along with a few diplomas on the wall are several photos of what could be family. Immediately Landers' psychedelicized eye locks on small paintings, purposely ranging from sentimental figurative through cubist, abstract and minimalist. His attention span on each is studied. Books all around, for a second, give him the safe feeling of Katrina's apartment. Behind a slightly cluttered desk, a small, serious man sits so still and silently Landers seems surprised when he actually focuses on him. Although stern, the man's thoughtful presence relaxes Landers and intuitively makes him feel slightly more secure.

With a slight, indiscernible accent the man introduces himself, "Hello, I'm Dr. Xylos. How are you?" He pauses to Landers' lack of reaction. "Please be seated."

Except for looking around furtively, Landers doesn't move.

With a slightly more commanding tone, Dr. Xylos repeats, "Sit. Please." Landers still doesn't move. "Son, I'm a psychiatrist, a doctor dedicated to helping people. All I want to do, right now, is find out why you're here. What is your name? And sit. I'd prefer not to have to ask again."

Landers does sit. He waits a bit. As if he's willing to outwait him indefinitely, Dr. Xylos waits, with hands clasped relaxed on his desk. In this setting with someone who appears thoughtful and intelligent, Landers turns off any intention of playing games, and finally says, "Landers. PFC Landers."

"Contrary to previous reports, he can talk," Dr. Xylos remarks and writes a bit. "If you don't mind, I'll call you Landers." Landers nods his head that this seems okay. "Now, Landers, would you tell me why you've come to visit us."

"I...I don't know."

Writing some more, Dr. Xylos continues, "Doesn't know. That's understandable and not even novel. Try this quiz. I'll read you five numbers, you tell them back to me, frontward and backward. Seven, three, six, four, two."

Not expecting to think in any way numerical, by the time Landers puts this question in place he fumbles with it, "Seven, three, ah, seven, three...four...could you say them again?"

"Never mind. Could you explain this saying to me, 'A bird in the hand is worth two in the bush.'"

This Landers takes up, trying to find some significant meaning but gets several twists on it intermingled, coming out with, "Because, because – no, that's not right – I disagree. Why would a bird want to be in a hand at all? It'd be better off in a bush, free."

Laughing slightly, Dr. Xylos writes, with comment, "The patient disagrees. That's a valid answer...for a bird. What type of drug did you take?"

"They didn't tell me. But I didn't want them to shoot me with that needle."

"Curious answers might get me to laugh; I like entertainment. But purposely misleading answers won't gain you sympathy in this office. Don't ever piss off a psychiatrist who's got you in a locked-down situation. In this case you needn't worry because I am absolutely not of a vindictive nature, but that's only by the luck of your draw. I do have your file here. That battery of tests they gave you, your first week after induction, was mostly written by psychologists. Not that psychology is an exact science, but it can predict certain personality traits, at varying degrees from better than fifty percent to nearly one hundred. You're smart, quite smart, and well-educated, so I'm going to at least pretend to have an intelligent conversation with you. If for nothing else, for my own amusement. Here's how I read these figures, in the order of importance I personally give them. Your morals are on the high end of what our society expects, particularly in your regard for others. You've probably been in a few disruptive incidences along the way, in and out of school. You've probably lied your way out, or at least tried to. You weight loyalty to family and friends quite higher than loyalty to institutions, public or private. You would probably lie to help a friend out of a scrape. Which tears both ways on an ethics fabric of when is loyalty more important than not lying. Maybe, another day, we'll discuss that, as I don't have any preconceptions even for my self. Though you like to appear casual and loose, you're quickly affected by everything you observe. You act out like you're content to just hang out, but you're actually self-disciplined and work oriented. You don't commit easily, but if you do you tend towards being a perfectionist, and you don't care how long it takes. You're social, like parties, but are comfortable spending a lot of time alone. Authority without logic offends you. You're stubborn, to the point of being willing to be in the unpopular minority or even get punished rather than let blatant injustice slip by. In sum, if you're clinically psychotic, it didn't show up on the tests at all. So, let's go on the assumption you're reasonably sane, unless full-blown schizophrenia set in, in the last six months. You are within the right age range for that to occur – particularly if you've been using modern street drugs – but I'm hoping that's not true and am inclined not to expect it. I'm not noticing the obvious physiological traits of amphetamines, opiates, psilocybin or mescaline. Still, excluding some total spontaneous brain combustion, it appears you're completely addled. Though I sense you've smoked marijuana in the last few hours…which doesn't make sense although I'm not going to research why…I think you're probably on LSD. If it's some other new designer drug, tell me, so we can both study it. Perhaps you're merely acting, which I always consider, especially these days. That of itself can be a symptom of psychosis. Still, I'm sticking with you're on LSD. Is that correct?"

"Yes."

"Progress. Is any of this hitting home?"

"I guess, since reading that file seems to have you knowing more about me than most people I know."

"On some levels. But having read this and said this, I don't consider that I know anything about your disposition or personality, as expressed in emotions. Emotions run the mind. Memories don't get registered or recalled unless there's an emotional catalyst in the reaction chain. Finding those catalysts, or their blockers, is my real job. And I can only get there by observing you, through my own senses. After having felt something, I can apply my training, but it's only a guideline to look for statistical predictions. You mentioned you think there's people who are possibly around you a lot who don't know much about you. That's undoubtedly true and it's partly by your choice. However, on the emotional level, not testable in the sit-down tests, you might be surprised that there are intuitive people…people who you might not even expect are even aware of you…who can feel right straight through to your values by your every reaction; or lack of reaction."

"Hm. I'll remind myself to look for that."

What the orderlies gave you was chloropromazine, which is somewhat of an antidote for the psychedelic effects of LSD. It should already be combining with the acid to give you a rather mellow high, without the fireworks and confusion. All that aside, I see here you have orders to go to Viet Nam. Do you want to go to Viet Nam?"

With all the bright flowing colors receding from his vision, Landers is beginning to see everything fuzzy. Dr. Xylos seems to be fading away. However, within this evaporation of visual clarity Landers' concentration is slightly returning. He feels the question is ludicrous, which starts him again feeling more angry than scared and

112

disoriented, "Doesn't everybody." He stops, pensively, not liking how that sounded. "Sorry. No, I don't want to go to Viet Nam."

"Are you trying to get out of going?"

Wanting sincerely to come up with an exact answer, he tries to articulate though his tongue feels bigger than his mouth, "Yes. But I'm not trying to say I shouldn't go and anybody else should. I don't like the Army. I want out. But I don't feel like I have the right to be out, not as a US citizen, even though I think the country is making a monstrous mistake. This circle of logic takes me nowhere at all. It makes me mad, it makes me confused, it makes me..." now a blast of emotion hits him that locks up his whole heart and psyche. He glares at a wall.

"It's enough to make you feel crazy, huh. Clinically, of course, that's a word I shouldn't use, even in irony. I suspect I'd feel caught in the same labrynth if I were in your situation. Anyways, I like your answer. I don't know if it's the drug, or you're just naturally honest. With me, that's going to help you. Do you trust me?"

"For some reason, yes."

"Good, because for some reason I can be trusted. I doubt you really belong here, Landers. But since you are here, we have to observe you for a week. If nothing else, get a good rest. It actually comes off your total military tour. There's nothing disciplinary going on. We'll be talking more, but mostly in group sessions. We're way understaffed, right now. Most people, if they want to, can learn things about themselves in this format. Any specific questions?"

"No, I guess, I'm getting pretty sleepy."

On that, Dr. Xylos calls for the orderlies, who lead Landers back up to the barracks area. One orderly, named Bobby, a tall, dumpling of a man, shows him his bed and explains the basic rules. They're less stringent than a normal barracks. Given no particular guidelines, Landers goes to the bathroom, which takes much longer than usual, while Bobby stands in the doorway. Very sleepy, but not wanting to shut down, Landers starts walking around, for another half hour. Bobby just watches. Finally, Landers works his way back to his bed. He's totally exhausted and has trouble talking, "Can I lay down...I kind of...Now. Sleepy now."

Bobby laughs, lightly, "You got a lot of will power, man. After what we gave you, it's amazing you didn't melt a half hour ago."

Falling off to sleep, Landers mumbles, "It ruined real good acid. Feels good though. Still see hallucina...Sort of." He drops out.

Nobody else in the room pays any particular attention, except one soldier in a far alcove. He's a wiry man, face and forearms as black as are ever see on the streets of America, with muscles and veins almost as defined as an anatomy diagram with the skin stripped away. His expression is so stern his age is indeterminate. He holds both hands up, as if observing all this through a telescope. For reasons he doesn't share – and nobody would understand or accept – he holds a crystalline rock "eye" as his implied eyepiece, through which he is intently inspecting Landers. As the interns walk away, Bobby, who sees everything in this place, looks to him and says, "Jameson, cool it. He's just another druggie. Keep your own eyes on your own self."

Jameson pays no heed and Bobby isn't in the mood to intercede further, so leaves. If he had watched he would have stepped in further. Jameson straightens up and stealth his way across the room, as if in some new-day awareness. Just a few feet away from Landers, he inspects him through his supposed looking glass. "They've found him. They've found you, man. Man, your life ain't never, ever gonna be what you thought was real again. And I don't mean here in the World. The Nam spirits got you, man. You're got." When he looks through his glass again, perhaps a droll lilt adjusts his abject seriousness. He bows, takes a few steps backward and stealths back to his alcove. And Landers dreams are about to illuminate.

8

Next time he saw Xein, Te asked a question he had been thinking about all month, "How can you know so much about our village? Why do you even come here at all?"

"How I know so much is there's a hiding place up near the top of the trail that I'll show you someday. And sometimes I watch from the woods. As for why I'm here, some day I will tell you about the two most important reasons, but it is more pressing that I teach you first about your present tribe situation, because you might soon have to make an instant decision and should understand the possible consequences. Now, I will explain why you have been taught that there are no other villages but your own. Eight days walk to the north is an area controlled by the large group of tribes known as the Katu. In one of their villages a group of two dozen men were banished from the greater tribe, partially for being extremely violent, but more so because some of them were an organized band of thieves. Stealing is very rare amongst all of the Myong people, extremely so in comparison with some of the other peoples I'll tell you about later. Even individual thieves are very rare amongst the Myong."

"There's never been a thief in our village. Although I know Aunt Rama and Mehra whisper that the Nie Drong have stolen Mehra's husband's land by decree. I'm not sure what they mean."

"It means they changed the rules. There's lots of ways of taking things that are not technically stealing but the result is the same. The

Nie Drong are specialists in these tricks, but we'll get into that later, also. Back to the Katu band of renegades. Before they had even found a place for a new village, they went looking for wives. Knowing how powerful the combined Katu were, they left their territory and went south, sneaking across the mountain ridges, crossing the lands of the Jeh, Duan, Sedang and Bahnar tribes. These are new names, I know, and you don't need to know them now. They kidnapped some women from the Jarai, but the Jarai sent a scout to catch up with them. They captured the scout, but he was smart and convinced them he was being followed by a hoard of warriors. He talked the renegades into negotiating for the hostages. The hostages were released and the renegades were paid off. With all this new wealth, the renegades tried to buy wives from the Ha Lang tribe. Nobody would deal with them, but Jom, who would become the chief of your tribe, and several other Nie Drong clan of your tribe crossed their path and sold them information about when your tribe would be coming to a trading fair. The reason they did this was Jom and his wife S'Yu and their circle of Nie Drong were still maneuvering for complete control of your village and they saw a chance for altering the power structure.

"Though your village had been trading again with neighbors for several generations, they were still known to all your neighbors as the New Tribe, and none of them felt any particular loyalty or connection, except for the families that had intermarried. On the clan level, only the Nie Drong cared, as control is ever their obsession. The earliest Nie Drong in your village, since they brought wealth and their underhanded ways with them, managed to get your Jolong clan and the Biu clan quickly into debt to them. Yet the Jolong were quickly becoming wealthier because their jewelry and fabric traded so well. They had bought all of their own out of debt to the Nie Drong. And the Biu clan were slowly becoming wealthier too because the Jolong compensated them very well, for their labor. Most of the Biu were bought out of slavery to the Nie Drong and many of them were also totally out of debt, too. This would seem fair, but not to the Nie Drong. Worst of all, for the Nie Drong, was that one of the Jolong and two of the Biu were about to have their fiftieth birthdays and there was no way they could be kept from becoming *Kra Polie*. At that time, your village *Kra Polie* council of elders was much more powerful than they are under Jom and S'Yu's current rule. Between those three about-to-become *Kra Polie* and the rest of the elders, they'd already claimed they were going to ban slavery altogether, and change the debt system.

"So S'Yu's and Jom's spies told Katu renegades where and when to hide, to surprise a selected advance party of villagers on the way to the trading fair. Before and on the way to the fair, the Nie Drong plotters purposely lagged behind, and selectively conspired to hold back all but the most independent and aggressive Biu & Jolong. However, all their teenagers ran ahead on their own, pretending not to hear their parents calling them back. The Katu renegades set upon the Biu and Jolong party, just as the teenagers caught up to them. Since the renegades all had crossbows and spears, while the Biu and Jolong had only their knives, the Katu tribesmen simply took all the teenage girls and youngest women, two dozen in all. Several of their husbands, brothers and boyfriends were foolishly brave and tried to fight or insulted the renegades. They were killed on the spot. All the rest of the Biu and Jolong men ran back to the village to get weapons to take chase. The Nie Drong pretended to go with them but they split off, supposedly to beat the renegades to the other side of the great bridge. Instead, they lagged behind, and when the Biu and Jolong men went across the bridge, in chase, the Nie Drong cut it, behind them. The Biu and Jolong continued chasing the renegades anyway but without the Nie Drong they were outnumbered. Most were killed or injured and the rest scattered." Xem paused, as Te looked almost overcome, but still realized he had to say, "Your father died bravely that day."

Both were without words, for a moment. Though shocked and hurt, Te braved up and asked, "And my mother, she was taken?"

"Yes, as was your sister. Your sister died later, giving birth, as did her baby. But your mother managed to escape, several years later, one night when the man who'd claimed her was drunk. She could have done this before because he was drunk almost every night, but right away he had impregnated her and she had waited until her children were strong enough to go with her, which was when they were one and three. You have a half brother and half sister. They are seven and nine now. She found her way to one of the small Katu villages, where she worked as a servant and even though it was difficult and she only had the privileges of the lowest free caste, she was treated honorably. But then these giant people came from far, far away, with horrible weapons – I'm not even going to try to describe who they are. For now, just call them the newest invaders – and took her whole tribe away to a strange place, a huge village of numerous tribes all forced together, in hooches with metal roofs. Some other day I'll try to explain it all, but it is much more complicated than you can imagine."

"What of the Jolong and Biu men who crossed the bridge but weren't killed?"

"Of most of their fates, I don't know. Some may have died later of wounds. There are two in the place where your mother is now, but they got there a different way. How they ended up with the new invaders, I'm not sure. For years, before that, they were forced to work for another peoples of the lowland, not Myong at all, who call themselves Vietnamese. And that'll be another long subject for another day, too.

"Some of the men who were scattered did try to get back directly. But being on the other side of the great river, without a bridge, during the monsoons, they had to walk weeks up into the mountains, through strange territories to even find a place to cross the river. Even if they could have returned in a day they would not have found the village. The Nie Drong knew that their betrayal would have been exposed if anyone returned. S'Yu and Jom overrode the *Kra Polie*, claiming total control under this time of siege, deciding to move the whole tribe again, to a place where they'd never be found. Everyone was so distraught, there was no resistance. For a month, they wandered, trying to pick such a hidden place. This here is where they settled. They thought they had found the Lost River Valley, but they were wrong. Still, it is one of the most beautiful valleys in these mountains, virtually inaccessible, with the raging rapids on two sides and the steep mountains there. Of course you know that. I'm sure you haven't been told that they built a tree bridge to get in here and then destroyed it, forbidding anyone to try to rebuild it. By S'Yu, Jom and the Nie Drong manipulations, they had almost all the positions on the *Kra Polie* council, so they decreed that there would be no contact with any other tribes, in any way, as surely the other tribes would figure out the betrayal themselves.

From that day, in your village, the penalty for even mentioning other people or the day all the women were abducted, was threatened to be death for the talker and banishment of their family. You were only one year old, and the oldest children were just three or four and had never actually been away from the village, so they had nothing left to remember. They were told that all the rest of the people in the world had caught a horrible type of leprosy, as had all their older brothers and sisters, and that most likely they were all dead or terribly disfigured. It was just an odd anomaly that there were already no children in your tribe between five and ten, at the time, as disease killed all the youngest children one year. S'Yu and Jom tried to convince the Biu and Jolong adults that this was the best for everyone, because then you children wouldn't think there were any other people, and wouldn't ever try to seek them out. Then they decreed it forbidden to even talk about."

"I can't believe nobody ever talked. When the Biu get drunk they tell everything."

"Maybe they have between themselves. They do have enough common sense to keep their secrets within their clan. You Jolong usually obey the law, and probably feel that not telling the children was protecting them, so why risk it."

He paused again, as Te was breathing heavy and becoming very agitated, "I hate the Nie Drong. I've always hated them, but now I hate them more."

"Don't hate. It only turns to poison in your *ae*. Leave payback to the gods, if they so choose. In the ninety reincarnations of the soul, all the evil that people do will be paid back, many times over. And that's just the beginning if they don't achieve overwhelmingly positive karma. If you always try to make moral and kind choices, you will always progress upward. Nobody's perfect but the stopping to think and making the moral choices does accumulate. Of course you're angry but you must learn to control it. You must try to not show any change or let anyone in on this knowledge, and I don't think I have to tell you why. Someday, in some way, having this knowledge will help you change the order of rule of your tribe. But for now, be patient. I feel your life is about to change. Someday I may have to ask you to help me in my great mission but it is not yet time. And I promise you I'll try to unite you with your mother again. Above all, be patient. The world is very, very complicated right now for the Myong. If the Nyang will it, it will be right again someday."

So Te left again. His mind and heart were reeling, considering all those other peoples, other tribes, other clans. Not to mention the place he thought humans had lived since creation was actually chosen to be isolated, and it was not the only time the tribe had migrated, even in recent tribal history. As evil as he'd already thought the Nie Drong were, these revelations were as awful as the worst tales of betrayal in their ancient Hamon lore. He barely got back to his gourds before Aunt Rama came down the trail. Since he would have had plenty of time to fill them, she scolded him that all his early morning trips were merely an excuse to come down here and avoid responsibility. She forbade him to ever go down there alone again.

This distressed him but before he even had time to mull over it, other events would soon totally change his attention. That very afternoon, Amba called the *Kra Polie* council to a meeting in the spirit house. Other than the normal ceremonies of the new moon, which occurred at dusk, this was not a usual festival or ritual day, so the word soon passed all around the village that something serious was coming. All manners of rumors arose, some even that Amba was dying. When the shadow of the spirit pole was as long as the pole was tall, the six *Kra Polie* came to the pole, touched it and prayed to have wisdom and make fair decisions, if that would be necessary. One had to be fifty years old to be a *Kra Polie*. There were more people over fifty in the village but they weren't accepted for various reasons. Te's great-aunt Meyhra was over sixty but, even though having great knowledge, she couldn't get along with anyone; plus she drifted in her concentration. There were several Biu over fifty, and it seemed they should have been represented. But one of them was seldom sure to be sober. One was always hopelessly in debt, partially because he was constantly taken of advantage of by the Nie Drong, but also partly his fault, for being forgetful such as leaving dikes half-built so his fields drained or letting animals wander off. There were three other Biu who should have been on the council but the Nie Drong found or invented some trifling reasons to exclude them.

Consequently, five of the six *Kra Polie* were Nie Drong. The only Jolong was named Tho, Mehra's second cousin. Once, they'd conspired to have him removed too, but Tho was so honorable they could find no reasonable way to disqualify him. Also, he was the smartest man in the village and could sing or cite many more stories of the ancient lore than anyone, except Amba. In almost every decision, he was confronted by Ham and Kdam, the senior Nie Drong members. The other three Nie Drong hardly ever spoke and simply went along with Ham and Kdam. Most often, even the opinions of Ham and Kdam were pre-ordained by Jom, the village chief. Just over forty, Jom wanted to be on the *Kra Polie*, and since he couldn't change the rules, he tried to have the *Kra Polie* banned entirely, but this was simply beyond precedent and Amba invoked that the Nyang would not hear of this. Actually Jom's wife, S'Yu, even then had much more influence than he did. But for her, he would never have become chief in the first place, as his reputation when he was young was more of a bully and lay-about. Yet he was the favorite of all the girls. It was rumored that S'Yu married him more to laud it over the other girls than actually loving Jom. Because most land and possessions were passed down through the women, she was by far the wealthiest person in the village, ever since her parents had died within a few weeks of each other. This was only the year before she married Jom. S'Yu was always pouty, petty and mean. Cross her once in your life and she would plot to get back a thousand times over, every chance she could. Even though Amba was her aunt, S'Yu even tried to get around her whenever she could, but Amba was much wiser and could anticipate S'Yu's machinations. Although Amba was not particularly wealthy any longer, she had started out with similar wealth as her younger sister, S'Yu's mother. Over the years, Amba had given away so much or loaned it to various people, that she hadn't much to show, in actual tradable possessions. Many people owed her, but she never put out any pressure to collect debts, some of which had lingered for thirty years or more. She never asked for offerings for her position, which was not at all uncommon with shamans in other villages.

When Amba came out onto the lanai of the spirit house, she wore a necklace and elaborate headdress that nobody had ever seen before. Last time worn was when she was picked to be the shaman, at age six, so nobody else in the village was even alive except Mehra, who was two. Asking permission from her patroness Nyang, La-Kon-Keh, she let down the stair pole and the *Kra Polie* entered the spirit house. After leading them in a prayer to all the Nyang, she announced that it was time to pick a new shaman. That previous night, the last of the moon cycle, she had dreamed of being visited by an ancient patriarch with white hair, which was the customary embodiment of Bok-Hoi-Doi, the Creator and governor of all the other gods and spirits, be they good or bad. As he walked across the river towards her, Ket-Droig, the Lord Frog joined him. When they reached the bank, Ket-Droig turned into two boys, though she couldn't see their faces. When Bok-Hoi-Doi walked back across the stream, one of the boys tried to follow him and was washed away in the current. Her interpretation was that the next shaman trainee would be a boy, but that there would be two nominees, with possibly some trial involving water. By ritual law, the choice must be made by the full moon. She said she would make particular note of her dreams, as should the *Kra Polie*, of any other notable reoccurring dreams of other villagers, and by the *roiq pong* half moon they should come up with the candidates.

At the meeting on the half moon, the two Nie Drong *Kra Polie*, Ham and Kdam, said they had had dreams. Since Han was assigned a demi-shaman role of calling the rites of life and death, he felt he should have more sway. On three different occasions, he said he had dreamt of Pim, the son of the chief Jom and S'Yu. Kdam had a lesser demi-shaman role of saying any prayers in the sacred house, other than those which Amba said. This he maintained would give his opinion the second most weight, and he described similar dreams of another Nie Drong boy, a second cousin to Pim. Although Tho of the Jolong said he had no related dreams, he said that on three occasions his wife had a very clear dream of Te emerging from a waterfall.

After a minute of bickering between the *Kra Polie*, Amba stopped them short. Although she had no distinct dreams herself, in her original dream the boys she saw were wearing symbols of two different clans, even though they were not of any of the current clans in the tribe. Still, she felt this meant that the boys had to be from different clans. Having much more to fear from the Jolong, politically, Kdam and Han argued that the other nominee should be a Biu boy. They had no convincing logic for this, but it didn't matter anyway because Amba saw through their whole campaign as being a plot by S'Yu so that her son Pim would be shaman. However, she was careful not to even hint of her suspicion, as even she did not want to be any higher up on S'Yu's target list. Since S'Yu had already made it clear that her older son Pim would be the next chief, for him also to be shaman would concentrate much too much power in one family. There was no specific law against it, but nobody had ever heard of such a thing. Besides this, Amba would have picked any of the Nie Drong boys over Pim, because he hadn't showed any signs of ever being able to do all the work it would take to memorize all the *Hamon* lore and the sacred rituals, let alone all the herbs and medicines that a shaman needed to know. Even though she would never try to affect the process if she did not feel she had a clear dream, Te would have been her choice, far and away. Though he wasn't fastidiously disciplined he wasn't lazy, and in her mind he was the most intelligent child in the village, by far.

Kdam dropped his nominee, so Han's choice, Pim, was decided to be the other candidate. On the full moon, Pim and Te were to sleep in the spirit house. They would be observed by Amba and the *Kra Polie* and woken, to tell their dreams. If neither of their dreams seemed to have enough relevance, they would try it again on *nhil nah*, the next new moon. If then there was no clear vision it could be interpreted that the Nyang weren't settled on their choice.

When told that Te would be one of the choices, S'Yu was furious, because she had planned to make sure the other Nie Drong boy would tell of a dream that would disqualify him. Although Jom suspected S'Yu was manipulating the whole process, he was actually glad that she couldn't do it this blatantly, as he was one of the most superstitious people in the whole village and thought nothing good could come from manipulating in the name of the Nyang. Nor did he want anyone else, even in the most secret inner society of their own clan, to ever be able to say he knew it happened. Though he was not particularly qualified to be chief when he was selected, nor had he the natural *dyut,* leadership charisma, having been in the position for five years he'd absorbed significant political savvy and could at least act the part. Though he strutted the role, S'Yu always got her way, and he had lost all faith that S'Yu ever said or did anything without it being a step in some plot or another. To compound his feelings, he doubted that his own son Pim could ever be a good shaman, though he would never mention this to his anyone. He had not one confidant with whom he might keep any counsel secret. Just to pretend he was concerned that the Nyang were not violated, he did initiate a pact with S'Yu that they would not try to coach Pim on his dreams. This he did knowing his wife would fully coach Pim, but by stating this opinion he felt he could assume no guilt for subverting the process. S'Yu called him a coward, but she did this so often he didn't attach any particular importance to it. To S'Yu, it was not so much that she believed her wealth and influence could buy her absolution, in that she intended to invent Pim's dream, but that once she decided to do anything she would cycle it through her obsessive mind so often she could convince even her own twisted conscience that she was justified.

In a conversation with Mehra, Aunt Rama expressed that she hoped Te would not be chosen. They would have to hire one of the

Biu boys to carry their water, and in fact they would not even have a married man in their own household, for several years ahead. When she paid attention, Mehra could still be wise, and convinced Rama that Te could help them considerably if he was shaman, without compromising his devotion to the Nyang. What was more important was that if Pim become shaman, there would be absolutely nothing to keep S'Yu from having total control of everything and everybody. Rama had to agree this was undoubtedly correct. As for Te, he wanted nothing to do with any of it, and was distressed he wouldn't have time to discuss it all with Xem.

9

For Landers, just the complexities of that day's turning points would have been emotionally draining enough, but add in the exhaustion of any LSD trip, particularly one ended by powerful suppressants, the totality has him in a deep, numb sleep. After many hours, he pulls into a long session of very realistic, run-together dreams with no segues between images. For a long time, he's trying to paddle out through surf, with that sensation known as "noodle arm", when the arms go around but have no more strength left to propel the board forward. Finally, a giant wave tears his board out of his arms. Then he's swimming, right in the impact zone, diving under wave after wave but making no progress in any direction. He hears someone calling, "We'll come get you." He sees Caves paddling his way, fully dressed in dry clothes. Then he is also on a board, astounded, looking down that his own clothes can be dry. Looking up, he's sitting in an empty classroom. Katrina is the teacher. Over and over she keeps asking him, "Michael, why you? Michael why you?" He never can form an answer but she keeps asking anyway. The sound of his mother's voice turns him around. He's in the hallway of his home. From another room, she keeps saying, "Michael, Michael, where are you?" He stirs in his bed, mumbles in his sleep, "Mom, Mom, I meant to say good-bye. Mom, where are you? I can't see." He consciously fights to get his eyes open, which he does just long enough to make his subconscious register he's in the Army. But he drifts back into dreams. He's locked in the large chain-linked area of the departure warehouse in Oakland, with Johnson, Smith, Jones, Mayborough and Clives circling around the outside, repeating, "You want us to get you out of here...out of here...out of here?" The chain link keeps growing until it and the guys outside fade into fog. Out of the fog steps the Elderly Man from the plane, walking around in circles, saying over and over, "Don't go easy. Don't go easy." Landers follows him, even up stairs into the plane. Inside the plane, it seems to be flying but there's no one else in it. Then the plane evaporates and he is falling. Though he can't see him, he hears the Elder Man keep repeating, "Don't go easy." Just before he would hit the ground, Landers fights off the falling and wakes up.

Though the barracks lights are out there's plenty of ambient light from outside and from bulbs in the restroom and the orderly office. Absolutely disoriented, Landers takes a long time to figure out where he is, to create some current order and even be sure he's totally awake. A very faint, jazzy blues tune being played on a harmonica that he can't shake out his mind gets him to concentrate enough to convince him that he's really awake. Looking around, almost all of the bunks seem to have someone sleeping in them. Very groggily, he gets up and works his way to the head, having to steady himself on bunk posts, as he goes. All the time the music gets louder. He's so unsteady he has to sit down to urinate. Now the music, though faint, seems all around him. He slowly bends over, but sees no feet in the other stalls. His curiosity won't let go, wondering if this is a total hallucination. In the last stall, he finds a skinny white guy sitting on the back of the toilet, with his feet on the seat. He's bent over playing the harmonica with his face buried in a pillow, another pillow over his head. Taking this all in for a bit, he is impressed how well he is playing, with unbound feeling. Only he's startled for a voice right behind him. "What the hell is going on here?" Landers spins to find himself only a few feet from a broad face, more Afro then he'll ever fully understand. There's nothing angry or sinister about him, but his overall demeanor says he absolutely should not be messed with.

The white guy comes out of his pillow sound studio, looks at the black guy and smiles, saying, "Say, Whistler, couldn't sleep, you know. Wolves start howling, you gotta play."

The black man, apparently named Whistler, says, "I could be diggin' that, bro. But it's three-thirty the fuckin' o'clock in the AM."

"So? Nobody hears me but you."

"Fine, but I'm only speakin' for me. So what if I'm the only dude tuned in to you. That's just the way it is. It isn't no other way." Then both of them look at Landers, for long enough to make Landers uncomfortable. "Except who's he supposed to be? I never even seen this cat before."

The white guy says, "They escorted him in today. Stoned on some mobster strength bella psychedellia."

"No shit. Got any more?" Whistler asks.

"No," Landers responds, not knowing if he should elaborate.

Whistler goes on, "Can't get nothin' in this place. Except for these jive-ass mood suppressants they load you down with for desert, after ever meal."

"They're better than nothing," the white guy says, then asks Landers, "So what are you doing in here, anyway?"

Landers answers, "I just came to take a leak. Then I heard the music and couldn't see anyone, so I thought it was going on in my head."

The white guy says, "Yeah, that's where it's all going on. In the head." This starts him and Whistler quietly laughing, and they exchange a soul slap. Landers has no idea what to make of this, but asks, "So where am I? What is this place, really"

Whistler says, "It's the real to the deal Fruit Bowl, man, they didn't tell you. S-2, gateway to the end of the mind."

"Fruit Bowl? "Landers repeats, "Yea, someone said that."

"Who sent you here? I'm Spandrow, by the way. My man here is Whistler."

"Landers is my name. It was just some MPs, from over in Oakland."

Spandrow says, "You're lucky. Oakland MPs are pretty cool. They're on a real base, with real soldiers. This Presidio is a fort for no reason, except to guard a stockade and a hospital, I guess. The MPs over here are a bunch of goddamn Nazis."

Whistler clarifies, "They're not all that bad. Just the guards who get around the asshole Macree. He's screwed up a lot of good dudes. He'll get his, in the final assassin-alysis. Were you locked up in Oakland?"

"Not really. Some MPs just picked me up in the street. In Berkeley. Walked me right through check-in and brought me over here. Amazingly cool dudes. Especially this black guy, name like a cigarette, it was..."

"Mayborough," Whistler said."

"Yeah, Mayborough. You know him?" Landers asks.

Smiling appreciatively, Whistler says, "Not really. I seen him once. The dude's a legend. Shows up when the right people really need him. Like some guardian angel of the underworld."

"The underworld?" Landers asks.

Spandrow says, rocking to some cool blues beat only he hears, "Yeah, you are in the underworld, man."

Whistler adds, "The Gulag Archipelago. It's worldwide international. With all the ones society said, 'you ain't nothin' but beyond gone. You've been caught in the deliberate act of thinking.'"

"Best dudes in the Army pass through here," Spandrow adds. "The musicians, the poets, the philosophers. The people who just care too much to walk straight into the lawn mower without asking why. Going ways the Army never meant them to go."

They hear an orderly walks in behind them. It's Bobby. He says, "Oh, it's you clowns. I should have known."

Whistler says, "We're partying, man, nobody said we gotta sleep, just 'cause the light's out."

"Gimme a break," Bobby says. "I don't need any more complaints on my shift. You know who they'll put here if I go?"

"Miss Universal Delight, that's who," Spandrow says. "So bang the drums slowly, man, us spooks'll be gone."

Bobby snickers, "Crazy mother fuckers. Get crazier every day. And I don't say that about the truly insane. Come on, back to bed, before you wake up all the bonafide loon-atics."

Spandrow makes a funny face at Bobby, goes, "Boo". They all laugh softly, a bit. They do go back to their bunks.

Next morning, the inmates are awakening. This resembles an average barracks except there are no bunkbeds, the soldiers range from eighteen to seemingly eighty, and all are wearing their heavy cotton ward garments. Spandrow comes over and shakes Landers' bed. Sifting through the cobwebs of his mind, Landers has to totally reorient himself, again. Spandrow says, "Come on, get up. Let's eat, before the potatoes turn to mush."

Groggily, Landers gets up and follows him. Behind a half dozen inmates, they get in line before leaving the room. Orderlies give everyone some sort of pill in little paper cups, and check off their names. Sensing it's useless to resist, Landers takes his. An orderly checks to see if he swallowed it.

Spandrow comments, "Alright, man, you're getting a purple and a blue. You be kiting high today. Hey, Drughawk, how 'bout shooting me up with a blue this morning. I need it. I feel a fit coming on."

The orderly addressed as Drughawk simply stares and says, "Spandrow, where the fuck do you come from? You only gotta know I wish I could put you on a permanent I.V. blue. So I'd never hear your voice again."

"I make their life a joy," Spandrow says as they move on to breakfast. The mess hall is in a building adjacent to the barracks. It too has grated windows. A few women enter from another door. Most people show no abnormal behavior. They all get their food on indented plastic trays, with flexible plastic spoons and forks. As they eat, Landers and Spandrow watch a group of six who are carefully led in by two orderlies. They escort them through the line and only let them pick up spoons. They're led to a separate alcove. The casualness of everyone else in the room leads Landers to believe that nobody except perhaps those protected six are considered serious psychopaths.

After breakfast, Spandrow shows Landers the arts and crafts room, well stocked with paints, papers and miscellaneous supplies. They stand and watch an artist in his late 20s intensely work on a canvas as large as he is. This soldier obviously has a lot of schooling or experience, or both. It's a vivid, finished composition, with sophisticated and inspired paint application. Spandrow comments, "Man, another one. You're really cranking these things out."

Without stopping, the artist comments, "Nobody's more amazed than me. My dealer wants to pay the Army to keep me in here. Outside, I never stay sober long enough to finish more than one a month."

"Maybe we'll get some critic to give you a bad review and you could throw an artistic tantrum. Or just paint some foam around your mouth. That always tweaks 'em. Maybe get you a couple more weeks."

"Yeah, maybe I will. I would really like to finish this series."

"You seen Whistler around?"

"No. He never eats breakfast, anyway."

As they walk on, Spandrow commentates, "Only three ways out of here. Their favorite, they rehabilitate you back into the Army. Our favorite, they turn you loose on the people, saying, 'This can't be no military man, you take him back.' Third way is nobody's favorite. They put you under loon-lock, over in that heavy security building. Sometimes for good."

They wander into the rec room, take up a game of ping-pong, slowly picking up the pace. Landers misses as easy slam, reacting a bit displeased with his effort.

"Don't sweat it, man," Spandrow says. "You're playing fine considering how stoned you are."

"Funny, I don't feel all that stoned."

"That's chlorpromazine for you. Does make you mellow but doesn't give much of a buzz. Too bad, huh. Why they give you that, anyway, you an acid-head?"

"Not as a habit. Yesterday – was that just yesterday – I got pretty out there."

"Good, almost half the guys in here are heads. I love it here. Some of the most aware people I ever met."

"How long have you been here?"

"Three weeks. That's about as long as anyone gets, just being checked out. Maybe I can stretch another week." Spandrow pauses, reading Landers' inquisitive look. "You want to know why I'm here? Well, started from when I was in Nam, ten months. In a line company, bad place, bad shit going down. Went to Hawaii for my R&R. Everybody said it's a mistake to do R&R anywhere resembling the States. Once I saw normal American's just walking around safe and free, and not caring nothing for my boys in Nam, I knew I couldn't go back; I couldn't see one more person blown into ant food. So I just swam out to sea, about five miles and was still going...Some outriggers found me."

Landers considers this, without comment. They start to play ping-pong again, but Spandrow spots Whistler, walking into the music room. They follow him and find him rapping with three other black guys. Whistler says, "Eh, it's Spandrow, my man, and the night crawler. You play an instrument, night crawler? What's your name again?"

"Landers. I can play a few chords on the piano. Or I can play rhythm.

One of the other black guys says, good-naturedly, "I'll believe that, when I hear it."

"Shush, give the dude a defining chance," one of the other guys says. "It's been done before."

Spandrow takes his harmonica from his pocket and fits it in a harmonica brace. Picking up a guitar, he begins tuning it. Playing a few riffs, it's clear that though a bit out of practice he's a superb guitarist. He announces, "Alright, let's try a couple verses of Whistler's Mother." He lays down the groove and defines the beat.

Whistler plays bass on just a few notes, hardly fancy, but with a solid beat. One of the other guys plays starts strumming out a basic but adequate rhythm guitar. Another plays a somewhat sloppy but very soulful saxophone. The other guy plays drums, unrefined with the pedals but keeps steady beat with the sticks. Landers picks up a few percussion devices and sits at the piano. After a verse or two, he taps out a rhythm on a Latin sound box, getting nods of approval. Keeping this up, with his other hand he picks out a few simple chords on the piano, gets more nods of approval. After about a dozen verses they have laid down a reasonably clean orchestration. Once he's satisfied with their background groove, Spandrow cuts loose on a five-minute solo. The others start adding in some intuitive harmonies and counter-rhythms. Soon, a dozen or so other inmates wander in to listen. An orderly walks in and, for a few minutes, listens too, then waves for attention.

Spandrow says, "Aw, man, why you always bust in just when we get into it?"

"Sorry," the orderly says, "We have to do Groups. Whistler, you're going on a field trip."

"Man, tell 'em I'm sick," Whistler says, keeping playing. "Let us play."

"If it was my call, I'd be playing with you. But it isn't. I'll give you five minutes, but don't hang me up."

The orderly leaves. All decide Whistler will sing a popular tune, "Sitting by the dock of the bay," currently top of the pop charts, recorded by Otis Redding. The lyrics, about sitting on a dock in San Francisco Bay, feeling very alone, coincides with all their dispositions. Messing up the last verse, they just let it fade away. Perhaps Whistler sang it too well, as they all seem depressed and walk off in their separate directions.

After trying to read a book, but not being able to concentrate very well, Landers browses through a few periodicals. He goes to lunch and eats alone. As the same six men from the other side are herded in again, he watches, trying not to be obvious. Feeling a powerful presence off to his rear, Landers notices that he's being watched, intently. He is. Briefly looking over his shoulder, he sees that same guy, Jameson, who Bobby had told to, "keep his own eyes on his own self." Although actually only about the same age as him, Landers thinks he's much older. Feeling a truly unique discomfort, Landers finishes quickly and leaves.

Wandering back to the barracks, he's beginning to feel ever more isolated. To dodge it all, he takes a nap. Soon, he drifts into an odd dream of moving through thick vegetation with shadow figures lurking just out of sight. Palpably sensing a powerful presence coming right up behind him, wakens him with a start. On the bed right next to him, the same black man from the mess hall sits, staring right at him. Landers gets the shivers, although he tries to appear unaffected. The man asks, "Yeah, don't I know you? Remember me? Jameson? From Fort Hood, huh? Only your name wasn't't Landers, then."

Landers says, "No, man, I don't think I ever saw you before. If I did, it wasn't Fort Hood. I've never been there."

"Yeah, I think you were. You're in CID, aren't you?"

"CID?"

"Yeah, you know. Criminal Investigation Division. Don't tell me you don't know what it is."

"Yeah, I know what it is. I suspect, about now, they might know who I am, too. But I'm damn sure not with them."

Jameson starts, as if dodging some invisible presence. "Man'd, you feel that?"

"Feel what?"

"How could you not feel it? It went right through you. I let the dream people out, last time I was asleep. Something woke me up so fast they didn't get a chance to get back in. They been cruising around, looking for someone to fall asleep, so they can get back in. They must've gone in you."

Landers tries not to credit this with any reaction. Jameson continues to stare. Landers does not want to start playing a game of running away, so pretends to fall asleep. An orderly comes by and says, "C'mon, Jameson, time for your Group. Anybody around here know a new guy named Landers?"

Landers is more than glad to acknowledge this distraction, but isn't particularly pleased that he and Jameson are led off to the same Group Therapy Room. Just outside the room, Whistler joins them. He and Jameson nod their heads slightly, in a distinctly Asian gesture. Clearly, they have an understanding and acceptance of each other more from just having returned from heavy combat assignments than from any social identity. Jameson seems nervous and goes in alone. By his facial expression, Whistler indicates to Landers that this guy's playing in his own sandbox and don't even try to share his toys. Landers nods that he's already picked this up. Three other guys walk in, followed by Landers and Whistler. Inside, Landers is slightly surprised that there's a middle-aged woman there. All sit when Dr. Xylos walks in and casually waves them down. He addresses them, "Good afternoon, everybody. We have a new member today. Private Michael Landers. Landers, why don't you just watch a bit. We'll ask you to tell us who you are, later."

The woman raises her hand and speaks, simultaneously, "Can we talk about me first, today?"

"Yes, Marge, we usually do," Dr. Xylos says, with a twitch of amusement. "Any particular subject."

She says, "I just want to know when I can be an out-patient again. If the Admiral ever finds out you've locked me in here..."

Dr. Xylos cuts her off, "Your husband knows you're here. Until you figure out why you're so hostile to everyone, he thinks you should be here too. I heard he'll visit tomorrow."

"So what? Who needs that cranky old grouch." At this, several people in the group snicker. After a flash of exasperation, Marge herself actually smiles, shyly.

Dr. Xylos says, "Well, I'm glad to see your sense of humor coming back. Jameson, do you feel Marge is hostile towards you?"

One of the male patients, named Jeffers, says, "Unfair question, Doctor. He thinks everyone's after him."

This starts the group snickering again, but Jameson turning sour stills them. Regardless of his idiosyncrasies, he projects a powerful confidence in his ability to take care of himself. He says, "I don't know who you all think you're fooling. And I know why you put his bed next to mine. He's CIA, isn't he? CID couldn't find out nothing."

Dr. Xylos comments, "I wished we knew what you think everyone wants to find out about you. So, Landers, are you CIA?"

Looking straight at Jameson, sincere and unmocking, Landers says, "I'm hardly CIA. No more than I was CID back in the barracks. And I've never seen or heard of you before I got here."

"Which you should believe, Jameson, but we've gone over this enough," Dr. Xylos says. "So, Landers, who are you?"

"Just an everyday guy, who got drafted when he didn't want to. And who got orders to Viet Nam where I don't think any American should go. And who got so high on acid, yesterday, I guess I lost touch with reality."

Jeffers, smiling, comments, "Yea-ah, another head. We've got a clear majority now. We'll have the whole country, soon. Doctor, why can't we run this place? We're in a democracy, aren't we?"

"In widely varying degrees," Dr. Xylos says. "Well, Whistler, you're quiet today. What's on your mind?"

"I'm getting tired of it here. I don't belong here in the first place."

"I tend to agree with you, but for some reason you did totally shut down, back at Fort Hood," Dr. Xylos says. "In all my years of doing this, I've never seen so many people who don't belong here. Yes, I understand that previous wars put a lot of people out of step with what they thought should be their normal lives. And those were wars that the vast majority of citizens couldn't fault. That's not the case anymore. However, while we're here, let's all look to tell each other exactly what we observe about each other, including me. Maybe each of us can get something that will help us all our lives. Unless there's someone here who thinks they don't have any problems at all. Is there anyone?"

"Well, I don't think that I really..." Marge starts to say, but pauses as all eyes turn towards her. "Well, maybe...It isn't ever easy, is it?"

So the session goes on. Other than Marge's egocentric take on everything and Jameson's paranoia, none of the others seem particularly odd, in any psychotic way. Jeffers and one of the other guys are in for getting too flipped out on acid, both on a military base. Another is clearly trying to make everyone think that he's crazy, to get out of the Army. He's not intelligent or sophisticated enough to keep track of his own stories. Nobody holds it against him, particularly, but little that he says is acceded any value. Whistler actually seems to Landers to be not only one of the most aware people he's ever met, but quite grounded emotionally. Exactly why he is there doesn't come up, and Landers doesn't feel it's his position to ask.

For the next few days, life falls into a loose routine. Other than meals and the daily Group Sessions, there's nothing scheduled for them to do. There's a few light details, to sweep the barracks, and the halls, but the orderlies clean the bathrooms and civilians do all the kitchen work. There are more music jam sessions, ping-pong, cards and board games, and even a picnic at benches in a grove of trees for a dozen of them, one day.

Landers tries to read as much as possible, but finds it difficult to concentrate long enough to get into any serious books. He doesn't know whether to attribute this to the daily drugs, or to the perpetual bombardment of thoughts and feelings about what is going on around him, and self concern over why he's doing any of this. Every day, at least one person tells some new story of the predicaments they've gotten into for being stuck between their conscience and their will. All of them have been severely hassled, on numerous occasions, for daring to wonder why the war is going on.

After a two-day barrage of non-letup rain, Landers lies in the barracks, with a numbing cloud of depression taking over everyone. Looking around, he sees nobody seems to have the energy or desire to do anything, not even go down to the recreation rooms. Even the orderlies feel it. The blues can really set in, in this place. A surf session would be Landers' normal savior from this circle trap, but even thinking of surfing makes him feel worse. When he expresses this at group session one day, Dr. Xylos has the presence to know something needs to happen, to shake the place out of its doldrums. He gets permission for the inmates to go swimming, a dozen at a time. Many don't accept, but at least the ones who do get back into a playful mood.

On the way to the indoor pool, Spandrow and Whistler are challenging each other to swimming races and snapping towels at each other. Only drawback on their mood is Jameson is part of the group, staring at them and anyone else they pass. Per usual, everyone tries to ignore him as best they can. As Jameson rants that there are no locks on the lockers, the others quickly change into swimming suits provided to them and head for the water. Headlong they all jump in, playing like kids.

When Whistler goes to the diving board, the orderlies seem concerned but he executes a flawless full-gainer, with classic form.

Inspired, and thinking he's pretty good diver himself, Landers tries to match him with a front one-and-a-half flip, only he opens to late and nearly belly flops. At the edge of the pool an orderly asks if he's okay. "Yeah," Landers responds, "the flop was nothing. But I can usually nail that dive."

"Because you guys seem to keep to forgetting that you're drugged, all the time."

"Yeah, I guess that's all it is," Landers said. Spandrow has organized a swimming race for a half dozen guys. Whistler and Landers are clearly much faster than the rest, with Whistler pulling away decidedly, at first. Not wanting to be beat in the water, Landers keeps pushing hard as he can but can't overtake Whistler until the middle of the third lap. They keep going, with Landers slightly gaining, but unable to run away with it. Spandrow keeps gamely in pursuit, though his technique is failing him. After a half dozen laps, they stop. Landers watches the other two finish, amazed that neither one of them have particularly good form, but seem like they could go on forever at that pace. Their competitiveness is from being in extraordinary physical condition.

As they dry off, all toned up from the vigorous exercise, Landers notes that Whistler, Spandrow and Jameson, even though lean, look stronger, pound per pound, than anyone he'd ever seen. More so than the best surfers he knew, more so than the scores of all-American athletes from a variety of sports around the gyms and playing fields at UCLA. He'd run into plenty of guys in the Army who were just plain stronger than him, a few that were better athletes, but perhaps none who had more stamina. These three all do. The whole process served for shaking off the doldrums. Guys are laughing and goofing around, until they get back in the locker room, where Jameson is on a rampage. He thinks someone was stolen something of his, though nobody is sure what. For procedure, the orderlies do line everyone up and search them, which doesn't take long, with these outfits. They do search the locker room and the pool area, with Jameson trying to supervise, while keeping a wary eye out that whatever he thinks is stolen isn't being shifted around behind him. Eventually, the orderlies herd everyone straight to lunch.

After lunch, Landers, Whistler and Spandrow play music for awhile, but the other musicians aren't there and they lose interest in this incomplete grouping. Spandrow does pick the guitar, sparkling as usual, but talks, "This Jameson dude, is unanimous nominee for must likely to graduate into perma-lock."

"Yeah, I'm not qualified to diagnose clinical paranoia," Landers adds, "but he's got seven out of seven symptoms."

"I'm no psychologist neither but I've run across plenty of people who get labeled paranoid, by those who know them best. Especially around any sort of drug scene. Except which I don't think is his problem. This guy is not vaguely like anybody I ever run upon. I think he thinks he's got demons."

"Demons, huh? He did pull a scene about dream figures touring around the barracks," Landers says, but stops short of saying that Jameson had mentioned them going into him. "When he's not flipping out, he's max aware of everything that happens."

"That's just an anyday Nam thing," Spandrow says. "Anybody survives a few months in the bush catches that trait. I don't think your day-by-day Nam-inanities did this to him. Call me an oversimplifying fool, but I think he's just a general-issue, brand-name, fuckin' lunatic."

"I'm kind of thinking his whole paranoia is an act to convince himself that he is paranoid of people, and not accept that he's possessed. Watch him, when no one's near him."

"I'll watch," Landers said, "but I don't know what I'm watching for. I never thought to look at anybody like they're possessed before. I'm not so sure I even believe in ghosts or demons. Not that I categorically disbelieve. But I haven't run into any. Don't want to."

"I do believe in them, and so does he and he thinks something is zoned in on him."

"Did he say anything to you about it?" Spandrow asks.

Looking inside, into another time of his life, Whistler relates, "No, I'm getting 'it' from a way my grandmother, who raised me, used to talk about her cousin, who was going after everyone, in the same way. That cousin lived in a house that was so haunted nobody but nobody but her would go in there after dark. One day she just got angry enough, told the spooks to at least quit messin' with her clothes. Once accepted she was destined to live with haunts, she became normal in every way. Jameson hasn't accepted his demons."

"Why do you say demons and not ghosts?" Landers asks.

"Say, not like I'm studied on this, but it seems to me a ghost is assigned to a place, not a person. I think he's dragging this thing with him."

"Yeah, well nothin' against him, but I don't need him or his demons playing in my band," Spandrow said. "And no insult implied to his ghosts or demons, neither. I figure what I don't believe can't hurt me."

"That's just my take, that's all. But don't unload all your ammo on it. As for my official opinion, so as to not get labeled freaky by the gatekeepers, here, I'm maintaining that he's just plain ol' home-cooked paranoid." He and Landers exchange an expression of understanding. They've built a strong sense of trust and appreciation for each other's awareness.

"You guys are nuts, you know. I'm so glad I got the guitar. At least it doesn't jabber in circles and contradict itself."

Soon, the orderlies lead Landers and Whistler off to their group session. It's the same main group as before, except two of the drug-abuser guys have been switched for two of the same cause. Dr. Xylos opens, "Well, another cycle is ending. Looks like we're going to lose four more of you."

"How about me?" Marge asks.

"We'll see. You are going to get to walk around the base, with your husband. Because you're listening to yourself tell yourself that you need to undo some locked-in cycles in your behavior. Does anybody have any general comments, not necessarily about things we've already talked about?"

Jeffers said, "Man, Whistler, that was one spectacular dive you did, at the pool."

"Thank you," Whistler says, with a soft, shy smile that they'd never seen before.

"Where did you learn to dive?" Dr. Xylos asks.

"In high school. I dove for the swim team."

"And where was that?" Jeffers asks.

"I don't want to talk about it."

"Why not?" Dr. Xylos asks.

"Because what I really wanted was to swim on the team, except they said blacks are sinkers. But they couldn't say I couldn't dive, because I just walked over to the board and showed them. Anyways, I said I don't want to talk about it. It got to be a pretty heavy prejudice thing. Not so much with my teammates, but on the road. Or maybe I was just seen as some sort of circus freak show. Either way, I get mad thinking about it, so I don't. I'm past it."

"Alright. Did anything else interesting happen at the pool?"

Landers asks, "I was curious, Jameson, did you find whatever was missing?"

Very sheepishly and totally uncharacteristic of him, Jameson answers, "Yeah," seeming to want out of the subject, quick.

Whistler, surprising everyone, picks up the dialogue line, "It was in your foot locker, huh? Is that where you'd left it?"

"Yeah."

Landers and Whistler exchange a glance that they're going to run with this. Landers says, "So, man, do you realize what you put everyone through. Not just that, you specifically accused us of a conspiracy."

Jameson stammers, head down, "Yeah, ah...well, I guess I was just wrong."

"That's right man," Whistler says, not antagonistically, "You were wrong. But what you're really wrong about, is everyone isn't out to get you."

Landers adds, "You're one of the sharpest guys here. You know that, too. What could anyone have done that the Army would assign a whole barracks to watch him? I heard you accuse your family even."

"What business is that of yours?" Jameson says, looking defensive and perhaps angry, which backs everyone down.

Everyone except Whistler, who says, "What he's saying is this; you're really paranoid. In the sense like everybody says paranoid is. How do you ever expect to get over it if you don't admit it? Or do you like it?"

Hanging his head further, Jameson says, "No. I hate it. Well, well, maybe I...I don't mean to be...just something..." he stops on the verge of tears. "I want help. What I really want is just to be left alone in my dreams. Visitors come to me in my dreams, only I seem like I'm only half asleep. I can't shake awake or nothin'. Mostly this old guy just watches me. I can't make out his face, but he's a Montagnard. It seems way too real. I'm scared. Will you guys pull watch over me?" In a very touching moment, he grabs for Whistler's wrist, then quickly pulls back.

Whistler puts his hand over Jameson's wrist, on the table. He nods his head, "Yeah, I'll take guard."

"Me too," Landers says. "Wake me if you want, and say exactly what you're seeing. Not that I like being scared, but it does make you pay attention. Far as this place, I've never felt safer in my life."

Dr. Xylos speaks, "Jameson has every right to be scared. Is it okay if I go on with this?" he asks. Jameson barely nods his head, that it will be okay. "He was the only survivor in one battle and one of two, in another. After the second one, he spent weeks lost in the jungle, until some engineers found him, in a delirium. Besides his infections from multiple shrapnel wounds, he had malaria. Part of his story has always been consistent, that some old Montagnard tribal doctor did tend to him at one point. Apparently, we're not sure on this story because Jameson isn't sure. But how could he be? It's a miracle he survived. Jameson, you are a survivor. You know that. A survivor's survior. You'll shake this off. By talking it out, every time. You feel that people are afraid of you. It's true, they are, because you show fear, so that's what they feel back at you. That doesn't mean they're against you. Everyone's on your side, at least here." He stops for a moment, the most emotionally moved that they'd ever observed him. "This is when I really like my job...When you people do it for me. This is the best group I've ever had."

After lights out in the barracks, only a few guys stay up any later. This is partly because they did rise right at dawn, partly because everyone was on some sort of mood suppressor drugs, and partly because virtually everyone just wants time to pass by, with sleep being the best hideout.

With a little shifting, Whistler and Landers end up in bunks beside Jameson. While Jameson is off in the latrine, Whistler says, "Can you believe I talked us into pulling guard? My boys back in Nam would be staring at me like I was indeed fading from reality. Ah, here he comes. Alright, Jameson, crash. We'll stay awake an hour or two then trade off."

"Maybe you don't really..." Jameson starts to say, but seems to be distracted by something only he can see. "Alright, but I'll pull guard too."

"I thought the idea was for you to get a good night's sleep," Whistler says.

"Heh, for whatever you think of me now, I pull my turn on guard," Jameson said. His exchange of expression with Whistler confirms, between them, that the trust of pulling guard is the most sacrosanct affair in a soldier's routine. "It's only when I'm asleep that it all goes wee-ird."

They don't even like the way he says weird, but the routine begins. After the second round, about three a.m., it's Jameson's turn again. He tells Landers, who's supposed to be next, "Just sleep straight through, I'm not tired. Sorry to put you through all this." Landers drifts off instantly into the most near-real dreams of his life. If he'd had his eyes open to watch Jameson, he'd not even have let himself go to sleep. Not that Jameson does anything sinister, he simply opens up his hand, revealing that same rock he'd been telescoping through, back on Landers' first day in here. In a near trance, he simply sits looking over Landers. The rock is lucent, liquid-green jade, with a translucent emerald naturally embedded in it, and a thin iris of deep-green jade outlining the emerald.

10

As the full moon is about to set, a streak of moonlight from the far window focuses directly on Landers, awakening him. Although he knows this time exactly where he is, he feels peaceful and content for being here and for what he'd just dreamt. Nothing specific happened, that he can remember, nor were their clear figures, but he felt like he'd traveled to other places in the clouds, as if he was flying and could sometimes see down at the world, places he'd never been but seemed so familiar. It was sometimes a verdant world, sometimes dark and shadowy, and all along he felt accompanied, though he never saw who was with him. Awake, turning his head, he sees Jameson still sitting there staring at him, with perhaps the faintest smile. That this doesn't bother him strikes Landers as odd unto itself, rather he feels that as loopy as Jameson appears, that he would protect him, very competently if need be. Jameson nods slightly and walks over to the window to stare at the moon as it sets. Landers watches it too, from his bed. He's not sure if he's ever watched a full moon set, but this one seems so large, close and – in an acceptance of circumstance he would never normally allow – with special implications for him. When he gets up, he feels he'd never been so rested.

That whole day is odd, like everyone is walking through their paces but disconnected to the scene at hand. Landers and Whistler are told informally by the orderlies that they'll be released the next day but there is no meeting or anything else scheduled, this day. That night, after lights out, the three don't feel like sleeping so move to the restroom, where their talking won't bother anyone. Whistler says, "I'm actually gonna miss Dr. Xylos. He's a right-down upright dude."

"If he's so special, why doesn't he do anything for you guys?" Spandrow says. "He just releases you as A-okay, all-American beef. Do either of you guys really think you fit the Army's program?"

"No, but speaking only for my case it's a matter of personal choice," Landers says. "I could go through the paces, if I it weren't for this insane war. In that irrational playing field, what could Xylos do for us to make it all right? He's a doctor; it's not his job to set the whole country straight. He just deals with individuals."

Spandrow mulls this awhile, "I'll just miss you guys, that's all. I want out too. I'm not going to commit suicide. I'm not so sure that's what I was trying to do in Hawaii. I just had all this screaming energy inside me that once I started swimming, I couldn't stop."

"So what's wrong with staying here? You for sure don't want to go back to Nam for four weeks. And if all you gotta do otherwise is kill your tour time at some base out in the backlands, this is a lot better set-up. Hell of a lot more interesting people, for the most part. I kind of wished I'd been more convincing, myself. Maybe I still could be; stay over a couple more weeks," Whistler says, looking like new drums are beating in his psyche.

Landers picks up his rhythm, "You thinking of doing something to convince them to let you stay?"

"I am," Spandrow says. "But it ain't that easy to out-psyche these guys. Whether we do fit or not, it wouldn't be like we're the first soldiers trying to convince the Army we don't. On the other hand, there is always new precedent to be set."

Whistler knows Spandrow is indeed capable of absolutely unique, creative bursts. He asks, "Spandrow, what would be this expression I see swarming over your raggedy-ass mind."

Exhibiting the pride of a master inventor, Spandrow produces an oddly bent piece of metal. They don't ask, letting him run his show. He opens the window and sticks his tool through the security grate. They watch as he loops it around one of the lag bolts, which lock down the brackets. After a few taps, the bolt starts unloosening.

Impressed by the technique but not necessarily the plan, Landers says, "So what, if you can break out of here. It's not exactly Alcatraz."

"Not just break out," Spandrow says. "Disappear, without a trace. Then pop back, in a couple days, claim we were never gone."

"Who's we?" Whistler says, dubiously. "Plus, being smart enough to pull it off isn't going to make them think you're any crazier."

"It takes raw genius to enter the ranks of the criminally insane."

Landers does a wry take, "Is this some new enlightened groove you think we ought to join you in?"

"I'm not trying to talk you into nothin'. But it'd be more fun to go together."

Whistler muses, "Let's just see if you can actually get it open."

Spandrow's tool slowly but reliably gets the bolt out most of the way. Then he produces two pencils, which he uses like chopsticks to grab the bolt and pull it in, through the grate. He puts his hand out for a slap of recognition and receives such from each of the other two. They hear footsteps. Having his pillows and harmonica with him, Spandrow quickly covers his head and starts playing his harmonica in his personalized sound studio.

Bobby, the orderly, appears. Shaking his head like a bemused kindergarten teacher, he says, "Wouldn't I know, it's you zombies again."

Whistler says, "Let it go, man. We're out tomorrow. We're just doing a good-bye party."

"It's still a full loon moon, man. You're gonna get all the real howlers cranked up. Aw, hell, who cares anymore? Go ahead, just keep it down to this level or below."

After he leaves, Spandrow goes back to work. It takes a while, but he removes the four necessary bolts. He pushes the grate out and grabs the drainpipe, up above them. To test its strength he slips all the way out, hangs from the drainpipe and even bounces a bit, then slips back in. He says, "Who's coming? I want to go last, so I can put the bolts back in."

Whistler says, "Why bother? Nah, I guess it's only appropriate. Don't want to damage any property. Hell with it, I'll go. I'm not ready to be normal yet."

They both look at Landers, not trying to guilt him towards their plan but clearly wanting him along for the ride. Landers shrugs, raps off a current military cliché, "Ah, alright. What could they do to me? Put me in the infantry and give me orders to Nam?"

In sync, the other two chime, "Precisely."

Whistler volunteers to go first, but gets leery as he looks down thirty feet at the concrete below. "You sure there's a ledge around the corner?"

"Yeah, I'm sure. I been casing this deal ever since I got here."

"Alright, move it out," Whistler says. Extraordinarily strong, particularly in relation to his body weight, Whistler grabs the drainpipe and gracefully overhands along, easily swinging around the corner, onto the ledge. He leans his head back and nods that there's nothing to it. Landers follows. Spandrow has the hardest part. Putting all four bolts in his mouth, he hangs alternatively by one arm and then the other, while he replaces the bolts, but only finger tight. By the time he works his way over to the ledge, his arms are shaking.

Meanwhile, Whistler has been scouting their next move, and is more than leery. "Man, we're sitting cool on this ledge. Yeah. Nobody'd ever find us. Or maybe next time they fix the roof they might find our skeletons; 'cause there's no way off."

Doing a silent imitation of his favorite movie stealth, Spandrow says nothing but walks over to the edge of the ledge. At its end, the building has a three-foot wide recess, about two feet deep, going all the way to the ground. Putting one foot across the gap, he slides his back against the other side, then holds himself suspended in place by pressure, in a classic mountaineering "chimney" climbing technique. By controlling the compression against his back, he simply horizontally walks himself down the recess.

Whistler whistles lightly, "Well, let's be check it out, man. You're the hi-town bonafide Spiderman." In minutes, all three have worked their way down. Playfully, like slinky cartoon characters, they slip from shadow to shadow, until they're in a brushy, wooded area near the fence. Hopping the fence, they move into the neighborhood. Trying to stay in alleys and side streets, they cross through San Francisco's Marina District, all the time wary of civilian police.

Yet, as careful as they have been, they've been followed the whole way, by a character much more wary than they.

While Landers and Whistler hide in an alley, Whistler walks into a Western Union office, convinces the clerk that he's an intern at a hospital (their clothes are similar) and, showing his military ID, talks the clerk into sending a wire asking for his uncle to wire back two hundred dollars. Although he's used to being very convincing, Whistler himself is amazed that, after a tense while later, he walks back to the other two with the money in hand. At a local second-hand store, Landers and Whistler buy decent corduroy slacks and cotton shirts. They purposely adapt a style that could cross a broader swath of society than just the hard-core anti-war and hippie factions, though not stand out against them. Spandrow goes for a hipper, musician look: worn jeans, paisley shirt, denim jacket, cowboy boots and old cavalry hat, to hide his short haircut. Both Landers and Whistler had been adept at slipping by military haircut standards, so wouldn't stand out in the general populace. Whistler ups his fashion level with a heavy leather belt and brown, Italian, buckled boots, in never-worn condition. Landers opts for ankle-height all purpose desert boots, completing an outfit that would fit within the dress code at any restaurant or club in San Francisco without a coat-and-tie standard.

"Let's get a long way away from here," Landers says.

"I want to see all these hippies I've been hearing about," Spandrow says. "Get some of that good ol', home-style, free lovin'."

"Fits within my mood. All we're doing is killing time."

Landers says, "So it's up the yellow brick road to the Grand Central of hippie-hood, Haight-Asbury."

"Why they call it hate-ass berry, if it's about lovin' a piece of ass?" Spandrow asks.

"Hate spelt H-a-i-g-h-t. It's a name," Whistler says. "Which I only happen to know because my main man in Nam was from there. The hippest dude you ever saw. Truly believed the peace and love thing, too...well..." he drifts off, looking sad, which clicks him emotionally into a play on the lyrics of his favorite song, "Why don't we slide by a 'dock of the bay', or two, on the way."

"And I say, why not," Landers said. "We're general issue public, as I see it.

Moving down to the Marina waterfront, they take in the extravagance of the perpetual kaleidoscope of the Bay. When moving together, they all emulate fun moods, but individually, when they stop and stare off, all become quickly broody and pensive. The beauty of the dancing waters kindles no romance, only the melancholy of their individual libidos. All feel the need to keep moving so cut inland, up the steep, winding, postcard-hall-of-fame

Lombard Street, up over Russian Hill. They slow to a crawl pace through the ever raunchy North Beach neighborhood, its reputation fixed over a century ago by rowdy sailors and gold seekers as well as those out to take their money and any other lingering buds of innocence from them. They stop into a neighborhood bar. Not knowing if they are being overly paranoid, still, they feel they were getting too many askance looks and move on after quickly downing beers. Walking into the second bar, they pool observations and figure out the over-attention they had received was because the last one was a gay bar. They check out photos outside a strip joint, of girls on show with tight orchestras and full balconies. None of the three seemed overly interested, at least not enough to pay a cover charge. Landers generally knows his way around San Francisco and leads them up Telegraph Hill, through Chinatown, and Pacific Heights. Then he gets lost and they wander all the way over to the Mission District, before he realizes they've gone too far. They work their way back up the ridge, north, until they run into the spacious and lush Golden Gate Park. By now it's late and, although not particularly sleepy, they realize the rest of the city is almost totally asleep, so they stop in the park, to rest. Recovering some cardboard, in an alley at the park's edge, they find bushes to lie under, naturally settling into a one-man-awake guard rotation.

Five local derelicts have been watching them, from when they had taken the cardboard from the alley. They have started stalking them and know the area much better. Making no noise, since they're walking on grass, they've circled the bushes where our three lay. Just as they seem about to pounce, a large rock clomps against one of their heads, thrown by the character who had been following our three, all along. A loud grunt alerts Spandrow, who is on guard. He would have spotted them in a few seconds anyway, but maybe too late. He shakes Whistler and Landers awake.

They come to with a start, with Whistler knowing the exact meaning of every type of wake-up shake, so is instantly crouched to fight. Landers simply wakes up confused, but picks up the character of his friends' positions. The derelicts decide to descend on them anyway, though having lost the element of surprise. Even in the dim light, they are visibly of dangerous disposition and dimension. One demands, "Just drop your money and run, or you're done for." Both Spandrow and Whistler are already on their feet. This is the first time Landers gets a glimpse of how confident and imposing these very recent combat soldiers can carry themselves. Even though one of the derelicts has a knife and another a stick, Whistler and Spandrow, with Landers right beside them, easily back the derelicts off, by nothing more than glares and walking straight at them, showing no more fear than if about to march through a field of daisies. After the derelicts take off, Spandrow and Whistler look at each other, with sighs of understanding of how much they hate to be reminded of what fear can be. They don't share this instance with Landers, either verbally or by body language. Spandrow does say, "What was weird though, was that one of them grunted, loud, while they were sneaking up."

"Probably hit his head on a branch," Whistler says.

"Wasn't that type of grunt," Spandrow saws. He looks askance, but soon shakes it off.

Dawn is glowing through a sparse fog. None of them feel sleepy, so they explore the park. Again, Landers sees another side of the other two. They intuitively move towards the thicker bushes, walking very lightly and continually scanning all around them. Yet they exude an air of exultation, of enjoying the beauty of the greenery, without the threat of what thick greenery so recently meant to them. Whistler seems ever more relaxed and enjoying it all but, after awhile, Spandrow starts looking very depressed and torn. His war ordeal is far from over. He quickens the pace, until they pop out of the brush, a mile west, on a bluff overlooking the infinite gray Pacific. Down below is San Francisco's Ocean Beach area; a residential beachtown, with no scene faintly resembling San Diego's Ocean Beach. While the other two take in the whole breadth of the panorama, Landers finds himself rapt, staring at the endless peaks of swarming, ten-foot waves pounding the shallows, agitating the sand bottom into rivulets and gullies about to become powerful riptides streaking foam lines back out to sea. The affect seems to calm Spandrow. Driven more than ever to get into the hippie world, he takes the lead, but circumvents the park, as if he doesn't want to go back into the world of green. He and Whistler seem to communicate their emotions, exactly, with no words at all. Landers just follows where they lead, other than generally pointing them towards Haight-Asbury.

Picking up pastry and coffee from a bakery, they sit on a wall where Haight Street meets the park. Architecturally, the street is mostly several stories high, mainly commercial, with almost no space between buildings. Some remnants of the Victorian era, homes, apartments and businesses, survive all the decades of building since then, though there are few post-war buildings. Mostly, it's a neighborhood on its low budget ebb, turning some sociological corner nobody's ever been around. Eating, they watch the golden age of hippie-hood unfold before them. Hair is almost universally much longer than the mode of the times, mostly left to hang free. High couture and hair permanents don't exist. Clothes are more towards eclectically composed costumes than adherence to any known mode. Many fabrics tend toward colorful patterns, many from the Indian sub-continent, mostly because they wiggle so well on LSD. Some stick with basic earth tones, baggy and monk-esque. Beads, ribbons and the ubiquitous flowers are displayed anywhere hair or clothes will hold them, on males and females. Scents of marijuana, incense and patchouli oil permeate the light breeze, amplified by the soft fog. The mean age is late-teens to mid-twenties, but much younger kids wander freely behind decidedly-stoned young mothers and a few older folk flow through the parade looking like re-invented beatniks. Sandals and boots and not much in between are basic footwear. Not only is the overall look airy if not fairylike, the mood is free and spontaneous, with unprecipitated smiles and frolic encouraged, and often mirrored. Expression of peace and love are not just an affectation, but a genuine belief system. Psychedelic art and decorative crafts are worn or hung in every available window opportunity. Elaborate posters on any spare wall advertise dance extravaganzas of the top rock music groups of the era. Even though it being morning, a distinct majority look and act high on some mind-altering substance, playing off the highness rather than restraining it. Nobody seems concerned that "the man" – any law enforcement agent – will infiltrate their world or descend upon them to remove anyone from it.

Meandering down the sidewalk, our three emulate the carefree mood and seem easily accepted in this circumstantial club without any order of membership other than wanting to be in it. On a struggling lawn, in front of a set-back Victorian building commandeered by a hippie commune, a half dozen groovers sit and listen to a guy barely able to keep a rhythm on a guitar, strumming mis-chords in all dimensions. Still, the drug wayfarers nod and tap to whatever concert of music wonders they must be hearing. After listening a bit, Spandrow manages to invite himself to play a bit.

Retuning the guitar back from the key of alphabet soup he starts into a set of psychedelic rock. Landers and Whistler exchange a glance of surprise, never having heard Spandrow play this style. Yet, he manages to make that old wooden guitar sound like everything from a sitar to a vibrato-amped Fender Stratocaster. The Pied Piper would slink off in jealousy. In five minutes there's a group of a few dozen groupies, mostly delicate, panting-to-be-deflowered damsels closing near, to hear and touch him if they can.

A half-hour later, the princess of the Haight herself, irradiant in all the beauty nature can compose, the ebullient, perfectly-named Sunkitty has hooked her love beads around his neck and leads him, straight-away, into the commune. This is an easy parade for Landers and Whistler to tag on to. Aside, Whistler says, "If you can't be a guitar player, next best thing is hang out with one."

They're led around the once-grand mansion that considerable surface patch work and a coat of paint could return to glory. All react to the thick air, sniffing a condensed blend of all the social scents of hippie life combined with seventy-five years of wood and cloth mold. It's decorated as a mish-mash Kasbah of hung fabrics. Floor, ceilings and walls are draped with Persian rugs, Navajo blankets, random elaborate-patterned cloths from India, batik prints from Indonesia, as well as any fabric with paisleys or any other pattern that would vibrate organically on a psychedelic excursion. The tall rooms, all with patterned wood floors and elaborate corner molding, are broken up by the hangings into a labyrinth of tunnels, with lairs off in any skeltered direction, usually with a mattress and an arrangement of someone's clothes, in the order they fell. Whatever sparse furniture existent is set up in small party cloisters. Most of the art on walls is dance posters from the Fillmore and Avalon Ballrooms, the reigning dance and concert venues of America, that year. Highly stylized lettering is virtually illegible as it flows around their fields, colors picked to trigger overlaps in the cones and rods of the eyes of the perceiver. There aren't many people around, except a few lumps that seem to be bodies passed out in available soft spots. Two couples sit by a scratchy stereo, passing a joint back and forth, with a large plastic bag over all their heads. In the kitchen – oft eaten in but seldom cleaned – they watch three teenagers pull food samplings from bags and dump them altogether in a large mixing bowl, adding beer and milk as folding ingredients. Everyone who sees them gives Sunkitty a grand smile, if not a hug and lingering kiss.

Our three get the revered guests appraisals, just for being with her. Stepping up a staircase with eloquently carved banister and complex molding, they do a tour of a half dozen bedrooms, decorated by the same lost tribe as the main floor. Opening a skinny door leads to a steep, twisting, staircase, up to a tower, with beaux-art, beveled windows all around. The light refracting from all these bevels, combined with a dozen, suspended, twirling crystals transforms the chamber into a daytime dazzle of fluxing rainbows and star flashes.

Another phantasmagoria of cloth covers the wall-to-wall mattresses with half dozen people sitting on them, four girls and two guys, all of them pure form hippies. Other than a big stereo, with bigger sound, the only object in the room is an elaborate towering pipe ensemble. Presumably some deviant scientist has assembled it from the surplus of several chemical labs, with pipettes and gyred drip tubes interconnected with functionally shaped Pyrex beakers, culminating in a half-dozen mouthpieces at the end of long, snaking tubes. A self-proclaimed drug-guru, with pretentious air and name, Captain Khayam, appears to be holding court. He uses their entrance to affect a bit of an introductory ritual; somewhat pompous but more for mocking the establishment than flaunted for effect.

Captain Khayam asks, addressing the chandelier suspended in a clerestory, "And who be these three newcomers from the netherlands?"

"Navigators from the way, far outback, seeking the love of the Haight," Sunkitty purrs, as if her words were floating away in comic strip bubbles. As if in on the joke, the others follow her eye movements and giggle a bit. Our three can't help but laugh with them but tone it down, to not seem disparaging.

"That's the easy part," Captain Khayam deduces. "But for love and peace one must first consume the passport. Smoke? The blend of the day."

Having enough street sense to not walk into unexpected nightmares, Whistler tests, "Ah, sure, only would it be impolite to ask what the blend of the day would be?"

"Pure organic ganja, man. Chemicals are to be ingested, not burned," Captain Khayam decrees and all the communal heads nodding in unison seem to agree to this proclamation. "A zodiacally aligned potpourri, *fleur*-de-weed of the Pacific seas, if you please. Thai, that's why, Peruvian gr-roovian, and the ultimate gift of her royal Juana, Maui Zambowee." He ceremoniously takes the lid off an urn, unleashing an aroma so redolent it perfumes the room. He packs three separate pipe bowls connected in the same vacuum system with generous wads of pot, and invites everyone to toke up, simultaneously. With a candle, he lights each of the bowls and they all take a couple hits, accompanied by a chorus of coughs and extended, "Wow's".

For a minute, everyone silently elevates to the next zone. Landers catches himself being so mesmerized by the kaleidoscope of refracted light swirls that he perceives himself as inside a whirlpool light cloud, with the squared walls and corners disappearing altogether. His intellectual sense starts thinking of electron-cloud models from some physics class. Sunkitty's movement shakes him back into the moment. She produces a bag of what looks like jelly beans, only it's a multi-hued array of capsules. She invites, "We all dropped acid. Want some?"

Our three look back and forth at each other. A tinge of caution clicks on, in Landers. All these people look friendly enough, but do they even have any idea of what they're really high on. And then, there's his companions. In so many ways they seem as aware, strong and protective as anyone he's ever met. Yet, considering where he met them, in his survival mind he can't really be sure. He ducks the issue, "Ah, you know, sounds cool...but, ah, maybe not today...'cause, well, actually, I dropped just a couple days ago. Hate to waste good acid if it doesn't have much affect."

"It affects. We drop every day. It's easy," Sunkitty pronounces so easily it's hard to fault the results. She is so dazzlingly beautiful and happy in that moment. She gets up and starts dancing, as do the other girls.

Whistler looks tempted, but is quite more out of his element than any of them. "You know, I've never done it. I'm gonna, one day. But this is all so new to me, I'd rather wait; 'til I'm somewhere more familiar."

"That's the wise prescription, for the first trip," the other guy says. Up until then he hadn't said a thing and seemed as stoned as anyone, but his words are clear and honest, as is his soft, yet steady gaze. His brown, straight hair is so long he must have been in this environment for many years – where else could he have existed three years before, looking vaguely like that – yet somehow he seems the least phased by it all. This gives Landers a bit more confidence.

Spandrow, on his own track as usual, proclaims, "What the hell, I'll do it."

Whistler and Landers make eye-contact, questioning the wisdom of this move. Landers says, "Like was just said, first time, familiar surroundings and all isn't a bad idea. Or at least in a place with a private garden. This stuff can be very disorienting. Way stronger than the strongest pot you ever imagined, which in my case is what we just smoked."

"Me too, I am so grooved, man. I want to go higher, higher, higher," Spandrow says, ever more trapped by Sunkitty in her nubile dance of seduction.

"So let the man drop," Captain Khayam decrees, reaching into the bag of pills. "I conceive to believe to let the violet be his cosmic ray, today."

"No, man, if he's really gonna do it, just give him one of the small greens. If he can handle it, maybe take another in an hour," the other guy advises. Captain Khayam twitches for a second, like his air of charisma is tweaked, but the other guy is clearly the strongest personality of the group. The Captain holds up a green capsule, like it's a Holy Communion wafer.

In her form, Sunkitty kneels before him and he places it on her tongue. She spins around and sticks it into Spandrow's mouth, but doesn't retract her tongue, once he has it. She stands up, still kissing him and enticing him into her dance. Once he's entwined in her every twist – and she has some fancy ones – she starts shedding her clothes. With the other girls' help, his start wandering too. Once she's all naked, the other girls start covering her in body oil, which she proceeds to rub all over Spandrow, without the use of her hands.

"Ahh, yeah," Whistler, enticed, says aside to Landers. "Just like your average afternoon tea, back on the block."

Picking up his tone, "Yeah, high school date night. It's how it is."

Two of the other girls go for Captain Khayam. He seems to be going along but appears oddly unaffected. Basically, he's just a cold, shallow person.

On a primal level, Landers and Whistler are awestruck, but trying to play cool. For a minute, they aren't sure what move to make, but are hoping at least one of the spare girls might turn some attention their way. Yet, the other girls, quite comely themselves, seem dedicated to being Sunkitty's assistants. It's some elaborate ritual they've worked out or are making up on the spot. This leaves Landers and Whistler in an awkward, new-to-them situation. All the wonders their fantasies could ever conjure project them into Spandrow's position, but they aren't comfortable watching and, although they've never had any reason to discuss it, both are too self-conscious for a full-fledged orgy, anyway. Apparently the guy who had been the voice of at least some reason is on their tract. He stands and starts to leave. Torn, Landers and Whistler follow. They can't even bear to look back, to not have any more of this vision perma-burnt into their memory; that it might have been them.

At the bottom of the stairs, the other guy shrugs, smiling, "Just not my scene. Don't ask me why, man; sometimes I wonder if I didn't go wrong somewhere in my upbringing. There is probably pleasure to be had." They all laugh. The guy wanders off.

Whistler says, "Man, I am so high, I don't want to do nothing but lie down. And if I do that I'm gonna fall asleep, for sure. You feel like just staying near, for awhile, make sure Spandrow don't wander off?"

"No problem. I'm not sleepy, and it's not like this is suffering. Sleep as long as you want," Landers says. Whistler looks around for a comfortable place to lie, there on the second story. Everywhere looks comfortable, so he finally crawls under a parachute tent, waving with his hand under the edge as he disappears. Landers picks another tented area nearby. For awhile, he sits and relaxes, enjoying the whole scene. Only his mind kicks in and he starts to scramble to make any sense of why he's here. He feels like he's on an Odyssey from nowhere to nowhere, with every turn taking him farther from a life that he has any control over. It takes a constant rotation of rationalizations based around a vague mantra of, "just flow with it, stay in the moment," to keep him from getting truly vexed. Each cycle of heaviness seems to be coming on quicker and more oppressive.

He doesn't really feel like he's close to panic but definitely accepts a breath of relief, when Sunkitty's two assistants descend the stairs, smile, and virtually float to his side. One takes out a notepad and writes, "We're sworn sisters of silence, this morning. Can I visit your friend?"

"Sure. He might be sleeping, but I don't think he'll mind. He's in there," Landers says, pointing to the parachute. The girl low-crawls under the edge. The other girl writes on the pad, "Can I rub oil on you? But we both have to be silent." Landers doesn't run this around his psyche very long, putting his hands out, like to say, I can't imagine any reason to decline, here. She undoes the ties on her almost see-through blouse, with nothing underneath. He starts to undo his shirt, but she stops his hands with kisses and unbuttons it for him. She indicates for him to just sit on his haunches and writes only the words, "Kama Sutra," on the pad. She reaches behind her and pulls a curtain aside, for privacy, which he appreciates. He tries to say, by sign language, that he needs to be able to see the staircase, that Spandrow won't get by. She seems to read his improvised sign-language, perfectly, giggles and says softly in his ear, "He won't be going anywhere, for quite some time. Neither will you. Shhh." She kneels, facing him and very slowly rubs her whole body with oil, lingering the longest on the places that turn pinker the most. Slowly, clearly expecting to spend as long as she wants, she enjoys her entire version of the Kama Sutra on him. He never remembers having seen a more continuously happy girl.

After what seems hours, she gets a wet and a dry towel, and bathes him all over. Slower and sexier than she took them off, she puts her clothes back on, blows him a kiss, backs away and disappears, slowly, behind the veil, her lithe bare leg the last to leave. There's not a single DNA molecule in his body that hasn't been unwound, tuned up and rewound. He had a vague idea of what the Kama Sutra is, but makes a mental note to check out the book. He finds it hard to stay awake. Putting his clothes on, he has to stand and pace a bit, to keep from falling asleep. In a few minutes, he's relieved that Whistler crawls out from under his parachute tent, buttoning his shirt and looking beguiled and bewildered. He says, "Bro, that is some pot. You would not believe the dream I had." He sniffs his arm, "Man, why do I smell like scented oil? And what's this?" He pulls a cloth blindfold out of his pocket.

Landers laughs, says, "Yeah, real good pot. I'll bet that was some dream. I had mine awake. I'm thinking I'm glad we snuck out on our curious Mister Spandrow." They share the slowest, most complete soul slap ever performed. Landers yawns, in utter relaxation.

"Go ahead, nod out awhile," Whistler says, totally at peace in the moment. "Got you covered. Got the whole world covered."

After a few hours of deep sleep – and a short dream of sitting on a very small cloud that he can't get off without falling, all the while being gently scolded by fully-winged angels looking suspiciously like Sunkitty and whoever that other Haight-angel was – Landers wakes up, only because someone has cranked a stereo to max amplitude. It takes him awhile to sort out what's real and what he was dreaming. Wandering around the house for a while, looking for his friends but purposely leaving the tower room for last, he runs into the guy with the very long hair, looking concerned, as a rather dirty couple of hippies are romping around what was originally the living room. Landers intuits his concern, "Everything alright?"

"More or less. No, less. This whole commune thing is running its course. I think I'm going to close this place down."

"Whose house is it?" Landers asks.

"Mine. Come on up to the real side of the house and have a beer," he invites. He leads off and Landers follows. They go up another staircase to the master suite, on the top floor and with a locked door. With pride, he waves for Landers to feel free to look around. It's some suite, with a large bedroom, an attached den, and a spacious bathroom, tiled from floor to ceiling and the biggest tub with legs ever seen, complete with faucets overhanging both ends and a panoramic view through multi-beveled windows. The guy walks into the den, where he has a small kitchen set up. He pulls out a couple of beers, hands Landers one and taps bottles in a toast. "What do you think of it?"

"Stunning. This is San Francisco I always imagined." Everything in the room is quality, selected over a century by loving and discerning eyes. Although the fabric is somewhat worn, the couches and chairs are collectors pieces from the Victorian, Art Nouveau and Art Deco eras, artfully arranged. The art is of value, eclectic and tastefully matched to the decor. Everything is tidy and very clean, all the wood and metal are freshly polished. Even the windows are squeaky clean and provide views of the city in all directions. "This is all yours, huh?"

"Well, sort of. You guys are soldiers, huh? Recent vets, I'm guessing."

"We're trying not to look it, but yes. Although I'm not a vet. What tipped you off?"

"Familiarity. My brother just got back a year ago. We inherited this place together, from our grandparents. Our parents died years ago. Only he joined the Army and was gone for four years. Green Beret. Gung-ho, jerk. In his last letters he seemed to be coming around. I just stayed here, maintaining it all 'til he got back, keeping tabs on our inheritance. Only he came back from Nam tweaked beyond the zone of anything I'd ever dealt with. He couldn't fit anywhere; just wandered off. I haven't heard from him in years. I took in a few borders, to meet expenses. I hadn't cut my hair since high school and for some reason I liked my grandfather's old clothes. Little did I know I was a hippie before its time; not until this invasion just swamped the neighborhood."

"It is quite a scene. Beyond what I'd expected, and I'd heard a lot of reports. You seemed a little less than impressed."

"I can't totally bitch. It was an interesting run, while it was developing, but the whole rest of the world caught the news and are pouring in here, now. The first tide is definitely ebbing. Though most of the new arrivals don't know to see it, the innocence is long gone. Since psychedelics were made illegal, a whole lot of hardcore dealers are trying to exploit it. And hard-core criminals are evolving overnight. Not to mention a newer drug is turning people into walking time bombs. Methamphetamine crystal; they're even mainlining it now. Total burnout in zero to 60 days or less. Ah, I'm just bumming, ignore me. Can't knock the free love, though. You drew the absolute miracle of all nature. Where do you think she learned all that stuff? Kama Sutra would be proud. I'd be jealous, except she never goes back for seconds."

Landers laughs, "I'll see if I can break down that routine, if I ever see her again. Is she one of your regulars?"

"Better that you should consider we both be glad she's not a black widow. That's part of the problem, there's too many people trooping through here. Can't keep track. Man, you know, most of 'em are like baby mallards; they just follow the first person they see who seems to have somewhere to go. Then you get these sheep dog types, like Captain Khayam, or whatever his real name is, who just herd them up. I'd eighty-six him except he does round up an amazing horde of chicks. I don't think he's dangerous...at least not violently...just a creep. If he evolves up from sheep dog to wolf, I'll run him off. I'm just more of an alley cat, by nature. I don't direct the flow, until my territory is compromised. On that note, I think I'll go delve in the owner's privileges. One of your buddies is up off the tower and the other is in the kitchen. By the way, my name's Mike."

"Mine too, although for some reason people started calling me Michael a couple years ago, without me asking them to. Michael Landers, glad to meet you, formally. Thanks for the hospitality."

"No problem, at least you guys have manners and don't act like you're automatically entitled to the accommodations," Mike says. Landers goes looking for Whistler and finds him precariously sitting on the rail of a small balcony. Looking over the edge, Landers seems concerned at the forty-foot drop.

"Don't worry, man," Whistler says, reading Lander's expression, "I don't die easy."

"I didn't think you would. Have you seen Spandrow? I fully conked out, for a few minutes."

"More like three hours. Spandrow's roaming around the house. He can't leave. I can see both doors from here. Which is why I'm here. I got tired of the scene. It's groovy enough, just reality has me somewhere else. I need to be moving."

"Yeah, I got a lot of nervous energy that needs burning off, too."

They find Spandrow in the kitchen, performing a mess while trying to make and eat a peanut butter and jelly sandwich between his fingers, without bread. Sunkitty is watching, ever giggling, with her five-foot strands of love beads still around Spandrow's neck. Whistler and Landers laugh. Landers says, "Just make sure to count his fingers when he's done."

Spandrow turns to them, with a smile of acidified bliss.

"C'mon, man, we're getting restless. Let's go for a walk."

"Not without Sunkitty," Spandrow says.

"I'm his designated guru-ette, for his first trip. Yeah, let's go."

As they leave, Captain Khayam and the two girls he'd been with fall in step behind them. Landers' and Whistler's free-lovers are nowhere to be seen. They all parade up Haight Street, towards the park. Almost everyone, at least in the groups of loitering locals, seems to know Sunkitty and Khayam. Since she still reins in Spandrow with her beads, they also seem to know her ritual, and comment on him being on his first trip and Sunkitty's initiating services, of which she unabashedly radiates pride. They wander into Golden Gate Park and watch an improvised jam session. These guys are real musicians and although Spandrow works his way in and shines, as usual, he's not as polished as a few of the others. Whistler drops off asleep.

Captain Khayam tries to direct the group; he likes to be boss. "The sun's getting ready to set. Come on, Sunkitty, let's go watch."

"Cool, I want to see it while colors are still flowing," Spandrow says.

Landers looks at Whistler, who seems totally out, "I don't want to wake him. He needs the sleep, and I don't know where we're going to end up tonight."

"I'd want to stay too, but I do want to see the sunset," Sunkitty says, honestly concerned. "Can't we meet you guys later?"

"For a variety of reasons, I think us three ought to stay together. And I'm not so keen on him running around loose on his first acid trip."

"I got it handled," Spandrow says, "it peaked hours ago."

Sunkitty says, "We can meet you at the Fillmore at ten. It's the New Year's eve party of all time. Gonna be Grateful Dead, Jefferson Airplane, Big Brother with Janis Joplin, Jimmie Hendrix, Santana, Steve Miller, Quicksilver Messenger Service, Buffalo Springfield, maybe even Dylan and Joan Baez. Or maybe some of them are at the Avalon Ballroom. Ah, it'll be most of them, anyway."

"Kind of the who's who of rock. Can't miss it," Spandrow says, adding, to Landers, "I'll be, okay. I'm not exactly helpless, you know."

Whistler says, with eyes still closed, "Go ahead on. But do make it there...And, Miss Sunkitty, please, don't give him any more acid before then." There's an authority to his voice that nobody would contest. Landers seems a bit concerned as Spandrow leaves, still towed by love beads, but doesn't resist.

Spandrow says, to Whistler, "It's covered, man." There's no doubt between him and Whistler that he means it.

11

The entire day of the *truc* full moon, the village is abuzz about the selection ritual for Te and Pim, to see who will be the next shaman. Taking all afternoon, Rama and Mehra dressed Te in ceremonial cloth, with geometrically sophisticated and elegant red, black and white patterns, woven by many generations of the Jolong clan's women. On his wrist is a new bronze bracelet, along with the one he already wore, with two notches in it signifying passages in his spiritual growth. The whole family said a prayer, that all the Nyang pay special attention that the correct choice be made and no malevolent spirits or deities should try to invade his dreams.

Likewise Pim was dressed by S'Yu, but in a much more lavish garb, with several new bracelets along with the half dozen he already wore. Also he wore a necklace that had been made by Te's great uncle, long ago, who was a legendary jewelry maker in the tribe. Immediately after his death, S'Yu had confiscated it from his ailing wife to pay a debt, before she too died. Nobody thought the debt was any where near that large but S'Yu demanded a single payment for the loan even though she hadn't even made the original loan but had bartered by threat for the right to collect it. Though most wouldn't have thought it highly inappropriate for Pim to wear such an extravagant necklace, the cruel irony of its origin wasn't lost on any of those who knew the story. Most also considered it an overt statement by S'Yu that she could do anything she wanted and nobody could stop her.

Special mats had been lain beside the spirit pole in an arrangement determined by the Jolong clan elder Tho, who was the demi-shaman in charge of the overall *feng shui* of the village. When the full moon arose, Te and Pim kneeled on the mats on separate sides of the pole, placed their foreheads on small carved rests and reached over their heads to put both hands on the pole. Han of the Nie Drong led the whole village in a prayer that the Nyang would come that night and make the correct choice. As they entered the sacred house, Amba asked permission for them to enter. All except Kdam of the Nie Drong entered directly, as he pulled up the stair-pole and placed taboo icons on the four corners of the structure, to ward off malevolent spirits of the Earth plane, as they often enter animals and plants and some might have ulterior or unclear motives. As he entered the door, backwards, he said a prayer further asking that the Nyang of the higher plane not allow the nyang or other spirits of the middle plane to enter, as their intentions can be even more arcane.

Amba brought out the ceremonial rice wine in seven gourds with long cane straws, for the Kra Polie and her to drink. She was careful to not give them too much, as they were expected to stay awake all night to watch the boys. So that they are part of the wine ritual, she sprinkled a few drops of the wine on the boys, but didn't let them drink it in case false spirits from the fields might be in the wine and internally influence the boys.

Lying on two central mats, Te and Pim were told to fall asleep, with the others going to wait for the rapid eye movement that indicated significant dreaming. Their optimum plan was to wait until both might be dreaming, at the same time. Te had no problem going into deep sleep and to have long, detailed dreams was his nature. Three times, once at midnight and twice a few hours later, Te had a dream similar to the one when first felt the presence of someone watching over him. Even though it was again a figure watching him and it also was a man with almost as much hair on his skin as a monkey, it was not the familiar figure at all, but much larger and sterner. Nor did Te feel the same sense of well being; scared of the image, he tried to run, but his feet didn't seem to stay and the ground and he couldn't get traction. Although he couldn't make significant progress away from the image, it showed no inclination to come any closer to him. At least Te felt safe; never to be dismissed.

Very restless and wanting nothing to do with any of this, Pim had a hard time getting to sleep. Even when he did, he kept waking up every hour or so and never actually made it through all the levels of sleep to allow significant dreaming. When it was getting near dawn and Pim still had not shown any significant movement under his eyelids, Kdam claimed that some slight fluttering was actually Pim's normal way of dreaming and that they should both be woken. His motive was that if by dawn Pim had no dreams and Te had a significant one, Te would be chosen by default. Quickly, the Nie Drong majority on the *Kra Polie* voted that Pim must have been dreaming, so they wakened them.

Right away, Pim told the elaborate dream his mother had prepared him to say, that he had dreamed of an old women dressed in rags, who was very dirty but not mean. She had taken him by the hand and they took a long walk, up to a high mountain. Since this was exactly the dream image associated with La-Kon-Keh, Bok-Hoi-Doi the Creator's wife, and since she was the second most powerful Nyang, this was considered irrefutable. Ham didn't even want Te to be asked because he claimed no other deity could be more important except the Creator. He cited that if Te did say he saw the white-haired patriarch embodiment of Bok-Hoi-Doi, either Te would be lying or it would invalidate even Amba's original dream, since in their sacred *Hamon* the Creator had never appeared in one village twice in one moon cycle, in all eternity. In lore, if there were two visits, one had to be a false image and could portend that the deities might be at war against each other, with possibly dire consequences for their village. Even if Te also had dreamed of an old lady in rags it could mean the same thing. Amba agreed that this was indeed the sacred principle on that matter, but still Te had to be questioned or the ritual would not be complete.

When Te told of the actual dream he had, all were relieved it wasn't of the Creator or his Wife. Kdam was quick to assert that most likely Te had dreamed of the Dragon, the over-god of all the Yang-Dak, the water gods. Even that could not be sure, Han contested, as it could have been a lesser Yang-Dak, maybe a middle-plain spirit of only some small stream. At any rate, La-Kon-Keh was the more powerful Nyang.

Then an unprecedented twist came into the decision making. All three of the Nie Drong who almost never spoke at the councils seemed very concerned. Though they meekly echoed Ham and

Kdam on civil concerns, all three were fundamentalists on religious matters and had more courage when they believed their souls were invoked. Their concern was that although La-Kon-Keh was indeed powerful and had great influence with her husband, who had created the universe, the sun, the moon and the stars, it was she who had created Earth and all the creatures on it. As important as this was, her work was mainly done and she might not venture down from the higher plane for long periods. What's more, she wasn't malevolent by nature and seldom got involved in the day-by-day lives of humans, except to protect some of her favorites.

On the other hand, Yang-Dak the Dragon, who controlled the monsoon and everything else to do with water, could be very angry and vindictive if he felt he was disrespected. Not only could he shut off all the streams, he could cause any number of leech, worm, mosquito or other plagues to come from all their water sources. This was not unusual Nie Drong logic, because their deceptive and vindictive nature also made them highly suspicious, so they often made decisions from fear of retaliation, be it from deities, spirits or humans.

Tho of the Jolong was last to speak and could have ended the vote in favor of Te. Yet he voted from his most sincere conscience, siding with Han and Kdam to proxy for La-Kon-Keh, and thus Pim of the Nie Drong. This left a tie and though a tie in civil matters would be turned over to the chief to decide, normally Amba would vote in case of a tie on spiritual matters. In this one case, however, Amba felt she should in no way directly affect the choice of her successor other than conveying the message to start the process, by her original dream.

Since there was no resolution, even though Pim and Te both seemed to be valid possibilities, it was decided there would have to be some ritual ordeal to decide between them. Since La-Kon-Keh was so wise and patient with humans, it was considered impossible to insult her without intending to. Yang-Dak was never predictable in any way, so not to slight him it was decided that the contest must have something to do with water. Since Amba had recused herself, the final decision of the *Kra Polie* was that the chief would determine the details of the trial by ordeal.

Everybody knew exactly what Jom — or in actuality S'Yu — would devise though to make it seem more ceremonial he waited three days to make his decision. Four days later on the *roiq pang* half-waning moon, the whole village went in procession up to the far corner of the valley to the deepest pool in their territory. Each boy was to hang onto an appropriately marked ceremonial stone and leap into the middle of a pond from an overhanging branch. They were to keep hanging onto the stones until they were unconscious; with whichever one passes out and lets go first being the loser. Since the current in the pool was strong, if either let go it would be only fifteen seconds and they would be at the top of a small waterfall where they could be retrieved and revived, as the tribe knew an affective means of artificial respiration. If death occurred, that would be irrefutable. Everybody assumed Pim would win easily, as he was much more developed physically than Te, as well as the best swimmer of all the kids.

Standing on the branch, they simultaneously recited the prayer Amba had taught them for this ceremony. Pim had to echo Te for most of it. Each then stepped off into the pond, letting the heavy stone pull them down to the bottom, four times overhead in death. Te had never even been in this pool or down this deep although Pim had been many times, as he and the other Nie Drong boys considered it their private swimming hole. Since one of their games was to try to grab the rocks and then pull themselves as far upstream as possible, hand over hand, Pim already knew every major stone and handhold at the bottom of the pool. So he let go of his stone and started to work his way over to Te, reaching from stone to stone. Te saw him coming and wrapped himself around his stone in a pre-natal position. Since he couldn't immediately dislodge Te, Pim picked up a rock in one hand and tried beating Te's hands to get him to let loose, but all he could hit was Te's head and shoulder. This hurt Te but soon Pim's effort had caused him to lose that much more breath and consequently his strength. He gave up and picked a random stone to hang onto, still intent on beating Te by holding his breath.

With Te's coaching from Xem, the contest was now decidedly in his favor. Soon Pim hadn't even the courage to hold on until he passed out so he let go, pretending to be in a deadman's float. Even this did not get him to the waterfall before he panicked and thrashed his way to the surface. This caused a simultaneous disgruntled sound from almost everyone, with S'Yu's feared grunt being the loudest of all. Although having lost some energy because of Pim's efforts, Te soon got back into the rhythm of letting out small breaths and relaxing in a few seconds of comfort. Over and over he did this, so

164

long that those on the banks feared he must have fallen unconscious, with his hands pinned under the stone. Rama even called out that someone dive in to save him but Jom, after having been jabbed in the ribs by S'Yu, ordered that nobody make any move to help Te. Eventually Te was fading anyway but was determined to hold on until he passed out. Just before he actually did go blank he hadn't enough strength so his hands slipped off the rock. He too feinted the deadman's float, only it took him so long to get to the falls that he was beyond his limit. He actually did pass out so that when two men retrieved him, his authenticity was assured as he choked up considerable water and bled from his nose. This nosebleed had actually been caused by Pim, as well as several large contusions, which later appeared on the back of his head. Although various people guessed what had happened they were afraid to outright accuse Pim, as they knew S'Yu would react harshly. Besides, Pim was absolutely disgraced anyway and some even felt pity for him because they knew S'Yu would punish him repeatedly.

Later, Amba asked Te how he had become injured so severely but he would never snitch, so said he had no idea other than he must have bounced his head along the bottom when he was passed out. Although he hadn't yet been fully anointed, after which point he could never lie to Amba, she was glad he didn't tell her even though she was quite sure what had happened. Before all this, she had always admired Te's sensibilities and talents but was not as fond of him as she was of Te's cousin Mya, whom she had always hoped would succeed her. Now she was taken with an absolute spiritual as well as maternal love for him. To the whole village, except for the most dark-souled Nie Drong, Te was quite the hero. They were relieved that, since Pim had given up, they would be free to express this admiration. One should surely admire the next shaman.

In the village that night was a great festival. It took a while to build momentum because many of the Nie Drong clan didn't want to appear very festive, being afraid that Jom and S'Yu might feel slighted. Although Amba was Nie Drong, she had always tried to show no partiality. Even if Te would end up as just and fair as she, still the fact that he was Jolong would change the order of the power structure. It wasn't until Jom and S'Yu came out and went by the houses of their closest supporters, calling them out to follow them, that most of the Nie Drong felt they should even make a showing. That both Jom and S'Yu were in somewhat subdued ceremonial outfits was duly noted, as they normally tried to outdo each previous showing at every festival. Pim wasn't seen all evening and things didn't really loosen up until S'Yu went home early, saying she didn't feel well. Enjoying these events much more than her anyway, Jom then felt comfortable breaking out many gourds of their better rice wines. After a bit he was laughing and called for the performances to begin. By order of the performers' ages, oldest last, many of their favorite rhythms, dances, songs and skits were presented. In her best form, Amba, who was once the best singer before tobacco had scratched her voice even though she'd quit smoking years before, sang several stories none of them had ever heard before, since they were reserved just for this rite. Having been able to cook all day, old Mehra was in higher spirits than anyone had ever seen her and even joined Amba in songs they sang as girls. After the formal performances, she kept all the old people laughing late into the night as she kept getting drunker and ventured into some bawdy tales, long forgotten or perhaps made up, in her ever-wandering mind. Not a young girl in the tribe took her eyes off Te. More than anything, he was embarrassed by all the attention.

Next morning, the village came to life languidly. Amba had her servant go over and send Te to see her, immediately, then go fetch the water for Te's family, himself. Already Te's selection paid off for his family, as Amba's servant, H'Go, was effectively theirs for second bidding. At fifteen, H'Go was gracious and ambitious, particularly since he had always had his eye on Lieu, Te's 12-year-old cousin. Immediately, this began talk of them being a match, since H'Go was from one of the best of the Biu families and there wasn't really any other appropriate Jolong boys available for Lieu, when it would be time. Though grateful for this extra hand, their was a different brand of task tradeoff for Rama; to keep them from wandering off together.

When Te arrived at her hooch, Amba was already at the spirit pole and taught him a multi-layered prayer for permission to begin this long transfer process. Taking him on a walk to the highest nearby rock, she made him repeat it over and over, so he would never forget it, as the next time he would say it was when his successor was selected. On the rock they sat silently, while she notched her symbol onto his new bracelet, and had him notch his new life-long symbol on hers, which symbol he designed, right then, as a variation of his family's symbol. This rocky tor was exactly as high as dips in ridges to the west and east, so they could watch the full moon set simultaneously with the sun rising. This is the only day of the year this could happen, she taught, as both would shift away from the dip by the next day. This is one of the most important days of the year to pray, particularly for aligning the allegiance of the heavens to protect from the dark nyang Bok Rok of the east mountains and bid assistance and balance from the good nyang Bok Xet, of the west mountains, so that no harm would come to Nyang of the sun and moon while they were sleeping.

Whether he understood them or not, she taught him to echo, as quickly and automatically as possible, every syllable of her prayers and songs. Later, they could go over the various levels of what they all mean, but she wanted him to develop his memory in a cyclical, direct rhythmical and tonal sense. On numerous occasions he had been schooled in the Nyang before, at home and sometimes when the other children gathered under a giant ficus tree where Amba or one of the other elders would teach them. This was different because he had to get every word, tone and rhythm correct. She started as if he'd never been taught anything.

Originally all a holy universe, she began, and all *ae*, the *mana* and soul force, were held by the Nyang. There was only one plane, a heaven beyond the clouds where the oldest Nyang lived. She told of their specific contributions to the new universe and how to never actively give one Nyang preference over any other, both because this could imply that some Nyang was a lesser Nyang and it could infer that Te felt he had a right to judge or order the Nyang. For their reasons, the higher Nyang created a middle plane where lesser nyang that served the higher Nyang existed. To complete a balanced triad, the Earth plane was created. Many spirits from the middle plane served as go-betweens and messengers, as well as represented living things on Earth.

First Nyang were Bok-Hoi-Doi, the Creator of heaven and the universe, and his wife, La-Kon-Keh, who created the earth and all its creatures, except humans. Amba tells of her special affection for La-Pom, their daughter. It was La-Pom, known simply as the Goddess, who came to Amba in her dream long ago that led to her becoming shaman. La-Pom is the older sister of La-Bok, the ancestor of all humans, and since La-Pom loved her sister more than anything she was very generous to humans, and protective by nature. An extremely powerful and potentially scary Nyang is Bok-Claik, lord of thunder and lightning, who spent much of the year sleeping, but would awake noisily to call in the monsoon season. This noise was important because it woke his sister, Yang-Sori, the god of the rice field who should be given praise with every meal. A complex Nyang is Yang-Kong of the mountains, because although he mostly existed in the higher plane and oversaw the individual nyang of each mountain, sometimes he had little control over them, as they were all stubborn. Specifically, two of his daughters disobeyed him and taught sorcery to the humans, which caused many problems on Earth.

Te asked her if she had every run across a sorcerer and how to tell if someone was one. For a long while she looked sternly at him, then she said only that that was a subject for another time. What he really wanted to ask was what she knew about Xem, The Wanderer, and might he be a sorcerer; but he knew he might never know the proper way of phrasing that question without drawing suspicion. Somehow he felt a very similar sense of awe and safety when he was with Amba, much like he did when he was with Xem. Because Te was sponsored by Yang-Dak, the Dragon, she told him he should give thanks every time he crossed a stream or drank water. Since every stream had its own Yang-Dak, who can be spontaneous. Though they do all answer to the Dragon much more harmoniously than the mountain nyang do to Yang-Kong, any encounter with the Dragon or any of his kin could be complicated and elusive. All shamans teeter over many arcane questions but since Te's sponsor was always changing not only his size and shape but also his moods, Te might expect to have to be shaman during times of extreme change.

She sang a condensed prayer to at least acknowledge the spirits of the lower plane, who dwell on earth, usually in animals and plants. Always begin with lord tiger, Bok Klia, and always refer to him as Mr. Tiger, being aware that besides his power he could also imitate the sounds of the other animals as well as the speech of people. Only Roi, the lord elephant, the embodiment of power and perseverance could stand up to Mr. Tiger of all the lower plane nyang. Don't just respect nyang because of fear, she taught him, because even the weakest animals have their purpose. Particularly even lord frog, Ket-Droik; though his embodiment seemed so weak if he didn't show up in great numbers at harvest time, the harvest would be poor.

Not quizzing him on any of this, except the morning prayer beginning the transfer of shaman role, they sat for a long time in meditation. When they came out of it, timed to be when a certain rock's shadow uncovered them, they drank tea and ate breakfast. At this time, they talked of light matters, mostly going over all their observations of the events of the day before, both ritual and social. She promised to teach him everything she knew of human behavior, on the social plane, as it would be part of his role to sort out the levels of spirituality in even the most mundane matters, to determine the balance of morality between conscious intention and instinctive reaction. Rather than talk about the order of Nyang again, he asked if she might sing stories from the *Hamon*, of the old legends.

For awhile she didn't answer. Asking permission from the heavens and forgiveness on earth, in a sing-song, enchanted voice she began the songs of the *Hamon*, the lore of all the Myong and that of their tribe. She began with one of his favorites, which he'd heard a hundred times, but it seemed clearer and brighter than he'd ever known it. "All the Nyang in heaven, after the initial rounds of creation were content with their work and sat back to watch it all play out. However, La-Bok, the younger sister of La-Pom, the Goddess, became restless. By Nyang standards La-Bok was thought of as a teenager; she moped and carried on that she had no real duties or purpose in heaven. She begged her sister to put creatures on the Earth with language and memories so she could teach them to tell stories, create art and perform music. The other Nyang were skeptical, but because La-Pom is so kind, she could not turn down her sister. So, from her own womb, she bore the Y Tung family of the clan of Ebing and guided them to earth. She gave them physical bodies so they could interact with the other creatures, though these bodies would be mortal and could never be brought back across to the other planes. At first La-Bok was happy with this, but soon she watched how quickly and complex the *ae* spirit, the Karmic soul, of these new creatures evolved. Soon they were carrying around far more accumulative turmoil and joys in their memories than the other animals. More critical, they quickly learned to manipulate events in the future. Since evil actions bear so much more dark weight if premeditated, for their spirits to return to the middle level carrying all these unresolved issues seemed unfair; not to mention, who among the Nyang would want troubled spirits in the heavens regardless. Between the sisters La-Bok and La-Pom, with counsel from the other Nyang – who had also been amused at first, but then became confounded with how disparate became the souls of humans – they determined that it would take at least ninety reincarnations for most humans to balance all the bounty and beauty with all the pain and tribulations that they could amass in a single lifetime. If they could build enough positive *ae* during all those reincarnations, they could spend all eternity in the middle spirit plane. Under special circumstances, some might be allowed to descend in spirit to the lower plane to guide their descendants. And some of the best among humans might be allowed to visit the higher plane, to be seen by the Nyang. Yet, if individual souls persisted in choosing evil paths or kept becoming *jolung* – sorcerers who aligned themselves with *molai* demons – and thereby tried to manipulate theirs or other humans karma by inserting evil spirits into the process, they might never be allowed to complete their ninety reincarnations. Or they might even be stuck as slaves to the evil spirits they had invoked into their lives. At any rate, there would be no gain in choosing evil, ever, even though there had never been any such thing as a perfect incarnation.

This was still all too moralistic for Te and he wanted to hear of real adventures of real humans. Could she tell him of how the Golden Tortoise gave Thuc Phan a crossbow with one of its claws as a trigger, and how he became invincible and used it to ward of the invasion of Trieu Da and the invaders from the north, five thousand years before. And what had happened to those invaders who survived?

At this, Amba became extremely troubled. Without even saying yes or no, she stood up and started walking. For awhile she trod along with a step that Te knew he better not match, staying five paces behind. She desired to pass on all the knowledge a shaman might need – which should be all knowledge possible – yet was deeply torn for being forbidden, by the decree of the *Kra Polie*, to tell of the recent history of their tribe, before they moved to this village. Particularly, she was not even to teach of other tribes and other peoples. In her mind, she searched the *Hamon* for a story of a shaman ever put in this situation, and she knew of none with such severe restrictions. Finally, she stopped at a stream and bathed her feet. This seemed to calm her and she signaled for Te to do the same. When she spoke, she said, "Humans cannot escape the truths in any of their incarnations, except by dying. If one dies bearing the weight of untold truths, which have caused others pain, they can not progress on their eternal path, until, in another reincarnation, they have suffered themselves an equal pain, for which holding back that truth had caused. In holding back some truths, sometimes one can actually cause less pain for others. When one dies holding truths of kindness, the Nyang might forgive the holding back of that truth, removing that weight from the bearer's soul." Again she paused, wondering if she was making sense even to herself. She prayed silently, asking for guidance, finally saying, "Te, I promise that I will try to tell you all the truths I know. But in time. Right now, some are forbidden to me to reveal, for human reasons. The Nyang will guide us through this."

If she only knew how much he already understood of what she was hiding, she might have known that he could console her more in this trial, right then, than she could him. For the rest of the morning they wandered through the forest, with her naming every plant, insect, and fungus that they encountered. If she knew its name, she identified the spirit within, and described how it might affect their human lives. "All spirits are interconnected," she said, "and just because we don't understand them, doesn't mean they can't affect us."

Making a point that Te be back to have the midday meal with his family, she told him to meet her the next day, early afternoon, that they might take a long walk and observe the sunset together. When he got home, he should ask to take on more complex chores, to compensate for not having to carry water every morning. Specifically, he should ask great-aunt Mehra to teach him to carve wood and to weave bamboo walls and floors, as Mehra's husband had been one of the best craftsmen of the village. She had mastered every skill herself, surpassing him in some. All in their household were surprised how eagerly Mehra took to this. Since Te's selection, she had become a different person. Not only was she not as contentious and dour, she often even smiled and joked. Had her change been defined it would have come from her new hope; hope that the tribe she was born into, then much more honest and open, would be the tribe she left, before becoming an disembodied spirit again. Mya begged to get time off from spinning thread to watch them. Even though Aunt Rama was anxious to create cloth for Lieu's dowry and wedding ensemble, which she sensed might be sooner than everyone else expected, she let Mya watch them and even gave her a small knife with which to whittle. Rama was so happy to see them all working together, with an ardor for creating exceptional things.

That afternoon for Amba was conversely an emotional pit-hole. For her whole life, she had sedulously prepared to take on an apt and talented student. Every day, for hours, she repeated and checked herself on all the vast lore she held in memory, to make sure she was not forgetting any story as well as getting all the prayers and songs exactly right, especially those prayers reserved exclusively for the shaman. The cruel irony of being restricted on what she could pass on seared at her heart and soul. Although she was acutely aware that even though it was decreed by the *Kra Polie,* all was caused by S'Yu's machinations, in cover up for the betrayal on that day of the kidnappings. This even though even Amba was not aware of exactly what happened that day.

While still eating her own meal, she felt her hooch sway from someone walking up the ladder-pole, then the porch creaked, unevenly. Not just because she could tell the weight did she know it was S'Yu, by far the heaviest of all the women, but by the trudging pace, as if she tried to impress her importance into the floor with every step. All the men who would be that heavy spent so much time walking softly out in the forest that their step barely caused any noise at all. Not announcing herself, nor asking permission – an unheard of incivility – S'Yu walked right into Amba's home. Rarely did the villagers come into her hut and even then it was almost never for a casual visit. Even though she always made herself available and did counsel on oftentimes obscure and even petty matters, mostly a session with her would be for an in-depth counseling regarding some illness or significant physical, marital or spiritual passing. Even though Amba was her mother's sister, S'Yu had only been to this place twice before. First time was when she was beginning to menstruate. Although Amba had tried to tell her everything this meant, for her hygienic as well as spiritual development, S'Yu barely listened. All she noticed were the objects in Amba's hut. Around all the walls were baskets and shelves piled with vestments, jewelry and curios, which had been collected by shamans for countless generations, for various ceremonies. There was also some of her family heirlooms, the few favorites she had kept for herself rather than give them to those in need. Few had much trade value but were only sentimentally dear to her. Never asking first, S'Yu had dug through the piles and baskets, pulling out cloth and dropping it wherever it fell, without refolding anything. As it was her way to observe all the villagers before imposing her suggestions, Amba was shocked how reckless and disrespectful this girl was of everything. Seeing that S'Yu was never going to stop, Amba had told her to squat in a specific place near the door, so she could tell her what she was expected to know. Soon tiring of this, S'Yu simply tromped off when she was bored, clearly pouting that she hadn't been allowed to see absolutely everything.

When S'Yu showed up for her traditional advice before marrying Jom, Amba knew what to expect. Though she usually enjoyed spending time showing the other girls and women of the tribe most of the various objects and letting them touch them, this time she showed S'Yu some of the important things, but wouldn't let her touch anything. Again, S'Yu barely paid attention and sulked that she wasn't allowed to help herself. When Amba turned to put some weavings back in a basket, S'Yu quickly tried on a necklace and wrapped another cloth around her. Amba became angry, as they were only to be worn once a year, on the new moon of the planting season. She commanded S'Yu to remove them. Yanking off the necklace, S'Yu tossed it across the room and simply dropped the skirt to the floor, before again sulking off. After she descended the stair-pole, she knocked the pole over, even commanding Amba's servant not to put it back up, though the servant did so, immediately. First day after S'Yu married Jom, thus making him chief and her first lady, that servant was beaten severely by several of S'Yu's acting thugs, on the way back from foraging.

This day S'Yu started out pretending she was on a light social visit. Though she looked around at all the baskets and visible things, she didn't try to go touch them. Going through S'Yu's head, Amba knew, was a jealous fit that if Pim had been made shaman almost all but the most sacred objects would have ended up in S'Yu's house. An even darker chill surged through Amba's senses, in realization that had if Te had not been chosen, S'Yu would likely have precipitated an earlier transfer to Pim, possibly by Amba's unnatural death. How Myong die can have as much or more importance relevance to the next path of their soul than how they had lived, since the soul has two counterparts, one good and one evil. If dying in positive spiritual balance, the good side of the soul would be able to warn and protect ancestors – in the case of a shaman, the entire village – from evil spirits. Dying by unnatural means, particularly suicide or murder, could cause the soul to have to remain on Earth as a haunted specter, causing havoc in the village, or roaming aimlessly, maybe even having to dwell for some time within a cobra or even a tiger. Committing suicide, particularly with an evil conscience, might result in having to be a slave for a *molai*. All this flashed through Amba's mind.

After chatting for a few minutes about inconsequential events, with no logical segues, S'Yu turned and looked menacingly down at Amba. She said, "Now, about Te's education."

"Te must be told everything I know about the Nyang and the *Hamon*," Amba said, "There is no other way."

"Well, the Nyang of course. And, yes, the ancient *Hamon*, since that is beyond our history. But as for the telling of how and why the tribe migrated here, any mention of that will be forbidden by the traditional taboo."

"How long can these children be kept in ignorance? Particularly Te, who is so intuitive and clearly wonders about how we, the oldest people on Earth, with such a rich, complex *Hamon* telling of thousands of generations, how could we be the only humans remaining in existence, in this tiny village. There's no doubt some of the Biu children know something. I've seen them wearing garments of old clans, and I've heard them say names of people who were killed in that day of battle with the renegades from the north.'

"Tell me their names, and their families will be punished."

Ignoring this, Amba said, "Don't you think accumulative logic will prevail, eventually. Most teenagers doubt the wisdom of everything their elders tell them, regardless. With this generation, when they combine their bits of information to conclude that they've been lied to in totality, then all rapport will be lost between generations. An honest history must be told and retold, that eventually its truths will prevail."

"Why? Who says? If remembering some event of history only causes turmoil and anxieties, why must it repeated? What is the matter with telling history as it should have happened? All that matters is that the tribe believes what most benefits the tribe. Don't you yourself teach that it does not necessarily harm the soul to retain truths in kindness."

"Truths in kindness are kept by the judgment of the person in question, not forced upon them by those who want to control what truths that person might say."

"Damn your automatic spiritual proclamations for everything. I hated them when you taught us as children. I hate them every time I think of them. I hate them every time I think of you."

"That may be your feelings but you still can't change the truth."

"I'm becoming very impatient and angry with this. I can and I will. If the tribe believes in the current leaders and the rules that we've taught them, they will be all the better."

"It is time to have a serious meeting of the Kra Polie."

"Fine. I'll alert the Kra Polie to go to the spirit house tonight."

"So it's you who orders the Kra Polie, now, is that it?"

"It always has been. Nobody else believes differently, so I don't expect that you should delude yourself."

"If the rules are always responsible to the Nyang, and if the rulers themselves follow them, then there should be no instance of history that can't be told."

"You and your Nyang. You are not a Nyang so don't speak like you are. You wouldn't even be shaman if it weren't for your sister being so jealous of you, for your weird little boyfriend."

"That's enough. Don't demean the spirit of your mother. You don't know what happened. It was much more complicated and impulsive than two sisters fighting over a boyfriend. I've long since forgiven her. She was a good person and died with an overwhelming positive balance. It can not..." Amba cut herself short. In her anger she was about to make a judgmental proclamation on the current state of S'Yu's soul, which was a domain reserved for the Nyang.

"Hah, you stop mid-sentence. Not so in control of your temper as you'd like, are you? Afraid to voice your own feelings about me? You're afraid of everything, old woman. Afraid of the Nyang, afraid of spirits, afraid of death, afraid of everyone in the village. Afraid of me."

"Yes, I'm afraid of almost everything. But I'm not afraid of the truth."

"You will be if you decide to tell truths in a way not decreed proper by the *Kra Polie*. And you have yet to know how scared you will be of me."

Not asking permission from either Amba or the Nyang, upon leaving this sacred house – this itself a sacrilege – S'Yu left with her usual stomping swagger. On the lanai, she stood with her breast and head high, as if daring anyone in the village to confront her. Although everyone was aware of this gesture, all those who looked did so out of the corner of their eye or through cracks in the walls. Instead of climbing down Amba's ladder-pole S'Yu stepped across the gap onto the lanai of the spirit house, stood there for awhile too, then she put down the pole and descended, without pushing the pole back up. Everybody turned his or her eyes away in fear. For S'Yu to dishonor Amba's position was bad enough, but for her to flaunt her power at all the Nyang, this was unfathomed blasphemy. Nothing but evil could come from this. As if gaining energy from her own display, S'Yu made a detailed lap of the village, walking in front of every single household and peering inside. When she returned to her home, she called for her servants to gather everything she needed to go bathe. They did so, but none could hold their head up as they followed her. Jom wasn't seen at all, until the next day.

That evening was the most dismal meeting of the *Kra Polie* that anyone could remember. With his eyes diverted and none of his usual exuberant hand gestures, Kdam of the Nie Drong recertified that there would be no teaching of how and why their village was built so isolated, nor would there be any teachings, in any way, of the existence of any other tribes or peoples. Nobody seconded nor challenged him. In ten minutes the meeting was over. None of them slept well.

Knowing she was not able to give to Te anything like the education she had received, Amba passed the next couple days working with Te to memorize the prayer songs to all the Nyang. To keep Te from asking questions, she avoided the old Hamon legends, because they almost always called for moral interpretations or had thought-provoking twists. And when Te thought, he asked questions. This was exactly what she wanted him to do and was distraught that she couldn't inspire his imagination to roam free. Knowing he became easily bored with the sacred work, she did tell tales of the wanderings of the earliest Myong, the clan of Ebings. Drifting off in his own mind, Te asked if they'd ever come across the Lost River Valley. He was startled how this turned her angry and flustered.

To come up with any answer at all, she said, "There is no factual evidence that such a place exists. So don't bring it up again."

Seeing how he was hurt by the rebuke, she was struck by serious doubts about all off this: of her role as shaman, as to if Te was a valid candidate, of her entire conception of the Nyang. She cut the lessons short and said for him not to come the next day, that she would spend the whole day in meditation and prayer.

This left him with the first free time he'd had in a long time. Knowing if he went straight home, Rama would find something for him to do, he wandered by the pool where the Biu boys usually hung out. When he stood on the banks, they barely acknowledged him. This was not that they didn't like or respect him; he was simply spiritually removed. Saddened and lonely, he wandered down to the watering place. Making sure there was nobody watching, he tried crawling through the ravine to the cave pool, but the spider webs were so thick he turned back. For a long time, he sat under the shower, trying to wash away all thoughts. Perhaps he did, or maybe he just fell asleep, because next thing he was aware of was the deep shadows and cool breezes in the vale meaning the sun was setting. He did feel slightly more at ease, though still very lonely.

12

Around dark, a chill of fog pours over Golden Gate Park, waking Whistler. This time he's the confused one. "Man, gotta get back to ground. C'mon, let's move out," he says, then mumbles, "Why the hell'd I let Spandrow wander off?" Walk they do, not saying much, other than brief comments on sights they came across. Landers is content to let Whistler lead. Having been humping a backpack, for the last year minus the last few weeks, Whistler finally feels more like himself after a couple hours of heavy urban hiking, including a few crosses through any park he sees, where he seems most at ease. Stopping to look at some shrubs, he comments, "Sure is nice to just admire a bush that's not likely to shoot you. Nam does have some admirable bushes, though. They patch it all up, I'd like to go do an extended nature hike. It's paradise, man. Not counting all those poison apples. But, at least there, you know one when you see it. Well, unless you're in VC country. Which we weren't, much. Pretty much NVA is what we dealt with. At least the NVA wear uniforms." Walking by a city college, they go into the gym to take a shower. Wending into a neighborhood where they are more black people on the streets, they walk until blacks are all they see. Walking farther, into a shoddier section, after dark, Landers is feeling nervous as is Whistler, realizing they are on claimed turf and are getting heavy stares, so he leads them into a more relaxed neighborhood and goes into a family-style diner. Still, everyone is black. "Just need to check the oil on the reality machine. This last twenty four hours hasn't reminded me much of the America I left back in Cleveland, say, a year and a few weeks ago."

"Compared to today, tonight ought to be a spectacle."

"Yeah, guess a spectacle's what I want, but I'm for turning our selves in, in the morning. I gotta get this whole Army thing way behind me, then check in for an extended tour of Mama's home cooking. After that...man, I can't imagine where on the planet I'm going to land this spaceship called me."

"Yeah, I haven't felt like I belonged anywhere, for over six months, and don't imagine how I'm ever going to get back in control of anything."

"Guess, I shouldn't be knockin' down so much. You got the whole monster still ahead of you. All I gotta do is shut my mouth and play tin soldier for a couple months."

After the first completely soul-food meal Landers had ever eaten, which does leave him feeling highly satisfied and grounded, they head back for the streets. For another hour or so they roam at random. Landers is getting anxious, "C'mon, let's head up to the Fillmore. I'm getting nervous about Spandrow."

"Don't worry, those people aren't going to hurt him. They're too flowered out. He is a boonierat, after all."

"You don't care for that scene much, do you?"

"Oh, it's probably a fine scene, for someone who just hit the streets for the first time in their life. I don't see you feeling all that comfortable either."

"It seems too impossibly innocent. Of course I could never afford to be a total dropout hippie. Most of them do seem to come from upper income and above; and know they can fall back into it. Not that I'm jealous. The girls are chewy enough but if it takes being a full-time druggie or candy man, I'm way out of my lane."

"Yeah, I like to get a ways high, when the time is right. But, that scene, I'm steady wondering when's the hangover's going to set in. I think of drugs, I think of some gangster up there top of the feeding chain. Where is he, here? Who is he? It scares me, but I can't even put a definition on why."

"Maybe that's part of why I'm leery. Spandrow sure fell for it all. You don't like that he never went back to Nam from R&R, do you?"

"I really don't know the details, but I know the guys in his unit should've been able to count on him. Everybody's at least half crazy in the field, but you gotta walk with it."

"Maybe it turned him all the way insane, for awhile. Maybe he belonged in the Fruit Bowl. Maybe I do."

"Or me, is your next addition. Nam or not, Bowl or not, you go crazy, you gotta lay most of the blame on yourself, short of some brain-eating germ. Spandrow's too much a drama junky to trust which way he's blowing. Hey, but you know I like him. He is one talented dude, man. But then you look how he dropped who he was, just this morning, and became part of that hippie train in an instant."

"Ah, he's on his first acid trip. That is a whole new psyche."

"Yeah, I guess. Man, the world's gotten too hard for me. You think that Jameson cat is paranoid? I'm so paranoid I'm afraid to even let people know I'm afraid. I'm afraid to let myself know I'm afraid. But, inside here, in my heart, I'm fighting back panic, all the time."

"I've been closer, in the last week or two, than I ever remember, too. But do answer me this; if you're down on Spandrow not going back to Nam, how come you tell me not to go?"

"Because the Nam has nothing to do with the World. The World being, which you probably know, is just Nam slang for anywhere but there. Your life in Nam doesn't begin 'til you get there. Baptism by very bad luck. Once you're there, you gotta take every sacrament it gives you. Carve each of 'em on your soul board and stand up and declare, 'Still here.' But you, you don't got that poison in you yet. Why start?"

"I just can't get over the feeling that I'd be running out on them...whoever them is."

"'Them', is America, man. America's ailin', right about now. Maybe healing America would start with you not going over. 'Them' are makin' nineteen-year-old poor boys make the moral decision for the whole country. Shit, we can fight; it's about all we can do. Which gives us the least rights of anybody. Like we don't count. Fuck 'them', man, we count too."

Both are getting way more agitated than they care to be, and go back to their defense of just keeping moving, to erase any consciousness of time passing. When they approach the Fillmore Auditorium, the highest temple of Hippiedom, the energy on the street becomes electrostatic. Hundreds of ultra-hippies converge, from all directions. Whistler smiles, "Now just what sorta circus is this comin' to town?"

Caught up in the mob, they work their way in through the packed lobby and into the main ballroom. One after the next, the top rock groups of the era ignite their disciples, all decked out in the costumes of a thousand antique chests, osterized in with the farthest-out accoutrements of hippie attire. Impromptu theater propagates throughout the whole scene. Dionysus would immortalize the dancers, on enthusiasm alone. Bliss and love abound, and not on a cheap or phony scale; these people believe. With phosphorescent paint and chalk, revelers psychedelicize the floors, the walls and each other. Nothing holds still, as a phantasmagoria of strobes, black lights, color wheels, mirror balls, slide projectors with telescoping focus, and tricked-out theater spots gyrate and pulsate through this soft-mosh mesmeria of surging libidos.

After taking it all in awhile, for pure wonder purposes, Landers and Whistler start looking for Spandrow. Up on the balcony, they find Sunkitty and Captain Khayam. Sunkitty gives them a grand smile, hugs and kisses but Captain Khayam seems to rebuke her for this. Whistler asks, "Where's our friend?"

Coldly, making no eye contact, Captain Khayam responds, "He's in here somewhere, totally tripped out.

"I thought you weren't going to give him any more acid," Landers says, about fed up with this guy's attitude.

"He didn't get it from me," Captain Khayam says.

Landers looks at Sunkitty, "And I thought you were going to stay with him."

"On his first trip," she says. "That was fading. This is his second."

Captain Khayam pulls her away, "Maybe he took enough this time to enlighten him."

"So you abandoned him?" Whistler says.

"We didn't abandon him. He's in a safe place. Everybody's a head in here," Captain Khayam says, then specifically addresses Whistler, "Everybody except you. So you're a Viet Nam vet? The killer type. This is a place of peace. You don't belong."

Landers seems more perturbed than Whistler but Whistler stops him from reacting, saying, "I want the peace too, brother. And I know the difference." He looks deep into Captain Khayam's eyes, with a life fire that shrivels him. He exchanges an indefinable smile with Sunkitty and says to Landers, "C'mon, let's find him. You were right. We shouldn't have left him. Not in these hands."

Near the stage, they spot Spandrow dancing, animatedly directing all fairies with his arms. When they get to him, he hugs them exuberantly. They have to actually hold him off, but don't mind. They watch him dance a bit. Someone hands them a joint, which Whistler smells and shrugs, as if to say, it might be okay, but how do you know. They pass it on without taking a hit. Since there are more girls than guys, they just start dancing and, since both are good dancers, they attract partners. At one point the Kama Sutra girl dances with Landers but doesn't seem to show any recognition that they'd spent hours making love, that midday. At this point, all any of them want is catharsis so they apply their entire psyche and souls to dancing the spectacle.

Almost without let-up, they dance until near dawn. The crowd finally starts thinning out, with most of them headed off for Golden Gate Park for a mass breakfast and more music. Once they're in the clear air, our three opt for peace and quiet. The magic moments of daybreak are on them, when the first violets of the sunrise bring up the details on the walls and trees. At this point they realize Spandrow is still completely tripped out on acid, "wow-ing" every squiggle he sees.

"Man, that acid must really be something," Whistler says. "I don't know where his mind is at but it's sure having fun. Maybe I'll have to try it someday." Alternatively, they don't let Spandrow get any farther from them than they can grab his wrist, if he bounds off. Outside a head shop window, crammed with psychedelic wares, Spandrow starts freaking out on a flashing peace-sign. This sets him off in a bad direction. He starts mumbling incoherently about peace, then things he saw in Nam. He starts to run, but they both grab his arms. He's shaking, but they slowly get him to sit down against the wall. A cop car starts cruising their way. "Oh, shit, here we go," Whistler says.

Stopping right next to them, the cops calmly survey the situation. One says, "Bum trip, huh? Is he breathing okay?"

"Ah, yeah," Landers says. "We'll take care of him. He's our friend."

"Just make sure he doesn't go running off," the cop says. They drive on.

"Man, if this ain't one weird ass town," Whistler says. "Even the cops turn their heads."

"They're obviously more concerned about the serious protestors than all this hippie flower stuff. It's kind of hard to put down peace and love. Except a lot of people do it; not sure whether it's with hate or fear as their motive."

"And I thought just the Nam and the World were different planets. This is another universe altogether. So what now? Technically, we're only AWOL for a day, two at most. We could try his original plan to sneak back in the window, but what's the use? Given they've already chalked us up as goofballs we probably won't get in much trouble if we just walk back in the door. Any luck, maybe they'll give you guys another week inside. Me, I just want out; gone."

"For his sake, maybe. But let's at least spend the morning checking out one other option, over Berkeley way. Spandrow, you feel okay to get on a bus?"

"Yeah, I can do anything. Let's fly over. You know the weirdest thing about last night, was they let the guys from the Fruit Bowl come over."

"They did what?" Landers asks.

"You didn't see them? Maybe it was only one guy, and I just saw him a bunch of times. I never did see his face. He was black, though. Weird costume for someone to go out in, don't you think, if he wasn't a real Fruit Bowler? I didn't want to sound paranoid, but I thought we've been followed all along."

Whistler almost looks like he's going to admit to this too, but just says, "Let's just call it weird, and leave it at that. I don't want to get back into a Nam thing of always looking over the shoulder. I say we walk awhile before we try any busses."

For an hour, they walk. To reintroduce Spandrow to humanity they try breakfast at a diner. Other than having a Sisyphus of a time trying to get his over-easy eggs to stand still, which has them all fighting back tears of laughter, Spandrow manages the public contact without any problem. They catch a bus and cross the Bay Bridge, over to Berkeley. Crossing the San Francisco Bay on any of the bridges is always dramatic. The bays many fingers and rias twist off in all directions. Hill vegetation runs from golden grass to pine forests, to a few spared redwoods. Heavy ocean clouds pour over the coastal ridges. East Bay has its interesting neighborhoods but is comparatively nondescript, on the flat-lands, though the hills above

Berkeley and Oakland run for miles, with thousands of unique and precious homes hidden in pine, cedar and eucalyptus woods.

At the Berkeley campus, they have coffee at a quad cafeteria. Whistler seems quite at home, but Spandrow watches it all like another new country. He'd barely made it through ninth grade. There's ample long-haired types, with beards and clothes in a hippie direction, but few of the students have the look of total drop-outs from society. It's not easy to get in this school. There are still plenty of athletes and fraternity types, as well as regiments of future scientists, in their studied bland styles.

Landers phones Katrina. Although always glad to hear his voice, nothing about the whole situation makes her feel anything but angst. He asks her if she can arrange a meeting with Arnold and any other legal minds that might be interested hearing in their positions. He specifically asks if she can do so without alerting Werner. Katrina says she's given up dealing with anybody near the center of the protest movement, because it seems impossible to isolate the reasonable voices from the show-boaters. Yet, she says she'll do what she can, to call her back in two hours.

By noon, she has tracked down Arnold, who pulls together a group to meet at a house just off the campus. Inside, it looks like a center for a political counter-action committee. It's also used as a launching pad for demonstrations and information blitzes, by various groups. Pamphlets from anti-war and anti-establishment groups cover the walls. The Black Panther Party, Students for a Democratic Society and Free Speech Movement – the three most publicized larger groups of the anti-establishment movement – have notices and literature scattered about; all were labeled radical, by the media. On the top of all anti-establishment hate lists was the war machine, which included not just the military, but the arms manufacturers and all its political and backroom corporate manipulators. Although there were undoubtedly some true communists in the closets – they were all inexorably branded as communists by that political wing as far right as they were left – not many people wanted to be outwardly labeled as such. In fact there were probably very few, not just because that label was likely to draw rejection from the borderline factions, but they still believed that when militant communists said they wanted to bury America, they meant it. Take Viet Nam off the table and the groups would have polarized, in minutes, mostly from the clashing egos of leaders.

When they enter, Landers sees Katrina and Jeffrey way off in the corner giving him slight nods, as if they're there out of loyalty but would rather be anywhere else. Arnold steps up and greets Landers, genuinely friendly, although it's not his nature to be warm, and he introduces himself to Spandrow and Whistler, who are holding back any signs of taking to any of this. Werner is off to the side with three other guys, who pay no attention to anything except some angry rhetoric they have running, which seems more a chant than a dialogue. A couple Black Panthers give abbreviated clenched-fist greetings to Whistler, who returns it even more abbreviatedly, but still with a sentiment of connection. Arnold runs the preliminary forum, which ends up being a lawyerly deposition of Landers about all three of their positions. Werner moves in and punctuates the air, with fragments of cliche anger phrases. Landers notices that the others not only don't echo him but seem to not even hear him. One of the black guys has a few emotional interjections of his own and sometimes gets seconded, though less fervidly.

Spandrow, wary in the first place, seems to retract more and more from it all, even though Landers somehow thought that he might have the most chance of stirring a precedent or recall of some soldier in a similar position. The basic defining fact of their being soldiers becomes ever more evident. Landers is quickly feeling very disappointed with himself, that he brought his friends into this snake pit.

Whistler seems to draw most of the general curiosity and eventually Arnold specifically asks him to define his position of how, having already served his combat tour, he had managed to get so disassociated from even the short career track that he as a draftee had remaining. Once he was directly confronted, Whistler slightly surprised Landers by not only not wanting to duck the attention, but by coming out with a different physical deportment and even accent. In the hospital and roaming the streets, Whistler certainly came across as intelligent and informed, but still had a personality style of a hip, street character, although not at all over-affected. He'd never mentioned much of anything in his past. Now he does, "When I got back, they wanted to train me to counter anti-war Americans, in the peace demonstrations, or riots, if they came. I couldn't do it with any stretch of conscience. I hate the war. I hate us being there. All I wanted was out, to go back home. They threatened and yelled, but I sat on my bunk and wouldn't move. After a few days, anytime they got near me, I growled. Then I went stonewall silent. Once you're back, they have no qualms about declaring you crazy; they don't need you any more."

Werner cuts in, "We really could use a disgruntled veteran to speak up for the poor, uneducated blacks exploited by the establishment war mongers."

Whistler waits, to let a few of his own trigger points ease off, then says, "I can attest that some of your suppositions exist. But I'm not the model you just defined. I wasn't raised poor. My father did well in his own insurance business and was a solid family man, the epitome of the American work ethic, until he dropped dead of a stress-induced heartache, when I was twenty. By then I was in my third year at Ohio State, doing fine. Had I not taken a semester off to help my mom, which got me drafted, I'd very likely already be a year into law school."

"Then you should have been above being drafted," one of the young women comments.

Landers' own agitation is increasing. He surprises even himself to blurt out, "We're not trying to define ourselves as being above anyone or anything. We're trying to redefine the country's war persuasion."

Werner snaps at him, "We're addressing him, not you. We've decided you're of no help to us." Others in the group exchange glances of wondering who are this "we" is he is talking about. Werner continues, to Whistler, "Won't you at least act it out, for the cause?"

The same woman piles on, "Being educated, you could act dumb so they'd lead the questions and you could answer them better. You know, be the even more underprivileged, ghetto black."

Landers and Spandrow look at each other like they want to bolt, right then, but Whistler stops them all, with a long, laugh; the first time they'd really heard him laugh out loud, other than a good-humored chuckle. "Now this is a cool switch. Exploit the educated black as being dumb."

Werner seems to miss the irony, "Whatever it takes, to add ammunition to our rally, next week. Governor Reagan's already alerted the state militia. He's even threatened to call up the National Guard. He wants to close Berkeley altogether. If we make sure he does that, we'll have all the media coverage we could ever want."

Landers and Whistler exchange a glance of who's going to take this one. Whistler nods for Landers to go ahead, so he does, "First off, with you going after increasing your TV ratings, I'm getting the feeling that your most important goal is confrontation, purely for the sake of it. Somehow I don't think that's going to win over many friends. More likely it'll piss off the pro-war people even more. No offense, but you're stirring up a civilian war here. We'd like to think we're civilians but we're not. Presumably, you really do want to stop the war machine. We do too. First we've got to get out of the Army machine. And I don't see any escape hatches around here. Sorry, if we wasted your time. No, sorry I wasted everybody's time."

"There's no time or room for individual interests in the revolution. The people must take charge of everything," Werner says, standing for emphasis.

Arnold has obviously had enough of Werner's provocations and cuts in, "When I see the people in a communist society elect a leader not shoved on them by the central party, we can have that conversation. It's moot in light of why we're here right now. Civilian lawyers have represented military personnel. There is precedent."

Whistler says, "Military law doesn't precede itself; it just makes up whatever is expedient, even in an 'undeclared' war."

Werner comes back, "That's why we need to tear up this repressive Constitution. If the people call the laws, the capitalists can't exploit everything. Power to the people, that's the answer." A few in the room second this last buzz phrase.

Landers says, "We're not exactly out to derail the Constitution. More democracy is what we're about, not less."

"Individual votes don't beat pirate industrialists. Committees do," Werner states. "We should be the committee. We're from the greatest public university in the land. Who better than us?"

Spandrow finally hits his emotional wall, "C'mon, let's go. We might have better luck with military justice. I'm not a poor, uneducated black, but I never got beyond ninth grade. And I'm damn sure poor. And my ma and grandma and great-grandma all were too. And we wanna stop the war. Man, the war's done me over. Stop it. But the real message I feel in here is if anyone's got to go, send the poor dumb kids. Ten years from now, all you people are going to be rich doctors and lawyers. And the poor are still gonna be the poor. Next war you're gonna be the establishment and the poor are still gonna fight it for you. I'm trackin' out o' here."

The air thickens, considerably. Spandrow stands to leave, looks at Whistler and Landers. Whatever they're up to, they know they're in it together. Right now they are collectively much less sure of what their position is, but know it's not currently improving, in any way. As they walk out, Landers and Katrina exchange an exasperated eye contact. The whole room erupts into a shouting match.

Our three walk steadily away, but Katrina catches up with them and grabs Landers' arm. The others walk ahead. Katrina is in tears, "Oh, Michael there's just too much going on...Too much I can't understand, let alone begin to control. School doesn't even make sense. I dropped out."

"You what! Why?"

"Because of you. No, not because of what you did. Because of what's happening to you. Because of watching you be torn apart. More than anybody alive I know how strong you feel. About everything. You don't have a destructive or vindictive cell in your body. Yeah, you're damn sure a survivor and will hit hard, to defend yourself if you really need to, but selfish is one thing you are not. You care about other people as much as you do about yourself. Thinking about where you are and what you're seeing has become an obsession. Looking around me, I'm bombarded by all the thousands of people that must be equally as ripped up."

"But quitting school? What're you gonna do?"

"Jeffrey and I are going down to San Diego, to work on that newspaper."

"Not because Werner put you up to it, I hope."

"You know what I think of Werner. No, actually you don't know what I think of Werner." She pauses and tightens her gaze just long enough for Landers to know she's holding back, but if she doesn't offer, he doesn't ask. "Not ever having to see Werner again is the only thing I like about it. Jeffrey's as flipped out as I am and really wants to do something against the war. Something besides shout and burn flags. Maybe we can put together some sensible articles."

"But can't you do that from here?"

"Michael, what is it that I like to do more than anything in the world."

"Read. So stay in school and read."

"I would if I could. But I'm so twisted up I can't even concentrate enough to read. That's never happened to me before, ever. Not for a minute. And you know I've had a couple reasons to get jacked up, along the way. Reading always worked as an escape. Not now. Now, just not being able to concentrate makes me instantly furious. I threw a book through a window the other night I was so mad. A precious book. That was it. I quit. I'll be back. I just need a break, before I really blow something out of whack. I don't hate America but I hate that it's carrying on this war. I could lose you, the best friend I've ever had, by far. For nothing. For goddamn nothing. And most of the country just goes on about their little lives. I've got to feel like I'm doing something to stop it."

"You better not be doing this for me."

"You're so wrapped up in this, now, it hurts me even to see you."

"Why didn't you tell me that in the first place. I'd have stayed out of your space."

"Michael, Michael. God, I don't know what to do. I just gotta get away from here."

"Yeah, I got other places to go too."

Neither of them could imagine a worse parting, but they have nothing left to say. They're both drained and the only thing common in their hearts are pain and icicles.

Riding the bus back across San Francisco Bay, our three say nothing of consequence. Without even discussing it, they walk straight to the entrance to the S-2 Ward. Upon seeing them, the administrators just huddle and get on the phone. In a few minutes, there are four administrators and two MPs inside the glass room, pointing and waving, all out of earshot.

Finally the MPs come out. The officer says, "Alright, boys, looks like you're ours, now."

Whistler mumbles, "Oh, man, now we did it."

The MP sergeant orders, "Shut up, soldier. You're back in the Army now. They march them a half mile to an MP holding station and turn them over to a Specialist 4 named Owens, who is way too old to have not moved beyond that rank. He locks all three in the same cell. The officer and sergeant leave. Once they're gone, Owens puts on his own lame power display, marching back in front of the cell several times. He's a shrill, redneck type, out of shape and probably never been in shape, but sure wants to sound tough.

"Welcome, boys, make yourselves at home. But don't get too comfortable. From here on out the beds get harder, the food gets harder, the walls get harder, the windows get smaller. There are no windows. So now that I've done the travelogue let's get in to introductions. He walks over and opens a door, ritualistic, like he's about to bring out Napoleon. Napoleon on a bad day would have been more welcome. Sergeant Macree, the one MP everyone has warned them never to get near, steps in, with his hands behind his back. He cockwalks a bit. For openers, he looks and smells like a highly toxic alcoholic. Even had they not been warned, they'd instantly know they were watching a sadistic sociopath. Spec 4 Owens says, "Here they are, Sergeant Macree. The trash of the day."

Macree stops a few yards from the cell, bringing out his hands and revealing he has a two-foot long, hard-rubber prod, which he swings, casually. "Well, what in the name of shit do we got us here? A faggot deserter, a faggot peace creep and a faggot nigger. Just what the party needed. We're gonna have you all three in the stockade in a day or so, then the fun really begins. But tonight, just a sampler." He swings out with the prod at Whistler's hands on he bars. Whistler barely pulls away in time."

Macree says, "Shit, this boy's quick. Good, I like to have some sport of it. You guys like to escape don't you? Yeah, we like escapers. Not because of the competition. You ain't no competition. We just like to discipline deserters." He unlocks the cell, swings the door open. He turns his back and crosses the room to as far from the doors as he can get. Pulling his gun out of his holster, he checks it out. He takes the clip out and puts it in an ammo pouch and puts the gun in its holster. "Here's your chance. How long you think it'll take you to make that door. How fast do you think I can lock and load."

"Seems like we turned ourselves in, why would we run?" Landers says.

Macree clicks his head back and his eyes widen, like he's shocked to be confronted and about to burst. He charges the cell, winding up with his prod. But the outside door swings open. In steps the MP officer and Dr. Xylos, who they've never seen look even vaguely angry, before this. Macree says, "Just doin' a little intro drill, all part of policy."

His teeth gritted, Dr. Xylos says, "I don't know what you're pulling here. When I release anyone, as my patient, they go directly where I assign them, until higher orders come down. In this case that means the Holding Company, not the MP holding station. Who misunderstood that directive?"

"We're gonna take them over Doctor," Macree says. "With the morning shift. We do things by the numbers here, and that means no troop movements until we've done the proper paperwork."

Dr. Xylos, who also happens to be a lieutenant colonel, pins Macree with a glare that he can't handle, for even a second. Dr. Xylos says, "I'm learning how you do things here."

"We treat soldiers like men here, Colonel. And a soldier deserves the respect to be able to take a little static." He gets no reaction and sees the officer doesn't want to intercede in any way, silently conceding that he was the one who made a procedural error by not delivering the prisoners, directly. "Ah, hell, Owens, march them over to the Suicide Squad. Sorry boys, maybe we'll get to have some recreation again; someday soon."

As they're walking out, Dr. Xylos addresses our three, "Incidentally, gentlemen. Where do you think Jameson is at this time?"

Our three look at each other, totally befuddled. Landers takes the initiative to speak, "Not with us. He did not leave with us."

"I can tell by your reactions that's probably true. This is rather curious though. He certainly left the same night." He says nothing else and leaves.

Specialist Owens tries to get them to march in step, but they are so purposely incompetent at matching his cadence that he soon gives up. Then they start walking so quickly he has trouble keeping up, but won't admit it. They track a mile across the Presidio Fort. When they arrive at the holding company, Owens is sweating and panting. Out of the corners of their eyes, our three share quick smiles, at his discomfort.

"Ought to join the infantry, Specialist, might improve your marching skills," Whistler says.

"Shut up, asshole. Don't think we're through with you yet. You may not find yourselves alive after the next encounter."

Collectively, they decide not to push the point. These barracks, called Montgomery Street Infantry Row, are historic landmarks built in the 1890s for troops returning from the Indian Wars. They are by far the nicest barracks they've ever seen. Five in a row face a wide lawn quad, and lack of fences assure them they're not in lockdown.

Three stories tall, each has tall windows and wide, covered porches along their entire front. Up in the woods, senior officers live in spacious homes. This is a showcase fort in a showcase location. The lush evergreen ridges of the Presidio Park lead up to the Golden Gate Bridge, a half-mile away. The Presidio itself, over near the south end of the bridge, is a thick-walled fort, originally built by the Spanish, in 1776, to guard the entrance to the bay. Before the U.S. took over, in 1846, Mexico ruled here for 25 years. Before all that, the Ohione people and their ancestors farmed and fished the area for perhaps ten thousand of years or more.

Inside, this barracks is plush by infantry standards. It is spacious, with high ceilings, built-in lockers and heavy iron beds, spaced far apart, set up now for about forty men. It even has a combination lobby and game room, with a ping pong table and two televisions, both in use, with worn, but deep and comfortable leather chairs all about. About a dozen men and the cadre, a Specialist 4 and a first lieutenant, sit watching the TV and pay almost no attention to the arrival of our three and Specialist Owens. In the barracks, about twenty men sit or lie on the beds. Owens clears his throat for attention. No one even looks. When a commercial comes on the TV, the Lieutenant stands, looking bored, followed by the Specialist. As Owens looks about to say something the Lieutenant, with a distinct Texas drawl, preempts him, "We see 'em. Good day, Specialist Owens."

Owens looks like he wants to insert his last say of authority over the three. It's clear they've had dealings before and the Lieutenant does not like him at all. Owens does a military turn and marches out. The Lieutenant addresses our three, "Alright, here's the rules. We don't train, we don't exercise, we don't parade, we don't do anything. The only detail here is maintenance of the barracks. All we do here is 'hold' people. Got that?"

"Yes, sir," our three say in reasonable unison.

"Fine. Nobody leaves this building or the immediate lawn square around it without specific permission. When your paper orders come down, you leave. We don't care why you're here, we don't care where you're going. You know why they call this place the 'Suicide Squad'?"

"Uh, well, sort of..." Spandrow starts, but is cut off.

"It isn't because we're an elite attack squadron. Got it? We'd appreciate it, if you are so inclined, go facilitate the Golden Gate. Let the Coast Guard earn their pay. Preferably, with your new orders in your pocket. We don't need the paperwork and particularly we don't need the mess. Got it?"

"Yes, sir," again in unison.

"Fine. We're just passing strangers. You don't mess with us, we don't mess with you. And we're capable of doing it."

He goes back to watching television. Our three pick beds together. Just walking through the barracks they've already caught the eerie boredom of this place, from the expressionless men on their beds. It doesn't help that a PFC next to Spandrow's bed reinforces the emotion, "Welcome to boredom. That's what gets 'em. Sucked down into the mud of gray; nowhere boredom. These days, it gets a couple very month." Since he shows no expression, they're not sure whether he's being wry or macabre. The PFC turns away.

One of the staff from S-2 brings over Spandrow's and Whistler's duffel bags. Whistler loans Landers a set of slightly oversize fatigues. Feeling too dirty to put them on, Landers goes into the latrine, to clean up. Even the latrine is impressive, with white tile everywhere except the ceiling of the main room, and heavy, old Standard fixtures, still with most their chrome.

Back in the barracks, he writes a letter. "Dear Mom and Sis...Well, I'm not very close to Viet Nam, yet. Am stuck in a lavish country club by the Golden Gate Bridge. I've been trying to explain to them why I don't think the war's such a hot idea. They're not showing that they're impressed. I knew there was a lot of people on the outside who didn't think much of the war. I'm finding there's a whole lot on the inside who don't either. People with a lot more to lose. I'm more confused than ever. There's not much to write about what I'm doing, now. Don't even know the address and don't know how long I'll be here. I'll keep in touch...Love, Michael."

About a week passes, with heavy gray weather. Either the mood seems to keep getting edgier or our three just feel that way, in their own time sense. They don't talk much. Each morning, lunch and evening they stand in formation before meals and when orders are read. Few like what they're dealt. Sometimes, whoever gets orders simply gets their duffel bags and marches off to the bus stop on the corner. Sometimes jeeps come by and pick guys up. Other times MPs come and get them. MPs bring new people, almost every day. Twice, Mayborough and Clives drop guys off. Since he's standing in formation Landers can't signal to them. They show no sign that they've spotted him. After formation, they're marched off to a mess hall that's up to standards of the fort in appearances and substantially above normal Army fare. Even though all the military services have their menus made out, years in advance, one mess hall to the next can vary dramatically. There's always room for an artist in a kitchen. Without asking permission, Landers starts running on the sidewalk surrounding the lawn area, to get exercise. This seems to work better than anything to make him feel that he's still alive and, by the end of the week, he's running an hour, twice a day, and also doing multiple sets of push-ups, sit-ups and stretching. Whistler joins him sometimes. Nobody else seems to pay any attention.

Day ten, at sunset formation, Mayborough and Clives pull up in their wagon, but nobody gets out. The unit Lieutenant reads the new orders for the day, "Specialist 4 Whistler, return to original company, Ft. Ord. Whistler shows almost no emotion, until he hears, "Specialist 4 Spandrow, return to original company, Republic of Viet Nam."

Whistler and Landers make eye contact, to silently ask, "What now?" Spandrow barely glances at his two friends, trying to remain calm. His lips start shaking and his eyes twitch. He takes off running, looking straight at the Golden Gate Bridge.

The Lieutenant turns casually to the MPs, and points at Spandrow running towards the trees. Mayborough and Clives get in their wagon, but aren't able to follow him directly on any road. Since they can see Spandrow keep looking at the bridge, Landers and Whistler eye each other, and spontaneously take off after him.

It's a frenetic chase. All three are quick runners, in excellent condition. These two MPs are also very adept at this part of their job. They anticipate where to cut him off, but Spandrow keeps dodging them. At the old Spanish blockade, resembling a small crumbling Coliseum, Spandrow tries to hide. Soon all five of them are dodging through the various floors, doorways and gun emplacements. At one point, Whistler and Clives have him cornered, but Spandrow jumps twenty-five feet onto a slanting ice-plant incline, and slides and tumbles another twenty-five feet. This gives him a fresh head start, as neither want to risk this jump. Mayborough and Clives have determined that Landers and Whistler have the same intentions they do. Tackle this guy.

By the time they all get back on his trail, Spandrow has reached the bridge. Traffic is heavy and Whistler and Landers are making more headway on foot than the MPs in the van. Spandrow just keeps running, showing no intention of getting to the rail, even though he is over water and plenty high enough for a terminal fall. Eventually the MPs get into a clear lane, honking at Whistler and Landers to jump on the front fenders, which they do. Spandrow hasn't been looking behind him as much and when he does look back, the wagon has practically caught him. Now he does dash for a rail, only Landers and Whistler grab both his ankles as he tries to dive over. He kicks and squirms but the clamp him so he's backward and they have his calves grasped firmly over their shoulders, on their chests. They sit down on the inside of the rail, leaving Spandrow bent backward, over the outside of the rail. The MPs arrive and pull him back onto the bridge. Neither Landers nor Whistler will let go, until the MPs have Spandrow handcuffed, hands and feet. Then they all just lie still for a minute, panting.

Eventually, the MPs go to put Spandrow in the wagon. He's mortified and, with head turned down, lightly mutters, "Sorry."

Mayborough locks him in and turns back and sighs in a way that says everything about their day-by-day dramas is pouring over the surreal wall, moving into fully awake nightmare territory. Ducking mention of the situation at hand, because it's too difficult to express, he says to Landers, "Man, you're a lot quicker than last time we saw you."

"He's our friend," Landers said as if a reason would add more sense to the scenario.

"A rare entity, in these parts. Worth keeping. C'mon let's take you back."

Whistler and Landers exchange an expression, wondering how this is going to play out. Whistler says, "Ah, man, you can't ride us all the way off the bridge on the fenders. Can't we walk back? We need the unwinding."

Now Mayborough and Clives exchange a look. They shrug, like there doesn't seem to be any logic left in the world, so what would it matter. Mayborough says, "Alright. You know we're cuttin' you a lot of slack. Don't get creative on us." They get in their wagon and drive off.

Silently, Landers and Whistler walk back towards the Presidio side of the bridge. After a while, Whistler says, "Shit, man, you know I've said I didn't think he should have not finished his Nam time. Just for his own state of mind, later on. Not that it's for me to say that. But now, how could they send him back, when he's so goddamn short. Twenty-five days. They can barely process him in and get him out to his company for a week or so, before he needs at least five days to get out."

"Starts to add more confirmation to the theory that if the war serves for nothing else, it's a quick trial by incinerator for the undesirables."

"Yeah, undesirables...Fucking don't go, you're undesirable. Come back, you're more undesirable." Whistler starts lagging behind, running on in a tone of voice that he's talking to himself and doesn't want to be interrupted. "Black vet, the most undesirable yet. Just like the swim team. Can't float, man, you can't cut it. But I can dive. I can float through the air. Only guy in the league could do a clean two-and-a-half pike. Almost had the highest score at the state championships, my junior year, except for one guy from Akron did a three and a half tuck; with no style whatsoever. Man, I could've learned, they'd given me a coach. Maybe even a three-and-a-half pike...maybe even a four and a half." His voice gets softer and farther from Landers.

Landers looks ahead, at the MPs who have stopped at the end of the bridge. They start point and waving. Landers turns around and sees the Whistler is at the rail, climbing. He calls, "Whistler, what the hell..."

"Yeah, man, maybe even a five and a half," Whistler says, trancelike, holding his hands out and up on his toes, in a perfect dive preparation stance. And he dives. A perfect pike, spinning down and down and down. Landers runs to the rail, but doesn't even see the final fifty feet of the fall. He sees the splash though. And waits and waits. Being an avid cliff driver, he's considering if he can jump in to help. But Whistler doesn't come back up. The ever-raging current under the bridge is so strong he knows he could never find him underwater. As surreal as the last half-hour has been, now Landers just blasts clear out of body, to incomprehensive emotional shock. He closes his eyes even and shakes his head. Opening them again, it's not going away. Lost for any semblance of grounding to anything, he starts running fifty yards towards the Sausalito side of the bridge. Looking up, the golden hills just disorient him. He stops and runs back towards the San Francisco skyline.

The MPs aren't sure what to do and Landers almost seems to forget they're there, until he's about five yards from them. He stops.

"C'mon with us. You can sit up front," Mayborough says.

Numb, Landers tries to compute where this will lead. "No," he says. "Only thing I gotta do right now is keep moving. I can't go back to that pit. Not right now." Clives starts walking towards him, but Landers takes off across the bridge, through the heavy traffic, until he's over on the sidewalk on the other side. He looks across at the MPs but neither he nor they even make any physical signal. He runs off into the woods. Not in a position to chase after him on foot, nor able to follow in the van without some exotic lane and island jumping, the MPs don't bother. For the moment, they don't feel like doing anything. Like all law-enforcement officers, the calls they hate the most are emotional trauma scenes. Mayborough just walks over to the rail, looking back at where Whistler might miraculously pop up. Clives leans on the fender, looking blankly out to sea.

For an hour, Landers runs. For four hours he walks. He goes into a all-night, you-name-it store and buys a small ratchet wrench and a grabbing tool. Not even with a real plan or vision, he just feels like he has to be somewhere safe to sleep, and can only think of the S-2 Ward. He sneaks back into the Presidio. Doing a pressure chimney-walk up the chute on the backside of the building is harder than it was to get down, but he does make it, his muscles so strained they're twitching. Hanging from the drainpipe, like Spandrow did, the wrench makes it much faster to get the bolts for the window grating undone, only he does notice there are only three, instead of the four Spandrow removed and replaced. He swings in and replaces the outside bolts, using the grabbing tool and wrench in unison. Both tools he drops in an overhead water closet reservoir. Carefully, he checks out the scene in the barracks. There's an empty bed near the latrine, so he works his way over to it on his hands and knees, out of sight of any of the staff that might chance to look his way. Pulling the blanket over his head, he curls up into a cocoon and immediately passes into deep, dreamless sleep.

When he wakens to the sound of shuffling, he's again disoriented. Somehow, during the night, he's removed his fatigue shirt. When he looks down at it, on the floor, all he sees is Whistler's name patch. Anger becomes his sole emotion. Not wanting to wear Whistler's pants, either, he takes them off and throws them into a corner. In his boxer shorts and T-shirt, he joins the other men in the line to get their pills. Once the orderlies spot him, they quickly recruit help and escort him towards the security offices. He demands to see Dr. Xylos but they tell him he's been discharged, they're not going to have anything to do with him. As they pass the hall to Dr. Xylos' office, Landers tries to shake loose.

Right then, Dr. Xylos steps out of his office, "What's going on here?"

"He snuck back in, claims he never left. We're turning him over to the MPs.

"Dr. Xylos, I have to talk to you."

As if protecting Dr. Xylos, one of the orderlies decrees, "Once you're discharged, it takes someone else to readmit you."

"But it's not for me. It's for...it's for Whistler...and Spandrow...and me."

Dr. Xylos simply nods for Landers to come on. The attendants let Landers go, but stay close behind him as he walks by Dr. Xylos, who holds the door open. One of the orderlies waits outside, as the others walk off.

Dr. Xylos sits at his desk, with his hand indicates for Landers to sit down. Xylos just stares out the window for a bit, then finally says, "I'm sorry. I wasn't thinking. Of course we can talk. I heard about Whistler. That was a hard one."

"It was just, just that I, we, were so concerned about Spandrow. He was the suicidal one."

"I wasn't unduly worried about Spandrow. Except for that he'd been through a whole lot of combat too; that unpredictable factor. That guy qualifies as a hero in any book. For five months straight, he stayed back with his unit and didn't take his R&R because they'd just been in serious firefights and were way down in numbers. He couldn't leave his friends so undermanned. With five weeks left to go, somebody picks up his case and demands he go, that day. Spandrow wanted to go to Bangkok, but the only plane was to Hawaii. There's another idiotic thing the Army does that gets a lot of people sent here. Going straight from combat, to watch average Americans, oblivious in paradise, then let them try to reconcile going back to Nam with any sense of reason. Letting married men see their wives and kids is asking for lunacy. Actually, Spandrow handles stress well. Not in normal ways, but it works for him. He projects himself right on out of it. He's brilliant at it and knows how and when to pull himself back. He's an actor as much as he is a musician. Mainly, he's a drama junkie."

"That was what Whistler called him, too."

"I know. He introduced me to the phrase. It seems to be in general usage, all of a sudden. It's more definitive than prima donna."

"Man, Whistler. There was nothing I could do. He just got up on the rail...and...shit."

"How would you know? He had no patterns of discernible psychosis. Yes, he got depressed. Around here? That of itself is hardly a sign of problems. This can be one very depressing place, and clearly that Suicide Squad is no better. Humans must incur depression for a reason, or heredity would have wiped it out twenty thousand years ago. That we get depressed because something isn't working in our lives, and most learn to work their way through it, is one of nature's most sophisticated survival-skill gifts. Feel lost, recognize why, correct, adjust and move on. That's a healthy depression cycle. Other cycles might get you in here. Whistler, the only reason he was sent here – and there are people sent here all the time by personnel who simply want a clean desk – is that he had a streak of conscience about possibly being sent to fight American civilians, against the war. I'm appalled they'd even think to send recent combat troops to do it. From both ends of the spectrum. Don't they deserve a break from confrontation? And who knows how these line troops are cross-wired? Modern explosives have ten to twenty times the shock wave speed of even Korean War explosives. Just the bullet from the basic combat rifle sends Mach 3 shock waves pulsing, inches from their ear. In horrendous numbers. Thinking about the number of shocks they take, that all of them don't have shell shock gives me a drastically higher respect for how resilient the human being is. And Whistler's record showed he'd been through about as much combat as anyone in the war, in one condensed year, to date. With the possible exception of Jameson. Who we'll get to in a moment."

"Whistler never said anything about that. Neither did Spandrow, for that matter. If they talked about it at all, they mostly just swapped stories about partying. Smoking pot, strolling through paradise or playing cards in a bunker. Just said, they'd always been lucky."

"That, there, is a trigger word I look for, for those who've been in the really bad stuff. 'We were pretty lucky', is one degree. 'I was lucky', can mean much worse. When they step away from it a few years, then maybe we'll hear how much 'luck' they actually had."

"Whistler was so strong, in every way. So basic. Maybe more aware of himself and the broad scale of everything than anyone I ever met."

"I know. I thought that about him too. We had many, very interesting conversations. About him, about people here, about you."

"Hm, I didn't know that."

"He has about the same basic feeling about you as you had about him. Hm, now having said that worries me."

"More than anyone, he convinced me not to go. And tried to bolster me to be able to take all the hits of being called a coward. He and a chance meeting with an older man on a plane, who'd also been through a lot of battles. His advice was if I sincerely thought my values were compromised, 'Don't go easy.' And he seemed as noble as any person as I've ever met. There's nothing you can do to stop any of it, is there? I can't even justify asking you to help me."

"I know. Though there's no word root connection, Hippocratic Oath is just too close a word to hypocrite. To not be a hypocrite, I examine myself every day, to see if I'm not playing favorites, even with myself. My diagnosis, you're sane, by every medical definition. Wanting to go to this goddamn war is insane, if one is minimally educated or willing to think for oneself. You know that recent book, 'Catch Twenty-Two'".

"Yeah, I read it. And I've thought a lot about it. It's this tragic game with exclusionary rules that preclude any chance of winning; or escaping. The logic 'Catch' here being that being able to recognize the insanity of this war certifies you as being qualified to get sent out to kill."

"Right. You're a perfect case. Wait ten years from now; a lot of those who altered their whole life philosophy will say they wished they'd gone and would have, except for a glitch. There'll be lots of those who went who'll say they wish they'd have found a way out. I'll bet, twenty years down the road, you'll hardly find anyone who thinks this war was a good idea. Even amongst those adamantly for war, now, most will then tell you how crazy it all was. And probably very few will accept any responsibility for it. By then there might even be a fresh generation ready to blast away. That's the way sanity works. Now, Jameson. He didn't leave with you?"

"Hell no. Would you want to go roaming with that guy? Why, is he missing?"

"Disappeared the same night you did."

"Wow. I wonder, Spandrow said he thought he saw someone in S-2 clothes at a dance. I kind of think Whistler was kind of spooked we were being followed too. They both sloughed it off, though. Or maybe they didn't and I didn't pick that up, either. Aw, no, that's too wild that anyone could have kept up with us."

"Well, an experienced jungle vet is usually a pretty good tracker. What was your take on him?"

"First reaction was to run and hide. In the end, I thought he'd kind of adopted me, like a watchdog. Not that I had any idea why, and sure as hell didn't want it. I'm not nearly as trained or as experienced as you, but I've watched enough people flip out. But I don't have any category to put him in."

"Neither do I. When patients are in that category of 'hearing' voices in their heads, I feel almost helpless. I've made progress with some, but it's rare. Yet they usually have lots of other patterns recognizable as symptoms of that brand of psychosis. Psychosis meaning generally that reactions to events are conceived somewhere in mind patterns unrelated to the specific stimulus. His weren't. He's reactive, on short notice but, given time alone, he clearly thinks things out. Other than about what he thinks he's 'hearing', he is extremely observant and made clear evaluations."

"I was getting to that same evaluation. I'll admit to being curious as to what makes people tick but, in his case, I didn't particularly want to push it."

"I don't blame you. How'd you get out, anyway? If that doesn't offend your sense of not wanting to be a snitch."

"Not really. Whom would I be snitching on; myself, for sneaking back in? That grate over the bathroom windows can be unbolted from the inside by a properly bent tool. Spandrow figured it out. You know, though, when I came back in, there were only three bolts. There had been four, before. That must how Jameson did it, too."

"Well, he's still out there. He was one I didn't mind keeping in here, for awhile. Though I didn't expect him to stay. He clearly has the capacity to rationalize his position...some of the time. First place, he has nearly every combat award there is, five times over. He was the only survivor in his unit, in two firefights. One was the first

201

two weeks he was there, one was the week before he was due to come back. On that one he wandered out of the jungle, weeks later, babbling. Actually, there was one other survivor of that one. Whom Jameson won't talk about, at all."

"Whew. Man, you go through this all the time, don't you?"

"No, they go through it."

"Well, I'm leaving here, huh. Do you still have my clothes? I'm not wearing Whistler's fatigues. Accepting that the totally bizarre is highly expectable, anymore, seems to be something to learn from it all. What now?"

"Unfortunately, we have to hand you over to the MPs. Resist saying anything vaguely confrontational to them. You're not on my orders, even now, because you're not even technically here. Normal course would be for you to get transferred to a holding company over in Oakland. Which isn't normally as macabre as the one you were just in. It's mostly for people with genuine paperwork glitches unrelated to their own extracurricular activities."

"All a wasted effort, I wished I'd never done any of this."

"No you don't, and no it wasn't. Somebody has to stir the system if it's not working up to full reasoning power. 'Don't go easy' seems like sound advice. What I will do is write, with total honesty, that you are sincere and conscientious and would prefer to be a good soldier under sane circumstances; which does not mean being a robot."

"I guess there's an irony around here somewhere. Thank you."

"Thanks for coming back to talk. I need to be reinforced, as often as possible, that other so-called sane eyes see this place somewhat like I do. Sorting out the truly ill from the truly exotic is difficult at best. In these times, sometimes you just have to throw the manual out the window."

Under his breath, Landers muses, "Lot of books flying out windows these days." Whether he heard it or not, Dr. Xylos nods acknowledgment and shakes his hand. Landers is passed back through channels. He gets his own corduroys, T-shirt and sweater back. The MPs pick him up at the door. He hasn't seen these guys before and they make no effort to converse with him. They do take him straight to Macree's holding station. Saying nothing to the other MPs, who don't seem to want to deal with him in any way, Macree takes charge of Landers. Spec-4 Owens is at his own desk. There are now four other soldiers there, in two cells. After a purposeful delay, Macree finally looks at Landers, "Well, well, well. Look who's dropped back in again. Maybe we can make you feel more at home this time, so you can stay longer. In an individual cell, out of sight of everyone." Macree opens the door of a cell isolated from the others and shoves Landers in. Only thing in the cell is a toilet. "So, you think you're kind of a rocking rebel, huh. Let's see how strong you are. Put your arms out on the wall." He means for Landers to put them on the wall across from the toilet, straddling it. "Now keep stepping back. Small steps." Landers starts slow backing up, increasing the angle. With his hard rubber prod, Macree keeps tapping his toes back farther. Landers is starting to strain. "Hold on here, for a minute. I gotta take a leak." Which he does, standing behind Landers, aimed between his legs and about a foot below his head. "There, now, I can concentrate on the task at hand. Boy, you're shaking. Getting weak? Maybe a year in Nam in the infantry would really get you shape, huh, boy."

Landers, for all that he has against the war and doesn't like about any sense of glorifying it, has a sense of respect and camaraderie with the infantry troops he's been in training with for months. This triggers an unwise response, "At least the infantry will take me. You'd never make it, Fatboy."

Macree is instantly bright red and glaring. He kicks out Landers legs, causing him to fall and land full weight on his cheek, on the rim of the toilet. Macree shoves him down into the corner with his boot and handcuffs him. His sadistic smile replaces his glare, "A smart ass. Yeah, I like a smart-ass. Builds my resolve." He calls to Spec 4 Owens, "Seems about time you oughta go force march the other scum around the building a few times."

As Spec 4 Owens clears the building, Macree goes into his desk and comes back with a rope and a pulley. He hangs the pulley on a high bar and threads the rope through it, tying one end around Lander's ankles. Roughly, he hoists him, until he's suspended upside-down, over the toilet. He says, "You hippies like swingin' don't you. How you like my swing?"

"It isn't all that groovy," Landers says, too angry to think.

"Not groovy, huh? Let's see. Got any allergies? Salt, maybe?" He pulls out a packet of salt, pours it into his hand, holds one of Landers' eyes open and blows it in.

In wincing and squirming Landers starts spinning wildly. Macree stops him by shoving him against the wall. "Maybe you're not allergic to salt. I didn't hear any sneezing. Pepper maybe. He pries open Landers' other eye and blows a full packet of pepper in his face. Now, Landers is just blinking furiously and shaking his head, trying to somehow clear the pain. Macree says, "Pepper makes you thirsty, huh. Maybe you need to wash up and have a drink. Then we'll try the cayenne." He pours some liquid lye soap into the toilet and, with the rope, dunks Landers into the toilet a few times.

Sputtering and choking, Landers finally gets his breath enough to say, "Where the hell do you come from, Macree? You don't belong in the army, not the U.S. Army."

"Me? Who you talking about, yellow, fuckin' commie faggot. You and all your coward buddies? Too bad about the nigger, huh. Quite a diver I hear...until his final 'black flop'." He roars at his joke. Landers spits, surprised for a second even that it hits Macree in the mouth, where he'd aimed. Macree starts spinning Landers and striking him all over, with his prod.

This isn't going well, Landers is well aware, but won't give in. "You hit like a little girl. A weak one at that. Average day surfing you get more lumps than this. Can't leave any blood or bruises, can you? How about we meet outside some time? You get the first couple swings. Bring your club. 'Cept we both know you'd never show. You wouldn't hold up to a marshmallow if you had a blow torch."

Macree says, "Yeah, faggot, you think you're so smart. Smart of you to establish a record of being an escape artist. Every couple weeks, we get someone who tries to escape and maybe fights back. We're obliged to take serious means to protect ourselves. Looks like we need some protection from you." He starts hitting a whole lot harder. Even he knows he can only take it so far, and stops when he sees a large contusion on Landers' forehead burst open and start bleeding. While it's dripping he lets it fall in the toilet. As it slows down, he lets Landers down and removes his rig but leaves the handcuffs on. "Just keep it up. Spec 4 Owens would love to come in and take a few licks. And he might not have enough common sense when to stop." Landers opts to shut up at this point. Macree walks out and slams the door shut and says, "And that's all just a warm-up, asshole. Wait 'til we get you up in the real stockade. Be the last place you'll ever see. Lots of suicides up there too. I'll see to it."

13

Next morning, Landers sits in the corner of the cell, steadily staring at Macree and Owens. He hasn't slept all night, on purpose. In walk Mayborough and Clives. Mutual hate between the two duos of MPs is evident. Macree starts in, "What the hell you doing here? Things getting too rough over in Oakland for you amateurs? Need a lesson?"

Mayborough ignores this, says, "Private Landers is in our jurisdiction. Our CO would like a written report on why we weren't called to pick him up, yesterday afternoon. Unlock him."

Macree reluctantly unlocks the door. All three men look at Landers, covered with welts, bruises and splatters of blood, still in handcuffs. Macree says, "Yeah, these fucking hippie prisoners. Not so peace and love all the time, you know. Turn your back, they try to jump you and escape. Guess you've seen plenty too, huh?"

"No. I haven't," Mayborough says. "Not even one. And I've never heard of a real MP who can't handle any such situation with more control than this. Your day's coming, Macree. Soon. You're going to spend some time on the other side of those bars before you get bounced out. Maybe you think you've got a quorum between your whiny little Specialist here and couple sick-ass guards up at the stockade, but the whole rest of the MPs are just waiting for you to mess up big; just one time. And I mean the lifers, not us just passing through."

Macree looks about to burst again, but the coward in him is stifled, facing Mayborough's glare that could freeze lava. He turns away, and stomps out. Clives goes to help Landers up, but he bounces up on his own, for effect, shrugging off the injuries, which really aren't any worse than a bad day surfing. All three glare at Spec 4 Owens, who can't take a second of it and turns away. Mayborough grabs his shoulder and spins him around, to sign the form for Landers' transfer.

They drive back across the Bay Bridge, with Mayborough in the back, cleaning up Landers. Mayborough says, "That psycho-pathetic sewer rot. He always gots an excuse. Always gets away with it. What got him going, this time?"

With a slight smile, Landers says, "Guess I just never learned to take well to bullies. Especially of the sadistic coward kind."

Clives says, "He's definitely out for your ass, and he don't forget. Whatever you do, stay clean, now, because you don't want to end up in that stockade. There's dudes been in there swear he's murdered people, or pushed them to aided suicide."

"Soon enough his Karma wheel will run him over on its way down. You don't suppose you could sucker him to try to pull an arrest down in Ocean Beach, do you? I'll round up some surfers. He'd look good in an inner tube in the Wedge shorebreak."

"Man, you are truly not the standard breed of nut, are you. Maybe they should have kept you in the Fruit Bowl."

"I guess I liked it there too much. Gets you expelled."

"People do like it in there, huh?"

"Most of them are just in there because they care...too much. You know, complete with a conscience. It's nice to be with your own kind, sometimes."

"Damn, we're gonna have to wash your brain, fast. Clives, my man, would you pass us the necessary accoutrements for a quick scrub." Clives hands a lit joint back through the security grate. Mayborough says, "First off, we gotta point out what you gotta care and about what you don't. Without drawing flak. Blatant honesty isn't the only path up the mountain. This is wartime, man, you just don't seem to grasp that. You ever hear of tactics?"

Landers takes a hit off the joint and smiles, "You guys may not know it, but there's a lot of guys stuck in the swamp who've elevated you to angel status."

"Yeah? Hm. Now if I could only sprout wings and fly back to New York. I'm so over all this shit, some days, I feel my whole gut is going to implode." He talks a long lit, closes his eyes and holds it as long as he can.

Taking a few wrong turns to drag out the ride, eventually they deliver Landers back to the Oakland Departure Center. 1st Lt. Pearson, the same officer they'd brought Landers to after the Berkeley LSD pickup, takes charge of Landers. As the MPs walk off, Pearson carefully eyes Lander's bruises.

"It wasn't them," Landers says.

"I know that. Some weeds are harder to yank than others. Well, in your few short weeks in our little human ping-pong game, you've managed to reach celebrity status. There's a whole lineup of people who can't wait to yell at you. But I'll spot you a day in the bunk."

"Thanks. I appreciate the favor," Landers says.

"Wasn't a favor. It's just the way I see it should be done. I don't see that you deserve to be prime target for people who just want to see a red bulls-eye anywhere they look. Your file makes interesting reading. I liked what Dr. Xylos wrote in it, and he's the best thing happening on that side of the Bay."

"I'm surprised you looked," Landers said.

"Yeah, you're right in assuming I don't look in many files. Sometimes I just get curious. Knowing what's likely to happen to so many of the thousands of people that pass through here monthly doesn't induce me to want to learn much. I did a year in a line company in Nam. It's not a glorious situation."

"How come you don't wear your CIB?"

"It causes conversations."

Landers laughs, "Yeah, conversations. I've been way over-conversed of late. One irony that keeps whacking me, though, is I hate the war but the people I like best, in the Army, are the vets. Particularly the combat vets."

"Infantry priorities are clear only when you're fighting. Everything else is foggy. The rest of the Army is about protecting their own asses and they tend to take control when there's no fighting going on, so best we take care of our own, everywhere."

"I'll log that. And I'll try not to cause you any trouble."

"I won't take it personal if you do. Unless it's aimed my way. I'm not going to be on your case here; babysitting isn't my calling.

Just make formations in the morning and show up for your appointments. I don't cover for AWOLs. I'll take a dead drunk in formation over a coward who won't even show up. Go grab a bunk in that barracks, over there. I recommend the back of the top floor."

Finding himself suddenly all alone on his own recognizance gives Landers an odd sense of serenity that he opts to not diagnose. Totally enervated from everything that has happened since the last time he slept, he feels himself drifting into a sleep trance just walking to the barracks. He hardly notices a clerk who hands him bedding and a towel, looking only for a bed. Kicking off his shoes and socks he just wraps the blanket around him and curls up in a cocoon. He sleeps all day until his hunger finally wakes him. He follows some soldiers to the mess hall for dinner. After dinner, he cleans up, washes his socks and underwear in the latrine and goes right back to bed.

Next morning, he's woken by a private who walks through the barracks and shakes each bunk. In the latrine, he borrows some soap and a razor and cleans up. After breakfast, in a large mess hall with all the other troops getting ready to be shipped out, there's a formation of about fifty men outside his barracks. At roll call, the sergeant first class in charge marches up to right in front of Landers, who snaps to attention. The sergeant barks, "Just what the hell are you doing?"

"Standing at attention, Sergeant."

"Not dressed like that you're not, not in my formation."

"My duffel bag disappeared. That's in my file."

"We'll see. To me you look like living proof that all pussies don't come with a pair of tits." He turns and goes back to the head of the formation. Marking off a list, he sends everyone on either a work detail or an appointment. As the others all walk off, Landers is the only one left. The sergeant walks to right in front of Landers, who snaps to attention again. "Why don't you just stand there at attention, until someone tells you not to. You're sure as hell not worthy to get assigned a detail in my unit."

When the sergeant is out of sight, Landers softly orders himself, "At ease, soldier." For a while, he just stands. He doesn't know how literally the sergeant was likely to take his position and he truly does not want to get in any type of trouble, but his normal low-threshold of boredom is stirring. Just to be moving, he starts giving himself drill commands, and marches himself all over the formation area.

After about an hour, a private approaches. Landers orders himself back to attention. The private walks up to him and says, with no particular judgment, "Where in the demento universe did you ever come from? Here, take this paper and go report to CID. It's the farthest building to the north."

Walking across the base, Landers finds a small sign saying Criminal Investigation Division on the back door of a generic office building. Inside, Landers is directed by a civilian secretary, a middle-age woman, to an officer down the hall. Without a word the secretary's facial expression tells Landers that her boss is not likely to make her short list for Christmas dinner. Behind a desk is a thin-shouldered man with no apparent muscle tone, whose puckered expression probably makes him think he looks like a pit bull but his soft jowls makes him come across more as an attack chipmunk. His built-in whine completes him, "Well, you've been having quite a bit of fun on Army time, haven't you, Landers?"

"We must have different concepts of fun, sir."

"Right. And it's time to pay the fiddler. What exactly is it you want?"

"Exactly? Or just reasonably? Reasonable would be reassignment, any assignment, not in the Republic of Viet Nam. Ideally, I'd prefer a discharge, anything but dishonorable."

"Leave it to me, you'd never get discharged at all. We've got places for wimps like you."

"Like the Presidio stockade? That's your torture branch, huh? Is that your idea of fun?"

"Boy, don't get smart with me. What do you expect the Army to do about your ignoring your orders to go to Viet Nam?"

"I expect them to lock me up, but in Leavenworth Federal Prison or such; not an under-regulated way station. I'm surprised it's taking this long."

"That's what the CID is for. We've got enough offenses here to add up to twenty-four years. How old are you?"

Though not an unexpected tactic – he had heard plenty of stories, in the last few weeks, of guys blindsided with astounding figures of prison time that they had supposedly accrued – having this said to him is a scalding stake. Having had time to consider his turn, plus having discussed the parameters with fellow Archipelago denizens, he applies loose logic. First off, nothing is going to happen in this meeting that would add time, if he behaves. He knows there is actuality very little he could be charged with, other than ultimately refusing his orders to Viet Nam. The LSD entry and subsequent escape from S-2, maybe, but he had heard enough stories drifting back through the grapevine that "patients" were rarely, if ever, charged for events immediately connected to their observation period. Still, the stake singed. What the old man on the plane had told him gave him the most solace, "First day you show up on the front line, everything is forgiven." Lingering uncertainty about where he was actually going diluted the effectiveness of this mantra. The "don't go easy" charm at least gave him a banner to fight for. He answers, "Twenty one."

During a three-hour session the officer asks detailed questions about everything he can think of that would connect Landers to some communist, terrorist or criminal group. There is nothing at all in Lander's past or present that fits the man's desire to find a subversive or sinister thread. He asks questions about Spandrow, Whistler and Jameson. Landers says nothing but how much he respects them as individuals and as war heroes, however, not addressing his concerns regarding Jameson's vagaries. For all his shrillness and petty personality, the CID officer is very thorough and covers most of the questions that Landers might have asked himself, had he the assignment to define how he had arrived at his position. By the end, the officer even seems to lose any animosity towards Landers, perhaps surprised that he seems to make a concerted effort to give a complete and honest answer to every question. He doesn't ask for the names of Katrina or any other individuals encountered on his various visits to Berkeley. That could have tipped Landers off, but it doesn't. He lies that he had bought the LSD from a random street dealer on Telegraph Avenue and that he was astounded and terrified by how powerful it was. As the officer keeps rephrasing his question on this, Landers creatively asserts that it was actually the LSD that raised his consciousness, to see so clearly how morally despicable the war is. The officer asks how he feels about betraying his friends and family. Landers states that going to the war might be traitorous to them since, in his intuitive poll of most everybody who matters in his life, those against the war overwhelmingly outnumber those in favor. This is true.

After this session, he walks back to the barracks, feeling more drained than he thought he should. Talking about his feelings about deeper issues was not a direction he often took because he knew, once started, he'd just keep pushing his own questions and answers until he had pinned down the truth of the immediate subject, as best he could. At the barracks he lays on the bunk and falls asleep, missing lunch. Coming back from the lunch mess, other soldiers in the barracks awake him. They're all in fatigues.

The guy in the next bunk, compulsively loquacious, informs Lander's he's been there six weeks, which gives him senior status. He says almost all of them are there only because some part of their files or orders are not in order. Since there was a standing rule that if one male, potential breadwinner, from a family was already in a combat unit, then any other male assigned to a combat unit would have to wait, for him to come home. There are a dozen guys in this category. This limbo could be a gut-wrencher for the guys who have no desire to go, which was almost everybody. He says, "There ain't no real rules here, when you're off duty. Nobody's ever heard of a bed check. Just make the morning formation and complete any details they give you. Most details are over by lunch, anyway. After that, it's free time. Best duty in the whole US of Army. Technically, you leave the base you should breeze it with the OD but nobody does and nobody cares. They're so buried in paperwork, the last thing they want is a sideshow. Now here's the prime treat about being on hold; since they can't pay you until you get to your destination, you can draw fifteen dollars advance, every single day. Which I'm about to do. Want to join the parade."

In that he hasn't any money in his pocket, this has an appeal. At the quartermaster, all it takes is his holdover orders and ID card and he collects a crisp ten and a five. Not ready to test his apparent freedom, he hangs around the base, buying some toilet supplies, shoots some pool and has a beer in the base pub, which is practically empty. Because the word is so near in his memory, he chances across a tattered paperback of "The Gulag Archipelago", by Yevtushenko, in the USO club, then goes back to the barracks, to read. In four hours he finishes the book. The correlation of feeling like a political prisoner is certainly there, and he identifies about how the protagonist keeps his spirit mobile by being competitive to do more, better work than anyone else. How civilians would manage to get in the prisons for political crimes in America hasn't happened to anyone he knows but he's heard rumors. Plus, he's realizing that bureaucrats, particularly in wartime, can drastically alter lives, with a simple piece of paper. In the newspapers are plenty of stories of demonstrators being locked up and underground activists being held for terrorist crimes, with no definitive evidence or charges. In none of the cases does he have enough information to see civil rights are being betrayed but – though 6 months before he'd thought it impossible in America – he's coming to not doubt that's the case. Feeling so ineffective in affecting his own fate doesn't make him feel reassured that justice is available in equal doses to everyone. Still, he does think he's the one who's most responsible for his present situation. Besides, he's heard guys tell stories that seem a lot more unfair than his. With a modicum of foresight, he probably could have been able to stay in school. Yet, given the more and more guys he sees with nowhere to hide, the unfairness of why students should be protected weighs on his conscience. The majority of them had a hand up in the first place, to get them into college, especially the good ones, not that most didn't deserve to be in college. Many worked very hard and paid most or all of their own way, as he had. Though the scholarships helped considerably it was hard work in high school that earned them. He has worked at one job or another since he became a paperboy at age 9. Most of his wondering leads eventually to the question that if a few more of the children of elite were really in harm's way, how much longer could this stalemate war go on. The most adamantly pro-war seem mostly those with their own family protected; and/or the potentiality to make money off the war. Lonely is what it all makes him feel; more isolated every day.

Next day, at formation, he receives orders to go be interviewed by the CIA. In a nondescript building, actually across the street from the base's boundaries, he is directed into the office of a very sturdy man, looking bored as he peruses some papers, which Landers recognizes as his file. For a full minute he looks at Landers, then finally says, "In my day, we were proud to go fight for our country."

"The Viet Nam non-declared war isn't exactly fighting for our country."

"Yeah? Wait'll the communists take over. Then they'll be a puppet of China."

"Weren't the first of the what's now called Vietnamese people originally part of a political rebel clan, which left China, being somewhat out of favor with the dynasty of the day, a couple thousand years ago. Seems they've been holding off China ever since. China is backing the North but it seems they've long ago determined trying to rule down there is not worth the trouble."

"So what about the Russians? That's who's really running the show."

"I suspect if Russia tried to permanently move in, the Vietnamese would make them as unwelcome as they're making us. They'd probably come to us for backing. Which I understand Ho Chi Minh did try to do, fifteen years ago. Maybe he's the guy we should've picked for our side. Did we push him to communism as the only way he could succeed to rid his country of foreign domination?"

"I'm not sure. I suspect he'd have turned out communist, no matter what. Ever hear of the Domino theory? What if holding Viet Nam would be just enough dominoes knocked over for Russia to feel confident enough to attack America?"

"In the big wars, we tend to be on the same side. They have plenty of land. So do we."

"This war is over ideology, not land."

"That would make it a first, wouldn't it."

"What if China and Russia get together and attack America?"

"Given their thousands of miles of contested border, they're much more likely to go war against each other. And if that happened, I wouldn't be surprised if one or the other of them, or both of them, would be kissing our ass. Is this a history lesson?"

"You're here so I can determine if you're part of a larger plot or just another selfish whiner."

"How about just check me as independent, even from the so-called 'organized' independents. Maybe I slip and fall into a political discussion, from time to time, but if tempers rise, I'm gone. And if it gets boring, which is usually pretty quick, I'm gone faster. Incidentally, I thought CIA was supposed to operate overseas."

"We operate where foreign agents might be found. Are you a foreign agent, or have you ever been contacted by a foreign agent, specifically by an agent operating from overseas?"

"I wondered when we'd get to real CIA business. No. I never have been, never will be. In basic values I'm probably on the conservative side, in terms of individual freedom and responsibilities. Which makes it hard for me to be called traitor by perhaps honestly patriotic citizens who see the war as simply black or white. But it doesn't align me much with the self-proclaimed, ultrapatriotic, new conservatives who scream about freedom but are obsessed to control from their own safe clubhouses. They sound a lot more like royalists and Tories to me."

"In that regard, we run in parallel neighborhoods. I don't care much for dragging out political discussions either. Though you never heard me say this, I'm tired of being worked by politicians to push their agenda. Your internal matters with the Army don't interest us at all. Actually, there's no information in your file to stir our interest. Someone merely wants to make sure you are aware we're here, or has a long, long list of places for you to go before someone in the Army has to actually make a decision. They'd prefer that you make the one decision which clears all their desks in one sweep. What you can be assured of, is that there are plenty of people, particularly in the surrounding communities, who, if they make any contact with you, will get you on our lists. Be careful. I'm not unrealistically Red-baiting when I say there are foreign agents and provocateurs, who feel that this is a very good time and place to ply their trade. Don't get caught in the crossfire. You are valid bait for both sides. If you do suspect anyone, you'll come out looking a lot better if you're the one who tips us off, not some of our information sources. I do hope we're on the same side. Good day." He stands and actually shakes Landers' hand.

Walking back to the barracks, Landers feels stronger for the first time in a long time. Not knowing whether the CIA guy might just be playing the good half of the good-cop, bad-cop game, at least he hadn't gotten yelled at. Mostly, he felt that had just talked to someone who realized that this whole war matter was extremely complex, who undoubtedly knew much more than Landers, and wasn't the least bit judgmental that someone could be torn, particularly if their life was potentially at stake.

Back at the barracks he takes a nap, goes to lunch and comes back. The talky guy next to him says, "So, why're you hanging around? I got a girlfriend up in Oakland, so I'm not inviting you to hang with me, but I'll show you where to catch the bus out of Dodge."

Both shower and shave, walk by the quartermaster for their daily fifteen and go stand by a bus stop near the Post Exchange. The private who hands out the morning orders walks right by them, clearly knowing who they are, but doesn't say a thing. The guy with Landers' says, "Amazing cadre, here. No way do they want to know nothing about nobody." The bus picks up them and another twenty soldiers. Going out the gate, Landers' observes that the MPs barely pay attention to anyone coming or going. The other guy gets off in Oakland and Landers rides up to the Berkeley campus.

Guessing where Sarelle might have lunch, he hopes to meet her at an outdoor quad. He spots her, right off, and walks over to her, smiles and casually sits down. She smiles back, but looks wary. He says, "Don't worry, it's strictly a social visit this time. Can I take you to dinner?"

"Sure. You actually have money? With pictures of presidents on it?"

"Yeah, I got a travel expense account. Plus they feed me and give me a bed. I got over all that hassling BS and decided to sign up for the good life."

"Are you really in the Army? The US Army?"

"I truly don't have any idea what the hell I am."

"Ecch, here comes Arnold." Arnold does walk near them, but doesn't look like he'd meant to. He only gives them a cursory nod and walks away.

"You're on the outs?"

"He's seeing Miss Righteous-Galore of 1967, from that committee place where you and your army buddies got grilled. Seems her mouth is much less annoying when it's stuffed with foreign matter; like any ol' guy'll do. I'm not hurting. Not that I dislike Arnold, he's actually rather interesting."

"Yeah, he's alright. At least he's not a blind, obsessed, screaming-meemie like Werner."

"God, I'm getting so drained of this entire moral philosophy drudge. More beer parties and less political parties would suit me fine. Arnold did get a job over at Stanford Law, teaching. Pretty impressive. I wish him well. He's way more sincere than most."

"It is harder to separate the dedicated self-servers just riding a fad from to the truly sincere. The gaps seem to be getting wider...Have you heard from Katrina?"

"Only once, since she left. She's living in a sort of commune that runs that newspaper they're working on, whatever it is. Man, this sure isn't like her."

"No, it isn't, and I'm worried. She thrives on self-discipline and it's hard to envision her in any environment not under her control. And what about all her stuff?"

"I took her apartment. Yeah, I gave up my parents' paycheck and left the sorority. A small price to escape terminal boredom. But which means I dropped a class and started working. Except for the financial stress, it's way better all around."

"I don't have to be back until 7 A.M. Mind if I crash on your couch?"

"No problem. You'll be my first houseguest. You do run the risk of me dragging you into my bed in the middle of the night."

"Danger lurks in every shadow, when you're easily distracted."

"These days, distraction is growing in value, exponentially."

When she leaves, Landers goes to a phone booth and calls Katrina's family home. Given that it's daytime, he so expects her mom to answer the phone that he hasn't even formed a plan to hang up if Arthur answers, which he does. Pausing a second, he asks if Katrina is home.

"Where are you calling from? Aren't you supposed to be in Viet Nam?"

"There's been some glitches. I'm calling from Berkeley. Is she there?

"I don't like glitches. And no she's not here. Katrina isn't welcome in this house anymore. And if you're involved with all the Berkeley anti-war crap, neither are you," at which Arthur hangs up, forcefully.

A swarm of past and present angers churn in his gut. Walking is all he can think to do, crisscrossing all over the campus and high up into the lush Berkeley hills. Looking back across the whole Bay Area, the wispy clouds clinging to a hundred hilltops gives enough of a dose of wonder at nature to at least makes his problems seem less important. In the library he kills more time, finding it enjoyable to pick up random books and articles, with no goal or reason, unlike the days of perpetual structured study. Around dark, he meets Sarelle and they go to dinner in a tiny quiet restaurant of her choice, long on candlelit atmosphere and short on haute cuisine, but it's reasonable and the wine is decent. Any subject with immediate emotional content is ruled inappropriate. After a second bottle, near the fireplace, they're cuddling and happy to pretend they're entitled to a valid moment of romance.

Back at Katrina's apartment, both are a bit uncomfortable being together amongst Katrina's things. Sarelle has totally redecorated one area as her living space, which is where they settle. Her décor suggests someone who wants to be an established, independent adult, very soon. She offers to throw Landers' clothes in with a load of hers, downstairs, which has appeal since, the only time they were washed was in the shower at the Oakland Base. She gives him an oversize terrycloth robe. While the clothes wash and dry, she studies. This is a serious side of Sarelle, new to Landers, that reminds him of Katrina. He wanders around the apartment simply reading the labels of all the books. The range and depth of Katrina's collection is intimidating, especially knowing that she's read almost all of them. After Sarelle is done, she pours them a sherry and lights a joint. He remarks, "This new freedom of yours is showing a side of you I've never seen."

"I've kept a lot of sides buried under living life just like my parents designed it. Of everyone I know, I have the closest thing to a straight, successful, loving, normal family life. Not that I resent it; I have no angst about not having angst. I love my parents. But you have no idea how jealous I was of Colleen and Francina and all those wild surf chicks you used to hang with. They just absolutely didn't care what anybody thought of them; at least not what all us so-called society throbs thought."

"They're not the only girls I hung with. But they can shake the rattle, huh."

"I wanted some of that fun, too. I'm catching up, in my own way. You remember making out at that beach party, in tenth grade?"

"Unh-huh," he says as they lean together, his arm making its way around her shoulder.

"But not much, huh, because I wasn't much of a maker-outer. Do you regret not going farther?"

"No. What there was of it was fine. You said you'd hardly kissed anybody before, and I took you at your word. Which made you a natural wonder. Since it's not exactly my nature to stop, if I manage to get started, I have to just be content knowing it's the girls who call all the shots.

"I'm calling heavier shots these days. You have no idea how many times I've rewritten that night in my fantasies. I don't suppose you have your surf trunks with you, do you?"

"No, and maybe that's part of why I'm feeling so lost. Hm. Guess I've had a couple, ah, scenarios about you, too. It's strange to imagine anyone fantasizes about me."

"Michael, you are so smart in class and in the streets but so naive about what urges girls. Not that I'm planning on curing you. I'm simply planning on making up for lost time." She seductively undoes the top button on her blouse, then undoes another, showing there's no possibility for a bra, underneath. She leans closer so he can have a better look.

"The wonder of these days is that, after I put in so much effort to rev their motors, over all those years, girls – not counting girlfriends – almost always played it so coy. Now, all of a sudden, girls are making all the first moves. Which is nice, but nothing I ever expected."

"First, don't take things for granted, especially me."

"I never would. But I'd take you by consent."

"Back to your previous comment. Two things. Collectively, it's not that we might not have wanted to just grab guys by the hair and drag them off to the cave, before, but the penalty for bad timing was rather severe. The pill detonated that excuse. Throw in that a lot of guys our age are simply being erased from the picture. And the formula is increasing exponentially. So I'm not waiting 'til there's no one left. You're prime real estate. Here's my bid. How about you just keep any counter bids silent." With this, she starts kissing and undressing him, as a young woman who evolved several reincarnations higher up the Kama Sutra chain than that shy fifteen-year-old kiss on the beach. It isn't long before they're naked and entwined with a familiarity and easy desire, which surprises and enraptures them both. His being a bit conservative, to not overplay it, doesn't last long because she's either had plenty of experience or plenty of imagination and proceeds to show him everything she knows and wants nothing less in return. Afterwards, for a long time, they lay awake, just exchanging light kisses from time to time, both glad to talk about nothing that matters in the extraordinarily self-obsessed era they're stuck in.

Next morning, he's off before daybreak, to make sure he gets back in plenty of time. At the formation, he gets orders to go see the FBI. On another border of the fort, he goes into a large trailer. In the first office, with no windows but with a large mirror, an FBI agent greets Landers, overly cordially. He invites Landers to sit, offers him coffee and prepares some for both of them. On the desk, Landers sees a file that he's never seen before, beside his regular file. On it is stamped CONFIDENTIAL. The agent hands him the coffee, "Tell me how you like it. I've started grinding my own. Something I've learned since moving out here from DC. All this cultural regeneration has it's plus sides."

Landers sips the coffee, says "As good as it gets, thanks. And thanks for dispensing with the usual patriotism speech."

"Why bother? You can't argue with a communist. Just buying into that load of crap indicates a mind incapable of reason."

Landers laughs, lightly, "Guess I misread. Except I never thought I was a communist."

"So what are you doing conspiring with communists?"

"I don't know what you're talking about."

"Weren't you at two committee meetings for a Berkeley antiwar group that is nothing but a communist revolutionary cell?"

"Who told you that?"

Now the agent laughs, "Oh, God, maybe I would rather be back chasing hardened criminals. At least they aren't naive enough to ask an FBI agent who his sources are."

"Sources or not, I've never met anybody who described themselves as a communist."

"Well they're sure fighting on the same sides as the communists. We probably don't need last names, so let's just keep it familiar. One-by-one we'll discuss each of these people: Katrina, Jeffrey, Arnold, Sarelle, Werner, Whistler, Spandrow, Jameson, Dr. Xylos," and he goes on to name a bunch more who Landers may have met but isn't sure of their names.

One-by-one, Landers indicates he doubts that any of them are anything but sincere individuals, solid Americans and have no intention of harming the country in any way. He's tempted to unload on Werner's case, but decides to be equally as vague about all of them, to not lead unusual suspicion in any particular direction. This agent becomes more and more condescending and tricky, choosing questions that have no answer that won't lead into a new intelligence direction. Landers either doesn't answer these or asks him to rephrase the question, or rephrases them himself. The agent splays questions in all directions, fishing for a slip up.

Having nothing to hide, Landers answers as directly as he can but still, when it's over, he is drained. He gets back in time for lunch, eats and lies down for a nap. It's almost dark when he wakes up, so he showers, eats a light dinner in the mess hall and catches a bus back up to Berkeley.

At Sarelle's, after a brief greeting hug and kiss, which she seems to want more of than he does, he starts right in on his meeting with the FBI, "I could not believe how much he knew. Either somebody's planting bugs all over town or there's at least one FBI fink running around the neighborhood."

"Am I a suspect?"

"No. But, because he had my mind racing, I tried to match up everything he said with who said what, at what time, in what room, and who else was there. You weren't even at that big meeting down at the committee office with my GI friends and he seemed to know every word that was said there."

"Well, I'm automatically crossing Katrina off the list, as I'm sure you are. And I really doubt it's Jeffrey."

"Me too. They'd have someone more active in the system, though that newspaper thing they're supposedly working on in San Diego makes me nervous. Not having seen it, I can hardly judge it, though. I guess I'm not shocked, but the whole concept of the FBI spying on students tends to piss me off."

"There are some very serious revolutionary words going down around here."

"I know, and so much of it is mindless dogma, just to be in fashion; by being counter-fashion. Which is fine, when you're thirteen. Aw, I don't know, a lot of people really want to make a difference. That aside, I still don't like snitches, especially paid ones."

"Well, somehow I don't think it's Arnold, because he's just too much of a pure scholar. I'm sure he'll do fine in his arguments but I can't even imagine him being tricky enough to be an actual lawyer, in a courtroom. Now, his new girlfriend, the poison posy, she's a nonstop babbler, with non sequiturs as her specialty. And she's at every single meeting or demonstration. After which she screws whoever screamed the loudest. She's a pure-form rally groupie, and has a perfect set up for a mole."

"Werner seems to be everywhere, too."

"But he's such a fanatic. You think so? For sure he doesn't care about anybody but himself; which would fit the profile. Still, wouldn't you think a mole would be more low-key. He's the one who usually starts everything."

"Just one of the things I don't like about him. Man, this is all so shaky. How did we ever get to be sniffing out FBI plants? And what if they plain had that room bugged; which actually does make some sense, unfortunately. That's the easy part. I want to figure out how he knew about the stuff that was said here. You think this place is bugged?"

"I can't and I won't," she says. Needing to study, she ends the discussion, sending Landers out for a few hours. He takes in a movie. When he returns, she's falling asleep. They make love, ardent but without much elaboration. They do manage to climax together, which seems to be the emotional reset they both need. Wrapped up together, with safety in mind, they both go right to sleep.

Next day, his morning appointment is with an Army psychologist, who entertains the thought of some short-term counseling. Landers honestly doesn't feel this would be productive, says, "I don't know if rehabilitation is exactly the process needed. I'm saying that from the Army point of view. My deviancies are philosophical, not psychological or criminal. At least I like to think so."

"So why didn't you declare yourself a conscientious objector?"

"Partially timing, because I didn't get the chance before I had my actual draft notice. Almost day one, I was assigned to infantry. No way back. Plus, in concept, by the Army's definition, I'm not a conscientious objector. It just didn't make sense to lie in order to make a moral point."

"Hardly stops anyone else; particularly these days. Why aren't you a conscientious objector?"

"Well, start with the first few questions on the test. If, say, a Hitler attacked my hometown, sure I'd fight. From every alley, tree or seacliff; whatever it takes. And if some psychopath broke into my house, I wouldn't say, 'Peace, brother, please don't kill my family.' That's not quite how it'd play out. I'm never want to hurt anyone but self defense…assuming I had no choice…and defense of family are plenty valid reason. To me."

"Conscientious objector can be more of a religious distinction."

"In my understanding it's the only current distinction. Which seems unconstitutional that you need to have an established religion to back your own sense of God. If that ever gets to the Supreme Court, I'd like to see their reading. Even by religious definition, I don't think I'd fry in hell, for all eternity, for any of the above defenses. I'm not even vaguely sure if there is or isn't such a thing as hell. I sure don't react well to people who feel they have to power to assign people there. I don't have a direct line to God, so I don't speak for him...or her. And for sure I'm not going to go around telling God, 'You got things wrong.'"

"Do you believe in capital punishment?"

"Why ask?"

"It's on the CO form, later. How did you answer it?"

"Didn't see it. Once I knew I didn't qualify, I didn't read any further. No, is the brief answer. I don't shed tears over murderers, but courts do make mistakes. On purpose, sometimes. Welding a few doors shut and shoving a bowl of gruel under them every day or so wouldn't bother me much. Especially if they carried on their ways in prison. Plus if, in a democracy, the state derives its power from the accumulative rights if individuals, why should the state be able to do what individuals can't? And since so many claim our country is Christian, to the core, how come those most for the death penalty seem to be the ultra-Christians. I'm not specifically Christian but I'm not anti-Christ. Christ was astounding, by any definition, and I won't deny his followers claims but, as I just said, I don't have a direct plug into the Mysteries, so I can't testify, either. For sure, I can't imagine Him going to an execution."

"I'm sorry I brought up the subject. But have you even been to a chaplain?"

"Well, I checked Catholic on my enlistment papers, because my family is Catholic, and I went to Catholic school even. You do realize, there's no such thing as a Catholic conscientious objector. You have to be Quaker or some distinct sect. Plus, be able to prove you spent a lifetime diligently following some tenet. Which I didn't."

"Well, I don't feel like attacking your arguments, because on logic level I don't know where to say you're wrong. This war doesn't breed logical explanations anyway. Dr. Xylos was your psychiatric evaluator; I'm sticking with trying to define your sociological aspects. And I don't see your value system as psychotic. So, like everyone else, I'm going to pass you on down the list. It's probably a list without end. Good luck. Tomorrow you get a chaplain. He's Catholic. Should I request a change?"

"Why? I'm just not a congregator so what does it matter whom I don't congregate with?"

Next day, Landers enters the base chapel, as plain Government Issue as a church could be. Not having been in a church in years, he's uneasy, and still has enough Catholic in him to cross himself when he passes the altar. A lieutenant chaplain walks out from around a corner. Landers asks, "Hello, sir, are you the Catholic chaplain?"

"I'm a Catholic chaplain but I won't officially establish myself here for another week. Why are you here?"

"I'm supposed to meet a chaplain, to discuss the concept of being a Catholic and a consciences objector, at the same time."

"Hm. Ducking that issue, I'll say that you're at the right chapel, but I suspect, for your sake, that you're not going to see the right chaplain. Through that door, there."

Inside the door, Landers encounters a full colonel, with the chaplain's cross on his collar. He orders Landers to sit, then immediately goes on a twenty minute tirade about how Catholicism is the most patriotic thing to be, and lists dozens of sacrifices made by Catholics, back to the year zero. Eventually, Landers' mind wanders off, and he's looking out the window, which enrages the chaplain even more, "Look at me when I talk to you...And you sit there, saying you're afraid to fight for your country. What sort of coward are you?"

"I didn't say I'm afraid to fight for my country. No, that's not true; I'm extremely scared of going to war. However, my background has always been, 'Oh, yeah, you'll ride this wave, or you'll dive off that cliff, or you think I'm afraid of you. Okay, chump, watch this.' Call it macho junk, but being scared has never stopped me before. That's not what's stopping me now. The hardest thing about this whole thing is being called a coward, when I know, relatively speaking anyway, I'm not. But there are plenty of things I'm afraid of."

"I just think you're plain yellow. Do you have any idea how many Catholics have died protecting America? More than any other single religion. Be proud of that. And the Vietnamese murdered 150,000 Catholics between 1822 and 1856. They were martyrs for Christ. And Christ died for you. You should be proud to die for Christ and country."

This is all only stirring up old angers in Landers. His mind had been racing, throughout the whole diatribe, hitting the same blank walls and infinities he'd met back when he was trying to be a good altar boy and make sense of any of it. He'd then soon found memorizing the Mass in Latin as to be a more enjoyable use of time. He'd drifted from being a Catholic in the first place because of the fundamentalists who couldn't carry on a real debate without blindly parroting some phrase from the Bible. Or worse, the Catechism; to say that every possible issue has already been resolved, for all eternity, by some post-Christ scholar. Even in third grade he couldn't see a common spirit between the Catechism and the Testaments. He felt those characters in the Testaments would have been dumbfounded by the unequivocal liturgy that evolved after them. And who deserved to decide the arbitrary cut-off line for prophecy was first century, even for the Jews? Just the fact that Jesus wandered around in the desert trying to find himself seems to make the point that even to Jesus, understanding God was never close to a fixed or clear issue.

Sensing he'll only get blasted for even kiting a debate on liturgy, he simply sees this man as so obsessed with his own voice that Landers could have been anybody in that chair, for any reason, and would have gotten the same tirade. Plus, the more he looks at the man, the more he sees Macree. This pushes him over the limit of not caring who he's facing. At least having enough presence of mind to not punch the chaplain out, Landers decides to simply stand and leave. The chaplain actually pushes him back in the chair, but Landers moves faster the next time, and is already on the way to the door.

The chaplain roars, "Sit down. I'm an Army colonel, Private, don't you forget that, and I speak for God, in this church."

"I'm not challenged by forgetting you're an Army officer. But I do have trouble remembering you're a priest. Look it up under hypocrite."

Now bright red and livid, the chaplain orders, "Sit back down. That's a direct order."

"I'm already doing twenty-four years. I'll enjoy the extra year for disobeying your order. And I'll never be tempted to think your orders came from God." He walks out the door.

At the back of the church, Landers again encounters the lieutenant chaplain, and says, "He's far and away the most militant person I've dealt with."

"I'm sorry. I warned you, but I'm not sure anyone can avoid his attack when he's in that mood. I got it, first day, for not taking the trash out."

"Well, I'm glad you'll be taking over as chaplain in a week. This place needs one."

"We're in agreement, there. Please, don't walk away from Christ, over this."

"I have nothing against Christ. And I hope he has nothing against me. Sometimes I wish he'd come back and straighten out a few Christians though. They're some very scary people swinging their personal crosses."

After a few more days of meeting various Army personnel, he has dinner in the same small restaurant with Sarelle. He hasn't seen her for two days, because they both feel that if they're not headed in the direction of being in love, they shouldn't get stuck in a routine. Still, they do both realize they'd rather be with each other than with anyone else, and sex is the best balm they know to assuage their anxieties. Mostly, he's tried to avoid talking about his trials, with her, but it comes up and he says, "Every single day, almost the same scenario. They scream at me for an hour. Then I get to tell them my life philosophy. I almost feel like elaborating on it, just to kill the boredom. But what point would that make? Sometimes, they actually seem to believe I'm sincere. Even most power abusers want to believe they're sincere. But how am I going to outnumber the Army? Especially in power abusers."

"It'd have worn out my will, long ago. I talked to Arnold. He still might be able to help you. He is willing."

"You know how much I trust that group. I'm not even vaguely interested in being crucified for their cause, especially when they're making themselves the cause."

"He's split from Werner and all those committees. In fact he's not even at Berkeley; he's moved over to Stanford, to start his new job. Regardless of his pompousness, he's always open to setting new legal precedents."

Next day, after two appointments, both with some seemingly unrelated personnel-type officers, Landers heads for Stanford. This takes him back across the Bay Bridge on a bus, then on several local and express buses, down south through San Francisco and an almost unbroken chain of suburban towns and cities, to the small city of Palo Alto, some thirty miles south. The entire area has a distinct tidiness, sense of prosperity and calm distance from the world's worries. Hardly the edginess of most of San Francisco or in the conglomeration of street people, hippies and students that is Berkeley. Old growth trees and shrubs compliment the arcades, covered walkways and pristine scholarly buildings, with professors and students glowing of how select they are to even be here. Sturdy mission style is the overall theme of the corps campus, with red-tile roofs and arch-covered walkways resplendent; it speaks of an older California era than UCLA and even Berkeley. The larger buildings are of a more formal Romanesque variation. There are a certain percentage of students who've bought their way in, but with vaguely respectable scores on their college boards and a few A grades, even if they were bought at private schools. Once in, though, Stanford has a reputation for finding ways to keep you in, particularly if someone wants to donate substantially more than the very costly tuition. All in all, it's on anybody's list as one of the elite few of private universities in America. On sheer scale, Berkeley has equal aggregate brainpower, particularly in its extensive and disparate graduate schools, but at Stanford, at about a third the size, it's more condensed.

Peace symbols and posters do abound, as do long hair and equivalent attire. But there's so much to risk – for the sheer tuition cost and all the rigid standards to get in and stay in – that there's not the recklessness of Berkeley, nor anything near the zaniness of Haight-Asbury. Plus, since money could ease the way in, here, and that great money often runs in conservative circles, there are definitively a much higher percentage of legacy-bred conservatives. Overall, pure intellectualism inside both universities tilted left, politically, though much more so at Berkeley, partially because success in pure academics doesn't demand – even holds in disdain – the avid right-hand allegiance to the all-consuming, capital-driven hierarchy of anyone wanting to mine their success in the corporate universe. Yet Stanford had conservative think-tanks tightly linked with the administration, with considerable clout in the finance committees. Also all those Berkeley physicists and engineers destined to do nuclear research, at perhaps the nation's top labs that UC runs at Lawrence Livermore and Los Alamos, had to walk and talk a tight establishment line. A distinct majority of students here too were against the war – or at least leery of becoming military bait – and many were very aware of the fragile twist of favoritism afforded them over those who'd never be capable, financially or intellectually, of gestating in college past the upper age of the draft, twenty-six.

Finding Arnold's office is easy, but a sign says he won't be around for several hours. Landers goes to the library, always a favorite haunt. This is a good one. He wanders through the stacks, specifically picking out tomes about things that he didn't even know were things. Though it would be in his curious nature to do at least some research on life-relative matters and though he had read some summary history text on Viet Nam, he had avoided details of the people and culture, as if somehow this avoidance would keep him from being drawn in. By fate, he sets down at a table shared with a seriously studious coed, who's amassed a pile of books on Viet Nam. So weary of this constant bombardment of his consciousness, he almost moves on, but she is cute, in a nerdy way, and reminds him of Katrina for her pure intensity, so he asks if he can look at a few. Hardly glimpsing his way, she indicates with her hand to dig in. He opts for those with the most pictures. In training, particularly at Tigerland jungle infantry school at Ft. Polk, Louisiana, he had seen plenty of pictures but most of them were picked for military reasons. All these pictures of tranquil villages, rice fields and market scenes just upset him. No war film he'd ever seen took place in a setting vaguely like these. He flips through pages of an in depth study of the biome. The flora all looks so lush and inviting. The fauna, mostly overscale from what he is used to – centipedes, scorpions, spiders, snakes, bats and tigers – all look so dangerous.

Picking up a book on Montagnards, he turns page after page of people he'd never seen before. GIs along the training route had spoken of the 'Gnards, as they usually call them, with respect for their courage. They remind him of Peruvian and upper Amazon tribal people in stature and adaptation of dress and tools, though with distinctly different features. Their attention to details of style in attire and jewelry, and the elaborate spirit houses of some larger villages, show they are an older culture, with varying degrees of longtime influence from other cultures in the region. Though the French came up with the generic term Montagnard – literally meaning mountain people – they go by older names of Hmong, Myong, Meo, Man and the Dega People. Most of the detailed books are in French, which he can read from his and Katrina's summer jaunts into learning French and Gaelic – which caused him to forever mistrust the French to spell anything. So it isn't clear whether Myong and Hmong, in his skimming, weren't just French attempts to spell the sound, since they don't write themselves. Someone has decided there are 33 major tribes but there are thousands of isolated villages, with a wide range of development, from Bronze Age to significant familiarity with Vietnamese, Chinese, Cambodian and Laotian cultures. Some were converted and educated by French missionaries.

Language is mainly in three groups: Mon Khmer, related to that spoken in Cambodia, Malayo-Polynesian, anciently derived along with the migrations to those places, and Mùong, which faintly resembles Vietnamese.

Their ancient religions are varied but most describe a three-plane spiritual universe with an elaborate pantheon of gods, demi-gods, spirits, and demons. Not only people and animals but also every plant, rock and stream has a spirit within. There is a distinct, direct cultural lineage going back well past clearly defined history, back without a break to the first migrations, perhaps 50,000 years prior. All along, various peoples from the West and North had tried to move in on their land, the earliest eventually matriculating into the tribal system. Some 500 years BC, Chinese of the Han dynasty came to stay and to keep their own culture, which could be called the first of the many wars between the North and the South, of which the current war was just one more chapter. It is these early Chinese invaders who evolved into the distinct culture called Vietnamese and who, ever since, considered the Chinese warily as foreigners who often have designs to conquer them, in turn. Various warlords from the north, including Kubla Khan and the Mongols, have occupied the lowlands and tried to conquer these Vietnamese, only to be rebuffed. Both they and several dynasties of Vietnamese have attempted total genocide on the Myong. For survival, the Myong moved back further and further into the rugged mountains and deep forests, some losing contact with anyone besides their own village. Still, that terrain and those forests are so impenetrable there are thousands of valleys and ridges where humans have never inhabited at all; perhaps never set foot. For an hour, Landers slowly turns the pages of a French anthropological study, with hundreds of photo portraits of villagers. Standing out to him, before reading the captions, are a dozen or so shaman, male and female. He's held rapt, partly for the things they wear, but mostly by those eyes of responsibility and deep understanding. Though fascinated, it all just rattles him further, but oddly he feels weary instead of stirred up; still, his body says move. Besides, the coed doesn't seem even slightly interested in him, so he goes outside. With his back against a massive, impassive Pacific coastal oak, he nods away, instantly slipping into dreams, super-realistic dreams like the floating dreams he'd had in the Fruit Bowl, only this time he's walking, so light-footed he can hardly get traction, but doesn't feel threatened so doesn't care. Everywhere he turns is one of those shaman faces, watching him without greeting or retreating; all as if to observe him, for reasons he doesn't expect to understand.

14

Next new moon, Te stayed awake all night, ready to sneak out as soon as he felt everyone was asleep. However, Mehra was up coughing, most of the night. Eventually, while she was having one of her fits, he used the cover of her noise to get out. She heard him and commanded him to come back, but he ran off anyway.

Since the older boys had told others about Te going down early to the watering place, S'Yu and Jom's secret inner Nie Drong circle discussed what this meant. Because every day of the month had its moon name, they figured out that it was on the new moon that he went. One of the clan elders, who was prone to rambling off on subjects with no correlation to anything, did say maybe Te must be meeting with someone or some *rolung*, who was conspiring with Te to eat all their souls. S'Yu scoffed at this, as it was becoming clear that she wouldn't give the spirits credit for anything, because she couldn't control them. More in demeaning jest than thought out, she threw out that it was more likely The Wanderer had found them. Over the years, citing The Wanderer's influence was a cliché explanation for anyone's unexplained actions. Having said it, this time, she thought how to use this and said, "Perhaps this is how Te started getting so smart and having dreams, all of a sudden. Maybe he's being told things that it is outlawed to speak about. If so, then he's cheated us all out of our spiritual heritage." Automatically seconding anything she said, the others agreed this could be so, but didn't take it any further, mainly because they didn't want to believe there was a *rolung* or stranger down by the watering hole. On purpose, S'Yu didn't push the point, as her evil mind was racing.

Going out into the night by herself, S'Yu called on her two main enforcers, bringing them out of their houses by imitating birdcalls. It was they who beat up Amba's servant and carried out other "accidental" punishments to whomever she was displeased with at the moment. She paid them with copper bracelets and other baubles for their silence, usually those confiscated by deceitful means. Plus always making sure to threaten them that if they ever talked, that she would claim they stole these things and she could have them executed. They were told to follow Te and if he did meet anyone, they were to kill that person as well as Te. They should remove some personal object of that other person, or if nothing was clearly unique, they should take his scalp. Then they should push their bodies down the rapids. One of the men asked how they could justify killing a blessed one. Trying to sound as if she cared, S'Yu said that if Te had been meeting someone, and not told this to the Kra Polie, then he had been committing a grave sin against the Nyang, long before he was selected. This made it a mistake that he was chosen in the first place and his whole selection was probably plotted by a *rolung* or witch, within the village, who was probably Mehra. If this recourse were necessary, she would say that Mehra would have to be killed too, though with an exorcism, before the whole village.

This was inclusion of another plot she had been stewing on because she was afraid of Mehra's new spirit for life. Not only had Mehra adopted a new proclivity of telling stories of the past, sometimes addled by her rambling mind, but some bordered on defiance of the present rules of what could not be told. Most of the villagers were becoming more and more concerned with S'Yu's erratic decrees, though silently or very discretely whispered, even suspecting she was becoming deranged. Dementia was not her problem, even though anger could derange her logic; her real character implosion was she was not intelligent, disciplined nor organized enough to keep track of all her lies.

When the two men following Te reached the top of the trail, they were so scared of the darkness they couldn't even get up the nerve to follow. Whether they believed it or not, they convinced each other that they were on a holy mission, so would be protected. Mostly they were more afraid of S'Yu than they were of the dark. Had it not been a clear night, with some glow from all the stars, they might not even have seen what was waiting for them. Just under the high bank near the top bridge, the head of a tiger appeared from the bushes. Dropping everything, they ran and ran, screaming as they went that Mr. Tiger was coming.

Te heard the commotion and waited a bit, to see if anyone was coming. He even considered not going further, but was so anxious to see Xem he went in anyway. As he stepped into the mouth of the cave, he received the scare of his life. There was the tiger head in the shadows. He turned to run, but Xem was right beside him to hold his shoulder, which was just as well because Te was actually about ready to run face to face with the *kuba* spider, which wouldn't have been fatal but not a kind memory. As Xem calmed him, he pointed out that it was just a tiger's head, not a living tiger, saying, "It's an old trick, but sometimes the old tricks still work." As Te calmed down the head moved, which startled Te again. Shaking his head in disapproval, Xem said, "Oh, Gxunk, I told you not to move. Alright, come out. It's time you two met, anyway."

Whereat an old monkey lifted the tiger's head off of his own shoulders, as it was just a mask made of an actual tiger's head, shoulders and front paws, all supported by a bamboo mesh. This was by far the largest monkey Te had ever seen. Not only that, on introduction, it bowed to him as a human would. He bowed back.

"This is Gxunk. He didn't seem to want to meet you. Sometimes he's shy. He's my constant companion and my protector, especially when I dream in such a way that I can't instantly wake up. Don't ask me where that name came from, I heard that in a dream, too, and when I awoke there he was. Has been ever since. This is a story for another time."

In being fascinated by this introduction, certainly his first to a monkey, Te was distracted for a bit from what had just happened with the tiger head. When he looked at it again he became agitated and said, in the most cross words he'd ever used on Xem, "Why would you trick me like that? I almost ran into the *kuba* and..."

"Stop, I didn't do it for fun. I wanted you to know that same fear just like the two men at the top of the trail felt."

"What two men?"

"You heard them screaming. They were following you."

"Following me? How do you know this?"

"I watch at the top of the hill, every time you are to come here. This is so you will realize how much more scared they and all the other Nie Drong plotters will be of you, now. Because now they will think you are protected by Lord Tiger, Bok-Klia. Right now, we must stop and thank Bok-Klia as well as state that we did not intend for this to happen, that it was an accident, but if it works out that others read into it, it is not our fault and we will not exploit it without asking permission. That having been said, you must realize that now your enemies hate you ever the more for this new fear they carry. The greater the fear, the greater the hate, because there is no such thing as hate without fear."

"How can you say that? I try not to hate, partially because you and Amba taught me not to, and also that is so clear in the *Hamon*. It isn't easy to not think something that your heart cycle keeps beating on. But I think I've hated some of the other boys before, and I wasn't really scared of them."

"In some way you were, if only that you were afraid they would have influence over someone whom you wanted to be on your side. There are many types of fear besides just the fear of being directly physically or emotionally hurt."

"I'll think about that. Maybe I'll ask Amba to explain it to me, some day. Because she's teaching me now. I've been selected to be the next shaman. But you probably know that. You've been getting into my dreams, haven't you? How is that possible?"

"That's another story, for another day. But, yes, I have visited your dreams. That's how I got you here in the first place. If I ever come into your dreams it's only after I have been asked by Yang-Dak of the waters to do so, when He comes to me in my dreams."

"So did you make me have those dreams so I would be picked? If you did, I'm going to quit. If that's even possible."

"Always be sure that I had nothing to do with you being picked."

"Then how come the very first thing you taught me was how to hold my breath. And it is exactly that which allowed me to win the trial by which I became shaman?" Te recounts the night of dreaming in the spirit house, as well as whole water trial with Pim, this time including how Pim had tried to break his grip lose with a rock.

"Both that the Nie Drong chose the water trial and that Pim tried to cheat would be predictable. That you were chosen would not be. Until you just told me, I knew none of this, other than that the spirit winds must have thought it important to tell me that you were picked to be shaman, without any detail. Why I taught you to hold your breath is perhaps that you can help me on my ultimate mission for the Nyang, if that is where our fates take us. If the Nyang directed fate that I should teach you how to hold your breath so you could be shaman, or whether it was just a life coincidence, we shall probably never know. I don't even pretend to know whether the Nyang direct the small moments of our lives, or if that they only apply broad soul tests that allow humans to cause all their own circumstances. Perhaps it is exactly that the Nyang, knowing you had this skill, directed the circumstances which led for the Nie Drong specifically to try their deceit. Perhaps that that deceit was concocted was a trial for someone else's soul, totally independent of you. See how quickly our minds become insufficient in sorting out Karma? Don't second guess the Nyang; merely acknowledge that they are drastically more farsighted than the most brilliant human."

"You promise you did not help me be picked?"

"I had no previous knowledge, nor even premonition. It makes sense, but not because I wished for it to be so. It is all a creation of the Nyang. Don't ever doubt that. As many mistakes as I've made with people, and as many sins I've committed against the rules of the Nyang, I would never, ever attempt to impersonate a Nyang. Nor would I convince someone else that I was speaking for a Nyang, directly, unless I presented it as my interpretation of a dream. Nor should you. No person ever has the right to claim they know what the Nyang actually want. Some of what I have been taught I believe dearly, but in my travels I've seen so many other ways of considering the Nyang – or gods or whatever names others might call them – that I'm not sure what to believe. When in doubt, I try to fall back on what I was taught, first. That stems from faith that it is not random or chance that, in this body, in this reincarnation, that the beliefs I hold and present to you were my soul's first calling to awareness. All you can really offer to the Nyang is to be sincere in expressing that you mean to be true to them, even though you will never be enlightened enough to be sure you are right. Perhaps once you have completed the cycle of ninety reincarnations and if, so deserving, you get to go up to the higher plane of the human *ae,* some clear comprehension of higher truths might come to you. Whatever this is or wherever that plane would be isn't knowable, in your mind here on the earth plane, so don't stress your brain trying to figure it out. You will learn much more about all this from Amba."

"What is so hard about what Amba is teaching me is that she doesn't tell me anything about the history of our tribe and other peoples, like you do. She tells about the ancients, but not in the way that there are other tribes or peoples, right now. It makes me wonder about the truth of anything she teaches me."

"Partly, she is respecting the vows the Kra Polie made her take, which they have the right to do, in earthly matters. Plus, she knows the danger you would be in if she did tell you certain things. And it's very doubtful that she knows anything specific about the treachery regarding the renegades and the kidnappings, for I'm sure she would never have kept silent for any of it. As I told you, the Nie Drong have their secret societies and never let anybody even be aware they exist who isn't one of them, already. That's the only thing they're sincere about; hiding their deceit. What I do trust, and you should too, is that in her teachings of the Nyang and sacred philosophy, that Amba is giving you the truth, as she believes it."

"My brain hurts from so many things. She's trying to teach me so many things, so fast. Why can't I just skip all these days of tests and trials, with people teaching me not to think for myself, but for the tribe, and even telling me to not be vain or presumptuous, when I don't even know what any of it means, really? Why did I have to be born into this soul instead of an old one, or just plain old and wise, like you?"

Xem laughed. "First off, I am only older than you in earth years in this, our coinciding incarnations. You may be much wiser, and are not even aware of it yet. Wisdom occurs in the moment, not in the past or the future." Pausing until he became calm within, he asked "And just how old do you think your soul is?" It was asked in a tone that Te had learned to associate with being asked directly to his soul. Te's eyes closed, and he imagined himself as a falling feather, to get into a meditation state as soon as possible. He heard Xem say, in a way that didn't even seem to come from Xem's mouth but directly from a soul dream, "When the waterfall becomes a crystal suspended column, and there are no more distinct sounds, but only the constant noise of whiteness everywhere, then begin looking. Everything is simultaneous, so you needn't ever really consider anything but being in the now."

When Te opened his eyes, he didn't know if he'd learned anything but he did feel peaceful, for the first time in a long time. This only lasted until he got back to the village, where he was given a lecture not by Rama, but by Amba. He gave her the answer that he had made up, long ago, because he knew someday he'd have to justify these excursions. In that circumstances had changed – as a shaman student he was supposedly never to lie to Amba, particularly in spiritual matters – he'd also prejustified that since he had concocted that lie before his induction, and would have told it then, it was not currently as big of a lie. This was only one more moral dilemma, though a troubling one, of so many piling up so quickly on his soul-slate. He reassures himself that it all started in truth, when he first told Amba that he had been having a reoccurring dream. And he couldn't get it out of his head for days. Then his explanation digressed to; one day he found that only by taking a shower at dawn and watching a spider weave his web, until he was in a trance, then could he wash the visions away. Often he had to crawl into the stream and slide a bit into the ravine, to make sure there was a spider actually weaving. After time, it had occurred to him that it only came on the new moon, but he had no idea why. When she asked him what the dream was, he responded, "It's not so clear, just something about some strange people coming and taking my family away. I can't stop the dream. I have to go there. Maybe I'll learn to understand it." By the time he actually got to tell the fib, and elaborated on this last part, he was having such a dream.

Though his going there at dawn singed her intuition and judgment – plus making S'Yu ever more dangerous – Amba could not ignore anything this boy dreamed. As troubling as this was, she and the unbroken line of all those thousands of shaman she succeeded had always been taught, preeminent, to take all reoccurring dreams seriously.

Te was finding himself ever more confounded in sorting dreams from reality, and discerning which were more important; or whether it was up to him to take any meaning from dreams whatsoever. Either way, life's complexities and dangers were compounding on him, not the least being that he knew his visits with Xem would be ever more dangerous. Why were the men following him? Perhaps it was a blessing that he had no idea yet of how diabolical S'Yu was, nor that her anger was being flamed by a jealous derangement. Te had enough fears for the moment.

15

Same time as Te was being shocked by Gxunk in the tiger mask, Landers shakes awake, his back to the oak. Without opening his eyes, he overcomes alarm at whatever startled him, though he doesn't identify what it was. Momentarily, he feels safe but also thinks it is dawn and he isn't sure, at all, where he is. First take, opening his eyes, doesn't help but he soon ascertains the situation, only briefly marking how disoriented he'd been. So he goes on a hunt for justice, over in the Stanford law building. He knocks on the door of Arnold's small office. He's there, unpacking boxes and piling books on shelves. First impression, Arnold is much warmer than before, even glad to see him. Landers says, "So, you're settling in to lay down the law in the blackboard jungle."

"Yeah, maybe for good. Maybe it's not as lucrative, but minds are what matter to me. As do principals. If I run across a ripe precedent case, I might go to trial. Right now, I'm just enjoying massive relief from escaping that Berkeley fire pit. Though I didn't think that it was, yesterday. And it's not Berkeley or Boalt, just the 'right now is all that matters' obsession of those protest committees. Come up with an angle, yet?"

"No. Other than at least sensing a weakness in how uncomfortable the Army seems to be about anyone walking into a courtroom and saying they'd have fought in a justified, declared war, but not in this so-called police action."

"That would explain why you're at a perpetual stalling point. Actually, I'm not sure if I know of a case of somebody hitting it right on the nose like that. But I suspect a military court will only pay attention to you simply disobeying orders; no reasons need apply."

"When did my constitutional rights dissolve? When I took that oath with a hundred other guys, way back on day one, when nobody seemed to even know what we were up to? Disregarding my naiveté in thinking my rewriting of it would stick."

"Yep. But what do you mean you rewrote the oath?"

"First day you show up, they had everyone stand in a formation and swear an oath of allegiance to the country and the military. I told them I'd swear to the country, but to the military only if they amended it. So they dismissed everyone else and a couple sergeants screamed at me. I said it would have to include that I would not agree to fight in a war that was considered illegal by the Geneva Conventions and international law, that I considered Viet Nam to constitute an illegal war, and that I wouldn't fight there because it could lead to me being tried under the Nuremberg provision. I was winging that part up because I have no idea how Nuremberg or Geneva deals would apply to me but they at least recognized the terms. I told them I cared about words and if they didn't reflect my opinion, I wouldn't swear to them. They got tired of yelling, I guess, because they said go ahead, so I swore to the oath with my amendments. Not very affective, huh."

"It might be if it had made your file or you could get one of those guys to testify. Did you record their names?"

"No, and I got a clerk down at Ft. Polk to check my file. It's not mentioned, anywhere."

"That oath would be one thing that would keep me from joining the military too. Plus knowing, from the inside, I couldn't exactly write my own agenda."

"Given what you have in place, why ever would you want to join the military? Now?"

"Because I feel so helpless to affect anything from the outside."

"Take my word for it, stay outside. Can we skim by all that Nuremberg Trial stuff, since it's up? Basically, they came up with the tenet that even if one were following an order he could be convicted of war crimes, if that order was illegal. Right?"

"Right. That's how they convicted the higher Nazi military personnel."

"Then why couldn't they convict every soldier who shoots anyone in Viet Nam, under international law, since this is an undeclared war?"

"First off, that trial is very unlikely to come about unless, say, the Viet Cong occupy the US. International law tends to be applied from the strong down on the weak. Also, at Nuremberg, once they'd prosecuted the obvious political scapegoats, they mainly only brought people to trial for specific war crimes; like torturing POWs, or concentration camp personnel in position to make decisions. Nobody is going to try an infantry private for surviving on the field of battle."

"Nor should they. But do you know of American soldiers who've cited Nuremberg concerns in a courtroom, and having that appealed to a level which would interpret Constitutional law?"

"Citing and getting judicial appellate attention aren't the same thing. And to be appealed it has to be tried. Only reason soldiers usually get into a courtroom with a civilian jury is for criminal matters. Which is not likely, in your case; to date. Nor does civil court really apply to you. Who would you be suing, for what damages? In all the cases I know of where soldiers faced civilian judges, they had very specific technicalities, which you don't. Besides, they weren't in the infantry. And they hadn't received orders to go to the front line. No court in America, maybe the world, would touch that."

"In a sense of actually defending a nation I don't particularly disagree. Disregarding that this war is not about protecting the U.S., no matter where you draw the line somebody's going to straddle it. Like me."

"Like you. I'm sorry. I think about it daily and it comes up in discussions in the legal community, all the time. If I hear of anything, I'll track you down. These are difficult times for justice. As I'm sure you know, there's a lot a judges out there who'll throw the book at you without hearing a thing, if they even suspect an anti-war concern. Hopefully, soon, someone will at least be able to present a case up through the Supreme Court, to clarify all the injustices inherent in sending only a disenfranchised minority into battle, when Congress can't even declare it as the nation's unequivocal policy."

"Not that that, of itself, would end the war," Landers says. Arnold seems about to go on, but Landers simply chops off the conversation with a hand gesture. He's grown so weary of talking about the whole mess; it is such an oppressive daily routine, beating word circles to nowhere. Without asking, he starts helping Arnold unpack and straighten up the office, while turning conversation to the first book title he recognizes. They have lunch and explore the campus a bit together, both enjoying the protective feeling of the lengths of arch-covered walkways and the overall sense of peacefulness.

Having time to burn, Landers heads back up to San Francisco and wanders over to Haight-Asbury; it is an excellent show. On the sidewalk outside the Victorian commune of earlier visit, he runs into Mike, the owner, who lights up on seeing Landers saying, "Man, I'm so glad to see you. I've got to go down to San Jose to sign some papers. Having my brother committed, but not to a Veteran's hospital. Which is a major bitch; maybe we can talk about it later. Meantime, I need someone to stay here. I've thrown everyone out and am putting it up for sell. The speed freaks and now even heroin addicts are driving me zombie. But every time I leave, someone finds a way in. If you need somewhere to stay you can camp as long as you want. Bizarre as it is, growing up right here, I have no friends around, at all. They all either went crazy or realized they would if they didn't get away."

This odd out-spilling of info and trust intrigues Landers, so he decides to stay, awhile. The only people who try to get in are Captain Khayam and the hippie girl he made love with, that first afternoon, who still doesn't recognize him. Khayam gets irate, to the point of calling Landers warmonger and trying to push by him. A much harder push back sends him sprawling. Landers locks the door and goes up to the turret balcony, where he can see all entrances as well as the overall street scene. He spots Sunkitty and would actually like to talk to her – that beneath her groovy caricature was a very observant, well-raised, fun-loving soul – but watching her for two minutes convinces him otherwise. Having lost all her bounce and glow, she is skinny, even shaking at times, and changes direction on the sidewalk ten different times. Methamphetamine. When Mike returns with a cousin, the cousin remains in the house while they walk all the way over to the Marina District for dinner. Landers feels lucky to not be in this guy's lonely dilemma. Mike takes a taxi home.

Landers spends the evening in San Francisco, almost hooking up with a hippie girl in a club, although their entire intercourse is in dancing. This seems to be enough. After she's applied every seductive move applicable, with clothes on, she's latched on to him and they're even on their way out together, but her glazed-over eyes aren't for him, right then, and he absolutely doesn't want to wander into any commune scene. He apologizes and takes leave. She barely seems to notice. On returning to the Oakland Base he actually feels relief, for its protection.

Next morning at formation, he is pleasantly surprised to receive no appointment orders, for that day. In walking to the bus, later, he cuts by the area where the troops load from the chain-link cage, onto buses for the airplanes to Viet Nam. The side doors are open wide, and he spots a soldier he knew from basic training so stops to talk. Right next to him, he sees Jameson, who's trying to be incognito. When he realizes Landers has seen him, Jameson pulls him aside. Landers notices the name on his fatigues is Jones. Jameson says, "Man, how'd you find me?"

"I sure as hell wasn't looking. Sign, seal and deliver that one."

"Promise you won't turn me in to them."

"Absolutely not my business. You know, though, in case it amuses you, you sure as hell have them mystified, back at S-2."

"I had to get out. I have to get back to Nam. I figured it all out. Those people in S-2 weren't after me at all."

"Well, I'm glad you at least came to that true realization. Just for kicks, mind if I ask, were you tracking us, that night?"

"Yeah, because I couldn't let you get away. I'd realized it was only you who was looking for me, all along."

"Jameson, I have no idea where you're coming from. But I'm going to do my everyday best to make sure I'm nowhere anywhere near your life chart."

"You don't understand. It's not here that you're trying to find me, it's in Nam."

"Nobody has quite seen me in Nam."

"I've already seen you there, in my dreams. Time doesn't matter, there. You don't know anything about dream magic yet. But it knows about you." For the first time, he looks directly into Landers eyes. And Landers sees a real person, deep inside there. A person he realizes he'd never really seen before; and now understands even less. Jameson, seeing the main group of troops heading for the buses, quickly maneuvers to get in line. Landers does have to admire the extraordinary quickness and slyness of this guy. Not that, in this case, there's a comprehensive security plan for people trying to sneak into Viet Nam. Landers shakes his head and finds himself saying to himself, out loud, "Don't mind me, if I bail out here."

While walking to the bus stop he sees a few hundred national guardsmen milling around a dozen trucks and several jeeps. They're fully outfitted, including helmets, rifles and gas masks. On first take, this doesn't strike Landers as completely odd, only when he comes in closer he sees them line up to get live ammunition and what looks like tear gas canisters for the grenade launchers. This confuses him and the fact that the men seem very nervous tells his instincts that this isn't like any training operation he's ever seen.

Walking onto campus, he can tell there's a totally different atmosphere than normal. Finding Sarelle he asks her what's happened. "Well, Governor Reagan declared the Berkeley campus to be in a state of emergency and immediately it became one. I stole that quote from everybody quoting some newscaster. It is accurate."

"What's changed that caused him to declare it a state of emergency?"

"Nobody seems quite sure. Demonstrations didn't really seem out of the ordinary. But all of a sudden there seems to be a whole lot of new protestors around, coming out of nowhere. With mayhem in mind."

There are city and campus police buzzing all around the area. Hundreds of protestors mill around Sproul Hall, the main administration building for the entire UC system, and one of the normal areas to stage demonstrations. Some students appear to be having a "sit-in", inside. Neither Landers nor Sarelle want to be anywhere near the center of action. They move to a higher place where they can watch, from behind shrubbery. Moving down to the center of action, they watch Werner and the shrill woman from the committee group walking with six protestors, dressed like students of the protestor mold, but a little bit older and with a discernibly tougher demeanor. Sarelle questions, "I wonder who all those guys with Werner are? He's usually always with his regular pack. I've never seen any of them before."

"One thing, they sure aren't Berkeley students. I'm calling them a biker gang or redneck thugs. And they look like they're coming to fight."

"This is just not right. Well the media sure showed up."

Looking around, they see two TV camera crews with logos from local stations, and several dozen reporters with accompanying photographers. What stands out, to Landers eye, is one TV camera crew with an extreme telephoto lens, back in some bushes. There's no logo or any other marking. Also he sees a man who appears to be their director talking on a walkie-talkie, while looking up at the roof of a building on the far side of the quad. Following his line of sight, Landers sees he's talking to two men in dark suits, wearing sunglasses. He says, "If those aren't feds up there, they're trying their damndest to look like they are."

Right then, they hear and feel the whole verbal and tension pitch go up a few notches. Soon they see why. The National Guardsmen are walking on line right towards the quad area. Police are on their flanks. Any student who doesn't move is herded off to the sides, where the police arrest them.

Werner and his group push their way through the crowd. Werner stops and moves to stand on a wall alongside the building. Continuing to the center of action, two of the thugs pull out chains from their packs and start banging them on trash cans and anything that'll make noise, including taking out a few windows. Two others bring out an American flag, running right in front of the approaching Guard and ignite it, waving it defiantly as it goes up in flames. All six of them are spurring others to rush the Guard, but although a few people seem to take defiant stances, none want to rush into the wall of soldiers. Lots of the protestors are starting to retreat but Werner's six and other leaders try to get everyone to bunch together.

Then the National Guardsmen put on the gas masks and one pops a teargas grenade, tossing it. One of Werner's thugs has a mask of his own, chases down the grenade and tosses it back at the approaching Guardsmen. Then there's the loud thumping of helicopters approaching, low. One sprays the crowd with tear gas, which starts people stampeding in all directions. Landers and Sarelle take off running, to get upwind of it all. She can't keep up with him, so he slows down and they do get a whiff of the gas, which starts them coughing and tearing. Almost immediately, they get into fresh air, but the searing effects linger for several minutes.

Making a wide circle of all the action, they walk back to Sarelle's apartment. She says, "I'm staying off the streets. I suggest you join me."

"I'm way too wound up, to sit still. I'm just going to walk this one off, way away from here.

Seeing a police car cruising up the street, although he feels it probably has no specific reason to look for him, he walks into the front of the apartment building, to cut through to the alley. Walking out the back door, just as he gets to the alley, he hears his name called. Turning, he sees Katrina, a few doors down and across the alley, waving for him to follow her as she quickly ducks out of sight. Astonished, knowing just from her furtive gesture that something is way wrong, he takes off in her direction. Between the buildings where she disappeared he doesn't even see her, he almost runs right by where she is down in the entrance to a basement apartment. He jumps over the rail to join her. Quickly, she ducks in the apartment and slams the door behind them. Like a raging river is trying to pull her away, she grasps him and breaks down sobbing. She fights to get control and he just keeps holding her, until she at least stops sobbing. Finally, he asks, "What is going on? Where are we?" He looks around and sees they're in a tiny studio with just a bed, a desk, a dresser, and only one small window, up high, covered by blinds.

"We're in hiding. I'm in hiding. I just wanted to find a way to find you. I'm amazed I did."

"What do you mean you're in hiding. From whom?"

"From the police, the FBI, you name it."

"You? You never did anything illegal in your life."

"Doesn't seem to matter, anymore, does it. Because they're for sure after me and, as near as I can tell, it has something to do with being involved with the shooting of a policeman."

"Wait, stop. This just doesn't register. Why any of this?"

She pauses to at least make a concise statement, "In order of events; they apparently wanted to shut down the newspaper Jeffrey and I were working at in San Diego. And they did. They broke in and destroyed the presses and trashed all the files."

"Huh. I've heard a hundred stories, in the last few weeks, of dirty tricks, but no government official is going to physically destroy an American newspaper."

"Michael, believe me, they did it. As a starter. Jeffrey went down there, after midnight, to pick up a file, and watched them. With unmarked cars blocking off the ends of the street. Only he saw them and they saw him, apparently. So he ran back to house where most of the newspaper people were living. They came right in the door, right behind him, already with a warrant. Only reason I escaped is I just happened to be out in the alley, taking out the trash.

At which point I could only think to run. Ran scared and empty like never in my life. I ran five miles from Little Italy to O.B., ducking down every back street I could find, to Francina's place."

"Why did they have a warrant for the house?"

"Well, that's where it gets really bad. Meantime, Francina was freaked and didn't even want to stay at her place, which turned out to be a good instinct, because they came by to question her, early the next morning. Her new boyfriend was out of town so we broke in there; well, she knew where the key was hid. Anyways, she went out the next day and found out all she could. The raid of the house hit the headlines, but nothing at all about the raid of the newspaper offices. Seems that they claimed to have found a pistol at the house. And apparently it had been used in the shooting of a policeman in Oakland, a few weeks ago. Which they apparently claim that Jeffrey and I had transported down to San Diego. Michael, that never happened."

"I have no trouble believing that. This is nuts. So where's Jeffrey?"

"Locked up. Without bail. Several of the staff were booked too, but they got out on bail. They said the officers actually went out of the way to have them watch the cops search a closet. And sure enough, they did find a gun. Suspicions are running high that it had to be someone working for the newspaper that planted it there. None of them will even talk to each other. And nobody's speaking up against the closing of the paper. In fact, the other local media seem to be applauding the whole police action. After hiding a couple days, Francina arranged for a friend of her boyfriend to drive me up here. Kind of a sketchy biker, but he was totally cool to me. Berkeley's probably the worst place to run to, but I just had to see you, so you heard it first from me."

"Doesn't matter who I'd have heard it from, I wouldn't have believed you did anything wrong."

Then she breaks down sobbing again, while all he can feel to do is hold and caress her. Between crying she blurts out, "And, God, Michael, now it's all over. School, family, my whole life. All of it. I'm a fugitive. A fugitive for murder. I'm not so sure they didn't set me and Jeffrey up to go down there in the first place. Neither of us actually thought up the idea. Someone in the committee had gotten a call from that paper. Or so it was said. We were just so lost and it seemed like something to occupy our minds, so we did it. Even then, after a week, we were both about ready to quit. There was just too many agendas at the newspaper."

"I, just an hour ago, realized that there's some heavy-duty meddling by the feds with the whole Berkeley anti-war scene. Not to mention that I've given up any preconceived idealism of what the government won't do. Any power-goon with the right party line can destroy anyone's lives, fast, these days. What now? Where are we anyway?"

"At a friend of mine's apartment. A girl I had a few labs with, a few years back, who I hit it off with and we've kept in touch. She's got a street survival attitude, because she ran away at twelve. I picked her because we don't know anybody in common. She'll come by tonight to drive me out of here. This is the last day anybody's going to know where I am."

"We've got to figure out a way to fight it."

"Not me. Not now. I'm gone. It's not like you're in any position to help. We're both scratched off society's list. Nobody but nobody can or will defend us." There's a different person inside her that he's never seen before. Terrified, for sure, but with a fully-realized, mature anger and toughness in her eyes. Her look has always been so steady, but now her eyes flicker all over the place.

"When did all this come down?"

"Four nights ago. And they were haunting everybody I knew in Point Loma, by early the next day. They almost caught me, twice, because they were tailing Francina, but she figured it out and ditched them. I feel twenty years older than the few weeks ago since I saw you last. In fact, you know what, we're not even talking about this anymore. There's nothing left of my life but the moment I'm in. And here's where this moment is taking us, now." She lights some candles and turns the lights off. "No thoughts, no impressions, no questions, no answers. The last virgin I know, probably the last virgin of the whole free-love revolution is going down in flames, now. After I walk out that door, I don't know when I'll ever trust anybody again. So right now, it's all about honesty, all up front. I don't want you anxious. I don't want you in a hurry. I want it all."

"Call me crazy, which kind of rolls off the tongue these days, but you've said five hundred times you really want to be in love, the first time."

"'In love. Lofty ideal. Mine, I know. But 'in love' or not, I do love you, Michael, for who you are. More than anybody I've ever known. You going off to war fits all the romance requirements I ever had."

"What about off to prison?"

"That's pretty noble too, for these reasons. I'll take it."

"Is there any such thing as noble, these days?"

"Not around here. But screw it, I don't care. Right now, I'm in charge. Stand up, let's get this right. I think I want, let's see, your pants off. Stop, don't help."

He's spent so much time with her, with no romance other than a few slow dances which touched on wandering hot, that jumping every pretense in one assault makes him embarrassed. She undoes a few of his shirt buttons, top and bottom. Unzipping him, she slides his corduroys down, slowly. Pushing his shirt up slightly, hands against his thighs, she kisses him just below the navel and pushes him back against the pillows. Standing on the bed, she slowly strips her own jeans and blouse, having nothing on under it but a sleeveless cotton slip top with lace on the bottom, hanging to just above her navel. Having never even seen her in panties before, let alone bikini white cotton ones, both intimidates and excites him, aeons beyond anything he's ever felt with any girl before. From her purse, she produces a joint. Straddling him, with her warmth pressed right on him in his military boxer shorts, she lights it. "The only joint I've ever owned. I saved it for just this occasion, only I never dreamed in my worst nightmare this is the occasion that would be." She takes a big hit and covers his mouth, softly. Slowly she breaths the smoke into him, following it even more slowly with her tongue, licking ever widening and deepening circles. "All I want to see, right now, is rainbows and novas."

As their pulsing wanders beyond their mouths and they tumble in each other's grasp, their passion eventually needs air. They pause, panting. He says, "Man, you're likely to set off a quasar, keep that up. Are you really sure?"

"Yeah, damn it, and shut up." She holds the joint to his lips, but pulls it away, after he takes most of a strong hit. "Not too much, it's supposed to be nuclear reactive. Just a little more, just enough for us not to have to think. Or I'll start getting pissed."

"At me?"

"Yeah, at you, for letting yourself get drafted. Not that you planned it. Pissed at the Army for drafting you. And pissed at the whole fucking United States of America for running justice-is-blindfolded right into this insane fucking war."

He's heard her drop a cuss word or two along the way, all the usual ones, but this is a livid degree of swearing he's never heard from her. "Yeah, sounds like my first thoughts, every morning. I can't remember the last time I woke up with any other emotion."

Then they're kissing with a rough passion only abject anger could ignite. They grapple, grind and roll around the bed so animated but in sync, that they're not even aware of how the rest of their clothes came off, nor of any step of them touching and kissing everywhere they can find. Finally, when he's atop her, she holds him away, to look deep in his eyes, a moment. Holding tight, beside his hips, she guides every millimeter of her first entry. For what isn't even twenty minutes, but seems forever, they make love with a last cry desperation, until he can't stop himself any longer from climaxing and tries to pull back. She holds him, inside her. He says, "Wait, come on, are you using anything?"

"No," she says, "and I don't care. I don't care because if I never see you again, I want you to live inside me."

Still, he makes an effort to get out, but she locks her hands and wrists behind his butt and out-holds him. Their wrestling only extrapolates the passion, all the way through an eye-to-eye, long-throbbing conjunction and long, slow winding down. They have nothing left but to curl up into a mutually protective, prenatal knot. He pulls the covers all the way over them and they just lie, listening to each other breath.

After a half-hour that neither wants to ever end, he finally says, "How can I feel so rip-sawed right up the middle during the prime fantasy of my life?"

"It's all different, now, huh. And now I love you. I'm so far gone in love. I'm all of it. Gone."

He leans back just long enough to hold her gaze, "I love you too. Like I've never loved another."

"And now it's one way better and six million ways worse than ever. And we're not waiting for each other, because, because...because."

For a long time, she cries silent tears. He doesn't, not because he wouldn't, but that the emotion is too complex. After a while of lying in the dark, both emotionally imploded, there's a light rapping on the door, in a distinct pattern. Quickly, Katrina gets up, wraps a blanket around her and raps on a panel beside the door, getting another distinct rap pattern back. She opens the door. In steps a tall, distinguished young black woman, who says, "Come on, the van's out back. Man, this town's creeping and crawling with The Man. Hi, guy, whoever you are. Sorry, I don't do intros in this mode. All I can say about me is this isn't my usual."

Katrina quickly dresses. For the first time, Landers notices her backpack and a heavy duffel bag, which is undoubtedly stuffed with books. She turns to Landers, gives him one last, powerful hug and a brief kiss. She says, "Goodbye. I just don't know what's...aw, hell, just goodbye."

"Yeah, goodbye," he says. "Only decision I have to make now is how do I get back on the streets the fastest, to come find you."

"Make your decisions on your behalf," the woman says. "She's got ample baggage, as is."

Katrina says, "Besides, what makes you think your immediate future is going to be any safer?"

"Doesn't matter. Clearing your name is the only good reason for doing anything that I've heard, lately."

The woman says, "There are way too many things to do to keep track of reasons. This Viet Nam thing is just one battle of the eternal war against suppression of justice. We need many types of warriors to put it to rest, forever. Don't burn your credentials, too soon...Come on, girl."

Without looking back, the women leave. Still in bed, Landers is suddenly overcome by the strongest sense of claustrophobic compression he's ever known, as if all the dark, unnamed fears he's ever felt breathing on the back of his neck are coming to get him. Still buttoning his clothes, he gets out as fast as he can.

16

Walk, briskly, is all Landers is driven to do, away from Berkeley, away from all these people and official cars darting in all directions. Once into a working class neighborhood of Oakland he sees a neighborhood bar and feels a beer calling. Walking into totally strange bars alone is not natural to him. The only times he'd ever done it before was on leave from infantry school at Fort Polk, when he'd hitchhiked down to New Orleans a few times, on weekend leave. This place feels anonymous enough. It's a blend of white-collar and blue collar, with a few clutches of regulars. It's laid out like it wants to make it as a single's pick-up place, but this is a slow night, with only a few single women, not being particularly available. Not that it matters to him, he's definitely not looking. There's an Oakland Raiders football game on a TV down at the end of the bar, which attracts the attention of most of the unattached men. He orders a beer and settles. In walks four couples of college students, with slightly long hair and clothes just a bit towards counterculture, but much tamer than any dedicated hippies or protestors standard attire. One girl has a peace-sign necklace and another has a pin reading, "Give peace a chance," on her purse. Casually, they move into a table near the jukebox. Landers notices a couple of boisterous drinkers down near the TV are looking at the students, giving them hard looks. The students ignore them or are oblivious. The only other person who seems to pick up on it is the bartender. Landers feels a tap on his shoulder. It's 1st Lt. Pearson, in a loose sense his current company commander, seeming amused by Lander's jumpiness. Pearson is in jeans and a sweater, looking pretty much

like a grad school or law student, styled not quite establishment, but
not a rebel, either. He says, "What are you doing off the base,
soldier?"

Stuck for excuses and seeing no profit in making one up,
Landers responds, "Oh, great. This is all I need."

Pearson just laughs, says, "Don't worry, I'm not a lifer. The
only way I could afford to go to college was on an ROTC
scholarship."

"I'd sensed that you were somehow human. Not that all lifers
lack humanity, by any means."

Again, Pearson laughs lightly, "A small irony, which I'll go ahead
and accept. You're sounding bitter. Which, normally, you are not,
especially given your predicament."

"Sorry. Special circumstances. Yeah, I honestly try not to be
angry against the overall machine, in concept. But it gets harder,
every day."

"Anger is easy. Repair takes more time. Yo, bartender, a
pitcher please." The bartender brings one over, and the Pearson fills
both their glasses. For an hour they sit and talk, sometimes watching
as the football game ends and everyone cheers that Oakland won.
Sometimes they talk about their respective colleges or about anything
not newsworthy or regarding the military. They are getting a bit
buzzed and Landers is relaxing, slightly. Only both perk up to that
the rowdy drinkers are starting to be more antagonistic towards the
students, while the students continue to ignore them. This brings up
a more serious side of both the soldiers. Pearson asks, "Totally off
the record, how do you feel you're proceeding?"

"Backwards. All this bureaucracy is wearing me down. All I
want, now, is to just hear a decision. If that means jail time, fine, let's
get it over. Why won't they even charge me and try me?"

"Partially because they can't totally label you. You're not anti-
American and not even particularly anti-Army, at least in
acknowledging that the Army might have a valid reason for existence.
Plus, your existence is known to people they're afraid of. One thing
the Army doesn't want, these days, is specific attention. That
Berkeley crowd can really drum up press."

"But the military can always isolate itself. Why do they care,
really? Clearly, they can do whatever they want."

"It's that precedent thing. Almost everyone they deal with
who's dodging them has a scam. You just put it out directly that you

think the war itself is what's anti-American. They don't like to have their own last line of defense turned against them. That's not a principal they want to risk, especially if it gets aired in the media or, god-forbid, somehow leaks out to a civilian courtroom."

"They act like they have plenty to try me on, besides my war position."

"In a way. But it's all borderline stuff."

"They seem to have no problems twisting the borders."

"Making decisions about unwilling soldiers is never easy, in a military society that specifically does not want to think of itself as totalitarian, even when it is. Just putting you in the brig for a few weeks or even months, if it doesn't generate dismissal from duty – which is what you seem to want – puts you right back in their faces."

Right then, a national news program comes on the air, with a special on that day's riots at Berkeley. This catches everyone's attention. This is all too familiar to Landers; he even sees a scanning shot of the foliage he was behind, but is glad he is hidden. As the coverage of the incident rolls, he extrapolates the position of the camera and realizes that almost all of the footage comes from that unmarked camera. Mostly, it's focused on the thuggish group that Werner had been directing. There is no footage of the police or National Guard roughing up students. It fades out with two of Werner's guys burning the American flag, with horrendously anti-social demeanor. Almost nobody, short of a sociopath, would want to identify with these two.

When the TV goes on to another story, the boisterous drinkers start surrounding the students, who can no longer ignore them. One drinker says, "See that. See what you goddamn longhairs caused."

Another drinker adds, "We work our asses off paying for your educations, and you tear down the goddamn schools, that's what."

One male student says, "It wasn't us. I promise you."

The first drinker says, "You got long hair. She has a peace symbol on. That means you're anti-establishment, don't it."

"And we're establishment, aren't we?" a third drinker says.

A female student says, "If you think so. We're not here to protest anything."

"You hate our guts, don't you," the first drinker says, knocking the chair of the first student who spoke.

The student, looking scared, responds, "No. Please, we're not trying to bother you."

"Well you are," another drinker says. "Fucking peace creeps. Look a this."

He grabs a purse that has a "Make love not war" button on it. On its other side is a small burned-in peace symbol. She tries to get it back, but the drinker's start playing catch with it. The first male student who had spoke tries to intercept it in flight, which is all the first drinker needs as inducement to deck the student. A melee starts and the students are clearly getting stomped, pleading for it to stop.

Suddenly, with accumulative anger at Macree, a chaplain and a whole lot more, Landers doesn't attempt to restrain himself and enters the fracas, downing the first drinker with one punch. Two drinkers grab Landers but Pearson comes around the side, knocks one flying with an elbow to the side of the jaw, brings a round-house knee up into the other's ribs and, when the drinker let's go of Landers, punches him several times until he does a backflop on a table. The drinkers try blindsiding them from all sides, and do get in a few glance licks, but Landers and Pearson are clearly winning each isolated encounter. As the drinkers regroup, Pearson clears a path and tells the students to get going. They posthaste-it for the door, not looking back. Standing shoulder-to-shoulder, Landers and Pearson back out of the room. The drinkers make a few movements like they're going to rush them, en masse, but when the soldiers stop like they're willing to hold their ground, the drinkers back off again. When they back out of the door, they turn and walk deliberately, but in no hurry, towards the corner. A few drinkers pop out and yell, but none of them make any effort to take chase. Neither Landers nor Pearson look back.

Around the corner, Pearson stops to look at blood dripping from Landers nose. Landers wipes it off with the back of his wrist, says, "Aw, it's just a nosebleed. It'll stop in a second."

Pearson hands him a handkerchief and says, "Here, anyway. Say, you fight pretty well for a so-called peace creep."

"Part of the restraint I'm holding back, through all of this, is that I can't be totally hypocritcal about my nature. I confess that I might've received an overdose of that stupid Irish fighting gene. Some of my friends and I used to get in fights for the sport of it. I've just held it back, since I realized I could really hurt someone." With a slight smile, he adds, "Yeah, I never said I won't fight. I just won't fight if it's not for a just cause."

253

Pearson says, "Good, then we'll always be on the same side. You do have a pretty nasty left hook. And you're going to have to show me that escape move. Where the hell'd you learn that?"

"Oh, just intuitively, trying to wrestle away from some Hawaiian I used to surf with. Just playing around, he'd try to take on the whole beach. Playing or not, he could do it."

They walk off down the street, swaggering. Friends. The lieutenant has a car. They start back towards the base, but decide to swing by another bar for another beer and a bite to eat. Not to stir prying eyes, he drops Landers off a few blocks from the base, on a side street.

Tired, torn and outraged, it takes a long time for Landers to get to sleep. It takes repeatedly rotating color wheels, in the order of the rainbow, to turn off all his thoughts so that his exhaustion takes over.

When he wakes up, he feels like a heavyweight slugged him alongside the head and in the gut. At formation that morning, he receives orders to meet with the FBI again, only in the afternoon. Unable to turn off his rage, and ready to unload on somebody, he picks the FBI as a good place to start, so goes directly there, four hours early.

Walking up to the trailer, he hears a lot of laughing going on inside. Swinging the door open, jerkily for effect, he stills the room. Standing around the main room, all with coffee cups in their hands, are a half dozen FBI agents, a few in suits and other younger ones in disguise, as students or hippies. Right in the center is Werner. Given the way Landers and Werner look at each other, Werner's cover is blown. However Landers is not as quick to decode the discordance of this scene. His first take is that Werner might have been arrested, but he quickly ticks past that to think he's an informant. He never does get to the realization that Werner is an active agent, yet, but he lets in on all of them, "I don't know what the hell I'm looking at, but my instincts tell me that someone in this room knows about how and why one fabulous, honorable, upright, brilliant student named Katrina got framed in a phony gun plant. Somebody better straighten that one out, because the truth will bury you if you don't."

The agent he'd met with before steps forward and shouts, "You don't come barging in here and talking to us like that. Shut up."

"Alright, I said my piece, I'm out of here," Landers says, spins and is out the door before they know what just came down.

254

The same agent says, "Someone call the MPs," and sticks his head out the door and tells for Landers to stop.

Hardly looking back, Landers says, "You're not on my chain of command. Unless you're going to arrest me for something, right now, I'll see you at two o'clock, when the Army says I will. On their bad days they're not as low as you guys." But before he gets fifty yards, he can see the MP van coming. When it stops, he walks around to the back door, with his hands out.

Two MPs he's never seen deliver him to the Oakland stockade, putting him into a cell with a simple chain-link security door. They leave and when Lander's looks around the room, the only person he sees is Mayborough, leaning back in a chair, with his feet up on a desk. He says, "Well, well, welcome to our humble abode. Somehow I thought we'd meet again. You're turning into the cat with way beyond nine lives."

Although Mayborough has a hint of his wry smile, Landers just nods; he's about out of smiles.

Mayborough reads the mood, "Yeah, sorry, man, this ain't all that funny. Things are about to mobilize much quicker, on your behalf. And it's way out of my hands. You know I'd do what I can, but this here is my duty station. Here I don't bend any rules." The other MPs walk back in, so the conversation doesn't progress. Most of the day, Mayborough is out on runs, then goes off duty. They never get to talk.

Next morning, a military lawyer comes to see him. To Landers, he seems rather nervous and almost seems younger than himself. After an introductory chat, Landers asks him, "What I don't understand is, are you my lawyer, or the Army's?"

The lawyer answers, "I'm assigned to your case. This is not the same as a civilian trial."

"But you are a lawyer. A genuine, law-school trained, passed-the-bar lawyer.

"Yes, I am."

"Then can you at least tell me the exact charges against me?"

"It's not really a court martial you're going before. It's the military equivalent to a summary trial. There, the charges will be defined."

"I guess I'm still not going to get any specific answers, am I? Can't you even be proud of having some ability to answer legal questions directly?"

"I am a good lawyer. But this is not the element I thought I'd be working in."

In walks the lieutenant Catholic chaplain Landers had met at the chapel. Another officer, a captain, also with a chaplain's-cross pin on his collar, is with him. The Catholic chaplain asks, "Can we speak with Private Landers?"

"Ah, yeah, I really haven't any more to say, right now," the lawyer says, leaving the room and letting them enter. The chaplains bring in another chair and all three sit down. The captain starts pouring them all a cup of coffee, from a thermos.

The lieutenant introduces the other chaplain, "Landers, this is Chaplain Conners. I believe he has an idea that might help you."

"I'm glad to meet you, Chaplain Conners. Hm, good coffee, thanks. Somehow, it seems I should be leery of meeting chaplains on judgment day."

The lieutenant says, "I'm not sure of what judgment will come down today. Since you listed yourself as a Catholic, I've been able to get some rather specific information about your position."

Chaplain Connors adds, "They now list enough charges against you to add up to twenty-five years."

"This I know. So, they charge me for twenty-five, they give me five and I do two, maybe three years at most. Maybe a lot less, but unlikely."

Connors asks, "Do you really want to do that time?"

"Of course not. But I will, rather than fight in an unjust war."

The lieutenant says, "Chaplain Connors is a Quaker. Quakers, with the backing of their religion, are permitted to be conscientious objectors."

"Are there actually Quakers in the Army?" Landers asks.

"Yes, quite a few. There are even a few Quakers in Viet Nam. In non-combat roles. With church approval."

The lieutenant suggests, "We believe we can fit you into a program, a new program, in which you can be classified as a non-combatant, but still must go to Viet Nam."

Chaplain Connors adds on, "Would you agree to that stipulation? If so, they might drop all charges."

"I don't know," Landers muses. "I still seems like copping out."

"Why?" Chaplain Connors asks. "Believe me, there is plenty of room for charity in a war zone. Without at all compromising your principals."

Thinking awhile, Landers responds, "I know you're going to think I'm nuts. But if I'm told by the Army to go to Viet Nam, I'd have a hard time justifying going there without being in the infantry."

From the background, they hear Mayborough's voice, "You're right man, you're nuts. If they give you that offer, take it. Given the gumbo you've jumped in, there's not likely to be a better one."

The lieutenant reacts, "I really don't understand your reluctance either."

"Because it's not the infantry or the absolute existence of the Army that I object too. In today's world, unfortunately, it doesn't seem possible for them not to exist. As far as my experience and knowledge takes me, I haven't heard of a better system than democracy. So if the majority vote says I get drafted, and the luck of the draw says infantry, I won't like it, but I'll respect it. But I won't respect America being in Viet Nam. That I resist, specifically. I'm realizing that going to prison may be the only way I can make that statement."

Walking over to them, Mayborough inserts himself into their group, "Man, put your mind on it. Even after you get out, they could send you to Nam. Military brig time doesn't have to count against your duty time. Do you really think that you, one soldier in prison, is going to make any difference at all? It's for sure not going to raise the respectability of your voice."

"What matters most about my respectability is what I think of myself. No, I don't know how me being in jail, alone, of itself, would make a difference. But I know what would. Take all those guys out there who got out of the Army on a scam, or student deferment, or who went to Canada, or whatever they did – and I have nothing against them, if they were sincere, since it includes most of my best friends in the world, even most of the people I'd choose if I had to pick a squad to go to war with – take all those guys, have them put on suits and ties, bring along their families and wives or girlfriends, arm in arm, and altogether parade right into the draft board and demand, 'Alright, put us all in jail, right now.' Do that, and this war would have been over a long time ago."

"Maybe a lot of wars would," Chaplain Connors adds. "One thing history does tell us, asking individual soldiers to lay down their arms, in isolated cases, and ruin their own personal lives...well, that's just not enough."

Since Landers can't decide what choice to make, the chaplains leave. Mayborough repeats his position. "Take it, man. I'm no older or wiser than you but, from where I sit, I've seen this junk go down a lot more than you. Just take some off-the-wall job, any job, mark your time and get back to your life. That's all it's all about." Still, Landers can't decide.

Later that afternoon, Mayborough and Clives walk Landers towards a nondescript building near the center of the fort. Mayborough carries a file folder, which Landers recognizes as his normal file, though it's a lot thicker than the last time he saw it. He also carries a legal expanding envelope several inches thick. He comments, "Man, most guys don't earn this many pages for thirty years in service. At least you got a knack for mucking up their parade."

"The main advice I'm following, is don't go easy."

"I don't know what the hell sort of *bon mot* that's supposin' to be," Clives says, "but let it *roulez* on 'cause you sure enough got 'em on the A Train to confused-ville."

"You guys helped more than anything else. Especially the laughs. Thanks, to every degree I can say that."

"Our pleasure. I don't know what it's all going to come to, but you're on our A list of guys who deserve to come out clean," Mayborough says.

They approach and enter two heavy doors, into an empty room that looks like it was meant to be a storage place. There's nothing in it but a folding table, with a staff sergeant sitting very rigidly, behind it. Marching Landers up to right in front of it, Mayborough salutes and says, "Delivering Private Landers, as ordered. Here's his files."

"Fine. You can leave," is all the staff sergeant says. The MPs go. The staff sergeant doesn't look at or address Landers. He merely picks up the file, walks across the room and leaves through a single door.

For a while, Landers just stands there. An hour goes by. Restless, as usual, he starts stretching, does a few push-ups. Another hour goes by. More stretches, more push-ups, lots of sit-ups. Another hour goes by. All he can come up with to describe this place is Kafka-esque. What's it all for? It can't possibly have been that sergeant's office. As much as he's felt like an inconsequential pawn, for a month, now it's as if the whole scenario is being performed just for him.

Finally, the door opens. Another sergeant he's never seen before says, "Soldier, come in here," after which he closes the door and goes back in. Walking over, Landers stops just before the door, gathers all the aplomb he can manage, and goes inside. There are eight officers sitting around tables set up in a U-shape, ostensibly temporarily. They say nothing. Landers steps to the end of the open U, stands at attention. Neither of the sergeants are in the room.

After clearing his voice, a colonel at the center and head of the tables says, "Private, explain yourself. Why are you interrupting our meeting?"

"Sir, I'm Private Michael Landers. I understood that I'm here for some sort of summary court martial, although I'm not sure what that means."

"This is not any type of court martial," the colonel barks. "We do not recognize you. We have no idea who you are."

Looking around, Landers even considers leaving, but sees that there is no handle on this side of the door. He spots it sitting on one of the side tables. Spinning his eyes around the table, he recognizes various faces, but stops on an FBI agent, sitting back against the wall and not at the table. This lifts him from a sensation of being lost in unreality, to a twitch of anger.

"Sir, this man here. An FBI agent, I believe. I've met with him twice, including yesterday morning. He must know me."

"I've never seen you before in my life. There is nobody like you in the US Army," the agent says, without looking at Landers.

Landers looks around, picking out the colonel chaplain who he'd walked out on a few weeks prior, who glares at him, and the young military lawyer he'd met that morning, who looks very uncomfortable, particularly when Landers holds his gaze. The lawyer looks away. Landers says, "Sir, these two man, the colonel chaplain and the 1st lieutenant lawyer, I've spoken to them both for several hours."

The chaplain snaps at him, "I've never seen you before in my life."

This escalates Landers' anger and since he has no idea what's expected of him he says what he feels, "Are you lying as an officer or as a priest?"

This sets the whole mood of the room to a much sharper attention. Snapping to regain control, the colonel in charge says, "Silence. We do not recognize you. As far as we're concerned, you are not even in this room. Gentlemen, let's proceed with our meeting."

Landers makes the briefest facial expression of what his thoughts say, "Oh, right, what now?" Then he holds his best military blank look.

Papers shift around, all sorts of comments are made by the various members as it all begins to blur into a Twilight-Zone montage.

The colonel in charge starts listing off what sounds like specific charges, "First off, he disobeyed his written orders to depart for Viet Nam."

A lieutenant colonel says, "On three separate occasions, related to his written orders, he disobeyed direct orders from officers to proceed with processing."

Since there's a slight pause, as they write, Ladners jumps in, "Isn't that kind of like double, no quadruple jeopardy?" There is never any reaction at to his comments, like an aggravating child's tease. Even as he occasional inserts corrections or denials, the meeting goes on at its own pace, speaking right over him sometimes, as if neither he nor his voice are even in the room. All table comments are as if they're talking about some mythical third person, not even in their presence. Sometimes there are ad lib asides but nobody ever looks at Landers. A clerk writes as fast as he can on legal pads.

When the FBI agent reports, "He conspired with communist agents."

Quickly Landers jumps on this, "Never, under any circumstances, did I conspire with any communist or any other subversive agents. Nor am I aware that I ever came in contact with any."

A major says, "He admits to taking illegal drugs. LSD for one."

The low-ranking officer, a captain, says, "He broke out of security lockup at the S-2 Ward."

"That's one AWOL," the lieutenant colonel says.

"He was caught with marijuana in his possession."

Since this never happened, Landers does have to think of what they're implying. Before he can toss in his comments, the lawyer says, "Citing the record, there is no physical evidence that he was caught possessing any illicit substances."

Ignoring this, the major says, "He ran away from a formation at the Holding Company at the Presidio."

"That's another AWOL," the lieutenant colonel says.

"I tried to save a man's life," Landers inserts. "That's an AWOL?"

Directly over this comment, the major says, "He was a direct instigator in the death of Specialist 4 Spandrow?"

"No, it was Whistler who died, not Spandrow. There were a hundred witnesses and I was as helpless as any of them. But Spandrow, is he..." he starts to ask but is cut off by the chaplain.

In the Presidio lockup, he assaulted an MP, a Sergeant Macree."

"That's can't be true. And Sergeant Macree is a well-documented sociopath. He's the one person, in all of this, who I hope gets his due, fifty times over."

The FBI agent jumps in, "He conspired with Communist activists to instigate a riot at a public university."

"Again, I did not conspire with anyone. Besides, the prime provocateur at the only disorderly rally I was even near is an FBI informer. Or, more likely an FBI agent. Correct?"

Reflecting on his own off-the-cuff comment, Landers wonders if this is right and whether Werner really is an actual agent and, if so, how much was he involved of Katrina's plight. Was he actually the perpetrator?! Various other charges are made but his mind is barely in the room. Three more AWOLs and refusal to obey orders are listed; he isn't even sure what they're talking about. It's all becoming an distant echo chamber, until one comment by the lawyer stands out, "There are other witnesses who reported that Whistler jumped off the Golden Gate, in a surprise move of his own initiative."

His anger growing exponentially, the mantra, "Don't go easy," spins in his consciousness. Since this is the first hint of something he's said in the room having been noted, he leaps on it, "Wait. Dammit you're a lawyer. If I'm not here, and you didn't hear me, how come you use my statement, which I made in this room, and which is obviously contrary to the faulty information you received beforehand? I'm the one who said it was Whistler who jumped and that there were witnesses. Plus, I'd have done anything to save his life. He was an honorable soldier, a great warrior, unlike..." but he stops himself short of directly insulting them. They're all silent; possibly no one wants to be the first to be associated with the hint of where 'unlike' was going. At their pause, Landers just keeps right on going, "What more can you do? You're officers. Citizens of America. You can reconstruct, later, about whatever happened in this room, anyway. Why don't you quit the jerking around and jump to the end game. Who are you playing this charade for? Maybe you're impressed, but I'm not. Give me whatever you're going to give me, jail or a deal. I'm beyond caring anything about what this kangaroo court tries to pretend is a valid voice of the US Army or anything else American."

Though indignant, this does actually cause them to take pause; none of them are able to hold eye contact with each other. The colonel in charge takes back the forum and pushes quickly to a finality, which was undoubtedly worked out in advance. They call in another specialist to take notes and even turn on a tape recorder. In fact, the Colonel has a document, previously typed up, delineating the terms. Landers, weighing everything in his heart, knows the only strong motivation he has for doing anything is a resounding beat pounding in him to find a way to help Katrina. Being able to somehow drift through the rest of his active military tour, sixteen months, as anonymously as possible, seems like the way that will leave him with the strongest voice. Plus, he knows he can't stand up to many more situations of having to delineate his life philosophy, which is becoming so overwrought he can hardly be sure of anything.

He has already indicated he'll take their alternate deal of not going to prison by the time the Colonel cites, "Private Landers, when you sign this paper, which all of the members of this board have signed, you shall agree that you will, of your own free will, board a plane to the Republic of Viet Nam. And because of the action of this board, your MOS will be changed from infantry to a non-combatant MOS, yet to be determined. Will you sign?"

"Yes, Sir," Landers says. "At this point, all I want is to get as far away from here as possible. And on the planet earth, that's the Republic of Viet Nam."

The colonel snaps, "This panel will not support any more insubordination. Will you sign?"

Without answering, Landers steps forward and thoroughly reads the paper. He signs it.

Taking the paper back, the colonel decrees, "Private Landers, when you leave the room, you will again be a free soldier, returned to a state of normal active duty."

Landers salutes the officer, makes a military turn and walks directly from the room. Two MPs he's never seen before approach him from either side. Each places a handcuff on one of Landers' wrists. They march him to their wagon and put him in back, still in handcuffs. They get in and wait.

Even locked up and in handcuffs, he feels some relief that at least he seems to have escaped the debilitating psychological maelstrom that has made every wakeup for many months seem like a new day in a bad, old dream. He does come to wonder why they made such a point of stating that he was a free soldier again, oxomoronic as that might seem. All he can come to surmise is that they had to state something of that nature for their official record. In one day, it will hardly matter to him that he had even been through it all. Except for everything about Katrina.

ABOUT THE AUTHOR

The author was drafted into the Army in his senior year at UCLA. Did one year in the field, in the Central Highlands of Viet Nam, with 2/8 Infantry, 4th Division, 1967-68; ended up a sergeant. Returned to UCLA for 3 years on GI Bill. Has written seven novels, a dozen screenplays. Worked along the way in various arts fields: 5 years with architect Frank Gehry, ran several L.A. art galleries, in film production at major studios for a dozen years. Speaks French, Spanish, Italian and German. Professional piano player, jazz and classical. Lifetime surfer.

9406219R0017

Made in the USA
Charleston, SC
10 September 2011